Search for the
HEART
of the
BISON

Also by Glen R Stott

Heart of the Bison
Neandertal Book One

Spirit Fire
Neandertal Book Two

Dead Angels

Timpanogos

Robyn

Search for the HEART of the BISON

Neandertals

Book Three

GLEN R STOTT

Copyright © Glen R Stott.

All rights reserved. No part of this book may be reproduced in any form or by any electronic or mechanical means, including information storage and retrieval systems, without permission in writing from the publisher, except by reviewers, who may quote brief passages in a review.

ISBN: 978-1-64669-643-7 (Paperback Edition)
ISBN: 978-1-64669-644-4 (Hardcover Edition)
ISBN: 978-1-64669-642-0 (E-book Edition)

Some characters and events in this book are fictitious. Any similarity to real persons, living or dead, is coincidental and not intended by the author.

Book Ordering Information

Phone Number: 347-901-4929 or 347-901-4920
Email: info@globalsummithouse.com
Global Summit House
www.globalsummithouse.com

Printed in the United States of America

To Ch*Ki

To Chi*Ki

Contents

Acknowledgements xi
Prologue xiii

Chapter 1 – The Metcalf Report 1
Chapter 2 – The Cavern 27
Chapter 3 – The Dy-emeralite City 70
Chapter 4 – The Search 130
Chapter 5 – The Heart of the Bison 172
Chapter 6 – The History Room 221
Chapter 7 – Home 253

Acknowledgements

A special thanks to my wife, Conchita (Chi*Ki), for her love and support. The manuscript reviewer for iUniverse pointed out weaknesses and provided critical suggestions as I worked on polishing the plot and characters to meet the expectations of fans of this genre. The iUniverse copy-editor helped add a professional touch to the style, grammar, and spelling of the final product.

Prologue

October 2011 – A.D.

Solero felt hot in his conference room, probably because the meeting was getting tense. The floor, walls, and ceiling were made of dy-emeralite, a pale emerald-green material used for most of the structures in Solero's world. The dy-emeralite was impregnated with bionic LED material, which caused it to give off a soft light when excited by small electrical impulses. There was no other light source and no shadows in the office, but everyone could see clearly. The room was fourteen feet long and twelve feet wide with no pictures on the walls. At each end of the room there was a door, and along each side there were three faux windows. Through the windows on each side was a realistic hologram. On one side, the hologram was of a densely forested mountain scene in Oregon. On the other side, the hologram looked out on desert scene near Bryce Canyon in Utah.

Rajel's jaw tightened. He was in charge of coordination and execution of *Operation Reclaim*. He was of the Earth People race called Gatherers. He was seven feet-four inches tall. Except for his face, the bottoms of his feet, and the palms of his hands, his body was covered with straight, reddish hair. His black eyes were intent as he stared at Solero. "It was all Al Qaeda. No other group was involved."

"I need to be completely clear on this point, so reassure me again. Was *Operation Reclaim* connected with the attack at *any* level?" Solero asked again.

Rajel expelled a blast of air through his mouth before answering. "I do not know how to *make* it clearer. Our people were not involved. The attack was not connected in any way to *Operation Reclaim*.

"I cannot over emphasize how important it is that *Operation Reclaim* stay uninvolved in any terrorist activities until time to initiate the final phase," Solero stressed. Solero was the Minority Leader of the Earth People Supreme Council. He was also the leader of the secret program titled *Operation Reclaim*. "I have been assured we have moles planted in *all* the major terrorist groups, so you can see why I am surprised an attack of that magnitude could have happened without our knowledge." Solero was of the Earth People race called Watchers. Watchers were bred and taught to look and act like the Sun People; those who lived on the surface of Planet Earth.

"We have not infiltrated the high levels of Al Qaeda yet," Rajel replied. "But we do have four moles in Al Qaeda."

"You are supposed to maintain deniability on the operation. How did you get those details?" Rajel asked Solero, obviously surprised.

"When President Bush announced it was an Al Qaeda attack, I needed more information," Solero answered. "The question stands."

"This was a high level Al Qaeda operation. Our moles are still in the lower levels of the organization."

"Pulgo says *Operation Reclaim* cannot succeed without Al Qaeda," Pulgo spoke in the ancient language of the Earth People. He understood the English spoken by the others and they understood what he said. He was of the Earth People called Ancients. His four foot-nine-inch body was muscular and wide with shoulder-length blonde hair that was clean but uncombed. He had almost no chin or forehead. His big blue eyes looked out openly from beneath a large brow ridge covered with bushy hair. His nose was large and wide. His large mouth, filled with oversized, crooked teeth, was framed with full lips.

"The next referendum is in two years." Solero said. "At that time, I expect to be elected Majority Party Leader. But whether I am elected or not, we have to initiate *Operation Reclaim* no later than right after the referendum."

"Why the rush?" Rajel asked.

"Have you heard of EarthScope?" Rajel looked puzzled. "I thought not. What about interferometers?"

"What do those things have to do with our timing?"

"EarthScope is a Sun People project to map all slippage areas on the tectonic plates in North America. Some of their seismic studies involve mapping deep geologic structures."

"That is not the first time Sun People have gathered information about below ground geology. We have always avoided detection," Rajel stated.

"This is much more intense than their oil explorations. Our Thinkers are working to counter the effort, but we have not resolved all issues yet. However, interferometers are a different story."

"Interferometers? Sounds like a high school science project," Rajel commented.

"Do not let the funny name fool you. They are based on very advanced physics using Bose-Einstein condensates. With them, Sun People will get very accurate surveys of deep geologic features. They work like the cavern finder technology we are using to look for the Heart of the Bison. Soon, Sun People will be able to fly over an area in an airplane and pick out oil fields on a computer screen. All caves, tunnels, and other voids will also show up."

Rajel appeared suitably surprised. "When will this happen?"

"They are near completion of a prototype. Our information indicates it will work, but it will be too heavy to use in the field. It will take some time to do the miniaturization, but it will be ready in a few years. Our Thinkers are working to counter these technologies. Perhaps they will succeed, but it is just a matter of time before we are discovered one way or another. I want things in shape before the referendum. Do not give me details, but generally, how is the plan going?"

Rajel answered. "We have infiltrated the targeted terrorist organizations. In all of them, except Al Qaeda, we are in positions of influence. Other agents have acquired control over the required nuclear, bio, and chemical weapons. The weapons are in position and can be delivered to the appropriate organizations in a two-week period. The *Operation Reclaim* signal is set, and our plans to send it are finalized. But after the signal is given, it will take about four weeks' work to coordinate the groups and get the commitments."

"Why so long?" Solero asked.

"We have to put sensitive information out to the various terrorist leaders. Do you want that information out before we make the decision to move?"

"Streamline the plan," Solero ordered.

"I am already working on it."

"It does not matter how fast you can implement it; the plan is useless if we do not achieve complete destruction of infrastructure and technology,"

Tofraprin said. Tofraprin, who oversaw security and intelligence for *Operation Reclaim*, sat to Solero's left. Like Solero, Tofraprin was a Watcher. "In addition, there must not be more than one billion survivors on the entire planet ... preferably around a half billion. We cannot gain control over enough weapons to create that much destruction. The success of the plan depends on retaliation from governments that have stockpiles of weapons. In countries like the United States and England, the civil governments must be destroyed so low-level military leaders will be left in charge. None of our computer simulations achieve anything near that goal without the targets assigned to Al Qaeda."

"What about assigning them to the organizations we can control?" Solero asked.

"None of those organizations is capable," Tofraprin answered in a tone leaving no doubt he knew what he was talking about. "We could directly train a couple of them and bring them up to that level in six to eight months."

"No," Solero said. "We are on shaky ground as it is. Direct training would put us in too deep ... at least for now. Once we achieve Majority Party status, we could do that, but I want to be ready before then. What is the problem with our Al Qaeda moles?"

Rajel put the palms of his hands on the pale green dy-emeralite conference table and leaned forward. "Our people have spent a lot of time building trust, but as things stand, the positions of influence are held by the early organizers from the Afghan war with Russia."

Rajel leaned back in his chair. "The Nine-Eleven attack changes everything. There is no doubt the United States will attack Afghanistan ... probably before the end of the year. They will not approach this the way the Russians did. People in my office believe they will disrupt Al Qaeda. They will capture or kill many of its leaders. That will put stress on the organization and create openings our moles are prepared to take advantage of."

Solero looked questioningly at Tofraprin. "The U.S. will not destroy Al Qaeda, but Rajel is right," Tofraprin said, "they will do serious damage. President Bush's plan to attack Al Qaeda on financial fronts will open other opportunities for us."

"We cannot offer or provide any direct financial assistance to any terrorist group," Solero said.

"That is not necessary," Rajel said. "Our moles are prepared to respond to stresses on Al Qaeda in ways that will put them in favorable positions with the leadership. It is a matter of the U.S. damaging Al Qaeda, but not destroying the organization."

"Okay then, things look good on that front," Solero said. "However, something else has come up. You are all aware of the Iceman discovery in the Alps, and the fact the dagger found with it matches the Small Beaver artifact," Solero said. "Many think that proves the Sotif story of the Warmonger is true. Even though that does not add credibility to the Points of the Wisdom Skins, we can expect to lose some votes because of it. That, by itself, is not a problem, but something else has come up. Tofraprin?" Solero nodded to Tofraprin.

Tofraprin passed out copies of a report bound in blue covers to each one at the table. "The Supreme Council has an unpublished report of some work done in the Middle East by a University Professor from Arizona State. The man's name is Marc Metcalf. It appears he found some troubling fossils this past summer." Tofraprin passed copies to everyone at the table.

"You can read the report for yourself; it contains two astounding discoveries. Metcalf found the remains of a Neanderthal child in a cave in the Middle East. The child had four smooth black stones ... one in each hand and one near each foot. The skull has puncture wounds consistent with the bite of a large cat of some sort."

Rajel gasped. Pulgo remained stoic. Everyone else sat forward.

"Not far from the cave where they found the child, they found a grave. They did not have time to recover the skeletons in the grave, but they took pictures before reburying their find for later recovery. The report says the grave contained the remains of a Cro-Magnon man embracing a female. Alriel has examined the pictures."

"I have examined the report and photos," Alriel said. Alriel oversaw science and technology for *Operation Recluim*. He was of the Earth People race called Thinkers. He was five-foot-seven-inches tall and weighed a hundred six pounds. His body was completely hairless, not even eyelashes or eyebrows. In the green light in the dy-emeralite room, his pale white skin seemed to have a green tint. His face was compressed into the bottom of a triangle formed by a large, wide forehead and a small, pointed chin. His mouth was small with narrow lips. His nose consisted of two small openings above his thin upper lip. His eyes, however, were about twice as big as those of the Watchers. His thin arms and legs were disproportionately long. He spoke clearly, but his voice had a watery tone to it. "I have no doubt the female is half Earth People and half Sun People. The skeletons were not fully excavated, but from what I could see of the female's hips, I am seventy percent certain she had given birth."

"Tuka," Pulgo muttered in awe.

"Tuka and Sky Man, parents of Shekek!" Rajel exclaimed. "Then, it is all as Sotif wrote."

"This is all preliminary," Solero stated. "It is conjecture to assume these are Tuka and Sky Man. And if they are, it does not prove there is a Heart of the Bison cave."

"What if it is true?" Rajel asked. "What if the Heart of the Bison really existed?"

Solero pounded his fist on the table. "That is completely irrelevant," he stated in a controlled, quiet voice contrasting sharply with his actions. He walked deliberately to Rajel's seat at the large dy-emeralite conference table. "It does not matter what those ancient people thought. The world has changed. Sotif could never have seen the world we live in. Nothing in any of his writings relates to *this* world.

"Footnote number six of the report says the grave was discovered through a dream one of Metcalf's students had … a woman by the name of Sandi Hartwell. I don't know exactly how or when, but I expect to interview her about her dreams.

"When the Sun People discover us, we will not be able to resist them if we do not prepare. Their history is clear … they will kill or enslave us all if we let them! We *must* take control of this planet before that can happen. We could develop the technology to destroy them first. The Earth was ours before they ever came. It is only the old tales and superstitions of the wisdom skins that prevent us from taking it back. So now, we must trick them into killing themselves.

"Opinion is swinging our way," Solero continued. "By the next referendum we will become the Majority Party. Then, we can initiate *Operation Reclaim* in the open. In addition, we will be able to participate directly to depopulate the planet without the damage of nuclear weapons. But it is still two years before the next referendum. I am convinced we must prepare to act sooner! There are too many possible ways for the system to fail."

Solero walked to one of the faux windows and looked out on the hologram of the Southwest United States. "The Metcalf Report does not reveal the location of the cave where the skeletons were found. It is in or near Afghanistan. Because of the potential for war in the area, Ronaldo will not be able to put people there right away. However, he is already working on plans to find out where the cave is and get his people in."

"How will he do that?" Rajel asked.

"Ronaldo is working with influential Watchers in the Middle East. They should be able to bypass roadblocks. The Metcalf report is supposed to be secret, but a Watcher, Garret Chandler, managed to get the copy, which he sent to Ronaldo. Ronaldo is putting a team together to be led by Garret. Garret will trick Metcalf into revealing the location of the cave, and then the team will go in to begin the search for the Heart of the Bison."

"The Heart of the Bison may be irrelevant to us and *Operation Reclaim*," Alriel said, "but if there is a Heart of the Bison, and Ronaldo finds it, you will never be Majority Party Leader."

"That is exactly why we have to make sure Ronaldo does not find anything he can claim to be the Heart of the Bison," Solero said.

"Ronaldo has begun to form a team," Tofraprin said. "So far, we have one operative on the team, and I think we can get at least one more. We will know everything that is going on. Depending on what they are doing, we can disrupt and delay them."

Solero paced behind Rajel, who turned uncomfortably in his chair to watch him. We must make sure they do not find anything they can call the Heart of the Bison. And there is another problem. President Bush has declared war on all terror. It is hard to tell, at this point, how much success he will have, but anything he does to weaken terrorist organizations ultimately weakens *Operation Reclaim*. The people in *Operation Reclaim* know, whatever the cost, the Sun People on this planet must be conquered and ruled by Earth People."

"Pulgo wonders what Solero can do," Pulgo said. "This *Operation Reclaim* is not strong. This *Operation Reclaim* cannot be strong without Al Qaeda."

"We have challenges," Solero said. "Time works against us on many fronts. If the Heart of the Bison is found, we will lose the election. Then, we will have to set *Operation Reclaim* in motion without sanction from the Council. If President Bush manages to render too many of our terrorist friends ineffective, the destruction will not reach the critical mass required in the simulations. If Ronaldo somehow discovers our plans prematurely, they will be countermanded."

"This is a critical time for you, Tofraprin. You must make sure your operatives are close to all three situations. If it appears any one of those things poses a threat, I must know the details, so if a decision has to be made, I can do it. If *Operation Reclaim* fails, we will not be able to recover in time to save our world."

The meeting ended and the men filed out of the office. The sobering realization of the danger of their situation weighed upon each of the *Operation Reclaim* leaders.

Chapter

1

The Metcalf Report

One—August 2001

Sandi Hartwell woke with a start. What was it? A sound? A smell? She lay on her cot in the predawn darkness of her tent. She felt on the verge of the answer to an important question, but she couldn't figure out what the question was. Then she realized that it was a dream—only a dream. Was it about the child? The dream was an ethereal cloud that she could not catch. Sandi relaxed, trying to remember, but she could not stop thinking about the child. For days, the child had haunted her. Puncture wounds in the child's skull indicated coldly, forensically, how the child had died. Did he suffer? Forensics could not answer that question, but somehow Sandi knew that the child had not died quickly. The child was loved, else why had it been ritually buried in the cave? Sandi knew that a mother had felt heartbroken and abandoned by the death of this child.

This deep feeling about ancient people was something Sandi could not help. When she first read about the discovery of the bones of the pre-human hominid called Lucy, she wondered about her, even though she was only an australopithecine afarensis on the evolutionary path to modern men. What had Lucy been thinking the morning of the day she died over four million years ago? What did Lucy feel about death?

This child was different. Sandi had helped uncover this child. She had touched its small bones. It was a nearly complete skeleton of a Neandertal child. It was all packed away for transportation to the lab in Arizona where it would be studied on loan from the Pakistani government. The examination would tell much about the child. When had it lived? About thirty to forty thousand years ago, Sandi guessed. The child could have died yesterday as far as she was concerned. The lab would provide an age at death, but Sandi could already tell that it was just a toddler. So much could be known, but what Sandi really wanted to know, science could not disclose.

Sandi rubbed her eyes, blinked, and looked at her clock. 4:37. It was too early to get up and too late to go back to sleep. She sat on the side of her cot. It would be hot later in the morning, but it was still cool. She lay back down on the cot and relaxed, trying one more time to recreate the dream. At first, the images were vague. Then her dream began to return.

Sandi stood in front of a cave facing the rising sun. An eagle circled above trees north of the entrance and disappeared behind them. Sandi walked to a large rock about eighty feet from the front of the cave. It held a secret, so she started digging around the edge. At the foot of the rock, she found an important key.

Sandi only managed to get a small glimpse, and then the dream disappeared. She thought about the key but did not understand what it might unlock. She felt the world desperately needed the secret of the key. The cave in the dream resembled the one she and the crew had been excavating for the past six weeks.

Sandi had noticed a large rock in the location of the rock with the key, but it was in the bottom of a gulley, not on top of the ground as in her dream. She was wide awake now, so she got off the cot and dressed. She put sunscreen on her arms and face. She put on the long pants that she always wore on these archeological digs. Although her career required her to work in the field, she did not intend to have her skin cooked to leather by the time she was in her mid-thirties. Her hair, cut shoulder length for work in the field, was dark, but her eyes were blue, and her skin was fair. During her teen years, all her friends "laid out" in the sun to get dark tans. Sandi had followed advice from her father to protect her skin. He told her that the natural contrast between her dark hair and fair skin made her more attractive.

Sandi began her doctorate degree in paleontology at Arizona State in the fall of 1999. Last summer, she went to East Africa to work near the Olduvai Gorge. This past year, she had taken a course on Neandertals from Professor Marc Metcalf, a leading authority on Neandertals. It was his theory that Neandertals and Cro-Magnons must have cooperated in some locations.

Although Sandi's original area of interest was australopithecines and the search for the missing link, she developed an interest in Neandertals soon after the course began. Sandi liked Marc. It was not just that he was handsome—something about his personality clicked with her.

When Marc invited her to join his crew on this dig, she accepted. The area in Pakistan where he planned the dig was not known to have ever had a Neandertal population. Marc wanted to get to the very outskirts of the known Neandertal populations. He reasoned that in such an area, the potential for cooperation was highest. Sandi did not know why he had been so sure that he would find Neandertals here, but he had been able to convince enough others to get funding for this dig. The artifacts they had found proved conclusively Neandertals had lived in this area.

Sandi hoped to make a name in research and fieldwork. With that background, she could get a teaching position in a high school or college.

Sandi left her tent and walked up the slope to the cave in the face of an eighty-foot-high escarpment. The ground sloped down from the cave about sixty feet to the top of another escarpment that dropped about a hundred feet. From bottom of the second escarpment, the ground sloped steeply to the valley below. The cave faced east. She stood at the entrance, looking out at the black silhouette of mountains in the gray morning light about twenty miles across the valley. There were three peaks—the tallest was on the left. The sloped area in front of the cave dwindled going north until the two escarpments joined about two hundred yards from the cave. A narrow footpath wound down from where the escarpments joined to the valley below. Going south from the cave, the sloped area widened to about a hundred feet and continued south on a gradual slope for about a mile to the valley floor. They had come up that way in the three Land Rovers they rented for the dig. The area in front of the cave was barren, except for scattered scrub oak and dried grasses. Pakistan was in a drought this year. There were scattered pine trees north and south of the cave. About a hundred yards south of the cave, the top of the upper escarpment began to slope back. Eventually, the escarpment became a steep mountain slope. The pine trees on the slope were closely packed. The air was warm and dry, but it would be hot before noon.

Sandi wondered what it had been like when the Neandertal child had lived in the cave. The mountain and valley had probably not changed much, but forty thousand years ago, the weather would probably have been different. There could have been a whole different kind of vegetation in this part of Pakistan.

The camp tents and the three Land Rovers were down slope and south of the cave. As she looked out over the valley, Marc walked from his tent to the latrine. He was thirty-three or thirty-four; Sandi was not sure. He was tall and lean. The skin of his face had begun to take on the texture of someone who spent a lot of time in the sun—something that looked good on a man. When he came out of the latrine and started up the slope to the cave, the early morning sun came over the eastern horizon and shone on his sun-bleached blond hair. The sun, along with the breeze blowing up the side of the mountain, made Sandi's eyes burn. Marc wore a khaki short-sleeve shirt and cut-off cargo pants. She could see the muscles in his legs ripple as he briskly walked up the slope. Sandi stared out at the rock as he approached.

"Still bothered by that rock?" Marc asked when he reached the cave.

"It does not belong there," Sandi said.

"Well, I still don't understand how you can know that."

"Maybe like a sixth sense. This morning, I dreamed there was a key next to the rock."

"What kind of key?"

"Just a key ... symbolic of something."

"Okay, that rock out there. What is it that's different? Texture? Color? Density? What? It could've fallen from the face of the cliff and just rolled to where it is."

Sandi shrugged. "When I was growing up in Denver, my parents made an annual trip to Dinosaur Land near Vernal, Utah. This thing started the summer between eighth and ninth grade on the Vernal trip. For some reason, I just began to sense things about rocks."

"What things?"

Sandi picked up a rock. "Look at this rock. How long has it been lying here?"

"Well, it can't walk. If someone or something didn't put it there, I'd guess a long time."

"You might guess that it fell from the face of this cliff. If so, it has been part of this rock formation for millions of years. The Neandertal child we discovered in the cave was alive thirty, forty ... maybe as many as sixty thousand years ago. This rock was in this escarpment then. Who knows what games little Neandertal children played or what activities they engaged in with mothers, fathers, and siblings? But whatever they may have been doing, this rock was here for it. It was here when dinosaurs walked here. Maybe it was still deep in the rock formation. Maybe it was sediment that had not yet been compressed and formed into a rock. But it is fascinating what has occurred here over the eons, and the atoms and molecules of this rock have been here for all of it."

"It sounds like you should have been a geologist."

"When this first started, I thought I would be a geologist. But I soon realized my fascination has nothing to do with rocks—whether they are sedimentary, igneous, or metamorphic. I do not really care about that. What really interests me has to do with the life that must have gone on around them. Think of their ages. Rocks are the witnesses of geologic time. Living things come and go so quickly they never witness any significant change. Only rocks last long enough to witness the changes. So my interest evolved from rocks to all that has happened while they have remained. I became aware that I had an ability to tell which rocks belong in an area and which were imported. Who can figure a thing like that?" Sandi bent over and replaced the rock on the ground where she had found it.

"That big rock out there, for instance," Sandi continued. "I know it does not belong with the rocks on the cliff. It is the same kind of rock, and it looks the same, but it does not belong. Some people believe that inanimate objects have a spirit of some sort. I know some Mormons who say God created everything spiritually before creating it physically. Maybe I can tie into something spiritual about the rocks. Whatever it is, that rock came from somewhere else. Someone put it there."

"You're not a Mormon, are you?" Marc asked.

"No. I just give that as an example. Who knows? Maybe they are right. There may be something about rocks that cannot be measured with tools and instruments."

"So, do you think the people who lived in this cave put it there?" Marc asked.

"Cro-Magnons would have a hard time with a rock that big. Maybe it would have only taken a couple of Neandertal men to move it. So, yeah, I believe the Neandertals who lived in the cave moved the rock." There was something more that made Sandi think that the people in the cave put the rock there, something about the child, but she could not explain it—not even to herself.

"Why would they expend the effort to move such a big rock? What possible purpose could it serve?" Marc asked.

"I do not know. Maybe the rock is telling me something about the people who moved it."

"You want to dig around the base to see if there's a key to something?" Marc asked.

"Yes."

"We only have a couple of days left before we have to leave. We have to pack and close the camp down. I think we should spend all of the available time on the cave. Maybe there are some clues that can tell us why the child was buried with those stones. I know Neandertals sometimes buried their dead with flowers, but those stones, and the way they were placed, one in each hand and one at each foot, had some meaning that is more advanced than just putting flowers in a grave."

"I know," Sandi said dejectedly.

"You know how important this expedition is to me," Marc said. "I thought I was going to get in last year, but the visas got all messed up. The child will make it possible to get funding for an expedition next year, but the politics here are volatile. Coming back could be delayed. We need to concentrate our efforts to get everything we can from the cave."

They had found a lot of Neandertal tools and bone fragments in the cave and on the slope in front of the cave since their arrival in July.

"You are up early today," Sandi commented.

"Just getting a little excited. Time is running out. I just want to get something more definitive before we leave."

"What brought you to Pakistan in the first place?" Sandi asked.

"It started in the Battle of the Black Sea."

"The Battle of the Black Sea?" Sandi had never heard of it.

"You remember back in 1993 when the Americans had a terrible battle in Mogadishu, Somalia?"

"No, I guess not," Sandi said.

"Well, there's going to be a book out this year all about it. It's called *Black Hawk Down*. I did an interview with the author."

"Are you going to be in it?"

"I doubt it. When the battle took place, I was in the United States Army Rangers assigned to Mogadishu. The army headquarters was in the Mogadishu airport. I'll never forget October 3. We sent a force into the center of Mogadishu to arrest some Habr Gidr clan leaders in a hotel. I remember hearing the reports that everything had gone wrong. The more we heard of what was going on, the more I knew that my friends were dying out there. It was hours before we could get there to help. By the time it was all over, eighteen American military men had died. Some of them I knew; some were my friends. Then, in just days, Clinton ordered us all out. We left with our tails between our legs. A bunch of wild tribesmen had kicked the United States Army out!"

"Oh," Sandi interrupted. "I think I remember that now. We were trying to get food to the starving people there."

"Something like that, but if we had some good reason to be there, we should have stayed to get the job done. If we had no good reason to be there, those guys all died for nothing. Well, I guess they all died for nothing either way, didn't they? It just seemed so useless to be called out like that. That's why I mustered out as soon as my time was up."

"But what has that got to do with this expedition?"

"Well, just about everything. When we got in the city to get our guys out, it was with the use of equipment and vehicles that were supplied by the Pakistani army. We got lost. We got pinned down. I thought we would never get to our men. We went through something that builds strong ties with those who experience it and survive. After we finally picked up our men, we all went to a soccer stadium in Mogadishu that was under Pakistan's control. We spent several hours there. While we were there, I talked a long time with one of the Pakistani soldiers. That was Akhtar Siddiqui."

"Akhtar was a soldier?" Sandi asked. She knew he was in charge of arranging supplies and coordinating the local people on this dig.

"Yes. I met him in Mogadishu. He told me about an old *vidu* of his tribe … about a time when some very ugly men came from caves and helped men on the surface."

"What is a *vidu*?"

"Well, you know how the early Greeks passed their history down through memorized poems before writing was invented?"

"Yeah, Homer's works were first passed on that way."

"Right. Well, a *vidu* is sort of the same thing, except it's more like a hymn passed on among ancient inhabitants of this country. The stories Akhtar told me from these *vidus* were very old. He told me that he knew of some caves near his village that had artifacts from the time of those stories. The people in the caves were very ugly, but they lived and worked with his ancestors. According to the legends, the ugly cave people used tools made of rocks."

"You do not think there are verbal stories from Neandertal times?" Sandi asked.

"Well, not exactly. But what if there had been some cooperation between Cro-Magnons and Neandertals at the end of the time of the Neandertals? With help from Cro-Magnons, some small group of Neandertals may have lasted well past the end of the major Neandertal populations. No one can say where the last Neandertal lived or when he died. The macro record ends around thirty thousand years ago. But we don't know when the last Neandertal died, because we will never know if we find that fossil. After they ceased to populate the land in large numbers, there were surely small, isolated groups that persisted for some period of time. Where was the last group, and when did it die off? Can't say. This story of ugly people coming from caves and using rock tools ... well, I was most interested in the tools. And look at what we found."

"I know we have not dated these artifacts, but clearly they are from the time when Neandertals were still alive in numbers. So what have we found, Marc?"

"Maybe evidence of cooperation. I could make a name for myself. That's how you get funding in this business. I was always interested in paleontology. Before going into the army, I started work on a bachelor's degree in paleontology. When I got out, I used my GI benefits to get my PhD. I knew that I would come to Pakistan someday, so I kept in touch with Akhtar. I have worked on a lot of digs around the world ... working for the time I could lead my own expedition."

"Why did you join the army?" Sandi asked.

"My parents died before I started school. I didn't have a real family; I spent most of my time in foster homes. I was pretty much on my own at fourteen. I moved around a lot. No family. No real friends. The army seemed like a good place ... at least until politics got us kicked out of Mogadishu. I'm no quitter. That was just too much for me."

"It must have been very hard for you to grow up without parents. I just do not know what I would have done without my parents."

Marc looked out at the rock. "You know what? It won't take that much time to see what's around that rock. Go ahead and check it out," Marc said.

"Thanks!" Sandi said.

"But first, let's get some things done around the cave. You should be able to find what you're looking for later this afternoon."

Two—August 2001

As Sandi dug around the rock, she uncovered a pile of smaller rocks that were carefully arranged in a line out from the southwest side of the big rock. When she finished uncovering them, they stretched out about five and a half feet from the rock and were placed about three and half feet wide. The rocks reminded Sandi of some old Western movies where someone was buried with rocks piled on the grave.

Sandi ran to the cave. "Marc, I want you to see what I found!"

Marc shrugged his shoulders and followed her back.

"Well, I guess that explains it," Marc said after seeing the rocks. "It looks like your stone is a grave marker." He did not seem excited.

"Well? We should excavate it," Sandi said.

"There's no evidence that ancient people ever used stone markers or covered their graves with rocks. That's probably a rather recent grave."

"Come on, Marc," Sandi said. "Look how it sits in the bottom of this gulley. When it was put here, it must have been on top of the ground. In my dream, it *was* on top. Then sediment covered this area and buried it. Then water, coming down the slope, eroded this gulley and re-exposed the rock. It has to be at least as old as the *vidus*. We should at least check it out."

"You're right," Marc said, a little more interested. "Well, it's getting dark. I smell dinner on the fire. We'll check it out tomorrow morning."

Sandi could hardly sleep. She knew that there would be something important under the rocks—a key, but to what?

The next day, Marc sent Kelvin with Sandi to help. Kelvin was a Native American with keen sight and a nose for anomalies in a dig. He joked about being a Native American and often wore a headband with a single eagle feather hanging over his left ear. He was six foot three inches tall with a muscular build—without question the strongest man on the team.

To pass the time, Sandi asked him about his name.

"My parents named me Flowing Water. When I got to college, there were several guys who joked about my prostate, linking it to my name. So, I put an end to it by changing my name."

"To Kelvin?"

"Almost sounds like another joke. I got it from my physics class, you know … the Kelvin temperature scale. There's nothin' colder than absolute zero on the Kelvin scale. So, I was kind of caught up with that absolute thing. It seemed plenty clever then, but now, it's okay. I like it."

Sandi and Kelvin worked carefully for almost two hours before the first bone appeared. It was a human skull. The height of the forehead and large chin indicated that it was a Cro-Magnon—modern man.

"Should I get Marc?" Kelvin asked.

"No. Not yet. Maybe we can find some tools or something to give us an idea of how old it is first."

The skull was on its left side. As they carefully uncovered it, they discovered some teeth and claws near the neck. "All of these claws and teeth have a hole bored in 'em. Looks like this guy was buried with a necklace," Kelvin said.

Sandi picked one of the teeth up. "This is a pretty big tooth," Sandi said.

"Let me see that." Kelvin slowly turned it in his hands. "Him heap strong man," Kelvin joked. "Unless I'm way off base, this is from a cave lion."

"Cave lion? That is from the time of the Neandertals. Marc will be interested in this," Sandi said as she stood up.

"Wait! Look!" Kelvin said. There was a bone partially exposed about four inches below the skull's chin. Sandi and Kelvin carefully brushed the dirt away until they could see another skull at about the middle of the first skeleton's chest. It was lying on its right side facing the first skeleton.

"They were buried together in an embrace," Sandi said.

As they carefully brushed the dirt from the second skull, Sandi gasped. "You had better get Marc now!" she exclaimed.

"Right," Kelvin agreed.

Marc, Sandi, Akhtar, and Kelvin worked, with painstaking care, for the rest of the morning. By early afternoon, the top layers of the skeletons lay mostly exposed in their ancient grave. One was over five feet tall. The other was a little more than four feet tall. Six teeth and eight claws were exposed around the neck of the male. The couple had been placed in the grave facing each other with their arms and legs carefully placed in an embrace, just as Sandi had thought, but it was not the embrace or the animal teeth that had everyone's attention.

"Okay," Marc said as he paced beside the open grave. "There's no doubt that the big one is Cro-Magnon. But the little one. There are several very Neandertal characteristics. Look at the brow ridge. The forehead is low, and the chin is small. The other bones are heavy, but …"

"But what?" Sandi asked, even though she knew what Marc was going to say.

"Well, the brow ridge isn't that big. The forehead isn't that low. We could have a Cro-Magnon that looked very Neandertal, or a Neandertal that looked very Cro-Magnon. But I think what we really have is the best evidence so far that Neandertals and Cro-Magnons could and *did*. Unless I miss my guess, we have a Cro-Magnon/Neandertal … a half-breed female … buried with a Cro-Magnon man. I think we can conclude that they were connected in life."

"Judging by the broken ribs on the male and the cracked skull of the female, they both died violently," Sandi observed.

"Yes, obviously," Marc said. "Maybe they broke a taboo. Maybe they were killed and buried this way as a sort of warning to others. But there was crossbreeding, and there must have been interaction between Cro-Magnons and Neandertals for that to have occurred."

"Your doctorate proposed crossbreeding did occur," Sandi commented.

"Yes. I cited some pretty good evidence, but there has never been anything this conclusive. The boy they found in Portugal is supposed to have been a half-breed, but it has not been studied thoroughly. I know Erik Trinkaus studied it and said that it is positive proof, but others have a different opinion. There are some experts who say that the bits of Neandertal DNA that have been recovered are too different to allow crossbreeding, but other experts argue that they were close enough. Akhtar, we need several days to get these skeletons out properly," Marc said.

"No way, Marc," Akhtar responded. "It was hard enough to get the paperwork to do the dig in the first place. If you ever want to come back, you'd better not do anything wrong now."

"No chance that we can get an emergency extension?"

"The wheels of government turn too slowly. This dig is actually not important to any officials. There is no one interested enough to grease the skids, as you would say."

"What if we just stay and apologize later?"

"If you don't land in jail, I can assure you that all agreements you have to remove the artifacts on loan will be revoked. You won't be taking anything out, and you won't get back again—ever."

"Okay, if we leave now, what are the chances of getting back, say, as early as next spring?"

"I don't see any problem, so long as we comply strictly with the terms of this trip."

"Well, let's get photographs and a couple of bone fragments to date them," Marc said. "We'll take the animal teeth and claws, too. We'll just have to carefully replace the dirt and rocks back over the bones and fix the grave up before we leave."

"Could we do a little more excavating around the female's hips first?" Sandi asked.

Marc took a second look at the skeleton. "I see what you mean. By all means, we should check that out."

"What?" Akhtar asked.

"The hip that is exposed is a little out of position," Sandi said. "I think, if we can expose a little more, it will show that her hips are spread … maybe enough to indicate she had had a baby."

"That would be important," Marc said. "Because it would show that a half-breed was not sterile like a mule, which is half horse and half donkey. It was a mistake to come in the summer. It's just too hot and dry. I'm going to push for spring. I'll have to get a sabbatical from my class, but I'm betting, with what we have found, that we'll be able to get back. In the meantime, we'll keep information about the location from the public. We'll have it all documented in our preliminary report, but we won't publish it. We just need to keep a lid on what we have found here until we get back to finish the fieldwork."

The next morning, they all finished packing their equipment and were ready to start out of the mountains before noon. Sandi rode with Marc and Kelvin in the Land Rover that Akhtar drove, picking his way to the road in the valley below. "If dating can tie these three skeletons to the same time period, it'll show that the couple lived at the time this cave was occupied by Neandertals. We may even be able to show that the Neandertals buried the couple," Marc said.

"Do you think the Neandertals killed the couple?" Sandi asked.

"Maybe, but if they killed them, why would they take so much trouble to bury them and mark the grave?" Marc asked.

"They buried the child with ritual stones in the cave with no marker," Kelvin said. "Then they buried this couple away from the cave with no ritual things, but with an elaborate marker. Seems like a different set of people."

"The stone artifacts with the child must have had some important meaning," Sandi said. "The couple was buried ritualistically. You can see that from the careful positioning of the bodies, and who knows what meaning the cave lion necklace may have had? If the couple died in the same time frame as the boy, their stories could be somehow connected."

"Well, we'll never know exactly what happened, but we may find some useful clues back at the lab. I'm going to call the couple 'the lovers,'" Marc said.

"When you come back, I want to come, too," Sandi told Marc.

"You expect to find something else?" Marc asked.

"Yes … the key."

"But isn't that the half-breed female?"

"The lovers are *your* key, to prove *your* theory. There is something else about them, something that is my key. I just cannot put my finger on what it is right now."

"Well, you've earned the right," Marc said. "I won't forget the part you played in this discovery."

Three—September 11, 2001

"Sandi, it's Marc on the phone," Sandi's mother said as she brought the phone to her. Sandi had been glued to the TV all morning.

"Marc?" Sandi said.

"Are you watching it?" Marc asked.

"Can you believe it? I just flew out of New York two days ago! Where are you?"

"We just made it. I got back to Arizona University yesterday."

"What do you think is going on? I mean, they are saying that it was terrorists and Osama bin Laden."

"Well, I've been on the phone all day. Talked to some of my friends in the military. They're sure that this ties right back to Osama and Afghanistan. Bush is not going to just shoot a couple of rockets at his training camps like Clinton did after the Cole. My friends don't have any details, but all bets are that he'll go to a full-scale war against Afghanistan."

"But that is a trap. You saw what happened to Russia in there."

"Well, I don't know how all of this is going to shake out, but I'm pretty sure of one thing."

"What is that?" Sandi asked.

"That whole area is going to be a mess for the foreseeable future. I hate to sound so self-centered, but it's clear that we won't get back to the dig next spring, or for several years."

"I know. They are saying there may be ten thousand people killed... maybe even more. What difference do our little plans make?"

"Right," Marc said. "This is going to change the lives of people all over the country. I'm considering reenlisting. But whatever I do right now, one thing is clear."

"What?"

"Whatever plans you might have had about next spring; you can change them now."

"I cannot even think about my plans right now. The whole world is changing," Sandi said.

"Well, that's normal, but in a few months, we'll all have to think about continuing our lives. What I wanted to talk to you about is the status of our project. It was a mistake to leave the lovers there. I was so sure that getting back would be a cinch. Who wudda thunk this could happen? Anyway, I'm asking everyone on the team to keep quiet about the lovers."

"My mouth is sealed. You can be sure of that."

"Well, I still have to do the preliminary report, but it will be confidential."

"Do what you have to, Marc. My classes start later this month, and I am sure the professors will want a report of my summer's work, but I just do not know. I think I am going to drop out, at least for a time. I just do not know what I will be doing, but I will not give out any information about the lovers."

"Thanks, Sandi. I'll stay in touch."

"Good luck with the army. Bye."

"Did I just hear you say that you're not planning to go back to school?" Sandi's father said. Earl Hartwell was a very impressive man—strong, handsome—a man who always had an opinion.

"How can I think about school now? With this?" Sandi pointed to the TV.

"I remember my parents telling me about the attack on Pearl Harbor. It seemed to them that the world they knew was ending. But it didn't end, and their lives had to go on. I remember the day President Kennedy was killed. I thought no one else could stand up to the Russians. It was like the world couldn't go on, but it did. It will go on now."

"Dad, this is the worst disaster. They blew up New York," Sandi said.

"I know, I know, but believe me, life will go on, and you have to think about your future. You can't start thinking about giving up on your plans over this." Sandi's father had always been her strength whenever she needed something. Her mother, Jan, was a small, almost mousy woman, with brown hair and brown eyes—very traditional, very subservient to Sandi's father. Though Sandi loved her mother dearly, on important issues, she always listened to her father.

"Maybe, but right now, I just do not have the heart for it," Sandi said.

Four—July 2002

Sandi jumped when the phone rang. She was reviewing notes for one of her classes, and the ring startled her. She had transferred from Arizona back to Denver to finish her degree. It was not as prestigious as Arizona, but after 9/11, she wanted to stay near her home. "Hello?" she answered.

"Sandi?" It was Marc's voice.

"Hi, Marc."

"Can you meet with me for dinner?"

"Are you in town?" Sandi was surprised at how excited she felt at the possibility of seeing Marc. They had kept in touch by phone and mail, but she had not seen him since they had parted in New York the previous September.

"Well, I got in about an hour ago. So, how about it?"

"What are you doing here?"

"I've got some important news to discuss with you."

"What about?"

"Tell you over dinner."

Sandi hurried to get ready. After spending the better part of a summer with Marc in the wild, with dirty clothes and snarled hair, it seemed funny to be so interested in looking good tonight. Her father had been right. The attack on the Twin Towers did not seem so life changing anymore. Sandi had started back to school, and now she was beginning to think about what she would do with the rest of her life. Marriage and family had always been a big part of her plan.

She and Marc had never had any discussions about life besides their interest in paleontology. The news must be about the lovers. She had been thinking about them a lot lately. She wondered how they came to die so violently. Sandi had an inexplicable feeling that somehow, she would find out why they died. Perhaps the secret was in the grave or in the cave, but how long would it be before it would be safe to return?

It was just a short drive to the Sizzler where she had agreed to meet Marc. He was waiting for her at the front door when she arrived. He was dressed in a blue suit. Sandi wore a sports shirt and a short skirt. Marc looked so handsome. His hair was trimmed, and he was clean shaven. In the field, his hair grew tangled and unruly, and he never shaved. She was more excited than she had expected to be. Marc gave her a hug and a friendly kiss on the cheek as he greeted her.

"So, what is this all about?" Sandi asked.

"Well, let's get our order in and sit down first."

Sandi ordered Malibu Chicken, and Marc ordered a steak. When they finally had taken a table, Sandi repeated her question.

Marc answered, "What would you think about going back to the lovers' cave?"

"What do you mean? I know the war in Afghanistan seems to be pretty much over, but there are still a lot of problems in that whole area. I think they suspect that Osama's group might be holding up somewhere in Pakistan near the area of the cave. How can we possibly get paperwork and funding for a new expedition now?"

"I have a contact who says that he can get us in early next spring."

Sandi uncrossed her legs and leaned on the table. "You did not tell me you were applying for grants."

"I checked on it, but there are no grants available in that area."

"Then how are we going to be able to go? Pakistan is not going to let us in now."

"Well, my contact already has the financing, and he says that he can arrange the paperwork."

"Who is he? Akhtar?"

"His name is Garret Chambers."

"I have never heard of him."

"Well, I've heard of him, and I've done some checking. He's a specialist in Neandertal studies, and he has written a couple of papers. He thinks that Neandertals must have had extremely advanced hereditary knowledge, and he argues that their brain cases, being so big at the back, show capacity for a great deal of instinct. He thinks that they may have also had strong powers of sight, smell, and hearing, and he says that those strong senses would have been necessary for them to survive in the Ice Age with the primitive tools they used." Excitement bubbled in Marc's voice.

"So? I have still never heard of him."

"Well, he hasn't done anything really notable. Somehow, he got a copy of our preliminary report. He won't say how, but he knows everything. He says that he has developed connections and that he can get us in *and* get funding."

"And the catch is?" Sandi asked.

"Well, he wants to come with us."

"And?"

"He says that's it. He just wants to follow up on his theories and get more information. He'll probably do a paper. He says that I would be the leader, and the team would take credit for anything we find."

"And you checked him out?" Sandi asked.

"I'm satisfied … at least enough to give him a try to see if he can really make something happen. I mean, I don't know how he can have these connections, but if he does, he does, and that's worth a shot."

"So, you are going?"

"It's hard to resist."

"There are terrorists there that will saw your head off," Sandi said.

"Look, my report is out. I don't know how it leaked or how many others have gotten it. I need to get back right away to get the lovers' remains and lock that whole thing up."

"What about the others?" Sandi asked.

"Larry, Kelvin, Rick, and Gary are in. The rest don't want to go right now. I don't expect you to go, either. I've been in tighter spots when I was in the army. I don't have a choice. Well, the only reason I'm bringing this to you is because I sort of promised you a place. But I don't expect you to go. You'll always be on my team when things are safer. And of course, you'll be involved with the lab work when we get the lovers back here."

"You can count me in," Sandi said.

"What?"

Sandi could tell that it was not the answer Marc had expected. "I found the lovers. It was because of a dream … almost like they were talking to me. I must go back just as much as you do. They are connected to the key I dreamed about. Now I have to see what the key is and what door it unlocks."

"What about your degree? You have less than a year to get your doctorate. Are you sure you want to postpone that? You can be part of the examinations of the fossils when we get them back to my lab in Arizona."

"I need to be there when they are still in the ground. I cannot explain it, but you owe it to me."

"You know we're going to be in the middle of the current problems in the Middle East. Garret says that he can get us in, but no one will guarantee our safety. We're going into an area where Osama and Al-Qaeda might be hiding. Even if they aren't there, we have to worry about the tribal rivalries."

Sandi leaned back in her chair. "The same tribes are there as when we first went. As far as Osama is concerned, he does not intimidate me. I found the grave that started this whole thing. You promised me I could go back with you, and you could not possibly think of going back without me."

"Well, I wanted to let you know all of the risks. Of course, I personally would love to have you along, but it's much riskier than the first time."

"I am in," Sandi insisted.

"Okay, that's good enough for me," Marc answered. "I will set up the meeting and get back to you."

Five—September 2002

On approach to LaGuardia, it was hard not to notice the vacant space on lower Manhattan like a child who had lost her two front teeth. *All I want for Christmas is my two front*—the childhood song kept replaying in Sandi's mind as she thought of the terror and tragedy of that day. She took a taxi to Times Square. The meeting was scheduled at the Olive Garden restaurant under the giant Coca-Cola sign. When Sandi arrived at the table, the members of the crew were there, except Marc. It was great to be with them again and get caught up with what they had been doing since returning from the dig.

Sandi had had a deep interest in meeting Garret ever since Marc had confirmed that he could provide paperwork and funding to go back to the lovers' cave. She had always been attracted to powerful men who could take charge of any situation. Marc was like that. He knew what he wanted, and he went for it. Though some of that probably came from his military training, Sandi was sure it was basic to his nature.

Marc also had the ability to stand back from a situation and find novel ways of doing things. He combined advanced survey techniques and equipment with archeology, using global positioning equipment to document locations of his digs and artifacts.

Sandi really admired Marc and liked working with him, because he very rarely let anything stand in his way. But he had been stymied for months in his attempt to get back to the lovers' cave. This year was wasted as far as fieldwork was concerned. Now Garret Chambers had come from nowhere and found a way to get back in. According to Marc, Garret had access to many details about the cave that were not released for public knowledge. This was a man she wanted to meet.

As Sandi sat in thought, Marc and two other men came in. The first man was a little shorter than Marc. He was thin, almost wiry. His face was round, even a little soft. His hair was short and thinning on the top. He was probably in his early thirties; he would be bald before he was fifty. His eyes were a dark grayish blue like a deep lake on a dark day just before a storm. Sandi had never seen eyes that color. He wore black slacks and a dark blue polo shirt. This was the man Marc expected to move mountains to get them back to the lovers' cave? Sandi was disappointed. This man looked more like a postman than a mountain mover.

The second man was much shorter. He seemed stocky, but it was hard to tell because his clothes were so baggy. He wore a robe with a hood that stretched in front of his face and sagged down over his eyes like a monk's hood. He wore a scarf or something that covered his mouth. It was impossible to see his face. All Sandi could see in the shadow was a large, wide nose. He looked like the Sand People in *Star Wars*; except he was stockier. *Only in New York*, Sandi thought.

"This is Garret Chambers," Marc said, introducing the round-faced man. "He says that he can get us back to the area of the lovers' cave this spring. As you already know, Garret's main interest has been the study of Neandertals. Besides arranging paperwork, permission, and funding for this work, he is prepared to add his considerable knowledge about Neandertals. His assistant's name is Jektu. He was born with some defects that make it impossible to make the sounds of normal speech."

Marc introduced the members of the team and explained what they did. Sandi watched Garret. She began to pick up the same determination in his dark eyes that Marc had—the look of a man who would find a way to do whatever he had to do to get what he wanted. He moved with confidence and greeted each member of the team with respect and open friendship. His eyes fascinated Sandi.

By the time Garret shook her hand, Sandi already felt she knew him on some level. There was something familiar in the way he moved. He spoke with a slight accent that was almost unnoticeable but somehow familiar. It was not the accent one would have from learning a new language, but just a way of speaking that was natural to him. Even though they had just met, Sandi knew she would like him.

Garret talked about archeology and his interest in ancient civilizations while they waited for lunch to be served. He talked about how fleeting fame can be in the archeological field.

"The lovers' cave is one of the most significant archeological finds regarding the relationships between Cro-Magnons and Neanderthals," Garret said. "The evidence that the female was already of mixed blood shows dramatically that interbreeding had actually occurred." Sandi noticed that he pronounced *Neandertal* with the *th* sound instead of the more formal *t* that was accepted by most paleontologists.

"We are aware of the significance of the lovers' cave," Kelvin responded.

"Like all of you, I have specialized in Neanderthal study," Garret continued. "That is why I wanted to team up with you."

"When our paper is published and our find is verified, everyone will want to jump on the crew," Sandi said. She was thinking of how hard Marc had worked to get funding for the first expedition. Very few archeologists took his theories seriously. They would have to pay attention to his ideas when the finds at the lovers' cave were verified and published.

"My interest has always been in the Neanderthal studies, not in notoriety," Garret said.

"Then what do you want?" Kelvin asked.

"Two things. I have always thought there was some positive interaction between Neanderthals and Cro-Magnons. Two." Garret held up his little finger on his left hand as he said the number two. "Genetic experts say that modern man shows no evidence of DNA that could have come from Neanderthals. There are a lot of gaps in the available Neanderthal DNA, but current evidence indicates the theory that Neanderthals bred themselves out of existence by mating with Cro-Magnons is not reasonable."

"So?" Sandi asked.

"The DNA evidence suggests that a mass interbreeding did not occur, but the data is limited, so it does not prove interbreeding was impossible. The woman is clearly a mixed breed. I believe that the evidence shows conclusively that Neanderthals and Cro-Magnons did interbreed ... at least on occasion."

"And what is the other thing?" Sandi liked the enthusiasm Garret showed as he talked about his theories.

"Many of those who agree there may have been interbreeding believe that the offspring would have been infertile. I believe the measurements of your female's hips indicate that she was delivered of a child. One." Garret held up the ring finger of his left hand along with the already raised little finger.

Sandi was a bit confused by the way Garret used his fingers and counted down as he made his points.

"Well, you're a minority in those conclusions," Marc said. "Those I've talked with think that she's just a disfigured Cro-Magnon. Maybe she had the baby, or maybe the spread is part of the deformity, and there's really not enough of the hip bone exposed in the photo to reach a definitive conclusion about the separation, anyway."

"That is because you are going by pictures and field measurements. When you have her in the lab, I am sure it will be irrefutable," Garret said.

"But how do you know so much about our find?" Sandi asked. "This information is not public."

"The information came to me quite unexpectedly," Garret said. "These things are very difficult to keep under wraps. Of course, there are those who will not accept the idea that the female had a baby until more research is completed. That is why you should begin as soon as possible."

"Well, you needn't worry yourself about that," Marc said. "I have plenty of backers to fund extensive research as soon as the political climate settles down."

"You think that will happen in the foreseeable future?" Garret asked.

"The war in Afghanistan is almost over. They are kicking the Taliban out everywhere," Sandi said.

"They are kicking them into Pakistan where they can regroup and come back. This war is only just beginning. Things will be a mess there for years."

"But you told Marc you can get us back as early as next spring. How do you plan to pull that off?" Sandi asked.

"I have been working in the Middle East for years. I have developed influential contacts. If the area of interest is not in Afghanistan, I can get you in this spring."

"And if it is Afghanistan?" Kelvin asked.

"That would be more difficult. I do not have connections with the United States military there. But I know someone who does. It would take until midsummer to pull that off, but my information is that the dig is in Pakistan."

Sandi was shocked. Did he seriously think he could make arrangements with the US military for an archeological dig in Afghanistan? And how could he know the dig was in Pakistan? She could see the same shock on the faces of the other members of the team. "It is too risky with so many terrorists who want to take hostages and kill Americans," Sandi said. "I do not see how you could get funding for an excursion now."

"It is risky, but there are two reasons why you should go back now," Garret said. "The nature of your find will not remain secret for long. When this gets out, interest in your work will very high. Two." As he spoke, he raised his little finger. "When things open up for everyone, you can bet there will be a lot of other people refocusing their efforts in that part of the world. One." Garret raised his ring finger.

"Even if you could get us in, where would the funding come from?" Kelvin asked. "Right now, commitments from all normal sources are being held back until the political problems settle down. We've already knocked on those doors."

"I can get you in now, and I can arrange sufficient finances," Garret said.

"The area we're talking about is extremely dangerous right now," Kelvin said.

"What if we could prove that, in one small part of the world, Neanderthals and Cro-Magnons found a way to live together peacefully?" Garret responded. "Suppose we could find out how they did that? It might be a ray of hope to some people who wonder if Muslims and Christians can live together."

Kelvin laughed good-naturedly. "It would give hope to fools, but it would do nothing to improve relations. Besides, the lovers were killed."

"Why did you choose archeology as a career?" Garret directed the question to the group. "Not for money," he answered his own question.

Sandi was taken off guard by the question. Why *had* she decided to make this her career? Garret waited and looked at her with his deep blue eyes. She felt he wanted her to answer for everyone. "I wanted to …"

Sandi struggled with her answer. "I guess it is because I always wanted to know what life was like when men dealt with nature mano a mano, without modern inventions and technology, facing the world with sticks and stones and with a brain."

"The lovers' cave has a key to unlock a mystery about how those people lived together, a mystery no one else knows," Garret said. Sandi felt her face get warm when he used the term *key*. She wondered just how much Marc had said about her. "Think of this," Garret continued. "The first real humans were Homo sapiens neanderthalensis. Imagine them living in Ice Age Europe and the Middle East for 150,000 years. What a world that was! Neanderthals were the kings. They had tools and mental abilities that put them above all animals. It was their world, and as hard as that world was, they ruled it." It was easy for Sandi to get mentally caught up in that world as Garret talked. "Now imagine that aliens from another world invaded the land of the Neanderthals. First, they came in small numbers, but soon, it was a flood. The aliens came with a different culture, religion, and highly advanced technology. They were the Cro-Magnons. It was like H. G. Welles's *War of the Worlds*, only no local disease interceded to save the Neanderthals. Gradually, they were replaced and ultimately ceased to exist.

"This is one of the greatest stories of human development, and yet we have no idea about what actually happened when these two great arms of the human race came together. All the known evidence seems to indicate that they lived separately in the same land until the Neanderthals just ceased to exist.

"Do any of you buy that?" Garret asked rhetorically. "There must have been pockets where they interacted. Did they fight, or did they cooperate? Now you have discovered something that may show in at least one place … they may have cooperated. Are you really contemplating waiting for peace to blossom in the area before you follow up? Find another career. You will all be old before there is peace and harmony there."

"Well, you present an interesting challenge. Tell us how you would arrange to get us back," Marc said.

"Like I said, I have worked in the Middle East and Asia for years. I know people who know people. I can get us in, and I have some private sources of funding who are interested in this project. But you are right …

it is still risky. I cannot provide an army, but still, I do have some contacts with some of the tribal leaders in that part of the world. In the end, you have to decide what you would risk to answer the question that the lovers create."

Sandi sat in silence, thinking about what she wanted. Garret did have at least enough contacts to get the information on the lovers' cave. The possibility of getting back seemed real when he talked about it.

"I have asked Akhtar to do some checking on Garret Chambers," Marc said. "He has verified that Garret is known and respected in that part of the Middle East." Turning to Garret, he said, "I can reveal that the area of interest is in Pakistan, as you guessed."

Garret nodded. "Thanks for your trust," he said. "Some of my best Middle Eastern contacts are in Pakistan. I have money already in a bank account in my name." Garret produced a bank statement. "That should be enough, but I have a commitment for more, if it is needed. As soon as you give me the go-ahead, I can begin the preparations. Marc has told me you want to go as soon as possible. Weather would permit an expedition in early spring. If there are no objections, I will shoot for that time."

"Akhtar Siddiqui was born and raised sixteen miles from the lovers' cave," Marc said to the group. "He has strong influence with the tribes and clans in the area. He assures me that none of them have ties with Al-Qaeda. He can't guarantee anything, but he's confident that we will not be molested. I don't want to minimize the risk, but I am going back. I need a firm commitment from those of you who want to go with me."

Everyone in the meeting made the commitment. "We'll hire some of the locals to help with the work as a public relations gesture, if that's all right with you," Marc said to Garret.

"I completely support that idea," Garret agreed. "That brings me to my friend Jektu." Garret indicated the strange man that had come with him. "Jektu was born very different from you and me. His appearance causes people to stare at him. For that reason, he chooses to dress as you see him. He was also born with differences in his throat that make it impossible for him to make the sounds of most languages. He understands English, French, and several Arabic dialects. He speaks with the sounds he can make, with his own language. I understand his language. You can speak to him, and he will understand you. If he needs to tell you something when I am not around, he will write it in English.

"I have been told Sandi has an uncanny ability to understand rocks and geologic formations in an almost mystical way. Jektu has similar abilities with fossils. He has been invaluable to me, and I will be bringing him along."

"We have not heard of him or his talent," Sandi said.

"No, you have not, but he and I work well together," Garret said.

As they left, Sandi noticed neither Garret nor Jektu had touched their lunches. She liked them, but something was not right. She could not say exactly what it was, but she knew she would be watching them.

Chapter 2

The Cavern

One ... February 2003

As the Land Rover jolted up the winding dirt road, Sandi thought about the strange events that had brought her back. It had been a whirlwind of paperwork, shots, and packing ... all the while anticipating a denial of the mission at the last minute. Garret took personal charge of every problem and roadblock that came up.

In addition to all the up-front work, Garret had spent the last week working with Akhtar to make all of the local arrangements for the camp. Garret had met Sandi and the rest of the crew in Islamabad. He still had not been to the campsite, and he seemed as anxious as everyone else to get there.

Pakistan was suffering from a three-year drought. As they approached the mountain where the cave was located, the winter grass between the scrub oaks was tall and still green in areas protected from the hot sun. Everywhere else, the grass was already drying. There was still some snow in shady spots, but most of the area was dry.

They left the road and drove along the base of the mountains, following the path they had used on the first trip as it sloped up to the escarpment where the cave was located. Akhtar and his group had already set up the camp. He was waiting with three other Pakistanis ... two men and a woman.

After greeting Sandi and the crew, Akhtar introduced his companions. The woman was Hannan Faruqi. She was hired to cook and do camp chores and would share a tent with Sandi. She was a short woman who looked overweight in the pants and kurti she wore. Her head was covered in a black hijab. The two men were Tariq Kahn and Shabbi Faheem, both of whom wore black kurtas with black pants. They were large, strong men hired to help with digging and any heavy work at the site. Sandi remembered Shabbi from the first dig in 2001.

"This is the cave," Marc said when the introductions were done. Marc pointed to the entrance of the cave in the face of the limestone wall. Garret seemed distracted as he surveyed the clearing.

"The gravestone, where is it?" Garret asked.

"That rock." Sandi pointed to the rock showing through some low plants beyond the cave.

"And that is exactly how you found it?" Garret asked Marc.

"We didn't move that rock at all," Marc answered.

"Jektu and I just want to spend some time at the rock before we begin the excavation," Garret said.

"What for?" Sandi asked.

"Jektu may be able to tell us if the lovers were born in this area," Garret said.

"You really think that he may be able to connect directly to the fossils?" Marc asked.

"I hope he can. He has done it before," Garret answered.

"Even while they are still buried?" Sandi asked.

"Right now, they are as undisturbed as they will ever be."

"Okay, it'll take some time to move into the camp," Marc said.

After they moved their things into the tents, Marc and Sandi walked to the cave.

"Look." Sandi nodded her head in the direction of the gravestone.

"Garret sat on the rock when they first got there. Now Jektu is sitting on it," Marc observed.

"Garret is a very strange man. The way he acts about the lovers, if I did not know better, I would think that they were members of his family. I know he thinks that Jektu can sense something, but why would he go sit on the rock before coming to the cave?" Sandi asked rhetorically.

"He doesn't make a lot of sense. But I have to say that Garret really surprised me at how fast he was able to put this together."

"I still wonder what he wants, and now I am even more confused. I know that we need to get the bones out and packed, but it seems to me that the important new finds will be in the cave, and it seems that he could not be less interested in the cave."

"Well, I think I'll just go ask them what's so interesting about a rock," Marc said.

Sandi grabbed his arm. "Somehow, I think that would not be good. He seems to approach archeology almost ... well, with a sense of religious fervor."

"Look," Marc said. "Jektu is changing the direction he's facing. He started facing north, and then he turned west, then south. Now he's turning east."

"Now he is facing south again," Sandi said. "I am going to ask Garret what that is all about."

"You're going to ask him, but I shouldn't?"

"Not right now, Marc. I will pick a time."

"Good luck getting a straight answer from him anytime," Marc said. "Come on, let's get something to eat."

Garret and Jektu spent about twenty minutes more at the rock. "What did you find?" Sandi asked when they came to the camp.

"Not much," Garret answered. "A couple of times, Jektu thought that there was something to the east or the south. He thinks the man had nothing to do with this cave, but he is not sure about the woman." Garret did not seem disappointed.

"Have you ever seen him actually follow a fossil trail to its origin?" Sandi asked.

"That could be difficult to prove," Garret answered. "I have seen him go from one site to another, and there were some indications that the sites were tied together."

"So now what?" Sandi asked.

"As soon as Marc is ready to excavate, I want to see the lovers," Garret answered. He picked up a plate of food and went to his tent. He still had not gone to the cave.

Excavation of the lovers began right after lunch. Marc, Sandi, Garret, and Jektu worked at the site. Sandi was impressed with the skill and patience Garret and Jektu used as they uncovered the fossils. As they dug, Garret talked to Jektu in English, and Jektu answered in his very guttural speech. Mixed in with the guttural noises were some chirping sounds and whistles. He used his hands a lot. Sandi guessed that his hand movements were more an integral part of his communications than the casual way other people moved their hands when they talked.

Sandi had never formally studied any language other than English, but she enjoyed language. While she was not proficient in any foreign languages, she could discuss archeological and general camp subjects in two African languages, and she knew a smattering of French from a roommate she'd had at the University of Arizona. She had also picked up some of the Arabic dialogue that Akhtar and his people had used on the dig in 2001.

Sandi had a nagging feeling that Garret was up to something that he had not revealed. She began listening closely to Garret's conversations with Jektu to figure out some meanings from the sounds and signs that Jektu made. Because Garret spoke in English, she knew what they were talking about. Very quickly, she picked up the sounds for *yes* and *no*. It was somewhat deceptive, but she wanted to know as much as possible about Garret and Jektu.

By late afternoon, the skeletons were exposed. Marc stopped the work and set up some sophisticated survey equipment he had brought for the dig.

"What are you doing with that?" Sandi asked.

"Well, this is one of the latest survey gadgets," Marc said. "It uses lasers to gather closely spaced points. They call them *point clouds*. It stores the three-dimensional location of each point. The points are spaced mere millimeters apart. A computer can take these point clouds and create a virtual three-dimensional representation of the object you are looking at. As we remove the bones and clear away the dirt, I'll take shots, in situ, of each new bone that is exposed. Then I can put it all together and delete everything except the bones and artifacts. We will then have a three-dimensional file of exactly how these bodies and their artifacts were placed in the ground. With that, we can project the objects on a screen, rotate them in space, and look at them from any angle.

"Right now, forensic artists can take a skull, and, using clay and knowledge of how thick the soft tissue is over various parts of the bone structure, they can reconstruct a fair likeness of how the person looked. Someday, I expect to see computers do the same with a virtual skeleton created with point clouds. We could tell from the thickness of the bones and the structure of the joints if the person was muscular, wiry, fat, thin, and a lot more about how the body looked. With a little manipulation, we could actually create a three-dimensional model of these people, even including a pretty good representation of their facial features. Then we could add animation software, and they could walk and talk."

"That is fantastic!" Sandi exclaimed.

"There's almost no limit to the ways survey technology can be used to assist paleontologists. After the fossils and artifacts are removed and logged, we could digitally construct the archeological history of a site in three dimensions. It would be like looking deep into the floor of a cave with X-ray-vision eyes and seeing each tool, bone, or other artifact located in three-dimensional space, all at the same time. That will give us a whole new tool to correlate evolution of tool development, cultural changes, and evolutionary changes in the population.

"I'm collecting and storing the data now. It stretches the imagination to think of all of the applications that'll become available. It's just a matter of writing the programs, and I'm sure that there'll be many programs written. Once we have the data saved, the only limiting factor will be the sophistication of the programs that will come along to interpret it."

Garret and Jektu took many measurements and photographs of the lovers using the tried-and-tested methods. Akhtar had built a protective structure over the dig site. Garret and Jektu elected to sleep beside the grave.

Over the next few days, Sandi, Garret, and Jektu worked together to carefully recover and pack the bones. Along with the bones, they removed more cave lion teeth and claws from around the male's neck. They also found a piece of reindeer antler near the male's hipbone with several marks on each side. Sandi recognized it as being similar to one that was found in France. The marks seemed to be some kind of tally, but some archeologists had proposed that each mark represented different time cycles.

Kelvin and Larry worked on the excavation in the cave. Akhtar, Tariq, and Shabbi helped with that work. Although they were not experienced in this type of work, they learned quickly. Marc spent about 70 percent of his time at the cave, though he regularly went to the lovers' excavation to take shots with the survey equipment.

Two—Late February 2003

As time went on, Sandi began to figure a rhythm to Jektu's speech. She determined the sound he used for *Jektu* and *Garret*. He used those sounds so extensively that Sandi concluded that he must be using names instead of pronouns. He seemed to speak in very short sentences, perhaps only expressing a single thought at a time. Though his language seemed simple, he appeared to understand everything others said to him in English. Sandi was getting a flow to Jektu's language, and she had figured out many of the sounds that he used for the names of various members of the team.

The nights were cold, and the days were cool. One night, shortly after she had bundled up for sleep, Sandi had to make a trip to the latrine. Hannan was snoring loudly in her cot. Sandi quietly dressed in her warmest clothes. She put on her parka, and then she wrapped a blanket around her shoulders. It was overkill for the thirty-foot walk to the latrine, but it was a clear night with a stiff breeze blowing up from the south.

The camp was quiet except for the sounds of the wind. The moon was so bright that it created shadows on the ground. All the tents were dark, except the tent Garret and Jektu shared. Sandi wondered what they were doing up so late. They had lost interest in the project since they had completed packing the bones of the lovers and examining the grave. They were aloof from everybody else. They even avoided eating with anyone from the group.

When Sandi stepped out of the latrine, the light in Garret's tent was out. She stretched and then pulled her blanket tightly around her against the wind. As she started back to her tent, a motion in her peripheral vision caught her attention. Two men were just ducking into the trees south of the camp. One was short and stocky. Garret and Jektu were sneaking off for something! Sandi half ran, half walked to where they went in the trees. The wind stung her eyes as it blew in her face. She could just see them walking through the trees about sixty feet ahead of her. She had not been able to rid herself of the feeling Garret was up to something, so she decided to follow them.

After about a half hour, they stopped near a clearing. Sandi carefully edged closer. Jektu was talking. Sandi picked out a few words.

"Jektu —— not —— not late."

"I do not understand, either," Garret said in English. "I took the coordinates exactly. Maybe there is something wrong with my GPS. Maybe there is a higher than normal radar activity."

Jektu said something about a call. Garret took something that looked like a satellite phone from his bag. "It is on power standby," Garret said. "I must have bumped a switch. Section HOB calling Base One."

The instrument threw an eerie green light on Garret's face as he looked at it. "I made contact," he said to Jektu. "Power is low," Garret said into the communicator. "We are in the pickup area. I am going to use voice only to conserve power." The green light went dark.

"Mission was scrapped," a voice declared through the communicator.

"We are here. We sneaked out of the camp."

"Sneak back," the voice said.

"Why?"

"Too many questions. Five. A terrorist camp is too close. Four. It is probably not the Heart of the Bison. Three. You need to work with Marc for more info on lovers. Two. And you need to get more bone samples from the cave. One. That enough?" Sandi could almost see the owner of the voice counting up from his little finger.

"The longer we wait, the more likely the Sun People will find it," Garret argued.

"Ronaldo argued that, but the Council voted no."

"I cannot believe the Council would back out now. This is the most important discovery in archeological history."

"Ronaldo said you would feel that way. He said you should remember Rule Seven."

"That is just what I was thinking. Link in the coordinates," Garret said. The green light came on again. After a few seconds, Garret said, "Saving power, end." Garret clicked his communicator off.

Jektu said something Sandi did not understand.

"You are right," Garret agreed. "We will have to go on foot. I have the coordinates of the area where they think we can find the Heart of the Bison. This will really complicate things. We will go three or four miles more from camp, and then we will rest. We will start early tomorrow."

"Is good," Jektu said as they started walking south through the trees.

Sandi was torn. If she followed them till morning, Marc would be beside himself with worry. On the other hand, Sandi wondered what this "mission" was and what it had to do with the "heart of the bison." She knew that Kelvin was an excellent tracker. Sandi checked her parka pocket. It had her notebook, a pen, and a granola bar. She could leave a trail for Kelvin and write notes to Marc. This might be her only chance to find the truth about Garret. Clearly, it had more to do with a heart of a bison than the lovers' cave.

The two men continued south for about an hour and a half. Then they curled up to sleep with no fire. Sandi did not have any water and only the granola bar to eat. She considered going back to camp to get some supplies and returning before daylight, but she knew that she would not be able to find this spot again in the dark, and maybe she would not even be able to find her way back to the camp. Garret and Jektu were not carrying backpacks—they would not go far. Sandi curled up behind a large fallen log for protection from the wind. She scraped the dirty crust off some snow nearby and ate the clean snow beneath.

Three—February 2003

The sky was gray when Sandi woke, but the wind had stopped. She had been afraid Garret might leave while she was asleep, so she did not sleep well. She woke early and wrote a note to Marc.

> Marc:
>
> Garret & Jektu leaving camp. A mission to find something called heart of the bison. I am following. Will leave trail.
>   See ya later
>
> Sandi

As Sandi watched, the two men got up. "What is it?" she heard Garret ask.
    Jektu said something about the wind along with Sandi's name
"Is she alone?" Garret asked.
"Yes."
"Where?"

Jektu said something else using Sandi, Jektu, and Garret's name

Sandi froze. She was completely hidden by the log. She could only understand a few of Jektu's words, but it was enough to know he knew she was there. Somehow, Jektu must have seen her, but that was impossible.

"Tell me when she starts to move," Garret said.

Sandi peeked around the edge of the log. Garret went behind some trees. When he came back, Sandi stayed behind the log and slowly moved to her left.

"Sandi is ——" Jektu announced.

"Okay, Sandi, we know you are out there!" Garret shouted. "You might as well come into the camp."

Sandi stopped moving and Jektu said something more about her.

"Come on, do you want us to come hunt you down?" Garret shouted.

"Why are you sneaking away from the camp? Where are you going?" Sandi shouted back.

"I will explain. Come on in," Garret said.

"Tell me first," Sandi said. She moved back in the direction from which she had come.

Jektu said something else about her as if he knew she was moving again.

"You go back to camp," Garret said.

"Tell me first," Sandi answered.

"Sandi is —— back —— path ——" Jektu said. Every time Sandi moved or stopped moving, Jektu seemed to announced it. She knew that she was below the level of the log she was behind. It was scary how he could tell what she was doing without being able to see her.

"You go back to camp," Garret said. "Tell Marc we will explain everything when we return."

Garret stood up. "Time to go," he said to Jektu. They started to leave.

Sandi sat still, thinking about what she should do.

After they had walked about fifteen paces, Sandi started to follow them. Jektu said, "Sandi is —— Garret and Jektu."

Garret said something Sandi could not hear. Jektu answered—also too quietly for her to hear. They seemed to be arguing about something.

"Not!" Garret said firmly in the language Jektu used. His accent was thick, but Sandi clearly understood what he said. "Okay," Garret shouted in English. "If you are going to follow us, we might as well take you back." To Jektu, he said, "Come on," as he started back toward Sandi.

In a short distance, they came upon her sitting on a tree stump. She put a playfully smug look on her face. "How could you tell I was following you?"

"What are the chances of getting you to go back without making us take you back?" Garret asked.

"Why not just tell me what you are up to? I mean, you are not interested in Marc's work at all. What did you do? Use us as an excuse to get into the country?"

"Who got whom into the country?"

"Okay," Sandi said. She took her notebook from her breast pocket. "Give me good answers to these questions, and I might go back."

"Fire away," Garret said.

"What mission was scrapped? Who is the Council that did not authorize the quest? What is the quest? Who is Ronaldo? Who are the Sun People? What is the most important discovery in all of archeology? What is Rule Seven? What is the heart of the bison? And where are the terrorists camped?"

Garret seemed stunned. He began speaking to Jektu in his language. Sandi could recognize Garret had a significant accent. She could understand enough of the language to know they were talking about her. Jektu seemed to be saying they couldn't take Sandi back. Garret seemed to agree.

"Be so kind as to speak in English," Sandi demanded.

They continued their conversation, which now seemed to involve a cave.

"English?" Sandi said.

Now they were talking about telling or not telling Marc something.

"English!" Sandi shouted. "Just stop ignoring me, damn it!"

"Look, Sandi, this is all very complicated," Garret said.

"So? Your lies and deceit make it that way," Sandi said.

"My lies and deceit? Who listened to my private conversation?" Garret asked.

"Do not try to change the subject. What about the answers to my questions?"

"You do not know what you have gotten yourself into," Garret said.

"Duh! I already know that. What is it? What are you? CIA? FBI? Are you in the army working undercover? I should have known it was all too easy for you to get us visas and run paperwork. What kind of danger have you put Marc and his crew in?"

Garret said something about her to Jektu.

"When?" Jektu asked. "Sandi sees ——?"

"I am really getting scared here," Sandi said. She felt her voice shaking. She tried to control it. She did not want Garret to know how really frightened she was, but one thing for sure—she was going to learn Jektu's language as quickly as possible.

Garret said something to Jektu and then turned to Sandi. "Okay, only English from now on," he said to Sandi in English. "All except for Jektu."

"Just tell me what is going on!" Sandi demanded.

"If I told you everything, I would have to kill you," Garret said. Sandi felt the blood leave her face. The effect was obviously not what Garret was trying for. "I am just kidding, Sandi. Look, you are going to be okay. Having you along makes things different ... difficult. I am going to send Jektu ahead." He turned to Jektu.

Jektu asked Garret a question. Though she did not understand all the words, Sandi guessed that Jektu asked something about hiding her trail. She hoped that he would not find the note she had left, but there was nothing she could do about it now.

"Right. You had better take off now," Garret said in English.

Jektu left in the direction Garret and Jektu had started. Garret and Sandi followed.

Garret shouted something to Jektu in his strange language as he left. "Oops! Sorry, Sandi. I will be more careful in the future. Believe me, I am the last person who wants anything to happen to you. Come on, we need to get going." There was something in his tone when he said that he was the last person— something Sandi couldn't quite figure out.

"I thought the quest was cancelled," Sandi said.

"Rule Seven says, under certain circumstances, the person in the field may have to ignore a Council ruling."

"What is the Council?" Sandi asked.

"Trust me, everything will be okay," Garret said as he started walking in the direction Jektu had taken. Sandi tried everything she could think of to get Garret to explain, but no matter how she tried, that was all the information she could get out of him.

As the day stretched into evening, there was still no sign of Jektu. Garret did not have any food, so Sandi shared her granola bar with him. He broke off a small piece, put it in his pocket, and gave the rest back to her. When they finally stopped for the night, Garret said it was too dangerous to start a fire, but Sandi thought Garret was most concerned that Marc and the others would find them. They shared Sandi's blanket. Though Garret was less prepared to follow his Rule Seven by wandering through the wilderness than Sandi was, and she distrusted him, there was something about him that caused her to feel secure at his side.

That night Sandi and Garret found some snow in shaded areas for water. She was quite warm walking in her parka, so the cool snow had felt good.

The next morning, Sandi was famished. "What are we going to do about food?" she asked Garret.

"Jektu will take care of that," Garret said.

"Has he gone for food?"

"Jektu is a survival artist."

"We should wait for him, then."

"No, he will find us. Do not worry about it."

"That is not at all comforting," Sandi said.

"Look. I really am sorry that I cannot tell you everything right now."

"I do not believe you. You and Jektu have not been a part of this dig since we first got here. It seems like we have been just a burden to you since we got the lovers out and packed."

"Actually, I really like you guys, but, well, obviously there is ... I have some things to do. I hope you will eventually understand," he said as he started walking.

About an hour later, Jektu caught up with them. He had a couple of rabbits and some roots. Jektu dug a hole and filled it with some small, round rocks. Then he built a fire over the rocks. Sandi looked questioningly at Garret.

"A small fire in daylight will not cause any problems. Besides, do you want to eat the rabbits raw?" Garret said.

Jektu pulled a metal hatchet from a belt he wore around his waist and used it to chop the rabbits' heads and legs off. He chopped the legs at the first joint, leaving stubs on the bodies. Then he pulled a rolled-up skin from a pouch attached to his belt and unrolled it on a rock. Inside were several steel needles and other tools. Most of them were made of flint.

"What are those?" Sandi asked Garret.

"Jektu is really into paleontology. He can make all the tools Neanderthals and Cro-Magnons made. For most things, he prefers to use Cro-Magnon tools. Flint scrapers and knives are sharper and more durable than their metal counterparts."

As Garret talked, Jektu used a narrow piece of flint to run around the stubs of the rabbits' legs between the skin and the meat. Then he used a wider blade to skin the rabbits in a way that preserved the skins intact. He started at the neck and turned the skin inside out as he peeled it from the body. As he passed each leg, he pulled it from the skin. After removing the skins, he turned them back to normal. Then he prepared the rabbits so quickly Sandi was hardly able to follow what he did. He tightly rolled the openings on the legs and tails and used thin strips of the rabbits' guts to sew them tightly. Then he put snow and hot rocks from the fire into the pelts through the neck hole. He peeled the roots and cut them into small pieces using his flint blades. He mixed the pieces with the rabbits' hearts, livers, and other internal organs and put that mixture with more snow, along with bits of other plants, into the skins. He cut the feet off the legs he had chopped off and deftly skinned the legs, adding them to the mixture. Then he took some mixed herbs from a leather bag and put them in. Finally, he stitched the necks closed. The openings in the pelts were so tightly stitched that the melted snow did not leak.

Jektu dug another small hole, laid the skins in the hole, and covered them with a layer of dirt. Then he moved the fire over the skins. As the fire burned, Jektu cut the rabbit meat into strips and stuck green twigs through them, rubbed some of his herbs on them, and slowly turned them in the fire.

When the meat was done, Garret and Jektu took their meat to separate places in the forest to eat. It was the first time Sandi had eaten rabbit. It was delicious!

It had taken about two hours to prepare and eat the meal. Sandi felt much better with food in her stomach. Jektu put the fire out and removed the two stuffed pelts from the dirt below. As they traveled, Jektu and Garret occasionally talked. Garret always spoke in English, as he said he would. Sandi continued to use all her concentration to pick up on what Jektu said. Garret had a GPS device that they were following.

At the end of the day, they ate the contents of one of the rabbit skins. It was a delicious rabbit stew that satisfied her hunger. At the end of the next day, they camped at the bottom of a narrow gulley and ate the contents of the second rabbit skin. A small stream trickled easterly down the gulley. Sandi was surprised at how good the rabbit stew tasted after two days. Garret and Jektu ate separately again. Sandi figured that it was some strange ritual, but she had never heard of any kind of religion that required people to eat separately.

"When are you going to tell me what you are doing and why we are here?" Sandi asked when Garret returned from eating.

"If I told you, you would not believe me," Garret answered.

"Okay, tell me, and I promise I will not believe you."

"So, then I might as well make a story up for you to not believe," Garret said.

"I am listening," Sandi encouraged.

"Okay, I am an alien to your world. My ancestors once lived in this area, and I am looking for my ancestral home."

"Oh God! That is rich. So, you are a Martian?"

"If you like," Garret said. "My people lived in a cave near here. They had a secret of life, but when they left, they were not able to take it. So, we have been waiting for generations to come back and get it."

"I do not believe you," Sandi said.

"Thanks."

"How about telling me something that makes just a little sense!" Sandi exclaimed.

"Okay, I am not a Martian. I really came from Canada, but the rest is true."

"Ha!"

"You should not demand a person to make up a story and then laugh at it," Garret said with a smile.

"Ha. Ha. Ha. Now, how about telling the truth?" Sandi said.

"I told you, you would not believe the truth. Besides, I would have to kill you," Garret said playfully.

"Seriously, Garret, what is going to happen to me?"

"Seriously, Sandi, I will not do anything to harm you."

"What about the other Martians or Canadians or whoever the hell this council is?"

"None of the people I represent will ever harm you."

"And Ronaldo?"

"Definitely not Ronaldo."

"Then why not tell me who or what they are?"

"I have reasons. You will have to take my word that they are good."

"Am I in any danger?"

"We are in a place where there could be terrorists who would love to have an American hostage."

"What have you got to do with the terrorists?"

"I am not here to deal with terrorists."

"Then why are you here?"

"To find the secret of life."

"Back to that?"

"I told you that you would not believe me."

"Why should I?"

"You should not."

"Why do you always eat alone?"

"Different strokes for different folks."

"Tell me about Ronaldo."

"Ronaldo is an old wise man."

"How old?"

"Maybe about ninety."

"Why should I not fear him?"

"Because his life has been dedicated to peace and harmony among men."

"Well, that has not been working out so hot."

"So, it would seem."

"What has Ronaldo got to do with the Council?"

"He is the leader ... president, if you like."

"Council for what?"

"I cannot tell you."

"You are not a well of information, are you?" Sandi said sarcastically.

"Nope," Garret responded.

"Argh! I am going to sleep."

"Me, too."

Sandi knew that something about Garret was not right. He had lied, and he continued to lie. Yet that first impression stuck with her. Since he had started talking to her, she felt more comfortable with him despite the craziness that was going on. Something about Garret seemed almost familiar to her. *I sure know how to pick men*, she thought as she finally dropped off to sleep.

Four—February 2003

Sandi woke from a dreamless sleep. Once again, Jektu was gone, but he came back shortly after she got up. He brought some tubers and vegetables, which he cooked in the rabbit skins. He was incredibly resourceful at finding food and preparing it. When Jektu was finished cooking, he and Garret took their share of food in separate directions. Sandi ate alone again. They had been traveling east, following the small stream as it flowed from the mountains at the bottom of the gully. They had camped in the bottom of the gulley. The north side was covered mostly in grasses and scrub oak with a few scattered pine trees. The south side, protected from the summer sun, was thick with the scrub oak at the bottom, but near the top, the pine trees created a thick forest. About halfway up, just before the pine trees began to thicken, Sandi could see the opening to a cave.

"Are you looking at the cave?" Garret asked when he returned from eating his breakfast.

"Yeah. It is a steep climb to get up there. It could be some kind of shelter."

"You want to go up and check it out?" Garret asked.

"It looks small. Probably not worth the climb," Sandi answered.

"You can never tell how big it is just from the entrance."

"Okay. This is your hike," Sandi said. *This must be where the heart of the bison is*, Sandi thought. She wondered if it was something in the cave or near it.

The climb was difficult, but it was cool inside the cave. "Is your heart of the bison in here?" Sandi asked Garret.

"I do not know," Garret answered. "The cave I was looking for should be much bigger than this."

"Someone has been in here recently," Sandi said, pointing to the ceiling. Though it was blackened with soot from fires, Sandi could see no sign of the hearths on the floor of the cave. "Maybe they found the heart of the bison and took it."

Garret laughed good-naturedly. "The Heart of the Bison is the name of the cave I am looking for, and this cave is too small."

Sandi looked around the small cave. Near the back was a pile of rocks. There was one large, flat rock on the bottom with several smaller rocks piled on top. "Look at the pile of rocks," she said. "Someone put them there on purpose."

"So, are they from somewhere else?" Garret asked.

"No, but someone put them in a nice stack."

"So?" Garret asked.

"We should see what is under the big rock on the bottom. Maybe it is a grave like the lovers' grave."

"My very thought," Garret said.

They worked carefully to remove the rocks. They didn't find anything interesting among them. "The rock on the bottom is bigger than I had thought it would be. Now what?" Sandi asked.

"We will just have to move it to see what it is hiding," Garret answered.

"It will take some levers," Sandi said. "Maybe we should get Marc and his men to help us."

Garret looked at Jektu, and they nodded to each other. They dug around one side to get handholds under the edge.

"This rock is too big for two men," Sandi said as they dug.

"That your expert opinion on rocks?" Garret asked.

"I told you, I know my rocks. That is too big, even if it is not sticking in the ground."

"Nothing like an expert," Garret said to Sandi. Then he said to Jektu, "Ready?" Jektu nodded, and they both squatted with their hands under the rock. They were situated so that Jektu would have to lift the heaviest side.

"Be careful you do not hurt yourselves," Sandi said to Garret.

"On three?" Garret said to Jektu. Jektu grunted in answer.

"You had better wait until …"

"One," Garret said.

"We can get …"

"Two."

"Some help from …"

"Three."

"The other … what the …?" The men heaved, and the rock moved. They heaved four times, each time moving the rock a little to the side. At the end of the fourth heave, they had moved the end of the rock a quarter turn from the original position. Even before they had finished, Sandi could see there was an opening below the stone.

"That is impossible. What do you feed him?" Sandi said more than asked.

"He has always been pretty strong for his age," Garret answered. "Okay, there is an opening here," he said excitedly.

Jektu said something. Sandi could tell he was excited, but he spoke too quickly for her to understand anything.

"Maybe, maybe not," Garret said to Jektu.

"Maybe, maybe not *what?*" Sandi asked.

"Maybe, maybe not, this is the secret of life," Garret said.

"That again!" Sandi was getting tired of this game.

The two men maneuvered the rock to fully expose the opening. Jektu said something that included Sandi's name. "We cannot leave her here," Garret said to Jektu. Then he faced Sandi. "Jektu is afraid you that will spill the beans about the secret of life. I need you to give me your word that you will not tell anyone what we find unless I say that it is okay."

"You knew there was a cave here all of the way back at the dig. How did you know that?"

"Technological magic," Garret answered.

"I am no fool! I can tell this opening has been closed for thousands of years. There is no way you could have known about it," Sandi insisted.

"Right," Garret said.

"But you did know."

Garret turned to Jektu and then back to Sandi. "I knew? Who told us to move the rocks?"

"Yeah, but you came straight to this cave."

"Well, now that we are here, it seems that way."

"You did not know there was a secret under the rocks?"

"No," Garret answered.

"Then it is my cave! I found it. Maybe you should ask me if I will let you go in."

Garret laughed. "Touché."

"So? You ready?" Sandi demanded.

"All right, then, we all go in."

Jektu said something. Garret shrugged his shoulders as he unpacked his lantern. Garret went first. Sandi followed, and then Jektu came last. About fifteen feet in, they came to a very narrow place in the tunnel. Garret grunted as he squeezed through. It was tight for Sandi, but she made it in. Jektu could not squeeze in no matter how he twisted and turned.

"You will have to wait here or go back to the cave entrance," Garret said to Jektu.

Jektu responded. Sandi could hear the disappointment in his voice, but more, she could understand him well enough to know he felt it was ironic Sandi was going in, and he wasn't. Sandi thought about what Jektu had said as she and Garret worked their way deeper into the cave. Though she only understood a few of the words, she was sure about the meaning of his statement.

The going was difficult, but in a relatively short distance, the tunnel opened into a giant cavern. Their flashlights panned through the darkness like fingers of luminescence. There was a large, flat wall covered with paintings and handprints. Sandi had never seen or heard of so many paintings in one place. Everywhere the light beam landed, there was a new painting. After unknown thousands of years, the colors were still vibrant, and the paintings were so alive that they seemed to move as the light played across them.

As they stood side by side, they both began to shine their lights higher up the west wall. They both illuminated a large painting of an aurochs at the same time. Sandi gasped as she saw the size and beauty of the painting. She moved next to Garret, feeling his chest rise and fall as her right arm touched his left arm.

"What on earth have we found?" Sandi breathed reverently.

Garret switched his flashlight from his right arm to his left arm and began shining it across the aurochs. "I do not know. This is not an area known for cave paintings," Garret answered in a whisper.

"Have you ever heard of a cave with so many paintings?" Sandi asked, wondering if he had intentionally moved his arm away from her.

"No."

"We need to set up more lights. Get some floodlights, you know," Sandi said. "There is too much to see with just these little lights."

"This is a holy place. This is from the very beginning of religion. It was never meant to be seen with steady bright lights of our time." Garret's voice was shaking.

"What do you mean?"

"We should not invade this place with bright lights and cameras. At least not now."

"What do you propose to do?"

"We will make torches and light it as it was meant to be lit … the way it was lit when it was created. Look," Garret said as he panned his light. "There are eight small rock piles with open spaces in the middle. I'm guessing they were used to hold lighted torches."

"I see what you mean. We can give Jektu a note and send him to get the others. That will give several days before they get here with the lights and equipment… time for us set it all up as it was originally."

"I am not sure about telling Marc just yet," Garret said.

"But this is his expedition. We have to let him know."

"This place is not mine or yours or Marc's." Garret faced her and put his left hand on her shoulder. "What will happen? First, Pakistan will say it belongs to them and close it off to the world. Then maybe some fundamentalist, Taliban-like people will decide these paintings threaten their beliefs or their God. Then they decide to use bombs to destroy it. It has happened before. A find like this cannot be risked in this kind of world."

As Sandi listened to Garret, she felt his hand on her shoulder. It was as though he was sharing something very personal with her. Suddenly, a strong feeling came over her—like something she had never felt before. "We are not alone!" she said in a loud whisper. "Someone is in here with us!"

"Who?" Garret asked.

Sandi began moving her light around almost frantically. Then her light landed on it—it was a motionless shape against a large rock in front of the wall with the great aurochs. As she stared at it in the beam of her light, she began to make the form out. It was a skeleton—the bones of a man in a pile facing out from the large rock, as if the man had died sitting against it, maybe staring up at the giant aurochs.

Sandi held her light as Garret slowly moved toward the man. Carefully, Garret moved in front of the bones and shined his light on the skull. Garret fell to his knees and cried, "The Guardian!" Then Garret put his face on the floor of the cave. He looked like a Muslim man at prayer. Sandi could not move as she watched and wondered at Garret's strange antics.

Finally, Garret got shakily to his feet. Sandi had not moved. As Garret came to her, she shined her light in his face. She could see the courses of tears in the dust on his cheeks. The cool darkness outside the beam of their lights seemed to breathe, maybe sigh. Sandi realized that she was on holy ground. "Who is the Guardian?" she asked reverently.

"This cave is your history, Sandi. This is not the Heart of the Bison, but I know this place. We are on the cusp of eternity here."

"What do you mean by *my* history?" Sandi asked. "How come it is not your history?"

"Listen," Garret said. Sandi heard muffled noises behind her. "Jektu is calling. Come, we must go to him."

Sandi knew she would not get an answer to her questions—at least not now. As she followed Garret out, she realized she had shared something with him as important to him as his life. Even though she did not know what had happened, the intimacy of whatever it was laid in her heart. There was something about Garret and what he was looking for that she wanted to know—something she felt close to, almost close enough to touch, but not close enough to understand.

As Sandi climbed out of the cave, Jektu was excitedly talking to Garret. Sandi was able to determine that he was saying that Marc was coming. "What is he saying?" she asked Garret, pretending that she did not understand him.

"Marc is coming up the side of the mountain," Garret answered.

Sandi ran to the entrance of the cave. Marc was about thirty feet from the entrance. When he saw Sandi, he stopped. Sandi ran down the hill to him.

"Are you all right?" he asked.

"I am fine," Sandi answered. "I saw Garret sneak out of camp. I followed him, and then they discovered me, so I joined them. I am so glad you followed my trail and got my notes. Where are the others?"

"Well, Kelvin followed your trail for about a quarter mile from camp, and then it disappeared. I found one note just before the trail disappeared."

"That's all?" Sandi asked.

"When you didn't show up for breakfast, we started looking for you. Kelvin found your tracks out of camp, but he could not find any tracks for Garret and Jektu. That was as far as the trail went. I decided to continue in the direction you were traveling on the chance that I might catch up. Kelvin went back to camp to get Akhtar, Larry, and some food. I left a trail for them to follow. They caught up with me yesterday afternoon. We split up to look for some sign. We have been in contact on the satellite phone. They have been traveling roughly parallel to me.

"I had begun to think that we wouldn't find you. Then this morning, from the other side of the draw, I saw the three of you start up the side of the hill. I gave my position to Akhtar, Kelvin, and Larry. I watched until you disappeared in the cave, and then I started after you. The others should be here soon."

Marc and Sandi walked to the cave. "What's the meaning of this?" Marc demanded of Garret.

"I wanted to do some of my own exploring," Garret answered.

"Why didn't you talk to me about it?" Marc asked.

"Look, I got you permission and finances to continue your research at your cave. If I want to pound a couple of rocks on my own, why should that bother you?"

"I don't like to be used. You got me here so that you could go off on your own to … so you could beat me to the connection between Cro-Magnons and Neandertals."

"You are partly right," Garret said. "I have my own private reasons for being here. But what I am looking for is something beyond your find at the lovers' cave."

"You must have come from our camp by a very direct path," Marc said. "It's clear that you knew about this cave. So, what's up here?"

"You did know about this cave," Sandi said. "Did you know about the cavern, too? No, do not answer. Of course, you knew. What is going on here?"

"What cavern?" Marc asked.

Garret looked at Sandi—it seemed almost in disgust for revealing the cavern.

"Sorry," Sandi said. "It just slipped out. Besides, he is here now."

"What cavern?" Marc asked Sandi.

"I am not saying anything else. Ask Garret," Sandi said.

"What cavern?" Marc demanded of Garret.

"There is a cavern." Garret nodded his head toward the opening. "We only had a couple of minutes inside. It appears to be a Cro-Magnon holy room. There are Cro-Magnon paintings on the walls, but no signs of Neanderthal influence."

Marc looked inquiringly at Sandi.

"I did not see any signs of Neandertals," she said.

"How big is the cavern?" Garret asked Sandi.

"There is something about this cavern that is special, at least to Garret. I just do not want to say any more about it. Garret led the way here, and so I am just going to let him answer any questions you have," Sandi said.

Marc looked at Garret.

"Okay," Garret conceded. "There is no way to describe the cavern. You will just have to see it. I can tell you, judging by the size of the cavern and the sophistication of the work, this was not the entrance the people who did the work used. It is too small."

"Well, maybe we'd better find the real entrance and see what that looks like and if it is well hidden," Marc said. "Or do you already know that?" he asked Garret.

"What do you mean?" Sandi asked.

"We have been moving as quickly as we could in this direction. He must have come straight here. He must have known about the cavern," Marc said.

"This entrance was blocked off," Sandi said. "I observed the rocks very carefully as we moved them. This entrance has been sealed off for several thousand years."

"All the more reason to know that there is another entrance," Marc said. "Garret must already know where it is."

Sandi looked at Garret. "Is there another entrance?"

"I agree, there must be one," Garret said. "I have never seen it. This was my first time in the cavern."

"But you came directly to this cave," Sandi said. "You must have known something."

"I had some idea of a cavern in this area from some other sources and traditions. I am not at liberty to tell you about them. I did not know exactly where the cavern was or how to get in. In fact, this is not the cavern I was looking for."

"But you knew this cave was here," Sandi insisted.

"We spotted the cave this morning. I did not know it was there, and I have never seen it before. We all hiked up the hill. You found the entrance to the cavern," Garret said to Sandi.

"Well, you were going someplace, and this is where you ended up," Marc said.

"This is not necessarily where I ended up. It is more accurately where you caught up with me."

"All right, then, where were you going?" Marc asked.

"Do not worry about that," Garret said. "What I was looking for is not nearly as big as this cavern."

"So, this is not the Heart of the Bison?" Marc asked.

"What do you know about the Heart of the Bison?" Garret demanded.

"I'm not stupid. You keep your secret … I'll keep mine."

"What is the Heart of the Bison?" Sandi asked. "And where is it?"

"It is an ancient cave that is important to me. I can now say it is not anywhere around here," Garret said.

"But you thought it was," Sandi asked.

"After seeing this cavern, I am pretty sure the Heart of the Bison cannot be close to it."

"Does that have something to do with the Guardian?" Sandi asked.

"Who's the Guardian?" Marc asked.

"It is a legend," Garret answered.

"No, it is not," Sandi said. "It is a fossil in this cave. I wonder how he got there and how you knew about him … and especially how his being there means the Heart of the Bison is not here."

"Sandi, what I tell you is the truth," Garret said. "What seems to be a lie seems that way because of what you do not understand. However, there are things I cannot tell you. Rather than make a story up or tell you a lie, I just refuse to answer."

"Well, I'm not buying that," Marc said. "But it'll have to do for now. Let's see this big find."

"The others should be here soon. Maybe we should wait," Sandi said.

"The others?" Garret asked.

"Kelvin, Larry, and Akhtar came with me," Marc said. "Well, not exactly with me ... we were spread out looking for Sandi. I called them when I saw you all climbing up to the cave. They should be here in a few minutes."

Suddenly, Jektu said something. Sandi didn't understand all the words, but she knew that he had said that Kelvin and Akhtar were coming.

"How far?" Garret asked.

Sandi could not understand the answer.

"Jektu says that Kelvin and Akhtar are coming down the stream. They will be here in about ten minutes."

"How does he know that?" Marc asked.

"He has very strong senses. It is part of the pattern of his strange birth defect."

"I've never heard of anything like that," Marc said.

"Like I said, it is very rare," Garret said.

In about ten minutes, Kelvin and Akhtar arrived. Larry was about five minutes behind them. Marc and Garret explained to them what had happened.

"What do we do now?" Garret asked.

"The first thing is to get our equipment in and fully measure, document, and photograph everything in the cave," Marc said.

"This cave is pristine," Garret said. "No one has been in this cave since the last Cro-Magnon painted the final painting. It would be an incredible shame if you went down there with a lot of equipment and started tearing everything up."

"Garret is right," Sandi said.

"We won't touch anything," Marc said. "As it stands now, this is a new discovery. We would need new paperwork to disturb anything or remove any significant artifacts."

"Then what are you going to do with equipment?" Garret asked.

"Well, I don't think that the political climate is at all favorable to report a finding of the magnitude you describe. What you say we have here is a bonanza of ancient Cro-Magnon artwork. There are some fundamentalist groups who would feel threatened by a discovery of this magnitude. These groups have shown a willingness to destroy things like you say are in this cave.

"I want to completely document this cave exactly as it is today. My people and I are well trained in methods of documenting an archeological site without disturbing anything. We'll take some small, insignificant artifacts just to help us date the cavern when we get back to the lab. We'll work slowly and deliberately. When we're done, everything will be basically just like you found it. I want to find the main entrance. It would be useful to see what it looks like and to find out why no one has stumbled into this cavern in so many thousands of years. We want to make sure that no one finds this place until we can protect it.

"Once we have collected and digitized all of the information, we will close this entrance as it was found. When the time is right, and when the political situation is more favorable, we can open the whole thing up."

"How are you going to get all of this information out?" Garret asked.

"I brought several data disks with imprinted audio labels. They look like music CDs. I can use laser surveying equipment that I have adapted to work in caves. I can do point clouds that will allow us to recreate the cave walls in three dimensions later. I can digitize everything and store it on the CDs."

"I am glad you are of the same mind on the find," Garret said. "There is a very narrow section in the tunnel. The rock there is not dense. We will have to chip it out somewhat to get equipment and some of the larger crew members in."

"I have my rock hammer. Kelvin and Larry have theirs. Do you think we can get it done with them?"

"I think you should be able to do it. It does not need much," Garret said.

Marc contacted the camp by satellite phone and requested that Gary and Rick bring the equipment that he would need to gather the survey data on the cavern. Meanwhile, the men took turns chipping the rock to open the narrow part of the entrance.

In the evening, Jektu started work on two arrows. "What are they for?" Sandi asked Garret.

"Jektu is going to make torches to light the cave. He is an expert in how people lived back then. The torches would have been constructed of dried grasses and twigs tied together on the end of large sticks. To make them burn, he needs to soak them in tallow from a large animal. He will use the arrows and a hooked throwing stick to kill a deer. The camp will feast tomorrow."

"I have not seen any deer signs," Sandi said.

"If there is a deer around, Jektu will find it. He is very accomplished in the use of arrows like the ones he is making."

The next morning, Jektu was gone before Sandi got up. Sandi and Garret spent the morning documenting and describing the paintings and handprints in the cave. They counted seventy-two paintings of animals of various sizes in different locations around the cave. The west wall was obviously the central focus of the cavern. They counted 104 hands painted or outlined on the walls of the cavern. Most were made by shadowing. The person put his hand against the wall, and the pigment was blown around the hand through a hollow bone.

All the hands were left hands except nine right hands. The hands were of varying sizes, but obviously all were adult. However, just below the head of the great aurochs was a left handprint that was smaller than all the rest. Garret was interested in this particular hand, since it was placed in an honored place below the head of the great aurochs.

When they returned to camp for lunch, Jektu was preparing a large deer. Garret told him there were eight rock piles that appeared to have been bases to hold torches. The bases formed a large arc behind the large rock and the bones of the man Garret had called the Guardian.

Jektu had hung the deer from a large pine branch near the cave entrance. It was already skinned, and one hind leg had been removed. Jektu was working on it near a small fire that he had started.

"After seeing the deer hung out like that, I am not sure I can eat it," Sandi said to Garret.

"You will probably have a change of heart later when you are hungry, and it is cooked," Garret said with a broad smile.

After lunch, Sandi and Kelvin began to explore the cavern. They found two other tunnels that exited the cave. One was the continuation of the tunnel they had used to get in. Near the other exit, they found a pile of rocks. They were broken and pulverized as if they had been pounded to pieces with rocks. Sandi could tell that most of the rocks were from inside the cavern, but there were some small pieces and shards of rocks that came from somewhere else.

The most impressive thing in the cavern was the gigantic aurochs on the western wall. Many of the animals were higher than a man could reach, but the aurochs was highest—about thirty feet up. The people must have built some kind of scaffolding to paint it. The front and back parts of the aurochs were painted using different techniques.

While Sandi and Kelvin explored, Marc, Larry, and Akhtar worked on setting up control points to do the survey. In the evening, they all compared notes for Marc to produce the official diary of the day's work while Jektu helped cook the deer.

"I have never eaten venison, but it really does smell good while it is cooking," Sandi said.

"You will be eating a meal that is close to what the people who made the paintings in the cavern ate," Garret said.

"Like the rabbit stew?"

"Of course, we do not have their recipes, but that is a pretty good guess as to how prehistoric men cooked," Garret responded.

Sandi moved closer to Garret and looked over his shoulder. "You really take good notes," she said to Garret, hoping to keep the conversation going.

"Thanks. That is something I have worked on over the years."

"Keeping notes has always been a problem with me. I get all excited about the discovery part, but I cannot seem to generate much interest in keeping the notes."

"Maybe I could give you some pointers later," Garret responded.

Sandi began felt she was making a connection with Garret, but then at dinner, he and Jektu both wandered off.

"What's going on with you and Garret?" Marc asked as they were eating.

"What do you mean?"

"Come on. You can't tell me that you haven't noticed how Mr. Cold Fish is suddenly paying a great deal of attention to you."

"I am sure I do not know what you are talking about."

"Well, he's always looking at you when you are around, and he seems much more open to talking with you than the rest of the crew. And what's this about how he's going to teach you how to make notes? Your notes are fine. You don't need him to train you. What happened while you were traveling through the forest?"

"Nothing. I mean, I gave him part of a granola bar, and he took it behind a tree or someplace to eat. Look ... Gary and Rick are here with the survey equipment. You had better go down and help them carry it up."

"Yeah. That's what I'd better do." Marc gave her a sidelong look as he got up.

Later in the evening, as a form of entertainment, the members of the crew made up stories to explain the things they'd discovered during the day. This night, the stories were about the small hand. One was about a holy midget. It was fun and entertaining. Sandi's story of the son of a chief was voted most likely by the members of the crew. While the rest of the crew was making up stories, Jektu finished nine torches to light the cavern.

The next morning, they took the torches into the cavern, and Jektu positioned eight of them in the rock piles. Then Garret lit the ninth one. The crew followed him to the entrance where they had found the pile of broken rocks.

All the lights were turned off. The light of Garret's torch illuminated the area around him, but most of the cavern remained shrouded in darkness. It was easy for Sandi to feel the awe of the prehistoric men who had no electricity. This was how they saw their world. Sandi began to feel ancient herself.

Garret started at the first torch. As he touched it with the one he carried, it sputtered and sprang to life. In the light, part of the wall nearby seemed to come to life. The paintings danced with the flickering light that was compressed by darkness around the torch.

One by one, Garret ignited the torches. After the eighth torch, he stepped in front of the arc near the Guardian. Although the light was not strong enough to light the entire cavern, it brought the wall with the aurochs on it to life.

Sandi suddenly felt out of place. She sensed that this was a holy room for men only. All the others gathered around Garret to stare at the incredible effect the torches created. No one spoke. Sandi stood alone far to the side. She wanted to follow the others, but she was frozen in place.

Someone took her hand. She turned her head. Garret quickly tilted his head to where the others were standing and then back to her. Sandi slowly shook her head. Garret squeezed her hand tighter and began to pull her.

Sandi followed, still reluctantly. When they reached the others, Sandi stared at the floor, afraid to look up. Then, she had an incredible feeling the Guardian had expected her—had been waiting for *her*! She looked up. In the torchlight, the animals took on an eerie life of their own. The artists had used the texture of the rocks and the shading of colors to capture the flickering light in a way that the paintings seemed to move and breathe. Above all the paintings, the great aurochs seemed to come off the wall and float in the air above the herds below. The wall seemed to float in a dark universe surrounded by infinity.

Garret relaxed the pressure on Sandi's hand, though he still held it softly. She was transported to an ancient time. She forgot about planes, electricity, hair dryers, and tall glass buildings. She sensed a world of stone tools and dependency upon nature and magic. In this room, the magic of the earth permeated everything, and Garret held that magic in the power of his torches and his understanding of the mysteries of this people. Soon, the smell of burning animal fat filled the room. Sandi felt something about these people that she could never learn from fossils or books. The Guardian's bones sat behind her. Sandi thought of this man who had sat alone in this cave—the last living man of his people to look on the paintings and the giant aurochs. She felt a sense of awe for him and his people. Time seemed irrelevant, and space was all that mattered as she wondered what happened to the people and why they had abandoned this cavern. Sandi still felt the Guardian had expected her—died knowing that she would come. The feeling was so personal that she could not talk to about it.

Sandi had no idea how long they stared in silence at the wall with the living paintings before them. Finally, one of the torches flickered and died. The members of the group began to silently work their way out of the cavern. Sandi was still standing beside Garret; he was no longer holding her hand. They turned together and followed the others out. Sandi imagined that she had felt strong feelings from Garret when he'd held her hand. Now, she wondered if it was real or just something she wanted.

No one spoke until they were all back in their camp. The sun was nearing midday. They must have sat in the cave for more than an hour. Sandi was the first to speak as she fought back tears she could not explain. "What happened to the people who had such skill? It is hard to think that they are gone."

"The paintings were so impressive when we first saw them," Garret said. "But when you see them in the light they were created for, you get an entirely different perspective. The positions of the torches throw different shadows on the protrusions and indentations of the rock walls. Whoever did the paintings must have studied the play of light on the texture of the wall in detail before beginning a painting."

"Well, it's obvious that to do so many paintings must have taken generations, and yet every animal is perfectly placed and shaded to take advantage of the position of the eight torches," Marc said. "This isn't the work of one incredible artist … it's the creation of a culture."

"I have seen photos of other caves," Sandi said. "I have been in some of them, but this is the first one where you can tell where the original lighting came from. It is impressive how the other paintings use the texture of the walls to accentuate the shape and shading of the painting. Now I think if we could determine how they were originally illuminated, we would see something sensational … something similar to this cave."

"This cave is a living fossil," Garret said. "It needs to be protected."

"I agree," Marc said. "With the proper equipment, it can be perfectly digitized so that it could be completely recreated."

"What are you saying?" Garret asked.

"This cavern is a fragile thing," Marc answered. "It has protected these paintings for perhaps twenty or thirty thousand years, but an earthquake could destroy all or part of it at any time. There are two more tunnels leaving the cavern that someone could find. A fundamentalist Muslim sect might decide to destroy it just because it doesn't fit their idea of God."

"What do you propose?" Sandi asked.

"Well, with the survey equipment I brought, I can get general dimensions of the cave and collect point clouds of each painting and handprint. Along with the pictures, we can get enough information to create a model of the cavern for the purposes of acquiring funding, but I cannot get enough information to recreate the magic of the cavern.

"My proposal is that we get all of the information that my equipment can gather. At the same time, we need to follow the tunnels to see if there's anything that can be done to secure the cavern from accidental discovery.

"We do all of this with the minimal amount of disturbance to the cavern. When we're done, we seal this entrance as it was before we came. Then, sometime in the future, when it would be safe to do it, we come back with more advanced equipment. Then we could gather enough information to document every crack, indentation, and mark. With the right laser equipment, we could gather enough information to exactly recreate all of the paintings and the effects of the lighting."

"That would be expensive," Sandi said.

"Think of it," Marc said. "Suppose this cavern could be duplicated in several places around the world? People would pay to see what we saw."

"You would commercialize this?" Sandi asked incredulously.

"What you saw was something," Marc said. "But what you experienced was much more. Some people might look at photos or movies of that cavern and say, 'Hey, neat!' Others might say, 'So what?' But if we recreate the whole cavern, most people would experience something similar to what we all felt. You seem very elitist to want to deny the world that experience. It's obvious this cavern would not last if it was opened to tourism, but a duplicate would offer this experience to the world without putting this cavern in any danger."

"You propose a grand scheme," Garret said. "But it may take years before things are stable enough to do what you say."

"I know that," Marc agreed. "It may not actually come to pass in the foreseeable future. That's why we must all promise to keep this secret. If we leak it out, there will be incredible pressure to exploit it."

"What you talk about sounds like exploitation," Sandi said.

"It is," Marc agreed. "It is in the sense that, to properly protect this find for all time, it will be necessary to attract a lot of money. That kind of money has strings. But my plan is first and foremost to protect the cavern."

"Marc is right," Garret said. "We do not know what the future will bring, but, for now, the most important thing is to protect what we have found. The sense of participating in the magic of seeing how early man partnered with nature is peace inspiring. In this cave, the people cooperated with the material and texture of the rocks to create a living world ... an act of creation to foster goodwill between the people and the earth they needed to survive. In the cavern, we all could sense that. The more people that experience what we experienced, the better. Pictures in textbooks or murals on flat walls will not do what this cavern does."

Sandi knew that Garret was right.

The next morning, Garret, Jektu, and Sandi followed the small tunnel that was near where they first entered the cave. The tunnel was narrow, and the floor sloped up and down as they walked. The air was still and musty. Garret was first in line as they walked. They had not gone far when Garret stopped. The tunnel was blocked.

"These rocks have been placed and interlocked to close the tunnel off," Garret said.

"They also do not belong here," Sandi said.

"What do you mean?" Garret asked.

"They do not come from the cavern, nor did they come from the side of the mountain where we came in."

"You are sure about that?" Garret questioned.

"I am never wrong," Sandi answered.

"Never?"

"Never."

Garret picked up a rock and hit the face of the blocked tunnel. "There is no hollow sound. These rocks were packed in tightly far down the tunnel. We do not need to worry about anyone coming in this way."

Jektu said something to Garret. Sandi could not understand everything, but she was sure Jektu wanted to open the tunnel.

"I do not know," Garret said to Jektu. "We will talk about it later." Garret started back down the tunnel. He seemed frustrated. Sandi and Jektu followed him.

Next, they followed the second tunnel nearly a mile, where they found it completely blocked off. Rocks had fallen from the ceiling, apparently as a consequence of an earthquake. They tried several ways to get around the blockage, but to no avail. There were places where they could feel fresh air seeping in, but there was no space big enough for a person to crawl through.

It was late in the day by the time they got back to the cavern. Back at the camp, the main topic of discussion was whether to open the blocked tunnel. Some thought that there must be something behind the rocks that the ancient people were hiding. They were in favor of opening it. But Garret and Marc both agreed that it should not be opened, because it might open another way in from the outside.

In the morning, Jektu and Garret were in an animated conversation. They were away from everyone, but Sandi could see the gestures that Jektu used. He thought that there was something important in the blocked tunnel. Finally, their conversation was complete.

"I think we should open the tunnel," Garret said to Marc.

"You know what I think about that," Marc answered. "What's changed your mind?"

"I have worked with Jektu for several years. It has always paid off for me to follow his hunches. He is sure there is something pertinent in that tunnel."

"What?"

"He is not sure about what it is, but he is sure there is something."

"Well, it will take me a few more days to get all of the information from my survey equipment," Marc said. "Akhtar is getting anxious about our work here. It's outside the approved area, and it's also outside his biradare."

Sandi had not heard that word before. "What is a biradare?"

"It's a patrilineal organization. The members of the biradare look out for each other Usually, biradares cooperate with their neighbors. Occasionally, they get involved in feuds that can be destructive. Akhtar is concerned that our being here could raise some controversy with the biradare that claims this area. You can work on the blocked tunnel until I get the data collected and verified, but then we need to get back to the original dig site whether or not you find anything."

As soon as they got in the cavern, Sandi and Garret went to the blockage to plan how to get it open. Sandi took pictures and measurements. Garret and Jektu pried the rocks out and placed them in rows along the length of the tunnel. Jektu showed his incredible strength along with great endurance. He worked all morning. In the afternoon, Larry replaced Garret at the wall, but Jektu continued on as strong as he had been in the morning.

Meanwhile, Marc discovered a part of the wall where some of the paintings appeared to have been damaged by fire. Sandi took time from the work in the tunnel to examine the pile of rocks near the main tunnel into the cavern. Most of the rocks there had come from the cavern. It was a large pile, but they had not fallen from the ceiling. Someone had moved them to the entrance from inside the cavern. A couple of the rocks were too large for men to move without some form of machine or very strong levers.

The biggest rock seemed to have been placed so that it blocked the entrance. There was evidence that the rocks had been pounded and broken from outside of the entrance. It appeared that someone had piled the rocks in front of the entrance to block it, and then someone from the outside had pounded them into pieces to unblock it.

The mysteries of the cavern were a topic of conversation each night. Why were the tunnels blocked off? Who brought all of the wood necessary to build a large fire near the wall where the paintings had been damaged? Why did they need a big fire? Every day, there were more questions and fewer answers.

Five—March 2003

"Look! There's a cavity!" Larry shouted.

Sandi knew from the hollow sound of the rocks that they were close. "Stand back … let me see." Larry made room for her. Sandi shined her flashlight through the crack. It was open behind, but the crack was not big enough. As the work proceeded, Sandi carefully measured each rock and drew it to scale on her notepad. Rock by rock, the men cleared the face. The rocks stacked in front of the opening were all long. Each course consisted of two long rocks placed so that they extended from the middle of the tunnel beyond a ledge that marked a point where the width of the tunnel suddenly narrowed. The next rocks had been placed to hold the first rocks against the lip so that they could not be pushed or pulled out of the way through the tunnel on the other side.

"The rocks have all been placed to close the cavern off," Garret observed. "But the strange thing is they have been placed from this side, almost like someone was trying to lock themselves in."

"No," Sandi said. "The rocks at the main entrance were broken through. Suppose both entrances were open at one time. Perhaps two tribes shared the cavern using different tunnels. Then suppose the tribes from this tunnel decided to lock the other side out. They put the stones at the main entrance. Then that tribe managed to break through and get back in. So, they blocked this tunnel off to keep the others out, but they did a much better job, and the other tribe was never able to break back in."

"Maybe," Garret said.

After the pictures were taken, they began removing the last rocks. Finally, Sandi could look over the rocks with a flashlight. The musty odor from the space behind was almost nauseating. The air had probably been trapped in the space for thousands of years. The beam of light did not illuminate very much. Sandi was not tall enough to look over the remaining rocks and see the floor, but she could see that the small space was blocked off with more rocks at the other end. The tunnel behind the blockage was only about twenty inches wide. The rocks at the other end of the narrow tunnel were much bigger than the ones they had been removing, and they were not placed as carefully.

"What do you see?" Garret asked.

"Just a small room, about eight feet long. Here, you look." Sandi gave the light to Garret.

"There is nothing here to explain all of this elaborate rock work," he said. "There are no paintings … nothing except another wall. I do not see why they would use so much effort to build a wall to hide a wall. It does not make sense."

Garret stepped back, and Larry and Jektu each took a look.

Jektu said something, and Garret answered, "Are you sure?"

Sandi thought that Jektu had said something about a tomb.

"What did he say?" Larry asked.

"Jektu thinks the space behind these rocks is a tomb," Garret answered.

"It looks empty to me," Larry said.

"We need to finish removing the rocks," Garret said.

They all worked feverishly to get the rocks out of the way. When they were more than half done, Sandi took the light and pushed forward. The beam of light played along the floor of the tunnel as Sandi slowly raised it. Right in the middle, the light landed on a bone—a pile of bones.

Human bones. "Jektu was right!" Sandi exclaimed. The bones were piled in one spot as though the body had been dismembered and piled up piece by piece.

"Let me see," Garret said. He took a long look and gave the light to Jektu. "The body was not lying down when it was put here," Garret said. "It is as if the person died wedged in a standing position, and then, as the flesh and sinews decomposed, the bones just collapsed on one another."

Jektu looked in. He said something, and Garret seemed to freeze. Sandi knew Jektu's words for *earth* and *people*. He had used both of those words to describe the skeleton. He had said something about earth people! Garret took the light and crawled in.

"What is it?" Larry said.

"This body is a Neanderthal," Garret said as he handed the light back to Sandi.

Sandi looked in. There on the floor was the skeleton she had seen. How had she missed the obvious brow ridge? "Wow!" she exclaimed. "Holy cow! Larry, you had better go get Marc. Oh, my God! What in the world was he doing here? Why would the Cro-Magnons go to so much trouble to bury this guy?" Sandi could hear the thumping of her heart in her ears as she stood back. She wondered why Jektu had referred to the man as earth people. *Was Garret really just kidding when he had said that he was from Mars? What a silly idea*, Sandi thought.

"We should get this passage open," Garret said to Jektu. Jektu moved the rocks even faster than before. He lifted the biggest rocks with no help from Garret. He had cleared the rocks out of the way by the time Marc arrived.

"Larry said something about a Neandertal," Marc said.

"See for yourself," Garret said.

"Why would the Cro-Magnons put a Neandertal in a vault like this?" Marc asked after he looked. The excitement in his voice could not be hidden.

"The rocks at the back were put there, too," Sandi said. "Those rocks come from outside of this tunnel. You can see they are much bigger, and they are not placed as carefully as the ones we have been moving. It looks to me like this vault was constructed by Neandertals at that end and at this end by Cro-Magnons."

"What?" Marc said.

"You do not need me to tell you the rocks at the other end do not belong there ... or that they are different than the rocks we have been moving," Sandi said. Marc and Garret looked where Sandi pointed her light. It was obvious that the rocks were smooth, rounded, and weathered.

"Look at the size of those rocks," Marc said. "I agree that it would take a strong Neandertal to move rocks that size into his tunnel."

"There is no way anyone could move those rocks away from this side," Garret said. "You would have to break and drill them, and there is not enough room to work in that small space."

"Look," Sandi said as she pointed to one of her sketches. "On this side of the tomb, the long rocks were all placed across the opening so that the outside edge hooked outside the opening to the vault. Then they were all held in place by the rocks in the tunnel. You would not be able to pull a single rock back into that tunnel ... not even if you were a Neandertal. The rocks on the other side serve the same purpose. No one from either side could get through this tomb to the other side."

"You're right," Marc said. "At this point, there was a meeting of Cro-Magnons and Neandertals. Both sides wanted to place an indestructible barrier between them. God, I'd like to know what happened here."

"I would really like to get a closer look at the rocks on the other side," Sandi said. "I bet if we take some scrapings, we would find fossilized moss on them."

"Well, I don't want to disturb this cave any more than absolutely necessary ... at least not now. We can't take an intact Neandertal skeleton out of this cave," Marc said. "I say we take a small piece of bone for dating and analysis. Other than that, I say we leave it all as it is."

"We could say that we found the skeleton in the lovers' cave, just to get it out," Sandi offered.

"I can think of a hundred blind alleys that could lead you into," Garret said.

"Argh!" Sandi exclaimed. "I cannot stand it! You are both right."

Marc got a toe bone and some dirt from the floor near the body. Jektu and Larry spent the rest of the morning and afternoon replacing several courses of rocks to seal the tomb off.

That night, everyone made up a story to explain the strange facts. All the stories had good and bad points. For the first time, Jektu participated in the storytelling. Sandi was pleased that she could understand almost half of what he said before Garret translated it.

According to his story, the cavern was a sacred Cro-Magnon cave. It was known that Cro-Magnons went deep into caves to make their paintings. It was also known that they only used them for ceremonies.

Jektu postulated that the Cro-Magnons were off hunting, and the cavern was empty. A group of Neandertals lived in a cave near the entrance to the tunnel where the Neandertal body was found. Normally, Neandertals would not go deep into a cave. Something made them go deep enough to find the cavern. Perhaps it was an eclipse of the sun or the moon.

The Neandertals followed the tunnel to the cavern. They decided to stay, so they brought a supply of wood and built a big fire.

The Neandertals were surprised when a group of Cro-Magnons came in through the main entrance. There was a short fight, and the Neandertals drove the Cro-Magnons out.

The Neandertals may have thought that they had discovered demons deep in the earth. They moved all the loose rocks in the cavern to the entrance where the Cro-Magnons came in to keep them out. Soon, they heard the Cro-Magnons on the other side trying to break back in. The Neandertals left the cave.

The Cro-Magnons forced their way back into the ceremony cavern. They discovered the tunnel that the Neandertals had used to get in, and they blocked the tunnel to keep the Neandertals out.

After a time, the Neandertals came back to check on the path to the cavern. They found the tunnel blocked off, and they decided to block off their side also. Their strongest hunter volunteered to be sealed in the space between the blockages so that his spirit would forever stand between the demons of the cavern and his people.

Sandi clapped and cheered when Garret was through with his translation. "Bravo! That is definitely the best."

Jektu never took his hood off to expose his face, but Sandi was sure that she saw the campfire reflecting off something white under the hood. Jektu was smiling at her. Sandi was not sure if it was because of the cleverness of his story, his partially hidden smile, or the fact that she was beginning to understand his language, but she suddenly felt a new respect for him.

The next morning, they cleared all their implements and tools from the cavern, and Jektu and some of the stronger men replaced several courses of the rocks over the entrance to the cavern. With all the entrances to the cavern effectively blocked off, they broke camp before noon and started back to the lovers' cave.

Sandi walked with Garret. Gradually, they drifted behind the rest of the men. "I do not think I have been with anyone who showed as much reverence for these ancient finds as you. Why are you in paleontology?" Sandi asked as they walked.

"I guess it is just something natural for me. At a level, I can almost be a caveman. What brought you into the field?"

Sandi explained her strange sense about rocks. "Apparently, Jektu has similar skills with fossils. I wish I knew where this comes from," Sandi concluded.

"Shall I tell you my theory?"

"Any theory interests me."

"Consider a bat. It can fly around at night and catch flying insects."

"So, it just uses radar instead of light," Sandi said.

"A swallow also flies around and catches flying insects."

"Swallows can see. What is your point?"

"Because one uses light and the other uses sound, it seems that what they do is somehow different. The swallow's eyes cannot see anything. They convert light waves into electrical currents that the swallow's brain then uses to create a three-dimensional image with shape and texture.

Likewise, the bat's ears convert sound waves to electrical currents, which the bat's brain then interprets to create an image of the world around it. I believe the image in the bat's brain is as textured, detailed, and three dimensional as the image created by the swallow's brain.

"There are many more kinds of energy waves all around us. For instance, when you use a satellite phone, you are using an instrument that can sense certain types of energy waves and convert them into sound." Garret picked up a rock. "This seems to be an inanimate object. But if you look at it on a molecular level, you will see incredible activity. That activity creates energy waves. For instance, if this rock were heated, and you were blindfolded and asked to slowly move your hand toward it, at some point, you would know you were getting close. You would know that because your hand would intercept energy waves from the rock.

"The rock is constantly sending energy out at all temperatures. Imagine that some characteristic of its energy pattern is influenced by its creation. For instance, if it cooled from magma, it might have a certain pattern, or if was created by heat and pressure, it might have another pattern. Those patterns might be impacted in small ways by the location on the world where the creation occurred—perhaps by magnetic or gravitational fields. The information about where the rock belongs could be constantly coming from the rock. The only thing needed to determine where the rock belongs is a sensing device to intercept and interpret its energy pattern.

"Suppose, in the ancient part of our brains, there are cells that could do that. Maybe they are so ancient they have atrophied. Perhaps occasionally someone is born with the old cells in full force ... a sort of genetic throwback. That person would know a great deal about rocks just from the energy she could sense and interpret, but she would be no more able to explain it than a seeing person could explain the color red to a blind person."

"So, you think I am sensing signals from the rock?" Sandi said.

"Who knows?" Garret said. "I am just proposing something that makes sense to me. So far, no one has proven any of what I am saying, but this idea can explain a lot of the unexplainable."

"What?" Sandi asked.

"Suppose I am right. Suppose inanimate objects *do* send out energy patterns that say something about themselves. Now, suppose there is a gun that has certain energy patterns. Suppose that gun is used to shoot someone to death. The victim is going to have an extremely powerful emotional explosion about that. Mixed in with the emotions will be some images ... visual, audio, emotional, and a bunch of other stuff. That powerful emotional state will create an energy pattern in the victim's brain that will throw out energy waves as the person dies. Those waves pass through the gun and make an impact on the molecular energy in the gun, upsetting it and creating new patterns. Then along comes someone whose brain can intercept and interpret those new patterns. This person holds the gun and gets visions and emotions similar to those the victim had, and ... *voila!* ... you have a psychic who helps the police find who was holding the gun when the murder occurred. There are documented instances when psychics have actually helped solve crimes from inanimate objects near the scene. Some people say they communicate with the person's spirit … maybe so. Maybe my theory is right. Maybe it is something else entirely. All I am saying is the brain is a powerful thing, and there are energy waves all around us that have important information if we ever find a way to read them."

"You and Jektu can make up the most fascinating stories," Sandi kidded.

"How did you get involved with Marc Metcalf?" Garret asked.

"I took a class from Marc about Neandertals. He was working to prove some cooperation between the Homo sapiens neanderthalensis and Homo sapiens sapiens. That just seemed to catch my interest, so I got with him in the summer of 2001. We found the lovers' grave that summer. I have been trying to get back here since then. Why do you ask?"

"No reason … just passing the time," Garret said. "This Neanderthal/Cro-Magnon connection is very important to Marc."

"Well, of course," Sandi said. "After all, it is the premise of his doctorate. If he could find conclusive proof, it would make getting funding for future projects much easier. And you know how funding is everything in this business."

"The connection is important to you, too," Garret said.

"It is. But maybe for a different reason," Sandi said.

"What?"

"You know what this world is like. We are the Cro-Magnons. We have conquered the world, but just look at us. We kill one another over the stupidest, smallest reasons … color of skin, different religion, you name it. If there is a difference, we want to go to war and start killing one another. It would just give some hope if human beings as different as Neandertals and Cro-Magnons had at one time cooperated. Maybe if they did, there might be a clue as to how they did it."

"Do you think they did?" Garret asked.

"The violent way the lovers died and the way the Neandertal was walled in does not give one much hope, but for some reason, there is just some ray of hope inside me. It is like I can almost see it sometimes. I really think they got together in some places."

"You know, I hope you are right," Garret said.

"You do?"

"Yeah, I would love to see all of your dreams fulfilled."

"Huh?" It wasn't just the words he said but the way that he said them that caught Sandi's interest. It was more than just a statement, but Sandi didn't know what it was.

"I have never known a woman like you. I mean, working with you has been great. You really care about the work." Garret's answer was clumsy, which surprised Sandi. He was usually so in control.

"What exactly are you trying to say?" Sandi asked.

"Just that you are a very impressive woman."

Something about what he said—or the way he said it—felt personal. Of all the things she could have felt, that was the most surprising. Yet she instantly realized that she was flattered by the possibility he meant it in the way she felt it. But it was crazy. She didn't know anything about his life or who he really was. Maybe a Martian, if she believed what he had jokingly implied.

"I have really admired your work," Sandi replied, sounding to herself just as clumsy as Garret had sounded.

"Good. We have a mutual admiration society," Garret answered in a carefree tone.

Sandi quickly pulled back, too. Perhaps there could actually be something between her and Garret. After the dig was over, there would be plenty of time to figure that out. Besides, Garret was keeping a secret from her—something that might change everything.

CHAPTER 3

The Dy-emeralite City

One—March 2003

Two days after they got back to the base camp, they were packed and prepared to leave. Sandi was anxious to get back to the lab and examine the bones and artifacts. She realized that the field portion of the work was done for a long time. She hoped somehow that they would be able to finish the work in the ceremony cavern, but she felt incredible excitement about the work they would be doing with the many things they were taking back. She knew they were on the verge of discoveries that would change or challenge many ideas about Neandertals and Cro-Magnons.

Marc called all the members of the dig together near the lovers' rock. Before he could say anything, Jektu started looking around. He said something to Garret. His voice was low and tense. "What's going on?" Marc asked.

"Seventeen men are in the trees north of camp!" Garret answered.

"Where?" Marc asked.

"They are hiding in the trees and bushes!"

"How can you tell? I don't see or hear a thing," Marc said.

"Jektu can hear these things," Garret said.

Jektu spoke again. Sandi understood little of what he was saying, but his attitude was clear. He was desperate.

"In a minute or two, they will show themselves," Garret said. "They plan to kill everyone but the white woman and two men. They plan to take them as hostages."

"I don't hear a thing," Marc said. The rest of the crew was looking intently at the trees north of camp.

"When they come out, tell them we are armed," Garret said.

"Well, I don't see …"

Suddenly, four men walked out from the trees! They were dressed all in black. Their heads and faces except for their eyes were covered in black scarves. Black pants showed below the black robes they wore. Each carried a rifle pointed at the ground in front of them. Sandi didn't know much about guns, but these were big and had curved ammunition clips sticking out prominently. No one in Marc's party was armed; even the arrows that Jektu had made were packed up for the trip back.

"Too late!" Garret exclaimed. He pulled Sandi slowly toward the gravestone.

"Lie flat!" one of the terrorists ordered as they came from the trees. Jektu ran to a small hill and threw himself flat behind it. Garret pulled Sandi down behind the gravestone. The others laid down where they were, except Marc.

"What do you want?" Marc shouted.

"We just want to talk," one said with a heavy Arabic accent.

Garret pulled a radio from his pocket and pushed a red button.

"Stay where you are," Marc ordered the four men. Perhaps it was his military training, but his voice and tone carried authority. The four men stopped.

"Are you on the panic button?" Sandi could barely hear the muffled voice that came from Garret's radio.

"What?" the lead terrorist said to Marc. "You're in our country. We just want to talk to you."

"We have a terrorist group attacking us," Garret said softly into his radio. "We need a code red."

"Talk … but stay where you are while you do it," Marc commanded. The terrorists looked at one another.

"Coming in. We are twenty seconds out on my mark … mark." The quiet message on Garret's radio just confused Sandi.

"You don't give the orders here," the terrorist said. He seemed uncertain. Then he shouted, "Fire!" Marc fell and rolled to his left. The quiet morning exploded. Sandi could see some of the members of the crew get up to run, only to fall limp and broken to the ground. Then, in what seemed like a lifetime, it was eerily quiet again. Sandi could smell the sickening odor of gun smoke.

"You ... behind the rock ... stand up," the leader commanded.

"Why? So, it will be easier for you to kill me?" Garret answered.

"We are taking you, the girl, and Big Mouth as hostages," the leader answered with a thick Arabic accent.

Sandi looked over at Marc. He was sitting on the ground, and it looked like he was unharmed. The voice on the communicator said, "Ten seconds out."

Garret stood up slowly. Sandi started to stand with him, but he pushed her down with his hand on her shoulder. All around were the bleeding bodies of the men Sandi had worked with all summer. Just to her right, Hanna lay like a broken doll. Marc stood up. Sandi felt nauseated. She wanted to stand, but Garret still had his hand on her shoulder. She could see the four men standing as the cloud of smoke gently blew from them toward Marc. Other men, dressed in black, were coming from the trees.

The four men started walking across the clearing. "Don't anyone make a move. You'll be dead before you ... "

Suddenly a flying machine came over the hill behind the cave. At first, Sandi thought that it was a helicopter, but it was silent! When she saw it clearly, she could tell that it was disc shaped. It had no wings or rotors. It hovered for a second, and then it made a sound that was so low Sandi felt it in her chest more than heard it.

A loudspeaker from the flying machine gave an order in Arabic. Sandi understood enough Arabic to know the order was to throw down their guns. One of the four dropped his gun, two stood motionless, and one aimed his gun at the flying machine and fired.

"Oh, shit!" Garret exclaimed.

"Oh, shit, what?" Sandi cried.

"The EMF is not armed," Garret answered.

"What do you mean EM ..." Suddenly, the flying machine rocked, made a rotating maneuver over the four men, and then shot straight up. The four men and everything around them were flattened.

"That was clever," Garret said.

Jektu jumped from where he had been hiding and ran to the boxes that had been stacked for pickup. As Sandi looked around, she saw the men who had come from the trees dart back.

"Okay, now you are going to have to trust me," Garret said to Sandi and Marc. "Those four guys will be out for about ten minutes. When they wake up, they will be in a really lousy mood. The other thirteen guys are still in the trees. Jektu and I are leaving."

Leaving? Sandi thought. Nothing about the situation was real! *Leaving?* What did that mean? The flying machine hovered over Jektu. The air between it and the ground began to shimmer. Jektu lifted a box, put it into the shimmering air, and let it go. It floated up into the machine. *Leaving?* Nothing made sense! Jektu picked up another box. Sandi was shaking. She couldn't move. *Leaving!*

"You two have to make a choice now," Garret's voice droned on in a flat, businesslike tone. Sandi stared blankly at Jektu. "You can come with us, or you can stay to talk with the terrorists. They are going to have some pressing questions, and I do not think they will accept, 'I do not know' for an answer. They have some unpleasant methods to help you know."

"Well, I know what their methods are," Marc said. "I'm not waiting here."

"Trust me," Garret said to Sandi. "This is a little tricky if you have not done it before. I will help you." Garret took her hand. Sandi looked at him. Behind him, she could see Jektu put the last box in the air, and it disappeared into the flying saucer. Then Jektu floated up in the strange beam and disappeared. Garret squeezed Sandi's hand as the flying saucer slowly moved over them. "Sandi, are you all right?" She didn't know how to answer that. Something about her life had just changed forever. The flying saucer stopped to hover over them about fifteen feet above the ground. It looked about thirty feet in diameter. Sandi began to pull away.

"You do not have to do this," Garret said. "You could get away in the Land Rover."

"Then what?" Sandi heard herself answer.

Garret put his arms around her. Sandi felt secure there. "Will you come with me?" Garret asked.

Sandi looked up at him and nodded her head. He raised his left arm to wave at the flying machine above them. Suddenly, her insides seemed to flutter as though she had swallowed a dozen butterflies. Then she sensed the weight on her feet getting lighter, and then she was floating!

She lost all sense of balance. Garret was her only anchor, and she clung tightly to him.

They rose into a chamber that was twenty feet in diameter with a ceiling about eight feet high in the center and six feet at the outside. The walls and ceiling were a pale green color.

Something slid underneath them. Suddenly, Sandi's weight came back, and she dropped about an inch. She found herself standing on a metallic-looking floor. The smell was sweet and vaguely familiar to her, but she couldn't figure out what it was. There were other people in the flying saucer, but Sandi hardly noticed them as she focused on Garret. He led her to one side. Once she was on her feet, she began to feel a surreal calmness.

"I am going to get Marc. You wait here." The floor in the center slid open, and Garret jumped into the space above the hole and descended.

Sandi looked around. Jektu and another man were putting the boxes and bags of artifacts into a cabinet on one side of the open hole in the floor. On the other side, there were two circular rows of seats that went a little less than halfway around the room. There were three seats in front of the cabinets that faced the rows of seats across the open hole. A man in a silver-colored jumpsuit with a red-and-blue insignia on his chest was sitting in the center seat. He had his hand on a joystick. There were some characters under the insignia that reminded Sandi of hieroglyphics.

Another man stood beside the open hole. He held what looked like a control box with a sliding handle. He pushed the handle forward, and suddenly Marc and Garret floated up through the center. "Are any of the others alive?" Garret asked the man who was sitting in the center of the three seats.

"Only two," the man answered. "One is not serious, and the other is critical. I am sorry that we could not get here in time." The man spoke English with the same slight accent that Garret had.

"I will get them," Garret said.

"The others are still in the trees and armed," the man with the joystick said.

The pilot moved the joystick, and the flying machine began to move. A man tapped Sandi on the shoulder, and she screamed.

"That is just George," Garret said. "Do what he tells you to do."

"George?" Sandi heard herself say.

"George, this is Sandi; Sandi, this is George. We need to hurry before those guys in the trees decide to start shooting again, so just do what he says." Then Garret jumped back out.

"Come," George said. "We need to sit in the mass-compensating chairs."

"The what?"

George led her to the front row of chairs. "You sit here. Put your feet on the footrest, put your arms on the armrests, and hold these handles."

"No seat belts?" Sandi asked as she grasped handles built into the arms of the chair.

"Not necessary," George answered as he sat in the chair next to her. Another man seated Marc. George was wearing a jumpsuit. The insignia was the same as the pilot's, but the hieroglyphics were different. As she sat in the chair, she marveled that in all this confusion, she could tell the hieroglyphics were different. The chair had a dark blue cloth-covered seat and back.

Garret and Kelvin came up through the hole. "This one is unconscious. We will have to put him in the transporter."

The flying machine moved a little, and then Garret jumped out again. The man next to the hole pulled the lever back, and Garret dropped out of sight. Two men carried Kelvin and put him in one of three boxes that looked like glass coffins. Garret came up with Akhtar. Garret sat between Sandi and Marc. Another man helped Akhtar to a seat. Akhtar's left arm was soaked in blood. "Hold the handles. This is going to be very uncomfortable, but if you squeeze the handles when the red light goes on, it will not be bad," George said.

Sandi was about to question him when suddenly the red light went on. "Here we go!" Garret shouted. "Squeeze!" Sandi felt lightheaded and disoriented. There was an extremely uncomfortable sensation of tiny, sharp knives running through her muscles. She could feel her neck and jaw tighten up. She tried to concentrate on relaxing, but they just got tighter. She tried to scream, but her breath was just shallow pants. "Squeeze, Sandi!" Garret screamed again.

She didn't know what to do, so she started squeezing. The knives seemed to slow down, so she squeezed harder. The harder she squeezed, the more the pain in her muscles dissipated. Soon, the muscles of her jaw and neck relaxed.

She was still disoriented, and waves of nausea flowed through her. Almost as suddenly as it started, there was a sense of relief, and the red light went off.

"Okay, you can let go now," Garret said.

Sandi let go and took a couple of deep breaths. The nausea left, and physically she felt fine again.

"What the hell was that? Where are we? What is this? A flying saucer?" Marc demanded.

"You have a lot of questions, Marc," Garret said.

"A lot? A *lot*? That is the understatement of the year!" Sandi shouted.

"I second that," Marc said. "What the hell just happened?"

Just then, two men took Kelvin from the glass box and put him on a gurney-like table. A man that Sandi had not noticed before began to examine him. The man was about five feet three inches tall. He was very thin, and his arms and legs were disproportionately long. He had no hair on his face, arms, or hands. He was wearing a white jumpsuit with a green-and-yellow insignia. His head was large. His forehead was about one and a half times as high as a normal person. His eyes were also about one and half times as large as a normal person. His mouth was small and had almost no lips. He had a small, pointed chin. His pale, white skin had a barely noticeable green tint. With some exaggeration of his features, he would look very much like the drawings made by people who claimed to have been kidnapped by aliens. Kidnapped in flying saucers!

As Sandi looked at the alien and Kelvin, who was covered in blood, she began to shake. It was hard to focus.

"What's he doing?" Marc demanded.

"We call him a Thinker. You would call him a doctor. He is stabilizing Kelvin until we get him to the base laboratory."

Sandi tried to ask about the base, but she couldn't speak. She closed her eyes and heard Marc ask about the base, but for some reason, Sandi couldn't follow his words. She felt faint. The sounds of Marc and Garret talking faded from her mind, and then the smell was all she could think about. It suddenly dawned on her—the smell was like coconut.

Sandi relaxed and began to remember a trip she had taken to Universal Studios with her parents when she was in high school. Her mother didn't like scary rides, so Sandi went on the King Kong ride with her father. The thing she remembered was the strong smell of bananas just before the giant face of King Kong appeared. Instead of being scary, the whole mental image of stuffing tiny bananas in that face was hilarious. Sandi and her father had laughed about it, off and on, all day long.

Someone shook her shoulder, and she opened her eyes.

"Are you okay?" Garret asked.

"Okay?" Sandi felt confused.

"Yeah. You were laughing."

"What should I be doing?"

"I know this is all pretty strange, but believe …"

"Strange!" Sandi shouted. "You said you were from Mars … or was that Venus? Where *are* you from?" The anger felt good.

"Nothing as sinister as that," Garret answered.

"What, then?" Sandi demanded.

"Some things will have to wait. You sort of have me in a tight spot. There was not supposed to be this kind of emergency."

"Is this a flying saucer?" Akhtar asked.

"Not in the sense of how your people talk of flying saucers coming from outer space."

"Well, in what sense?" Marc asked.

"In the sense that it is shaped like a saucer, and it flies," Garret deadpanned.

"How does it fly?" Marc asked.

"Pretty good, actually," Garret answered.

"Do not be glib. You know what he means!" Sandi interjected, feeling strength in her anger.

"I do not fly these things, and I do not make them. They use gravity, magnetism, and gyroscopes, and that is about all I can say."

"Gravitation and magnetism are very weak in deep space," Marc said. "How can you fly these things out there?"

"You could not fly them there."

"Then how did you get this machine here?" Marc asked.

"We typically fly these at about thirty or forty miles high … not quite in deep space."

"So how did you get it here?" Marc demanded.

"And where did you come from?" Sandi added.

"Ah, the deep imponderables," Garret answered. "Who am I, where do I come from, why am I here? You cannot answer them about yourself, and I cannot really answer them about me."

"Well, what do you say we skip the deep imponderables and get to basics?" Marc said. "I was born in Oregon, and that's where I'm from. So where are you from?"

"A little north of Oregon," Garret said. "That is all I can tell you at this time."

"Where is this flying saucer taking us?" Sandi asked.

"To my base," Garret answered.

"On what planet?" Marc asked.

"I told you that this machine cannot go into space," Garret answered.

"Where? In what country?" Akhtar asked.

"I cannot answer that question."

"Is there anyone who can answer it?" Sandi asked.

"Ronaldo," Garret answered.

"Who is Ronaldo?" Marc asked.

"You will have to wait for the answer."

"Well, what questions can you answer?" Marc asked.

"Not many," Garret said. "Ronaldo will answer your questions."

"How fast does this thing fly?" Marc asked.

"It can go up to ten thousand miles per hour," Garret answered. "However, because we are carrying a wounded man, we are going at a lower speed."

"So, then, how fast are we going?" Marc asked.

"It will take us a little over three hours to get to our base. If I tell you how fast we are going, you could figure the distance, and then you would be able to draw a circle that would have our base somewhere on the circumference. That is more information than I can give."

"Who can give us that information?" Sandi asked.

"Ronaldo."

"What kind of weapon did you use on those men?" Marc asked.

"My people do not have weapons to use against other people," Garret said.

Sandi didn't like the cagey way Garret answered Marc's questions. "If you do not have weapons to use against people, what kind of weapons do you have?" she demanded.

"We have archaic weapons from a time when we depended on hunting. They are museum pieces now."

"You're lying," Marc said. "What do you call that *Star Wars* weapon your people used to kill those four terrorists?"

"That beam is not a weapon, and it was never intended to be a weapon."

"If that was not a weapon, what do you use it for? To clear land?" Akhtar asked sarcastically.

"That is the first time I have ever seen it used for anything. I must hand it to the pilot to have had the ingenuity to use it. We call that phenomenon an electro-gravitational vortex … an EGV."

"What is an EGV?" Sandi asked.

"As you are probably aware, a jetliner creates powerful air vortices behind it. If a small plane cuts too close behind the jet, the vortex can actually cause it to crash."

"Well, this thing was not flying like a jet," Marc said.

"Of course not," Garret agreed. "This thing flies by manipulation of gravitational and magnetic forces. When making certain maneuvers, these forces create an electro-gravitational vortex. It is a vortex similar to the air disturbance behind a jet, but air is not involved. When the vortex hits the ground, it causes a reaction in the stocks of small plants, such as reeds and grasses, which results in something like a small explosion that breaks them at their bases. The vortex itself causes them to fall in a circular pattern.

"At first, this was quite a problem for us. It left tracks on the ground. You call them crop circles. They are most obvious when they hit a cultivated field. They are not strong enough to knock a tree or bush down or damage a building, so they really only show up well when they hit grass or something like that."

"These vortices make all of the intricate patterns you see in crop circles?" Sandi asked.

"The patterns they make are not exact circles. Usually, they are a little bit oval, depending upon the angle of the vortex relative to the ground, and the edges are not perfectly defined. They tend to feather out a little. All those perfect circles and intricate designs are made by men on foot. They use boards to knock the plants down and strings and ropes to lay them out. We have actually hovered above them and watched them do it. They probably got their idea from our circles.

"We occasionally knock down a circle when we need to make a maneuver or the pilot forgets to apply proper procedures, but almost all crop circles you see now are done by people."

"You say they cannot knock trees down, but they sure knocked those terrorists down," Marc said. "Did they blow up their ankles?"

"The vortex did not knock them down per se. The effect on an animal is very similar to that produced by a stun gun. The terrorists were immobilized, but that only lasts a few minutes. It will leave them with serious headaches for several hours, though. They will also be very confused about what happened around the time they were hit. The effect is not powerful enough to cause physical damage to them."

"Does that thing know how seriously Kelvin is injured?" Sandi asked, pointing to the alien-looking being that was examining Kelvin.

"That thing is not a thing. His name is Miejer. He is a scientist who specializes in biology." Garret stood up. "Let me check."

A few minutes later, Garret returned. "Kelvin is pretty bad. His right lung is completely destroyed, and his back is broken. He is stabilized. Miejer says he expects a full recovery."

"Do you mean a full recovery as an invalid in a wheelchair?" Marc asked.

Garret responded, "Like I said, Miejer is a scientist. We have gone a bit beyond the stem cell research you are just starting. We can skip the whole stem cell thing and directly stimulate the lung cells to grow new lung material to replace all that was destroyed. It takes a bit more advanced technology, but we will also repair the nerves in his back. He will be like new in about a month. No more questions for now."

Time and space seemed unreal to Sandi as they cruised. She watched Miejer as he continued to work on Kelvin. Garret, George, and the pilot seemed normal enough, but Jektu and Miejer were both very different. They were as different from each other as they were different from Garret. Sandi wondered if all three came from different planets. Perhaps there was a whole *Star Wars* empire of wildly different humanoids.

Miejer came to where she and Marc were sitting. "I have done all I can for Kelvin here." His English was perfect, but his voice seemed a little watery. "He will be fine now. When we get to the laboratory, we will fix everything." Close up, Sandi could see that his skin was a very pale white, and the green tint was a reflection of the green color of the walls and ceiling.

"Laboratory?" Sandi asked. It almost sounded like Dr. Frankenstein.

"You would say hospital, I suppose," Miejer said. "We do not have doctors and hospitals. We have scientists and laboratories, or labs, if you prefer. In my world, there are people called Thinkers. You might call them scientists, because they spend their lives studying science. A Thinker is not a person who chooses to study science. A Thinker is born to be a scientist. I was allowed to choose what kind of science to pursue. I chose biology. I like healing people, and I am really good at it. You will see in a few weeks … Kelvin is going to be fine … better than before." Miejer went to look at Akhtar's left arm.

Sandi wanted to believe him but, how could she? Aliens had kidnapped her, and who could tell what experiments they may decide to perform?

Garret had been wandering around the ship. He took his seat between Marc and Sandi. "We are nearly at our destination. In a few minutes, the red lights will go on, and you will need to squeeze the handles again."

"What is the point of that?" Marc asked. "What do these chairs do?"

"These machines change direction and speed extremely rapidly. You know what g-forces are … they come as a result of rapid changes in speed. Unfortunately, that is related to mass, not weight. Even if we can make you weightless, that would not help compensate for g-forces. When we took off this morning, we reached nearly twenty-five g's. That would have crushed you. These mass-compensating chairs build up electromagnetic waves and gravitational flux forces that withstand the g-forces. They build up pockets of flux in your body that are painful and can lead to a condition similar to the bends deep sea divers sometimes get. When you squeeze the handles, they provide a path to bleed off the dangerous flux."

"What about Kelvin?" Sandi asked.

"We put him in the transporter. It does the same thing as the mass-compensating chairs, but it is more sophisticated. You do not have to squeeze handles. Everything is monitored by computer."

Sandi grabbed the handles and squeezed them as soon as the lights went on. It seemed like the deceleration was longer but less stressful.

Finally, the flying saucer stopped moving, and the humming sound was silent. The center opened, and there was a stairway going out.

"Follow me," Garret said.

Garret walked down the stairs. Marc followed Garret, and Sandi went behind Marc. Even when the terrorists were firing on them, she was not as frightened as she was now. She was sure Garret would protect her if he could, but someone or something called Ronaldo had the power. She had no idea what the paradigm of her life would be after this.

At the bottom of the stairs, Sandi could see they were in a large room. She had gone to a Neil Diamond concert at the Forum in Los Angeles several years before, and the area seemed to be about the same size. She counted twenty-three flying saucers of several different sizes as she followed Garret. The wall, floors, and ceiling were all the same creamy green-white color she had seen inside the flying saucer. It reminded her of the Formica on her mother's kitchen countertops, except these glowed with a translucent light. She could not see any lights other than the glowing green walls and ceiling. It seemed that the whole area got its light from that glow. The space was not brilliantly lit, but she could see everything clearly. There were no shadows. The area smelled the same as the flying saucer. She did not see many beings, but the ones she saw all seemed busy. Most of them looked like Garret, but there were several that looked like Miejer. She did not see any that looked like Jektu. Everyone she saw wore jumpsuits with insignias on their chests. Most were white, but there were some pastel colors. No one paid any attention to Garret and his group.

Sandi followed Garret through a doorway into a wide hallway where an open four-seat vehicle waited. As soon as they were seated, it began to accelerate. It ran toward a wall with four tunnels. Each tunnel had strange symbols over the entrance like the hieroglyphics she had seen on the jumpsuits. At the last second, their vehicle turned into the tunnel on the left. The tunnel was lined with the same creamy green material. The ride lasted about fifteen minutes and then came to a stop in another room about three hundred feet long and thirty feet wide. The ceiling was about nine feet high.

There were thirty-five or forty beings milling around. Several looked like Miejer and Garret. Others that looked like Chewbacca in the *Star Wars* movies were so tall their heads nearly touched the ceiling. The

Chewbacca look-alikes wore jumpsuits, but they had no shoes. The backs of their hands and feet were covered with long, shaggy, reddish hair. Their heads and necks were the also covered with hair. All the beings were humanoid looking. At least she hadn't seen any giant insects—so far.

Garret led them to a gate and into a vehicle that was like a bus inside. It was about twenty feet long with seats on one side. The inside seemed to be built of a metal that resembled that of the floor of the flying saucer.

"Take a seat," Garret said.

"Where are we going?" Marc asked.

"We are going to meet with Ronaldo and the Council. Sit comfortably. This thing gets its first acceleration from a gravity drop. It is sort of like going down a roller coaster, so do not be concerned when it starts."

Several other beings sat in the vehicle. They were talking in English about subjects Sandi could not follow. "What about Kelvin and Akhtar?" Sandi asked while they waited to start.

"They are being sent to a lab where their wounds will be treated. You will see Akhtar later today. Kelvin's wounds will require several weeks to treat."

The vehicle moved forward. "Here we go," Garret said.

They moved a short distance, and then the bottom seemed to fall out. Sandi felt weightless as they fell, and then she was pressed hard in the chair as the vehicle reached the bottom and leveled out.

"Okay, we are on our way. This will take about an hour, and then we will change to another tram that will take another hour. Ronaldo will meet with you at the end of that ride. You might as well use this time to rest up."

"What planet are we on?" Sandi asked.

"Earth," Garret responded matter-of-factly.

"What planet, or should I say planets, do all of those aliens come from?" Marc asked.

"You will have to save your questions for Ronaldo," Garret answered.

"Is this some sort of alien way station?" Sandi asked. "Is Jektu an alien?"

"You watch too many movies," Garret answered. "You will have to wait to talk to Ronaldo."

Sandi sat in silence wondering what kind of being Ronaldo was. As hard as she tried not to be, she was frightened of him. What had they all done to get into this kind of trouble? It made her sad to think about all the others they had left at the cave site. They changed trams at a station like the first one. After leaving the second tram, they rode a vehicle that could seat six people, though they were the only ones on board.

When the vehicle stopped, they got out onto a small platform. Garret led them through a tunnel about six feet wide and nine feet tall to a long room about thirty feet by twenty feet. The corners were rounded, so the room was almost an oval shape. All the way to this room, the floors, walls, and ceilings were constructed of the same creamy green material. This room was the same, except that there was a window on each of the long walls. Through the windows Sandi could see a dense forest. Looking out of the window on the right, she saw a wide river flowing away from the structure. They seemed to be at the level of the treetops, like being in fire observation tower.

"Where are we now?" Sandi asked.

"This is the central government meeting room in a place called Rodlu City," Garret answered.

"What forest is this?" Sandi asked, hoping to figure something about where they were.

"That particular forest is in Alaska, on the Yukon River."

"We are in Alaska?" Sandi asked.

"It is a very realistic display," Garret responded.

"Display?" Marc asked.

Garret walked to a chair with several dials on the table in front of it. He punched some buttons on a keyboard, and the scene quickly changed to a large river in a rain forest. "That river is the Amazon," Garret said. Just as she thought she was getting a handle on things, suddenly it was ripped out again. Sandi's legs started to shake. She took a deep breath to relax.

"Are all of your displays of Earth, or do you have some from the planets those aliens come from?" Sandi asked, hoping to trick Garret into an answer that would reveal more information.

Garret punched up the Alaska scene again. "You will have to wait for Ronaldo. He will be here shortly. Please sit here." Garret indicated the seats on one side of the table.

Just then, an old man entered. He wore a dark gray suit with a light blue shirt. The top button was open. His hair was white but still thick. He looked like a university professor. He moved slowly, and it was obvious that he was in pain as he sat down. "Arthritis is getting to me in my old age," he said. "The Thinkers say they can fix it, but I am not really sure about this newfangled stuff."

He looked like any old man Sandi had ever seen, but his eyes seemed especially alert and intelligent. Sandi thought he, at least, might be from this earth. She took another deep breath. Perhaps Ronaldo was not as bad as she'd feared.

Garret stood. "This is Ronaldo, leader of the Majority Party and keeper of the memories and the traditions of the Earth People." Garret turned to Ronaldo. "This is Marc Metcalf, discoverer of the lovers cave, and this is his assistant, Sandi Hartwell."

"Let me express my deepest sympathy for the tragedy at your camp this morning. I wish we could have gotten our EMF in sooner. I suppose you have a lot of questions," Ronaldo began.

"Where are Akhtar and Kelvin?" Sandi asked.

Ronaldo looked quizzically at Garret, who nodded. Ronaldo answered, "Kelvin is in intensive care at our main bio lab. He will be there about a month. Akhtar is in what you would call a clinic."

"That is what Garret says, but what do you say?" Sandi pressed, trying to quell her fears by acting aggressively.

"I have not received the report, but if Garret says they are in treatment, that is where they are."

"Where are we?" Marc demanded.

"We have existed among your people for longer than you can imagine," Ronaldo began. "We have had contact in many ways over many years, but we have never told anyone of your people everything about us. In fact, you could say we have allowed some of your people to be seriously misled. I am not going to tell you everything about my people, but I will tell you more than has been told before. I am going to do this, because I need your cooperation and assistance."

"You are wrong to think that we will do anything to help you do harm to Earth or any people who live there," Marc stated.

"I believe what I have to tell you will convince you we mean no harm to your people," Ronaldo said. "I am hoping you will maintain confidentiality after you have heard the entire story."

"Maybe you start by telling us where we are," Marc said.

"You are in Rodlu City, our capital, in the Northwest Territories of Canada. You are in the Mackenzie Mountains, about 250 miles north of the border with British Columbia. Our major population centers are farther south, but we moved the capital north after our flying machines were developed. We call the flying machine that brought you here an EMF. That is an acronym for electromagnetic floater. You landed at our main port on Banks Island at the north end of Prince of Wales Strait."

"What planet do you come from?" Marc asked.

"Let me give you some background information before we start a shotgun approach to questioning. Going back in Earth's history about two hundred thousand years, we find early humans living in Europe. These are the first of the human species to be called Homo sapiens. They are the Homo sapiens neanderthalensis, the Neanderthals." Sandi noticed that Ronaldo used the *Neanderthal* pronunciation just as Garret had.

"The Neanderthals were intelligent but simple people. About forty thousand years ago, Homo sapiens sapiens from Africa arrived in Europe. They were technologically and culturally far more advanced than the Neanderthals who had lived in Europe for more than a hundred thousand years.

"The Neanderthals could barely make a living for their small clans scattered across Europe. Culturally, they were separatists. Some trading and mate transfer occurred, but no official inter-clan organization existed.

"The Cro-Magnons brought a sophisticated culture. They lived in large tribes with strong intertribal relationships. They were highly successful in their hunting techniques.

"Ultimately, the Cro-Magnons, with their hunting technology and their advanced culture, drove the Neanderthals to extinction. It was not an evil plan, and there was no direct confrontation. The Cro-Magnons simply put so much pressure on the land and resources that there was no possibility for Neanderthals, en masse, to survive with their ancient technology.

"Twelve days ago, there was a well-executed burglary at the University of Arizona where the artifacts of your first dig in Pakistan were kept. The young boy and the four stones were taken. We have them in a lab along with the artifacts from this last dig."

"That is my dig and my find," Marc argued.

"Perhaps by your laws and standards, but there are other ways of looking at these things," Ronaldo said. "Do not worry. We have no intention of interfering with your studies and any fame or fortune that might work its way to you as a result of this find."

"Why are you interested in those old bones?" Sandi asked, directing the question to Garret.

"We have some important tests to perform," Ronaldo said. "When we are done, we will discuss options for returning some of these things."

"Well, what does all of that have to do with who you are and what you're doing on this planet?" Marc asked.

Ronaldo reached in his shirt pocket and pulled out a small electronic device. He put it to his ear. After putting the device back in his pocket, he said, "I know you have had a difficult day already, but I am going to release you to our scientists for the rest of the day. They will explain some of the tests we are running. You must be patient, because what you are going to learn is incredible … beyond your wildest dreams. I will meet with you tomorrow, and we will continue."

"What about the members of our group that were left behind?" Marc asked.

"I am very sorry," Garret said. "They were all dead."

"How could you tell that?" Marc demanded. "No one checked on them. You just left them for the terrorists. We do not leave our people behind like that."

"Our remote sensing devices can accurately sense life. No one was left alive."

"Dead or alive, we don't leave our people behind."

"The site is under surveillance," Garret said. "The terrorists all left in a hurry when the four woke up. You are expected out today. When you do not show up, the government will send someone to look for you. Your friends will be discovered and properly cared for."

The old man got up.

"What is the Heart of the Bison?" Sandi asked.

Ronaldo faced Sandi. "That is the entire crux of the matter. Everything that is happening now hinges on the Heart of the Bison. If it were not for that, you would still be back in Denver waiting for an opportunity to return to the lovers' cave ... an opportunity that would probably never come in your lifetime. Be patient, and you will know all."

It was surprising how comforting it was for Sandi to hear Ronaldo refer to Denver—something familiar. Sandi wished that she could go back in Denver now.

After the old man left, Garret said, "We have got to get you something to eat, and then I will take you to the laboratory."

"I thought Ronaldo was going to answer all of our questions," Sandi said. "He did not answer anything."

"There is a lot to know. It will take some time. Please follow me," Garret responded.

Garret took them on a six-seat monorail through several intersecting tunnels to what appeared to be an apartment complex. There was an open space on the right side of the monorail about twenty-five feet wide, two hundred feet long, and twenty-five feet high. The wall on the left side of the rail went straight up to the ceiling. The wall on the other side was a three-story structure from the floor to the ceiling of the cavern. It had doors, stairs, and balconies, but no windows. Everything was constructed of the pale green material.

Garret led them up to a second-story door. "These are apartments that have been set aside for government guests. We do not have any public restaurants. Food has been provided inside."

Garret led them into the apartment. "There are three rooms and a bathroom. This room is the entertainment room. Here we have satellite TV," he said as he pushed the button on a remote control. CNN came on a flat-screen TV on the wall. "This is also a room with a view." He pushed a button on a dial, and the curtain opened on a window overlooking waves breaking on a rocky beach. It was a window next to the door. Sandi knew that there was nothing out there but the monorail and a pale green wall, but the view of the beach was deceptively real.

"When will we see Akhtar?" Marc asked.

"In a short time."

"What is a short time in Rodlu City?" Sandi asked.

Garret pointed to a table with two chairs. There were two plates on the table. "I hope you like tuna fish sandwiches with chips and Coke. Something unexpected came up with Ronaldo. He wants you to see some of our lab in the meantime." With that, Garret walked out the door.

"You notice how he ignores questions that he doesn't want to answer?" Marc commented.

"What do we do now?" Sandi asked.

"I don't know. I'm thinking that it's probably not a good idea to eat that stuff."

"Who knows how long we are going to be here? Do you propose to starve yourself to death?"

"I don't know. I don't trust any of them."

Sandi sat at the table and looked at the sandwich. It looked like any other sandwich she had seen, and the tuna fish smelled really good. "Right now, I do not trust them or distrust them. I guess I will have to wait until I hear the whole story." Sandi picked up the sandwich and took a bite.

"Are you crazy?" Marc exclaimed.

"I have to eat. They have me now. If they want to pump chemicals into me, I suppose there are a lot of ways to do it without using food. Besides, this is pretty good."

Marc sat at the table looking at the food. "Before, Garret called the Cro-Magnons *aliens*, but that may be just a metaphor about Garret and his friends."

"Oh?" Sandi said as she chewed her sandwich.

"Yeah. You see, the aliens that came with a better technology. They flooded in with such big numbers that the world couldn't support everyone, so Neandertals went extinct. You see, these aliens have a beachhead now, and they're getting ready to flood the earth and make us extinct. Maybe they don't even have to kill us. Maybe they will just out-tech us."

"I do not know. Why are they so interested in the possibility Cro-Magnons and Neandertals may have cooperated for a short time?"

"I don't know, maybe it's a ruse."

"Maybe but think of this. They have been here for some time. Just from the facilities we have observed, it would take a lot of time to construct them. Some people think there is evidence of aliens from thousands of years ago, but there have been crop circles, sightings, and stories of kidnappings for as long as I have been alive."

"So, what's the point?" Marc asked.

"They have studied us and our archeological history. Suppose you are right. Suppose they want to colonize the planet. But suppose they want to do it peacefully. Suppose they want to avoid making us extinct like we did to the Neandertals. Maybe that is why they are interested in the possibility Neandertals and Cro-Magnons did cooperate. Maybe they are trying to find out how that happened and what caused it to break apart. Maybe, without knowing it, we have stumbled upon something that can alter the future of the world or even the whole universe."

"Nice bit of bullshit, Sandi." Marc got up, walked to the wall, and rubbed his hand up and down it. "Very hard … feels dense." He took a ring off his right hand. "This is a fraternity ring. It has diamond chips around the sapphire center stone." He rubbed it vigorously on the wall. He squinted at the wall and rubbed his fingers across the area he had rubbed his ring on. "This wall is not from the Earth," he concluded.

"What do you mean?"

"Diamond is the hardest thing on the planet. It should have scratched this wall, but there's not a mark."

"Maybe your diamond is too small or too deeply set in the ring."

Marc walked across the room to the glass on the faux window and rubbed his ring in the corner. "Nope. It scratched the glass easily."

"My sense is that it is from this earth."

"Your sixth sense about rocks?" Marc asked, sounding unconvinced.

"It is kind of confusing, but it feels like this earth."

"Still," Marc said as he sat at the table and picked up a sandwich.

"Look at the world, Marc. We are the survivors. We are the Cro-Magnons. We have subdued the world, but has that brought us peace? No, because whites and blacks will not live in peace. Muslims and Christians will not live in peace. Protestants and Catholics will not live in peace. Shiites and Sunnis will not live in peace. Some say we fight over land or food or oil, but those are just the excuses. We fight because we cannot reconcile our differences to live in peace.

"Think of it, Marc. The differences between us are minor compared to Cro-Magnons and Neandertals. If they found a way, and we can find their secret, that would be great … maybe the greatest thing ever."

Marc took a bite of the sandwich. "I guess we might as well cooperate. There's certainly no way to fight this."

"One thing Garret told me was that his people were near the area of the lovers' cave a long time ago. He said the Heart of the Bison was the name of a cave, and when his people were there, they lived in it. He said they had the secret of life there, and they had to leave in a hurry, and they left it behind. Maybe they used the secret to help Neandertals and Cro-Magnons live together in that area."

"That doesn't say anything about who they are," Marc said.

"Right," Sandi said. She wished she felt as confident as the words she had spoken. The two finished their lunch watching TV. According to CNN, President Bush had given Saddam a deadline to get out of Iraq, and if he did not get out, the United States would force him out. Another Cro-Magnon war was about to begin.

It had been a very long day. It was hard for Sandi to believe that she had been in a camp in the Middle East earlier that morning. She had seen many of her friends and coworkers shot down. Then, in less than four hours, she had been deposited in a secret world somewhere in Canada—that is, if she believed Ronaldo.

After they had eaten, an aide came to take them to the lab. The lab was a ten-minute ride from their apartment. It was an irregular cavern about a hundred feet by thirty feet. The walls and ceiling were irregular, as though the pale green material had been used to line a natural cavern. The floor was flat and smooth. Most of the beings in the lab were Thinkers. They all spoke English well, but they all sounded like Miejer. They were working on DNA extraction from the bones that came from the lovers' cave. Her knowledge of DNA was limited, but Marc had done some personal study in the science. Sandi was bored most of the time, but Marc was interested in the Thinkers' work. He asked a lot of questions that Sandi did not understand.

After about four hours, an aide came to take them back to the apartment. Sandi had not seen Garret since he had brought them to the apartment. Where was Garret? What was Garret? He looked human. So did Ronaldo and some of the workers at the lab. The Thinkers in the lab were in control of the work. Many of the people she had seen at the train stations also looked human, but there were plenty of beings like Miejer, and there were also plenty of the Chewbacca look-alikes.

Jektu had referred to the Neandertal in the ceremony cavern as "earth people." Sandi remembered there was something about Earth People in Ronaldo's title. Did that mean he was an earth people man? Were the ones that looked like humans actually earth people who had joined with the aliens?

"What do you make of all of this?" Sandi asked Marc.

"Well, I'll say one thing … their Thinkers are really intelligent. They are way ahead of us on DNA research. I know enough to understand what they have been doing and where they have been going. They were able to isolate the mitochondria from the samples we got at the lovers' cave. That is the DNA that comes only from the mother."

"I know that," Sandi said. "What are they looking for?" From Marc's tone, it was clear he was more excited by their science than worried about what it all meant.

"Remember when Miejer came in?" Marc said. "I overheard him saying something about a female they lost. He was saying something about trying to get her DNA. When they saw me, they clammed up really quickly. But all day, they seemed very interested in the mitochondria DNA from half-breed woman and the Neandertal child. They were not that interested in the Cro-Magnon's DNA. I think it's possible that they were visiting Earth twenty-five thousand years ago, and somehow, they left a woman behind with the Neandertals. I think they suspect that we found her daughter. The half-breed may not have been Cro-Magnon and Neandertal. She might have been half Neandertal and half alien. I think that they are looking for their own mitochondria in the half-breed. I don't know what they are looking for in the child."

"If the half-breed was half alien, then the whole idea of Neandertals and Cro-Magnons having a cooperative relationship is all a lie," Sandi said. "It is strange, but as you talked about the woman, I got a feeling that it *is* more about the woman than anything else."

"What kind of feeling?"

"Fleeting. It was strong then, but it is like a flash already going dim."

"I've been thinking about this all day," Marc said. "I'm sure that they have been stringing us along. I don't know why, but I plan to find out."

"I wonder if Jektu might have been expecting to find the alien female in the ceremony cavern."

"Why?"

"If you remember, he was the one who wanted to break into the tomb. He said it was a tomb before we found the skeleton, and when it was first opened, he made it a point to tell Garret that the skeleton was of the earth people."

"How do you know all of that?"

"I have been studying their conversations, and I have learned many of Jektu's words. I can understand about half of what he says, but do not tell anyone."

"Well, understanding half is a good way to misunderstand the whole."

"What do *you* think they want with us?"

"Well, there you have the sixty-four-thousand-dollar question. There could be an advantage if they say things in Jektu's language that they don't think we understand. So, you should really work on understanding it better."

"Do not worry. I am certainly working on that, but I hope they give us some good answers tomorrow." Sandi wanted to trust Garret. The way he acted toward her gave her a feeling that he cared for her, but whenever she asked a question that Garret did not want to answer, he got evasive or just refused to answer. She had not seen him since lunchtime. It suddenly dawned on her that his part might be over. Thinking about not seeing Garret again, Sandi realized how strong her feelings for him were growing.

Marc and Sandi ate the food they found prepared for them in silent thought. Each room had a bed. Marc took one room, and Sandi took the other. She had not realized how tired she was until she laid down. There were a hundred things on her mind, but she fell asleep before she could decide which one to think about.

Two ... March 2003

The next morning, Sandi and Marc found food on the table and clean clothes on the couch in the joint room. The day before had been so busy that Sandi had hardly had time to take stock of their position. Marc was wolfing down his breakfast as though he had not eaten in days. Sandi watched him as she picked at her food.

"Your attitude about food has changed," Sandi commented. His attitude about everything seemed to be changing. He seemed more excited about the things he could learn than worried about their situation.

"Well, I guess it's like you say ... if they want to do something to us, they certainly have a lot of options that don't involve food."

"I wonder how long we are going to be held here. What do you think the point of all of this is, anyway?"

"I don't know," Marc answered. "But I tell you, if they wanted to hurt us, they could have by now. They want something from us. We don't have any choice now except to play along and see what it is."

"I am going to take a shower." Sandi left her unfinished meal on the table. She was still tense and worried. The hot water was relaxing. When she finished, she put on a clean white jumpsuit that had been provided. She walked out of the bathroom and found Garret talking with Marc.

"Garret!" she called without thinking. He stood, and suddenly Sandi felt a wave of confusion. Was her life before yesterday real, or was yesterday all just a bad dream?

"Do I have time for a quick shower?" Marc asked.

"Sure, but make it quick," Garret said. As soon as Marc was out of the room, Garret asked, "How are you doing?"

"I do not know, Garret. I do not know why I am here or what is going to happen to me. What is expected?"

Garret approached her. She had a sudden desire to fall into his arms, but she instead moved away and sat on a chair. "I did not see you at all after lunch, and then I thought I might not see you again, and ... and it is clear now that you ... or maybe just those others ... I mean, someone is not from this world. What if you just go back to your planet and do not even say good-bye?"

Garret looked intently into her eyes in a way he had not looked before.

"What is it, Garret? Do you not see how frightened I am?"

Suddenly, Garret looked like he was not sure about something, "Say that again," Garret said.

"What?"

"What you just said."

"I do not know exactly what I just said, Garret. I am just saying do not leave me. Do not just disappear someday. That is all I am saying."

"I will not leave you." Garret looked even more intently at her as if he were trying to decide something very important.

"Will you ever tell me who you are?" Sandi asked.

"You will know who I am before the day is over."

"Ronaldo will tell me?"

"He will tell you who I am, but who are you?"

"What do you mean?"

"Nothing ... only that questions about who a person is can be extremely complicated."

Garret walked to the faux window and looked out. Sandi just stood looking at him, wondering what his riddles meant and wondering why she cared.

Marc came from the bathroom in the clean, white jumpsuit. "Are you two ready to go?" Garret asked.

"Go where?" Sandi asked.

"This morning, we meet Ronaldo again. He has a big morning planned," Garret said to Sandi as if the conversation with her had never happened.

Before Sandi could calm her nerves, they were sitting in Ronaldo's oval office. Ronaldo entered the room and hobbled to his chair. His face was old and wrinkled, but his brown eyes seemed young, alert, and intelligent. Looking at his eyes, she thought of her father.

"When we last talked, we discussed what is fairly well accepted paleontology regarding the appearance and disappearance of Neanderthals on this planet," Ronaldo began. "What I tell you now will be new and incredible to you." Ronaldo's voice was strong and clear.

"Twenty-five thousand years ago, most of the Neanderthals in Europe had already disappeared. The last remnants were barely holding on in the Middle East. Not far from where you found the lovers' cave, there was a young Neanderthal female. She was called Kectu. How or why is unknown, but she mated with a Cro-Magnon man. He was a great spirit man among his people. He was called the Guardian. He was the chief of a Cro-Magnon spirit cavern where their most important paintings were created."

"How could you possibly know those details?" Marc asked.

"To know the story is not hard," Ronaldo said. "I will explain that to you, but to know the story is true is something else entirely. For now, I will just tell the story, and later, we will talk about true or false ... and how I know."

"Good enough for now," Marc said.

"From the mating of the Guardian and Kectu came a daughter called Tuka. Tuka mated with a great hunter chief of the Cro-Magnons called Sky Man. They had a son named Shekek. Tuka and Sky Man were killed when Shekek was a child. The Guardian and Kectu raised Shekek.

"Shekek and the Guardian formed a bond between a clan of Neanderthals and a tribe of Cro-Magnons. They called it the Alliance. Kectu gave the Alliance a fire to remind them of the beginning and the promises of the Alliance."

"What were the promises of the Alliance?" Sandi asked.

"Shekek and the Guardian recognized that Neanderthals knew important things about the earth and survival. They also recognized that Cro-Magnons had important skills and technology needed for survival. The promises of the Alliance revolved around how these two peoples worked together, using their various skills and knowledge to make life better for everyone.

"The fire Kectu gave the Alliance was called the Spirit Fire. It was never to be allowed to burn out. It was to be the center of the culture and promise of the Alliance.

"Kectu was a Neanderthal, so the Neanderthals were the caretakers of the Spirit Fire. All Neanderthals of the Alliance were cremated at death. Their ashes were mixed in the Spirit Fire, and through the flames of the Spirit Fire, their spirits were sent to heaven. The ashes from the Spirit Fire were spread in the soil where Neanderthal food was grown. In this way, all Neanderthals were tied physically and spiritually through the eternal flames and ashes of the Spirit Fire."

"What happened to the Alliance?" Sandi asked.

"The Alliance thrived for thousands of years, spreading from the Middle East across Asia and across the Bering Strait when the land bridge existed. They moved down the coast of Alaska as far south as the Columbia River. When the Bering Strait flooded, the Alliance was ripped in two. In Asia, they thought that all of those on the east side of the water had drowned."

"You are suggesting that there were Neandertals in North America?" Marc asked.

"According to our legends and writings, the Neanderthals of the Alliance ranged from the Middle East to the mouth of the Columbia River," Ronaldo repeated. "After a time, the Cro-Magnons in Asia who were not part of the Alliance flourished. The Alliance began to decline. Then, about five thousand years ago, a large army came from Europe. At that time, the Spirit Fire was kept in a cave called the Heart of the Bison."

"Are you saying that there were Neandertals in North America and Asia as late as five thousand years ago?" Marc asked.

"You find that incredible?" Ronaldo asked.

"There have been no Neandertal remains to show any of that," Marc stated.

"What remains would you look for?" Garret asked.

"Bones and tools like anything else," Marc answered.

"They were in an alliance with Cro-Magnons. Naturally, they used the better tools of the Cro-Magnons. And as far as bones are concerned, their religion required them to cremate all their dead. Their ashes were scattered in their fields."

"But Neandertals did not have fires hot enough to consume bones," Marc said.

"Neanderthals, no, but we have clear evidence Cro-Magnons were building fire hearths that fed air into the fire so their fires were hot enough to use mammoth bones for fuel," Ronaldo said. "In an alliance with Cro-Magnons, the Neanderthals would have had that technology available."

Marc sighed. "Go on."

"In our stories the leader of the army from Europe is called the warmonger. He believed in a religion that taught there were strange people from caves who were evil. He was intent upon destroying every last one. The army brought with it a holocaust that nearly completely wiped out all the Neanderthals in the Old World. The Spirit Fire was doused, and the Heart of the Bison was sealed. The ancient stories of the Alliance had been memorialized in special paintings on a wall in a cavern in the Heart of the Bison.

"A great leader named Sotif gathered the few Neanderthals remaining in Asia and the Middle East on the shores of Lake Baikal in what is now Russia. He took a small group of explorers down the Lena River in boats to the Arctic Sea on the north coast of Russia. He followed the shore from there to the Bering Strait, where he crossed the sea and went up the Yukon River. There, he found the remnants of the Neanderthals of the Alliance in the East. Under Sotif's leadership, the two groups were joined together. The Alliance in the East had their Spirit Fire, which was originally started from the Spirit Fire in the Heart of the Bison before the Bering Sea flooded the land bridge.

"Sotif invented the first Neanderthal writing, using symbols in the same way the Egyptians used hieroglyphics. He wrote all the stories of the Alliance that were painted on the wall in the Heart of the Bison. We have many of his original writings, in his original hand."

"Wait a minute," Marc interrupted. "Are you saying that there still are living Neandertals?"

"I am saying there are Neanderthals and there is a rich Neanderthal history," Ronaldo answered.

"And where do you keep these Neandertals?" Marc asked. "I would really like to see one."

"In due time," Ronaldo said, ignoring Marc's sarcastic tone.

Suddenly, things began to make sense to Sandi. "Marc," she said. "I think you are looking at a Neandertal right now."

"Where?" Marc looked around. "Not him," he said, pointing at Ronaldo. "He is too different. Evolution doesn't go that fast."

"You are talking twenty-five to thirty thousand years or more with possible crossbreeding with Cro-Magnons," Sandi said.

"What? No. Are you saying you are a Neandertal?" Marc asked Ronaldo.

"You are getting ahead of me. Oh, well. Show the demo," Ronaldo said to one of the men at the table.

The three-dimensional display out the window in front of them suddenly changed to a pack of wolves running down a caribou. The picture freeze-framed on the bloody face of one wolf looking up from the carcass he was devouring. In the next scene, a German shepherd herded some sheep. The picture freeze-framed as the dog nipped the rump of a sheep that had gotten out of line. The next scene showed a

Saint Bernard as a hiker reached for the drink the dog carried around his neck. The next scene showed a greyhound in a race. Finally, there was a child playing with a small terrier.

"If you follow the ancestors of each of these dogs back a few thousand years, you will come to the wolf," Ronaldo said.

"What are you getting at?" Marc asked.

"You know the answer. All dogs come from wolves ... not by evolution, but through breeding. We know that by five thousand years ago, men had domesticated several kinds of animals ... goats for food and dogs for work, just to name a couple."

Ronaldo pushed a button, and a door slid open. Sandi recognized Jektu in his strange outfit as he walked in. He greeted her in his strange language, and she recognized his voice. Then he dropped the hooded robe. Sandi gasped. Jektu stood in front of her in a small animal skin waistcloth. His muscles stood out on his chest, arms, and legs. His blue eyes stared from under a large brow ridge and over a wide nose! He smiled at her with a large mouth showing huge, crooked teeth between full lips. There was almost no chin. She knew that she was looking into the eyes a living fossil—a Neandertal! Even Marc was speechless.

"Ask this Sandi what Sandi thinks of this Jektu now," he said.

Sandi did not understand every word, but she understood the question. "I do not know what to think yet."

"You understood Jektu?" Ronaldo demanded.

"I have listened closely when Garret and Jektu talk. I can usually guess what he is saying by hearing Garret's half of the conversation. I cannot understand every word, but I can sometimes get the gist of what he says. Surprised?" Sandi noticed a look of shock on Marc's face, but it was no use hiding her ability now. Everything was changing.

"Did you know this?" Ronaldo asked Garret.

"Yes and no," was all Garret said.

"Jektu is what we call an Ancient. He is original," Ronaldo said to Sandi.

Miejer walked in. "You know Miejer," Ronaldo said. "He is what we call a Thinker." He was followed by one of the big, hairy creatures. "This is Katyniel. He is a Gatherer."

Garret stood by Katyniel. "I am what we call a Watcher," Garret said. "Trace all of us back through our ancestry and you will come to the

Ancients. Some of your people have seen our Thinkers. You call them aliens. Some of your people have seen our Gatherers. You call them Bigfoot. Some of your people have seen our flying machines. You call them flying saucers from outer space."

"You are all Neandertals?" Sandi directed her question to Garret.

Ronaldo answered before Garret could say anything. "We are all Neanderthals in the same sense that all dogs are wolves."

"This is crazy, absolutely crazy." Marc had found his tongue. Sandi had lost hers as she stared dumbfounded at Garret. Ronaldo talked at length about the Neandertal breeding program, but Sandi's mind was racing. She picked up some bits and pieces. She could not keep her eyes or her thoughts from returning to Garret as she tried to grasp what this all meant. Each time her eyes turned to Garret; his strange blue eyes were on her. She could not decide what his look meant. How could she? He was something different, alien—a Neandertal! And then the morning was over. Marc was going with Miejer, and Garret was leading her through a door from Ronaldo's meeting room, and she could not even begin to think about what might be happening.

Three—March 2003

Sandi realized that she had begun to think about a relationship with Garret that was more than just one of friendship. His actions toward her seemed to encourage that. Now she could see it was impossible. "What does all of this mean?" she demanded when they were alone.

"The story of the Alliance is kind of like the story of Adam and Eve in your world," Garret said. "It is the basis of our religion. But many say it is just a story Sotif made up as a metaphor of life. As Marc pointed out, there is no archeological evidence pointing to the Alliance."

It was obvious Garret had missed the point of Sandi's question. In frustration, she asked, "What are you getting at?"

"I am just trying to show that you should give yourself time to let this all sink in," Garret said. "I know this is strange. Just give yourself some time to develop an understanding of what this all means."

"Maybe the first thing is to find out why I am here."

"I will tell you as much as I can."

"And Ronaldo will explain the rest?" Sandi asked sarcastically.

"I am confident all of your questions will be answered in the proper place and time."

"Okay, then ... what can you tell me?"

"The stories of the Alliance were first written by Sotif. He is our Moses. Sotif wrote of a cave called the Heart of the Bison ... the cultural and religious center of the Alliance. A large wall in the cave was set aside for paintings depicting the history of the Alliance. All the people knew the stories painted on the wall. However, some of the people were appointed to memorize the stories and pass them word perfect from generation to generation. They were called history men. Sotif was the last of the history men. He wrote all those memorized stories from the beginning of the Alliance. In his language, Cro-Magnons were called Sun People, and Neanderthals were called Earth People."

"Earth People? Is that what Jektu called the Neandertal skeleton that was walled up in the ceremony cavern?"

"Yes, I suppose so. Why?"

"I thought he was referring to earth people as opposed to spacemen. No matter how careful the history men were, in twenty thousand years of verbally passing a story, mistakes will accumulate, and in the end, the story will not be reliable. How can anyone trust a twenty-five-thousand-year-old verbal story with the detail Ronaldo gave us?"

"Many of my people are asking the same question. The verbal stories tie in with paintings in the Heart of the Bison, all done in original time. If the paintings exist and match the stories, that would prove Sotif's history. According to Sotif's writings, the Guardian returned to the Sun People after Shekek was grown. He returned to the Sun People ceremony cavern and died there guarding their paintings."

"So, you are saying the man we found in the cavern is the Guardian, and the cavern is the Heart of the Bison?"

"I am certain that the man is the Guardian, but the cavern is a Sun People ceremony cavern. It is not the Heart of the Bison. According to our legends, the Heart of the Bison is about two summers' travel by foot from the ceremony cavern where the Guardian died. Suppose we can salvage enough genetic material to prove the skeleton in the cavern is the father of the female lover?"

"I do not know how to respond to that. You cannot get good DNA from fossils that old."

"We are way ahead of your scientists when it comes to recovery of DNA from fossils."

"But there is no evidence that the Neander … I mean, that *Earth People* ever painted on cave walls like you talk about," Sandi said.

"The first leader of the Alliance was Shekek. He was three-quarters Sun People. He and the Guardian taught the Earth People how to paint. And remember, in the Alliance, there were Sun People and Earth People. Shekek painted the first painting showing his genealogy and the formation of the Alliance. He called the room where this painting was the History Room. The History Room was in the Heart of the Bison. It became the custom of the people to add paintings depicting important events in the history of the Alliance.

"The Alliance lasted from that time until the time of Sotif. The stories say the army from the West sealed the History Room and the Heart of the Bison, probably in a way similar to the way the Earth People man was sealed the ceremony cavern. So, you see, the Heart of the Bison contains proof the Alliance existed. You and Marc would like to prove there was cooperation between Neandertals and Cro-Magnons for a short period of time in a small area. How about finding evidence of cooperation for twenty thousand years from the Middle East across Asia to Alaska?"

Sandi bit her lower lip. "Suppose you find this Heart of the Bison. Are you going to announce it to the world?"

"Not right away," Garret said.

Sandi sensed that he was being evasive. "When, exactly?"

"I cannot say exactly. That depends upon the Sun People."

"How so?"

"Our law says we are not to expose our existence to Sun People until they live two generations without war."

"That is never going to happen." Sandi said.

"Not in our lifetime," Garret responded.

Then something Garret had said to her before came to mind. "You once said that if you ever told me where you came from, you would have to kill me."

"I was just kidding," Garret said. "I thought that was clear to you at the time."

"It was ... at the time. But now, you just told me your law does not allow you to have dealings with Sun People, and you just told me all about your people."

"We have had dealings with Sun People individually for generations. In fact, Ronaldo has contacts high up in your military right now. We can have such contacts, but they have to be secret."

"You are kidding!" Sandi said.

"I am sure you have heard of the Roswell incident."

"You mean when aliens supposedly crashed their flying saucers in the desert in New Mexico?"

"Your armed forces were developing advanced aircraft on a base near Roswell. Our EMFs were there to keep track of progress. One of our pilots made a mistake and created an EGV over the others in his squadron. Three went down. They were discovered and carried from the field before we could rescue them. Ronaldo was a Watcher working fairly high in the US military. He intentionally blew his cover by proving he was connected to the people responsible for the EMFs. Those he dealt with assumed the EMFs had come from another planet. Ronaldo succeeded in getting the bodies and most of our stuff back. He has maintained contact with the military ever since. We give them some information on developments we have made, and they help cover up our existence. We have made similar contacts with other governments."

"So that means Marc and I may be the only ones who know the truth about you. So that just takes me back to what you said."

"I told you, I was just kidding."

Sandi was not convinced. She turned away from Garret. "Oh, for Christ's sake, Sandi. You do not think I would let anything happen to you."

"I am not sure you are allowed to take the Sun People Lord's name in vain."

"Do not lose your sense of humor," Garret responded.

"I was not trying to be funny."

"Marc will be spending most of the afternoon with our scientists. Come with me, and I will show you some of what makes Earth People tick. I think, when you know us better, you will feel comfortable about your situation." Garret's words were more of a directive than a question.

"I suppose I might as well find out what I can while I am here. How long am I going to be held here?"

"We are building a cover story that the survivors of your party have been kidnapped by terrorists, so you can be released without compromising our cities."

"You cannot just let us go," Sandi said. "We will blab everything."

"You are going to say you were taken to caves in flying saucers by Neanderthals? The lunatic fringe will swarm all over you. Everyone else will wonder what the terrorists did to you and what was in the water they gave you."

"How long?" Sandi asked again.

"It will take about a month to repair Kelvin. You could leave before him, but I really hope you will wait until Kelvin is able to travel … that is, unless you decide you want to stay a little longer."

"Why would I want to stay?" Sandi asked.

Garret shrugged his shoulders. "Maybe to help find the Heart of the Bison."

"Find a secret to keep a secret?"

"Not for publicity or fame," Garret said. "Just to know."

Sandi was deeply concerned about being split from Marc, but she felt an excitement that overpowered her fear. *Just to know*, rang in her ears.

Sandi and Garret rode a monorail tram for about fifteen minutes to a place that Sandi recognized as the main station where they had come in on the previous day. Garret led her to a tram, and in a few minutes, they were off. Again, the beginning of the ride was like a roller-coaster drop.

"Where are we going?" Sandi asked when the train had settled into a boring hum.

"To the core of our beliefs."

"Do you believe the ancient Neandertals, Earth People, actually believed in spirits and gods?" Sandi asked.

"They buried their dead … you already know that. Our traditions tell us they believed in a spiritual essence from the earth leading to life. They call it Mother Earth."

"But Mother Earth, as you call her, is actually just a large puddle of molten rock with a crust around it. I guess a belief that ignores that fact would come from a culture that developed below the ground. I do not mean to sound snobby … it is just that people above the ground look to the heavens when they seek spiritual growth."

"In most Sun People religions, there is a deity that created the Earth and people on it. Mother Earth is not a being."

"Then what is she?"

"Let me explain a little first. The Earth is filled with fossil evidence of evolution, but evolution is so statistically unlikely that it is ultimately impossible."

"But the evidence is irrefutable," Sandi said.

"To get the first living cell, a strand of DNA is needed. The statistical probability of atoms joining randomly into such a chain is more unlikely than that a monkey playing with a typewriter will type out *War and Peace* with no errors."

"But there were more than a billion years for that to happen."

"Great, but we are talking about a universe of random actions. About a thousand trillion years of random chances would be needed."

"So, this planet was lucky," Sandi argued.

"Following the first cell, another universe of random actions would be needed to get the vast variety of plant and animal life presently existing."

"But not purely random. It was based upon survival of the fittest. Plus, we are talking about three and a half billion years."

"True, the first cells appeared three and a half billion years ago, but most of that time was used to evolve a variety of the single-celled plants and animals. There were a few cell colonies like hydras, but no complicated life. Then, at the beginning of the Cambrian Period, an explosion of evolution created the basis of every plant and animal in the world today over a period of only about ten million years. Sure, there have been a lot of changes since, but they are all based upon complicated systems developed during this period, such as; digestion, sight, smell, reproduction, the nervous system, mobility, and so on. Not to mention complicated behaviors needed for survival in a predator-prey environment. All those complicated systems came into being during that period, while all life was still in the ocean. The changes and adaptations of those systems are not nearly as fantastic as their development over ten to twenty million years."

"So, what is your point?"

"That we have to look for another paradigm about evolution."

"And that is?"

"Evolution requires astronomical numbers of random coincidences that lead to a complicated result. Earth People do not believe in coincidence as a creative force."

"Then how do you explain life?"

"Mother Earth is a property of this planet that moves things in favor of life, creating incidents that only appear to be coincidence."

"Like intelligent design?"

"No. More like a physical law … like gravity. You are at the end of an unbroken string of life that stretches all of the way back to the very beginnings of life on this planet. There is not one single break in that string. The shadows and inferences of that string are in your DNA. The DNA is the beginning of your life, and it will be the only physical part of you that will pass on to your children.

"When you look at the skull of one of the Ancients, you will notice most of the brain mass is in the back of the skull … the area we often refer to as the ancient brain. The ancient brain has the ability to examine itself through its own DNA, meaning it has the power to sense the history of its evolutionary track. The details are revealed through thoughts, visions, dreams, and feelings. From their knowledge, we know this earth formed itself from gases at the right location where water could exist naturally in its liquid state, a basic requirement for life. There is a purpose or law contained in this planet that is directed toward life."

"What has that got to do with me?"

"You are here because Marc went to Mogadishu where American soldiers needed to be rescued. In the process, Marc met Akhtar, who told him about his *vidus*. Marc worked several years to be able to go to Pakistan to check these stories. You met him just in time to make the trip to Pakistan. The cave Akhtar led you to contained the skeleton of a young boy. You felt a connection to the child that set your mind wondering. As a consequence, you dreamed of the stone that led you to the lovers. I found out about it and took you back to the grave. You got up to go to the latrine at just the time to see Jektu and me sneaking out of camp. You followed us to the small cave. You questioned what was under the rock, and as a result, we found the ceremony cavern and the Guardian. A rather unlikely string of coincidences.

"According to our legends, Kectu was at the cave with the small boy. Maybe she even saw him die. Kectu was in the ceremony cavern and most likely helped place the stone over the entrance. We know Kectu traveled from the cave where the boy was buried to the ceremony cavern and ultimately to the Heart of the Bison. As a consequence of all of those apparent coincidences, you have crossed Kectu's trail twice.

"My people do not believe in coincidences. There is an energy trail you are able to sense, and it is no accident or coincidence you are on that trail. The Mother Earth purpose for life is opening this opportunity for you. Mother Earth is a law of life. It has no more personal interest in life than the law of gravity has a personal interest in whether you fall or float when you trip. It just is what it is. But when you understand gravity, you can put satellites in orbit or fly discs in the air. When you understand Mother Earth, you can improve the life experience.

"You have a connection to the law, which neither you nor I can explain, but believe me, you are on an important trail based upon life force."

"But nothing was directing me. I do not have a clue where to go from the cavern to get to the Heart of the Bison."

"I do not say you have a map or even a spiritual guide ... only that you can sense when you are on the trail. Perhaps it has something to do with your sense about rocks. If you agree to help us, I can assure you there will be more apparent coincidences, and they will become stronger as you learn to recognize them."

"Why me and not one of the Ancients?"

"All of the Ancients are born with all of the knowledge they need to survive. They do not even have to learn their language. It is their hereditary gift from Mother Earth. Naturally, we expected one of them would lead us to the Heart of the Bison. It was shocking to read the Metcalf report. The discovery of the lovers was the first evidence of someone on the trail to the Heart of the Bison. Then, with the discovery of the Guardian, there is no doubt. Why you? I cannot answer that, but you have the needed gift ... that much I know."

"Here we are," Garret said as the train pulled into a station like the others Sandi had seen. They got out of the vehicle and walked to a large reception area. There were Thinkers, Gatherers, Watchers, and a few of the Ancients. They all wore white jumpsuits. Some of each breed were smaller and had developed chests, though there were no differences in hair, makeup, or dress.

"We are at the religious center of Mother Earth. The Ancients here will hear everything we say."

"Even if we whisper?" Sandi asked.

"If I can hear you, so can they," Garret answered.

"So Big Brother is always listening," Sandi said.

"It is not that they are listening … it just cannot be helped what they can hear. I have made arrangements to show you the heart of the Earth People religion. Come with me." Garret walked to one of several doors. He showed a card to a man behind a counter, an Ancient. The man nodded, and Garret walked through the entrance. Sandi followed.

The room was noticeably warmer than any of the other places in this underground world. It was almost circular, about eighty feet across. Most of the walls and ceiling were natural rock, but there were several veins and patches of the creamy green material. The ceiling was about forty feet high, with no paintings on the walls and no furniture—just a plain, almost empty cavern.

Across the space a little to her right, a fire was burning. Three Ancients stood not far from the flames. Sandi had been to several ornate, even opulent religious shrines and places of worship in her life. She always found them awe inspiring. Never in her life had she felt the spiritual awakening she felt in this simple cavern. Not even the living paintings in the ceremony cavern had given her such a deep reverence as this unadorned space. She had a thousand questions, but she was speechless as she stared at the fire.

Garret took her hand and led her closer to the fire. She could see that it was in a circular pit about fifteen feet across. The outside of the pit was constructed of the green material she had seen everywhere. There were ten symbols etched around the edge. The fire occupied a small space at the edge of the pit. The half of the circle going counterclockwise from the fire was covered with ashes. The rest of the pit was cleaned out. Sandi noticed four wooden trunks about three feet long by two feet wide by two feet deep. Three were closed, and one was open. The open trunk was about three-fourths full of ashes.

As they stood close to the fire, Garret turned to her. "This fire has burned continuously for twenty-five thousand years."

"This is the Spirit Fire!" Sandi gasped.

"Yes. This is the Spirit Fire of the East that Ronaldo talked about. This is the cave where Sotif found it. He brought ashes from the Spirit Fire in the Heart of the Bison, which he mixed with ashes of this fire so all the powers of the two fires were joined together. He took part of the Spirit Fire back with him to help the people fight the warmonger who was trying to destroy all the Earth People. For many years after the war was over, there were two Spirit Fires. Eventually, the two fires were joined together again in this cave."

Sandi looked at the flames as they danced yellow and red inside the green, circular hearth. Through the history of her people, this fire had burned. Through the great scientific discoveries and men walking on the moon, the great wars, and the origination of the great religions of the earth, this fire had burned. This fire was already ancient when the pyramids were first conceived.

"The Spirit Fire moves clockwise inside this circle." Garret's voice startled her from her thoughts. She almost resented it, but she was curious. "Those who feed the fire always add the fuel in the direction the fire moves. Each day, the ashes are removed from the circle at a point directly across from where the fire is burning.

"The symbols on the side divide the circle into ten equal parts. Each part represents a partial phase of the moon. The Spirit Fire makes a complete trip around the pit with each lunar cycle.

"The ashes are put in the four trunks. All four are used during a lunar cycle. Each month, the ashes from the Spirit Fire are taken to be scattered where our ceremony food is grown. Each month, we celebrate our heritage with a feast that includes the ceremony food. In this way, we are tied spiritually and physically into one family.

"Right after Sotif joined the ashes of the West with this Spirit Fire, the Spirit Fire was stolen by Sun People. A Sun People warrior named Small Beaver led a force of Sun People and Earth People to rescue the Spirit Fire. If it were not for Small Beaver, the Spirit Fire would have been lost. When Small Beaver left the land of the Earth People, he gave the point of a stone dagger to Sotif to remind the Earth People there are Sun People who can be trusted."

"How do your people know all of these ancient stories with so much detail?" Sandi asked.

"After we leave here, I will explain all about that."

"How come this room is mostly rock?"

"We have tried to keep this cave in its original state. We came in from a tunnel that was cut in by our people nearly a thousand years ago. When this cave was used in ancient times, it had an opening to the outside world. It was through that opening the marauding Sun People came to steal the Spirit Fire. That opening has been sealed off.

"The green stuff you see is called dy-emeralite. We used it to seal the opening and to strengthen weak parts of the cavern. We use it as sparingly as possible in here, but we do have to ensure the integrity of the cavern.

"We use dy-emeralite for all of our construction, because we can construct it in any form and because it attaches to rock better than anything known to man. The bond is molecular and seamless."

"What is dy-emeralite?"

"It is a compound made mostly from the rock materials we recover when we excavate our tunnels and living areas. We add some trace elements including aluminum, coal, and limestone. It is all ground to a fine dust, and then water is added. We get a heavy, plastic-like material that can be formed like you form concrete. After it hardens, we radiate it with intense photoelectron beams that cause the atomic structure to collapse. When that happens, it loses a little more than half its volume. Dy-emeralite is a combination of the words *diamond* and *emerald*. We call it dy-emeralite because it is harder than diamonds and green like emeralds. It is extremely dense and heavy.

"When we bore a tunnel, we bore it about twice as big as it needs to be, and then when the dy-emeralite is placed, most of waste material from the tunnel is used, so not only do we get a very strong tunnel, we use most of the waste material from the dig."

Sandi stood near the fire and looked into the flames. There was something almost mesmerizing about the Spirit Fire.

"Do you have any more questions?" Garret asked.

"I would like to just experience this whole thing in silence for a while."

"I always get the same feeling," Garret said.

Sandi stared at the fire. She closed her eyes and relaxed, feeling her shoulders sag. For a moment, she could see a wide valley. A river meandered down the valley. It was a bright, moonlit night, and some spots on the river reflected silver light. She felt something calling her to the valley. Sandi shook her head.

"What?" Garret asked.

"It is really weird," Sandi said.

"What?" Garret asked again.

"I do not know. Do you sometimes think that the Spirit Fire speaks to you?"

"What do you mean?"

"I think, when I relaxed just now, the Spirit Fire was trying to show me its home. But that is crazy. I do not know. Think of how many hands have fed this fire, and all those ashes of all of those people. I am Sun People, but in a way, I understand this Spirit Fire."

"During the twenty thousand years of the Alliance, the Spirit Fire was important to Sun People and Earth People. It was given to both peoples in the Alliance. I am not surprised it would have an impact on some Sun People. You are closer to an essence of the earth through your connection to rocks than many Earth People."

Sandi looked at Garret's eyes. She felt the same closeness she had felt that night in the mountains. Could a Sun People woman love an Earth People man? Could an Earth People man love a Sun People woman? The lovers that she had found indicated the answer was yes. But that was then. What about now?

Sandi was reluctant to leave the Spirit Fire, but she knew they had to get on with—with what? "I guess I am ready to leave now," she said.

Garret smiled, almost as if he knew her dilemma. "Come on, then." When they were out of the Spirit Fire cavern, he led her to a larger cavern. It was constructed completely of dy-emeralite. Several display cases were located around the room.

"This is our History Room. You would call it a museum."

Garret led her to the cases at one side of the room. In them were some leather skins with faded symbols that looked similar to hieroglyphics. "These are ancient goatskins. These are the first writings of our people ... some of the actual skins Sotif wrote on. The symbols were made by him in his own hand. They are old and very delicate. We still have over 20 percent of the original skins he wrote."

"And these are over five thousand years old?" Sandi asked.

"Yes. At the time of the great wars, Sotif invented writing and collected all the stories to preserve the history of the Alliance and the Spirit Fire. He spent many years carefully documenting the traditions of our people. We call those stories the *History Skins*. He also wrote new laws to govern our people after the fall of the Alliance. We call them the *Wisdom Skins*. These are the two great books of our culture."

"You think these are actual stories of things that really happened?" Sandi asked.

"That has become a major source of contention among my people. There is a growing faction that believes the traditions are just legends, and the precepts and laws of our people from those traditions are not valid in today's world. They call into question both the *Wisdom Skins* and the *History Skins*. That is why it is important to find the proof of the traditions of our people," Garret said.

"You think you will find that in the Heart of the Bison?"

"I am sure of it," Garret answered.

"It seems the findings at the lovers' cave and the ceremony cavern should provide the proof you seek."

"Those finds have definitely proved it to many, but some are more hardheaded about it. I am sure the cavern of paintings we found is the Sun People ceremony cavern. Unfortunately, the traditions do not contain any details about the cavern. There is still a lot of room for the doubters to wiggle in.

"The thing that would really seal everything would be the History Room in the Heart of the Bison. The traditions say Kectu was buried at the foot of the wall that has the first painting of the beginning of the Alliance. If we find the History Room and the bones of Kectu, by using mitochondrial DNA, we may be able to show Kectu is the mother of the half-breed female in the lovers' grave. Using nuclear DNA, we might even be able to show the Guardian in the ceremony cavern is the father. The paintings on the History Wall will verify the traditions as written by Sotif."

When Sandi got back to her room, she was physically tired, but her emotions were so high she could not sleep. Marc was also excited about the things he had learned. They watched CNN while they ate. The United States was getting ready to unleash an attack on Iraq they were calling "Shock and Awe." There was a surreal quality to the news, and Sandi wondered if it was real or something the Neandertals were faking for some purpose.

As interesting as the war news was, Sandi and Marc turned the news off after they had eaten. They spent the rest of the evening talking about the things they had learned. Marc had spent the day in the DNA labs. He was deeply impressed by the methods they had developed to capture DNA patterns from fossils that had begun to crystallize. Sandi tried to grasp the meaning of the Spirit Fire and all that it implied. If the stories were true, the religion of Mother Earth and the Great Spirit was twenty-five thousand years old!

Finally, she was so exhausted that she went to her room and fell asleep almost as soon as she hit the bed.

Four—March 2003

Sandi sat on a rock looking out over a beautiful, green valley. The sun shone brightly on a deep blue river as it meandered down the valley. In some places, the river reflected gold sunlight. At the bottom of the hill, there was an oxbow pond with a thick growth of cattails and bulrushes around the edge. The cattails gave life to the pond. Across the river, she could see a herd of elephants. They should have seemed out of place. Sandi then realized that they were mammoths. It was strange, but the sight of them brought a strong sense of home to her.

Someone was shaking her. "Come on, sleepyhead. It's time to get up for another exciting day in the Neandertal underground city." It was Marc's voice.

"What time is it?" Sandi asked groggily as she tried to clear her head. She wished he had not disturbed her dream. She was on the verge of knowing something important.

"Breakfast is already here. If you don't hurry, you won't have time to shower and eat."

Sandi took a warm shower, hoping that the water would help her relax and retrieve what her dream had tried to tell her, but it was gone. It had only been two days since she was in a camp in the Middle East, living under the sun and preparing to return with exciting new discoveries. Now she was in a new life, surrounded by phony, three-dimensional pictures and dy-emeralite floors, walls, and ceilings. She hoped that Garret would come to get them, but she knew he could just disappear down a tunnel at any time.

Garret did show up just as she finished stuffing a bagel with cream cheese down her throat, followed by a gulp of warm coffee. He was wearing a jumpsuit like the ones most of the people seemed to prefer. Perhaps it was just the stress of the situation, but when she saw him, she almost started to cry with relief.

"Are you ready for another day?" Garret asked.

"What is the point of all of this?" Sandi asked. "Why are you showing us all of this? What do you want?" After the initial relief of seeing him, she could feel anger from the frustration and the emotions she had experienced over the past two days.

"There is a point," Garret answered. "This morning, your questions will be resolved."

"Don't tell me. You can't say anything. Ronaldo will reveal all," Marc said sarcastically.

"You catch on quickly," Garret answered.

Sandi knew Garret had saved her life, but at what cost to her? She just wanted to know what the catch was—and the sooner, the better. As they boarded the tram, Sandi could feel herself shaking. She didn't know if it was fear, anger, or anxiety over what she was about to find out.

The three traveled in silence to the oval room. Ronaldo was waiting, wearing a suit and tie.

"I would like to know why we are here and what you expect of us," Marc demanded.

"A fair question," Ronaldo answered. "Our great history man, Sotif, wrote the traditions of our people. He also wrote a book of wisdom. We call it the *Wisdom Skins*, because it was first written on goatskins. The *Wisdom Skins* contain the laws of our culture. Our government and all our dealings are based upon the laws contained in the *Wisdom Skins*. Point Four of the *Wisdom Skins* states, 'The Earth People abhor war. The Earth People will not create or use weapons of war. War is a powerful seductress that is very difficult to remove once she gets a foothold with the people.' As Earth People, we have expended all our energy remaining hidden from the Sun People, because the Sun People have been seduced by war.

"We have used Watchers primarily to help us remain hidden. The search for oil in Alaska and the Northwest gave us many times of great concern. We had Watchers in the oil industry that used their influence to direct explorations away from our caverns and tunnels. We have put Watchers in environmental groups to spearhead protests on other developments. Meanwhile, our Thinkers are working on shields to disguise our facilities from technology Sun People use to locate geologic structures underground that might contain oil.

"The Roswell incident was one of our greatest tests. We made some deals and traded some information about radar. We have maintained contact in top-secret levels of the government of the United States since that time."

"Well, I get this cover-up idea, but this whole flying saucer thing is where your story falls apart," Marc interrupted. "I don't believe that you could have developed them."

"Really?" Ronaldo said. "You have seen them fly. Where do you think they come from?"

"You call them electromagnetic floaters?" Marc asked.

"EMFs are a class of areo-grav-levitators ... AGLs for short."

"All right then, AGLs are impossible."

"Of course they are possible. You flew in one."

"Oh, I agree that they exist. In some ways, your AGLs are better than our best airplanes."

"Yes, in most ways, they are better," Ronaldo agreed.

"And you want us to believe that you developed these fantastic flying machines in caves? That borders on the ridiculous."

"Oh, now I see what you mean!" Ronaldo exclaimed.

"There is no way that these things could be developed, tested, and perfected in a cave. And really, what would be the need for them? They can't be too useful in caves, and you can't use them on a regular basis outside. So, they must come from somewhere else, and that's the question that needs to be answered."

"Very good observations," Ronaldo said. "The Sun People developed science and technology consistent with living on the surface. The Earth

People developed science and technology consistent with living below the surface."

"Exactly," Marc said. "And that does not lead to flying machines, especially not such highly advanced flying machines."

"As you have pointed out, Earth People have some severe limitations on scientific development. We have no need for skyscrapers, bridges, dams …"

"Or flying machines," Marc interjected.

"True, we have no vistas that draw us into aviation, and Earth People do not stare at the stars and dream of going to them."

"Right," Marc said. "And I don't see any other point of view that makes any sense."

"The narrow scope of development that has been open to our Thinkers is a two-edged sword. You would not expect the wide areas of interest and development Sun People have followed, but, on the other hand, our narrow focus would naturally lead to an extremely high level of development in those narrow areas.

"Our aviation program actually started about four thousand years ago. At that time, the Bering Strait divided our culture. Most of our people lived hidden in caves in what is modern day Washington and Oregon. However, we needed to maintain clans in Russia and China, because we hoped someday to find the Heart of the Bison.

"In order to maintain contact and perform some sacred ordinances of our people, it was necessary to cross the Bering Strait in boats. This put our people on the surface and in view of the Sun People, from whom we always strove to hide.

"At about the time your people were building the pyramids, my people began the construction of the first tunnel under the Bering Strait. There were a number of failures and problems. It was over five hundred years before we were successful in making the crossing underground.

"When the tunnel was finished, another science became important … how to best travel the long distances in tunnels as rapidly as possible. Over the centuries, our tunnel technology developed in incredible ways. In the early 1700s, our smartest Thinkers began working with magnetism and electricity as a driving force. We developed generators and transformers long before Benjamin Franklin thought about flying kites to look for electricity. Strong permanent magnets were put on the vehicles, and electromagnets were placed at stationary points along the tunnel. As a vehicle approached the electromagnet, the polarity of the electromagnet was set to attract the magnet in the vehicle. As the vehicle passed, the electromagnet was shut down for a couple of seconds to let the vehicle pass, and then it was re-magnetized with the polarity changed so that it pushed the magnet in the vehicle away. Naturally, this required an incredible number of electromagnets and created a rough ride.

"Then our Thinkers discovered methods of shielding and focusing magnetic flux lines. This technology was used to send concentrated magnetic flux lines down the tunnel in a way like that of a laser light. Shields along the tunnel controlled the power of the magnetic attraction along the path between the stationary magnets. As the vehicle passed the stationary magnet, it was completely shielded from the flux lines for a couple of seconds while the magnet in the vehicle was flipped to reverse its polarity, so when it passed the shield, the magnetic flux lines would push it on down the tunnel.

"This method of travel rests upon focusing magnetic flux lines and shielding their effects, which is something that your people have not discovered. This method required fewer magnets, and the ride was smoother.

"By the late nineteenth century, we had developed highly efficient principles of friction, magnetism, and gravity. Our vehicles regularly hit speeds approaching two hundred miles per hour.

"A little over a hundred years ago, one of our researchers developed methods to focus and shield gravitational forces. Shortly after that, we learned to reverse the polarity of gravity. This totally outdated all the magnetic work that had been done. By 1911, we had completely switched to gravity as the driving force in our tunnels. With gravitational forces, we could maintain speeds nearing five hundred miles per hour. Magnetism was then relegated for use in making toys and games."

"That is all very good and interesting, if it is true, but how does speeding through tunnels lead to flying saucers?" Marc asked.

"Be patient," Ronaldo said. "When you have magnetic or gravitational forces attracting each other, everything is pretty straightforward. However, when the forces are repelling, there is instability. For instance, if you put two magnets on a smooth table with their north poles facing each other and then slowly move one toward the other, you know what happens. As soon as the forces that repel begin to move the magnet on the table, it will flip its south pole around and snap onto the magnet in your hand.

"If you put one magnet on a cart with wheels so it cannot flip around, you can push the cart just by bringing the magnet in your hand closer. If the cart could be held stable, you could push it straight up in the air and make it float. In fact, your people have toys that do that very thing. They spin a magnetic top and then carefully move it into a strong magnetic field. The gyroscopic force of the spinning top keeps it from flipping over as the magnetic force keeps it in the air. It looks just like a hovering flying saucer. And, in a way, that is just what it is. Our Thinkers had already done that, making toys for our children to play with.

"A couple of years later, some of our Thinkers began to experiment with applications of gravity flux lines to float things in the air. By the early 1930s, we had developed floating machines that could carry several people by manipulating gravity and magnetic forces. The machines allowed us to travel long distances to keep watch on developments all around the world. Not only can we keep watch on the Sun People, but by developing distribution centers in unpopulated areas, we are able to bring more supplies into our caves. Before AGLs, all our supplies had to be carried in by Gatherers. This new technology has facilitated major changes to our economy.

"We covered the machines in a material we had developed to reduce friction on our trams. It turns out our antifriction materials are nearly invisible to your radar.

"We use gravity for acceleration and deceleration, and we use magnetism for control and direction. The machine's stability is ensured using gyroscopes, hence the saucer shape. We get high efficiency from the antifriction material we use on the skin. This material also prevents heat buildup when we travel at super-high speeds in the atmosphere, and it makes radar detection difficult. All of this technology came from travel in tunnels, but the driving force to extend that technology to AGLs came from our need to keep ourselves aware of developments on the surface that might threaten our civilization."

"Amazing," Marc said.

"I still want to know what all of this is about," Sandi demanded.

"First, we will take a break," Ronaldo said. "Garret will take you to a room where you can get a snack."

Garret led them to a small room with a couple of chairs and some doughnuts and coffee. "I am not hungry, and I do not know why we have to take a break now," Sandi said. "You still have not told us anything about why we are here."

"I am sorry. Ronaldo has many things to deal with. He would not break the meeting unless something important had come up. I am certain it will not take long."

After Garret left them, Sandi said, "They seem to have an answer for everything."

"If they are lying, I have to admire how they are prepared for every question. On the other hand, if they are telling the truth, they don't have to prepare for any of our questions."

"It sounds like you are beginning to believe them," Sandi said.

"It does?" Marc said. "Hm."

Sandi did not know what to make of Marc's response. She felt mentally overloaded, and so she ate a doughnut and silently sipped coffee. Marc was also quiet and pensive.

Finally, Garret came to take them back. Sandi was getting tired of the information overload with no answer to the important questions.

When they got back in the oval room, Sandi impatiently spoke up. "You have been bombarding us with endless information, but what I really want to know is why we are here."

"You are right," Ronaldo agreed. "Many of our people are deeply concerned the Sun People will find us. There is no doubt the Sun People will not allow Earth People to live if that happens."

"I object to that conclusion," Marc said. "There are many people who would be really interested in having open dialogue and relations with Neandertals if they discovered that you exist."

"Sun People are warriors. They invented war, and they constantly work to perfect war. If Earth People were discovered, the first thing the Sun People would notice is our culture is different. Our culture says we should be the best we can make of ourselves. That is in direct conflict with major Sun People religions."

"No," Sandi interrupted. "If you knew our religions, you would see most of them teach us to improve ourselves. It is basic."

"I disagree," Ronaldo said. "Your religions say each man should try to improve himself within the moral culture proscribed by religion. Breeding is a well-known concept among Sun People. They use it to improve animals and crops, but to suggest using it to improve themselves is unacceptable. For five thousand years, we have intentionally bred ourselves to be better as a people and to break boundaries. Take our Thinkers, for instance … on your IQ tests, their average score is over 180. The average is climbing rapidly. You cannot tell me most Sun People would not feel threatened by that prospect.

"Now consider what levels of development we will be able to achieve with genetic engineering. Our culture and religion see no conflict in using genetics to make us better. Already, we are working in the realm of defeating the aging process. I am well past my prime, but I can look forward to many more years of productive life. Death from disease and old age will be a thing of the past in the next ten to fifteen years.

"Both of you take a moment to reflect. Can you honestly say that your culture and your religions are ready to welcome Earth People? Neanderthals are supposed to be the simple-minded cavemen. Our approach to breeding has clearly allowed the Neanderthals to surpass Sun People in science, and there is no limit to how far we might go now that direct genetic engineering is becoming available.

"Sun People have known the precepts of breeding for thousands of years, but nowhere is it acceptable for improving humans. Genetic engineering is even more controversial. Your religionists preach against it as though it would threaten their gods to allow people to select attributes they want their children to inherit. Would they welcome a race of people who have practiced breeding and who actively look forward to genetically engineering fantastic new people? Do you think they would not fear a stronger race that could outlive and outthink them in all aspects of mental and physical prowess?

"Sun People think in terms of force and war. They would not stand by and watch us become the most powerful beings the planet has ever seen. Our culture would threaten most of your religions."

"Our religions teach us to love one another, even to love our enemies," Sandi argued.

"Right now, your government is planning to love the Iraqis into their graves," Ronaldo responded.

"Well, that's different," Marc said. "They pose a real threat to us, not merely a perceived threat. We have to defend ourselves."

"Sun People can argue about what threats are real and what ones are perceived. In any case, it is prudent for Earth People to remain hidden from Sun People for the time being. It is our belief a time will come when we will again form an alliance with Sun People."

"Well, I don't agree that any of your arguments are absolutely true or convincing," Marc interrupted, "but that is an argument we can have another time. This is not getting us any closer to knowing why we are here."

"In the beginning, it was not our plan to bring you here. When the terrorists attacked your camp, Garret made the decision in the field to pull you out. It was the right decision. Of course, you are not the first Sun People to have been brought here over the years."

"What happened to them?" Sandi asked.

"The EMV that knocked the terrorists down also scrambled their short-term memories. We have small machines that duplicate that effect. They leave people confused about things that have happened over the past day or two. They tell somewhat incoherent and largely inaccurate stories about what has happened. In the past, we have treated visitors with the EMV and returned them to your world.

"After you were taken from danger, we could have done the same to you and dropped you off someplace where you could reach safety. Garret could have been dropped off with you, and he could have told a story that would negate the confused UFO story you might tell."

"Why didn't you do that?" Marc asked Garret.

"That was my call," Ronaldo said. "Your discovery of the lovers has given us a starting point to locate the Heart of the Bison. You and Sandi are important to us in the search. You have a strong background in paleontology. We will have Watchers with stronger backgrounds in a few years, but right now, you could be a great help. We need to find the Heart of the Bison now for two important reasons. There is a powerful, charismatic leader in our world who believes Earth People must do something to make it impossible for Sun People to ever threaten us. His name is Solero, and he believes he can do this by creating a massive war among different factions of Sun People so they will destroy themselves.

The existence of the Heart of the Bison would break Solero's influence. Two." Ronaldo held up the little finger of his left hand as he spoke. "Our geologic assessment of that area indicates there will be a powerful earthquake in Pakistan in the next four to six years. We need to find the Heart of the Bison in time to assess its ability to withstand the earthquake and shore it up if needed. One." He put his ring finger up with his little finger and then dropped his left hand.

"Your find at the lovers' cave is on the trail to Kectu and the Heart of the Bison. We need to follow that trail now. We cannot wait until we develop our own resources."

"What makes you think our find has anything to do with the Heart of the Bison?" Sandi asked.

"I told you the story of Kectu, the Guardian, Tuka, and Sky Man. Kectu had a son who was killed by a large cat. He was buried in a cave with four smooth, black stones," Ronaldo said.

"Maybe that was a custom in this area. There might be many boys waiting to be discovered who were buried with rocks," Marc said.

"The mitochondrial DNA test results are complete. The female in the lovers' grave and the boy buried in the cave both have the same mother," Garret said.

Sandi was stunned. Everything Ronaldo and Garret said seemed unbelievable, but something deep inside told her it was true. The fossils they had found had names and lives!

"We have done some work on the nuclear DNA," Ronaldo said. "It is more difficult, and results have not been completed, but right now, we are more than 70 percent certain the old man in the cavern is the father of the female lover."

"No, they are so far apart, and their lives are so different," Sandi said.

"I don't believe it. It's too much of a coincidence," Marc added.

"So, it seems, but it can all be tied together in the Heart of the Bison," Garret said.

"You and Sandi are important to us in our search for the Heart of the Bison ... that is, if we can get you to help," Ronaldo said. "That is what all of this is about."

"I don't know why you think we can help you," Marc said. "We don't know your history, and for sure we don't know anything about this Heart of the Bison."

"The trail to Kectu and the Heart of the Bison begins at the lovers' grave," Ronaldo said to Marc. "Whatever forces led you two, a Sun People man and a Sun People woman, to find the grave is a mystery. When we read your report, we did some aerial recognizance of the area. Some of our advanced technology discovered the existence of a large cavern south of the lovers' cave. We hoped it was the Heart of the Bison. We discovered three possible entrances to the cavern. We planned to fly Garret and Jektu to check them out. Solero was able to convince the Council to postpone exploration of the cavern, and the mission was scrapped. Sandi overheard part of our transmission to Garret. Fortunately, he evoked a rule that allows a person in the field to override an order when he deems his knowledge of the situation warrants it.

"It was clear to Garret the cavern was not the Heart of the Bison as soon as he saw the paintings. Then, when Sandi found the skeleton of the man, it dawned on him that he was in the Sun People ceremony cavern, and the man must be the Guardian.

"According to our stories, Kectu led the first clan from an area near the ceremony cavern to the Heart of the Bison over a period of two summers. We estimate men traveling without women or children could cover that distance in fifty to sixty days. Up until the discovery of the ceremony cavern, the only clue we had was that the Heart of the Bison was probably somewhere south of the Himalayas. Even with the information we got from the lovers' grave and the ceremony cavern, that still leaves a large area to search."

"Well, maybe it would be great for you to find the Heart of the Bison, but why should we care about your religion?" Marc asked.

"Because Point Four of the *Wisdom Skins* is the concept most under attack. We have many Watchers in many countries and governments who know of biological and chemical weapons that have been developed and hidden by your countries and organizations. Those who oppose Point Four say that they could gain control of many of those weapons of mass destruction. They would infiltrate groups, such as Al-Qaeda, Hamas, Hezbollah, and several other organizations, and then they could arm them and coordinate an attack on Sun People that would throw the whole world into a state of chaos."

"How would they get those organizations to work together? Some are Shiites, and some are Sunnis. They hate each other, and you could never get them to work together," Marc said.

"They would not know they were working together until the attacks were already underway. Imagine Watchers infiltrating various terrorist groups and arming them with WMDs. Imagine a plan using them in a coordinated attack on cities like Washington DC, New York, Los Angeles, Chicago, London, Paris, Berlin, Moscow, Mexico City, Sao Paulo, Tokyo, and others. Each terrorist organization would be given weapons and targets commensurate with its ability to use them. They would be given detailed training to accomplish their part of the overall plan."

"That's impossible," Marc said.

"Not really," Garret said. "We could procure the stuff, and we could get it into the right hands. We could develop our Watchers in positions with terrorist groups where they could do the planning and training. Each organization would be instructed to act on a signal they all would recognize. Since none of the terrorist groups would know what the others were doing, the magnitude of the disaster would be as much a surprise to them as it would be to the rest of the world. At a critical mass, representatives of your governments who control the major weapons of mass destruction would be compelled to retaliate.

"We could fan the fires of local wars and dissention all around the planet. Soon, the few remaining survivors would be desperate for anyone who could bring peace. Then we would take control of the planet."

"A one-world government?" Marc asked.

"Not so anyone would notice. Earth People Watchers would be leaders in different areas of different continents. Sun People would not know their leaders were not Sun People. The world would not even know of the existence of Earth People. Our people would completely cooperate with one another behind the scenes. All phases of life on the earth would be under the control of Earth People leaders.

"Solero and his supporters imagine they would then live in peace eternally," Ronaldo continued. "They ignore the warning of Point Four. I believe once Earth People embrace war as a means to peace, they will find themselves in the same trap the Sun People are in. Then there would be no force for peace in the world. The world would be caught in the trap of war until some scientist developed the true doomsday weapon, and some fool would set it off, and the end of all people would come."

"You think you can stop this with the Heart of the Bison?" Sandi asked.

"The Heart of the Bison would validate Sotif, and that would validate Point Four."

"I don't see how we can help you find the Heart of the Bison," Marc said.

"Some things cannot be explained," Garret said. "You found the lovers. You found the baby boy and the four stones. From that, we found the ceremony cavern and the Guardian. Perhaps this is just luck. Perhaps there is a spiritual essence to Mother Earth. I cannot explain it, but you seem to be on the path to Kectu and the Heart of the Bison."

"Maybe so," Marc said. "But we were not looking for the Heart of the Bison. Now you want us to go find it, but I don't have an idea of where to begin."

"I do." Everyone looked at Sandi. It was an idea that came to her mind, and she spoke without thinking about it.

"What do you mean?" Marc asked.

"I do not know what I mean. I have been dreaming of a cave overlooking a wide valley with a river. This morning, in my dream, I saw a mammoth herd. It is a dream of ancient times. I do not know where this valley is, but something tells me it is east of the lovers' cave. I will know it when I see it. I have a feeling the cave is the first home of the Spirit Fire."

"You've been reading too many of the Earth People books. They're going to your head like *Don Quixote*," Marc said.

"Maybe," Sandi said.

"Jektu has seen a vision of the Spirit Fire in the Heart of the Bison," Ronaldo said. "According to our traditions, the Spirit Fire was started in a cave somewhere west of the Heart of the Bison. The original home of the Spirit Fire was two or three days from the place where Tuka and Sky Man were killed. Already, you have narrowed our search area for the original home of the Spirit Fire. Our Thinkers have followed many clues trying to find the valley of the Heart of the Bison. Until now, the whole of Asia and the Middle East were our hunting grounds. We know Kectu and her group ran east from the original home of the Spirit Fire to escape the Sun People. We have no idea how quickly they traveled, but our legends say they traveled two summers to find the Heart of the Bison."

"It is obvious Sandi has some connection to the Earth," Garret said to Marc. "It is this connection that led to the lovers' grave and the secret entrance to the ceremony cavern."

"Why would she be connected to Neandertal things?" Marc asked.

"The things she has found are connected to Sun People. Sky Man was Sun People, and so was the Guardian. There were more Sun People in the Alliance than Earth People. It is possible some inherited knowledge of those things was passed to Sandi through Sun People DNA. It is possible the people of the Alliance left some kind of energy trail Sandi can tap into. The Alliance was between Sun People and Earth People, and it is right there should be cooperation between Sun People and Earth People in the discovery of the Heart of the Bison."

"My genealogy comes from Europe, not the Middle East," Sandi said.

"According to our traditions, a Sun People man called Small Beaver was instrumental in saving the Spirit Fire five thousand years ago. He came from the area where the Iceman mummy was found."

"The frozen mummy they found in the Alps … Ötzi?" Sandi asked.

"That is one of his names. There is a connection between him and Small Beaver."

"What kind of evidence could show a thing like that?" Marc asked.

"Small Beaver gave Sotif a small chip of stone as a reminder of the cooperation between Sun People and Earth People," Ronaldo explained. "It was to be a reminder there are Sun People who respect Earth People and can work with them. He said the stone chip came from the tip of his father's dagger. You can imagine what it meant to us when it was reported that the Iceman had a dagger with the point broken off. During the confusion about who owned the Iceman, we were able to procure the dagger long enough for our Thinkers to confirm Small Beaver's stone chip came from the dagger. We proved it by checking the broken surfaces for fit and the crystal structure in the two pieces of rock. We returned the dagger, and no one thought much about it. The dagger point Small Beaver gave to Sotif came from the Iceman's dagger.

"After saving the Spirit Fire, Small Beaver returned to his land with a woman from the Alliance as his mate, along with several other Sun People from the Alliance. Sandi could be a descendent from that group."

Sandi had studied the Iceman in one of her classes. The Iceman was discovered by hikers in 1991. He was not removed from the discovery site by archeologists, but by local officials who thought that he was contemporary. He was removed and taken for autopsy. The medical examiner recognized he was looking at ancient, mummified remains before damaging the body. Later studies showed he was about five thousand years old. The artifacts were recovered over a period of several days by different groups of people. They were collected in garbage bags, some of which stayed with the mummy, some of which were held by the sheriff, and some of which were collected by other officials. It was nine days before an attempt was made to collect everything in one location. On top of that, there was a serious discussion as to whether the site was in Italy or Austria. Sandi was familiar with the major artifacts, including the bow, arrows, axe, and the stone dagger with a broken point. She had studied photos and descriptions for a paper she wrote for one of her classes.

"You think I am a descendent of your alliance?" Sandi asked.

"Maybe, but always during important periods of great historical impact, cooperation between Sun People and Earth People has accomplished great things," Ronaldo said to Sandi. "The Guardian was there in the beginning to help create the Alliance. Small Beaver was there to help Sotif save the Spirit Fire. Now Marc Metcalf and you are here to help find the Heart of the Bison. I do not know if you have any connection to our past, but you're connected to the problems we face now. Sun People and Earth People have always worked together when serious threats have come. This is as it should be."

"That's all well and good," Marc said. "But our crew is all dead except for Akhtar and Kelvin. The area is full of belligerent terrorists, and we have no paperwork to go exploring through that area."

"There is no way to officially continue our search," Garret agreed. "If we go in, it will have to be without paperwork. We will supply all the crew you will need. Much can be done from our AGLs. We have already begun reconnaissance east of the cavern. We will do our search with three-dimensional photos that can be examined life size in our special viewing rooms, very much like the displays you have seen in our windows. We will only go in personally if it is absolutely required. When you are in, we will have our AGLs close by and prepared to make an extraction at the slightest sign of danger."

"Like the last time, when we lost most of our crew?" Marc asked sarcastically.

"You were in with legal papers," Ronaldo said. "We were too casual in our surveillance and backup. Under this scenario, we would have a large, specially equipped AGL to oversee the work. We will be able to extract everyone in less than three minutes if we detect anyone with weapons within four miles of you. We will only be in during daytime. I cannot say it would not be dangerous, but it would perhaps not be as dangerous as you imagine."

"If you are willing, we can review some of the recon photos this afternoon," Garret said.

"This is something to think about," Marc said. "Give us the afternoon to talk it over."

"What if we say no?" Sandi asked.

"Plan B," Ronaldo said. "Unfortunately, we would have to stun you to scramble your memories. You would be found wandering somewhere in Pakistan. You would tell a disjointed story of being kidnapped by Neandertals in flying saucers. Garret will tell of being captured and drugged by terrorists. His story will dovetail with your story, but it will be more reality based, if you know what I mean."

"Not much choice," Sandi said. "Help you or lose our minds."

"It is not that dismal," Ronaldo said. "You will not lose your minds. You will be confused about the last few days. In the past, the stunning caused some people to have recurring nightmares and other psychological problems. Our technology has improved a great deal. Memory loss is more complete, and side effects have been reduced. The other option, if the EMF had not dropped in when it did, would have been far worse."

"Oh yeah. Well, if it hadn't been for Garret's connections, we wouldn't have been there in the first place," Marc said.

"But you wanted to go, knowing there was a risk," Garret said. "You were not forced then, and you will be able to choose now. Think about it. Tell us tomorrow morning."

"What about the ceremony cavern?" Sandi asked.

"Yeah, what about that?" Marc asked. "Who gets credit for that discovery?"

"You had already decided to keep it secret, at least for a while, and besides, you would have to admit all of your data was lost when the terrorists attacked … unless you want to claim Neandertals picked it up in a flying saucer," Ronaldo said.

Sandi thought about the feelings she'd had when she first saw the Spirit Fire. "I will help you find your Heart of the Bison," she said.

"Let's think about this before we decide," Marc said to Sandi.

"I have thought all I have to," Sandi said. "I will do what I can to help."

Marc looked at her intently, but he didn't say anything. Then he turned to Ronaldo. "What if we help you?" Marc asked. "What if we find the Heart of the Bison? Then are you going to just let us go and blab all of this to the world?"

"If we do not find the Heart of the Bison in time to stop Solero's war, we will have to make contact with the United States government directly to stop what our people might try to do. In that instance, you will be put in contact with those people to help prevent worldwide terrorism. If we do find the Heart of the Bison, you will be allowed to leave with all your memories. In either case, we hope, by then, you will realize the damage your story would do, and you will maintain our confidence of your own free will. Even if you decided to publicize this story, the mainstream will not believe you."

"How can we be sure that you will let us go?" Marc asked.

"We cannot prove anything we have told you," Ronaldo said.

"Are you sure you want to do this?" Marc asked Sandi.

"I am. Not just because of the ceremony cavern ... I want to see the Heart of the Bison and the History Wall. If there is such a thing, could you possibly turn away from it now?"

"But we would never be able to publish such a find," Marc said.

"I do not care. I want to see it, not for fame and glory, but for the knowledge it would give me personally."

"Well, I still think we need to talk about this first." Marc turned to Ronaldo. "Let us have this afternoon to talk about it."

"There is nothing to say," Sandi said.

"Marc is right," Ronaldo said. "Take the time to be absolutely sure."

Chapter

4

The Search

One ... March 2003

Sandi did not know what to say to Garret, so she said nothing all of the way back to her room. She admitted to herself that she was developing strong feelings for him, but now, knowing he was a Neandertal, everything was different. After Garret left, Marc began, "I don't know what to make of all of this. But to start with, we have to assume that these rooms are bugged ... maybe even video surveillance or something even more advanced."

"I do not care if they hear what I have to say," Sandi answered.

"It doesn't hurt to be aware," Marc said. "What do you think of all of this Neandertal stuff?"

"I guess, for right now, I accept it at face value. They are definitely interested in some archeological discovery. I cannot think of any motive other than the one they have given us."

"Well, we don't have any proof or evidence of anything they say," Marc said. "I mean, for all we know, they are aliens from another planet. What they want us to do might be helping them destroy the world."

"What we know for sure is that they have flying saucers, and they live in fairly extensive cave systems, and that is about all we know," Sandi said.

"Well, I'll give you the flying machines, but I'm not convinced we're in any caves. This stuff they make their walls with is not from this earth."

"I asked Garret about it. It is called dy-emeralite, and it is made from stuff on Earth."

"Dy-emeralite?"

"Yeah. It is a word made from *diamonds* and *emeralds* because it is harder than diamonds and has that green tint."

"Well, you can tell where rocks come from. Is dy-emeralite from Earth?"

"They make it from rock dust from a lot of places, and then they radiate it. It is too messed up for me to tell."

"Convenient, I'd say. I think we're not in a cave. We're on some spaceship ... a large one ... probably hiding behind the moon."

"That would be too long a distance to travel in the time it took us to fly in the flying saucer."

"They can probably reach incredible speeds. How else could they cross deep space? Maybe we were unconscious part of the way. Those mass-compensating chairs were very strange. Maybe they messed up our sense of time."

"You make it sound like we are in a situation where we cannot trust our five senses."

"Well, the answers that they gave to my questions are all just too pat ... like maybe they've gone through it all before. I want proof that we're still on Earth, and I don't want them to put me in a flying saucer or a mass compensating chair to get me there. I want to be someplace I know and am familiar with before I make up my mind. I just don't feel like I have any kind of paradigm to decide from."

"Maybe their answers come so easily because they are the truth. When your five senses cannot be trusted, you have to look to something within ... a sixth sense. Ronaldo's description of how flying machines were developed makes much more sense than aliens from tens or hundreds of *light-years* away.

"But there is something even deeper. I have my own sixth sense of their Heart of the Bison. It touches something in me ... the same part of me that finds paleontology so important, the same part of me that feels closeness to the rocks. I believe Ronaldo because of all those things.

"Maybe some of my progenitors were a part of the Alliance. Sometimes, I feel I can see through the eyes of a Stone Age woman. Knowledge is passed in DNA. We call it instinct. For instance, when a baby turtle cracks out of its shell, it has no parents. All the knowledge it needs to survive is developed in its brain from the DNA. Why should Homo sapiens not have a similar source of knowledge? I believe some kinds of knowledge are genetic. I feel I have an instinct from the Stone Age world, maybe from the first Cro-Magnons who came from Africa.

"The Spirit Fire cavern I went to was mostly rock. There was very little dy-emeralite in that cave. The rocks were from this earth, I am sure of that. I am going to help them find their Heart of the Bison. What about you?"

"I don't know. I'll think about it tonight."

Two—March 2003

The first part of the morning was uneventful. Breakfast came, and they ate. Then Garret took Sandi and Marc to meet with Ronaldo again. When they got there, Akhtar was waiting in the room. Sandi was so excited to see him. "How is your arm?" she asked.

"It's almost like nothing happened. They used some kind of salve along with energy fields to speed up the healing process."

"What about Kelvin?" Marc asked.

"I wasn't in the same place. I asked, and they say that he'll be fine. Garret says they have explained all of this strangeness to you, and you are thinking about helping them find their cave."

"They've asked us, and Sandi wants to help, but I don't know. What about you?"

"I don't know about all of this stuff. What do you make of it?"

"I have given it a lot of thought. I believe that we could be on a space station someplace."

"You thinking about helping them find the Heart of the Bison?" Akhtar asked.

"Well, I still have a lot of questions. What about you?"

"If you and Sandi decide to go, I'll be going with you."

Just then, Ronaldo came in. "You have had time to give our offer some thought. What have you decided?" Ronaldo asked.

"What exactly are you offering us if we do help you?" Marc asked.

"When we have found the Heart of the Bison, we will drop you off in the Middle East with a good cover story to explain what happened to your expedition. You will have the ceremony cavern, which will make you famous. You will have to promise not to reveal anything about us or the Heart of the Bison. Most importantly, you will have the personal satisfaction of knowing you played an important role in preventing the destruction of a major part of your world."

"Well, I have one last question," Marc said. "You say that we are in caves in Canada, and yet everywhere we look, we see the pale green glowing stuff you call dy-emeralite. I don't think that it comes from this world. Are we really on Earth or someplace in a dy-emeralite spaceship?"

"You are familiar with the periodic table," Ronaldo began. "All of the possible stable elements and plenty of unstable elements that could exist in the universe are on that table. There is no strange, unearthly element. Dy-emeralite is a compound of basic elements common on Earth. Our dy-emeralite walls are impregnated with organic LEDs. They are lit with a mere trickle of electricity."

"How can dy-emeralite be harder than a diamond?" Marc asked.

"What is a diamond?" Ronaldo asked.

"It's a carbon crystal," Marc answered.

"Basically, the same material as coal," Ronaldo said. "But coal is soft, opaque, and black, while a diamond is hard, clear as glass, and breaks on well-defined and predictable planes. Yet the carbon atoms in coal are no different than the carbon atoms in a diamond. The only difference is in how the atoms are hooked together.

"Dy-emeralite is made of very common materials … feldspar, gneiss, some silica, and carbon. Our Thinkers have developed a process that makes it the strongest and hardest compound existing on the earth today. Dy-emeralite is harder than diamonds, but it is not a crystal. It has a small level of elasticity. It will not break under pressure like a diamond.

"I have answered your questions to the best of my ability. Now, what is your answer to my question? Will you help?"

"You can count on me," Sandi said.

"Well, I'd like some kind of proof that we are not on some spaceship," Marc said.

"That can be arranged," Ronaldo said. "Garret, have a Gatherer take Marc out. If you find everything I have said is true, will you decide?" Ronaldo asked Marc.

"Well, if I'm satisfied that we're still on Earth, I will try to help."

"What about you, Akhtar?" Ronaldo asked.

"I'm with Marc and Sandi. I'll go with them."

Garret made arrangements to take Sandi, Marc, and Akhtar out of the caves. They took about an hour ride through a tunnel, and then Garret led them to a room about thirty-five feet in diameter. There were a lot of security devices in the room. Six Gatherers were there. Each put on a large backpack that went from their shoulders to their buttocks. The backpacks had a hairy covering that looked like the hair on the Gatherers. None of them were wearing any clothing, but their hair was so thick that Sandi could not tell if they were male or female. When the backpacks were in place and the hair around them was combed, it was impossible to tell they were not part of the Gatherers. All six appeared to be some sort of wild primates—like Bigfoot.

After the Gatherers were ready, they all walked down a dy-emeralite tunnel about fifty feet long. At the end of the tunnel, a dy-emeralite door slid open, and they entered the back of a cave. The inside of the cave consisted of all natural rock. The door closed behind, and there was no way to tell where the door was. Even though Sandi knew where the seam should be, she couldn't find any sign of it. It was about twenty feet to the entrance of the cave.

As they walked from the cave, there was a slight breeze carrying the earthy smell of rich, moist soil mixed with pungent pine. The area was a thick forest of tall Douglas fir trees and fern undergrowth. Having spent several days in the dy-emeralite caves, the sight of the forest was comforting to Sandi. Being surrounded by the beauty and variety of the outside world was calming. No wonder Garret's people tried to duplicate it with the three-dimensional pictures in their faux windows. But, as realistic as they were, it was nothing like stepping out into the middle of a forest.

The Gatherers left the cave without saying a word and spread into the forest. Though this cave was obviously a well-used entrance, Sandi could see no sign of a path leading away from it. She doubted that Kelvin would be able to see anything, either. As they left the cave, the Gatherers walked with very short steps in a manner that looked clumsy. Marc walked to a baby pine, crushed some of the pine needles, and smelled them. Sandi looked up through the tall pines to a deep blue sky. A white cloud moved above, making it seem like the trees were moving, making Sandi slightly dizzy.

"Why do they walk that way?" Sandi asked Garret as she watched the Gatherers taking their separate ways into the forest.

"Normal steps cause the heel to come down heavily, followed by a strong push off from the ball of the foot. They walk that way for about a hundred yards to prevent concentrated pressure from beating the ground down around the cave. With loaded backpacks, they can weigh over three hundred pounds. However, even when they walk normally, they rarely leave a trail. Sometimes, they might leave one or two footprints, but never enough to form a trail that can be followed."

Marc let Sandi smell his hand as they started out. It had a strong pine smell. After about a mile, they passed what appeared to be a logging road. In another half mile, they came to a two-lane, paved road.

In about five minutes, a blue 1998 Ford F-350 with a silver shell pulled up. The driver was a Watcher. The Gatherers removed their empty backpacks and loaded full ones from the truck onto their backs. After packing the empty backpacks in the truck, they started back to the cave.

It was late when they got back to their room. When they were inside, Marc approached Sandi. "Well, I said I would go if they convinced me that we are on Earth. I'm convinced, but if you want out at any time, I'll support that."

"I do not think much will happen," Sandi said. "I do not believe I can figure out where the Heart of the Bison is from holographic maps. I think I am going to have to be in physical contact to feel the spirit of the rocks."

"This Heart of the Bison is really important to these people. I don't think that they'll just walk away. Are you sure that you want to go back in the field?"

"Yeah, I think so," Sandi answered. "I am as curious about this Heart of the Bison as they are. Maybe I am descended from the Sun People of the Alliance. What about you, Akhtar?"

"I'm with Marc on this. I go where he goes," Akhtar said.

"Are you staying in our room now?" Sandi asked.

"No, I have a room three units down."

"Well, I reckon we'd better get some sleep," Marc said.

After Akhtar left, Sandi crawled into her bed, exhausted.

Three—March 2003

The next day—after a short meeting with Ronaldo—Sandi, Marc, and Akhtar returned to the AGL base station on Banks Island. On the way there, Garret explained how the mission would be carried out. They would be taken by a large AGL that would hover over Pakistan. It was called a hovering surveillance station—an HSS. They would not be orbiting in the sense that satellites orbit. However, they would hover on the edge of space. Each day, a small AGL called a shuttle pod would take them down in the morning and bring them back up at night.

When they entered the base station, Sandi was once again impressed with its size. She could not tell how many AGLs were in the station, but she could see about a dozen from her vantage point. When Garret pointed out the HSS that they would be using, Sandi was surprised at its size. It was at least one hundred feet in diameter and close to twenty feet high. "How can you possibly fly this thing without being seen?"

"There are only two places on earth where this can land. This is one, and our base station in northern Russia is the other. Both areas are uninhabited. Our flight patterns take us at a low altitude over unpopulated places until we are near the North Pole. From there, we climb rapidly to thirty or forty miles high and then take a heading toward our destination. By the time we fly over any populated areas, we are just over sixty miles high, out of sight to the naked eye. This has the most advanced stealth coatings available. No radar can pick us up. The coating also absorbs light, so there will be no reflection when the sun hits us. At those high altitudes, we are invisible."

They rode up a short escalator to a door that slid to the side as they approached. "Why don't you just beam us in?" Marc asked.

"The HSS does not have the antigravity beam. It does not get close enough to the ground to load or unload anything except in dock at a base station."

Inside, there was one long, rectangular room. All the surfaces had a metallic appearance. There was a large, round table at one end. There were several doors on each side of the room. Around the walls and between the doors, there were desks with computers on them. There was a long, rectangular table down the middle of the room. Several people were sitting around it. They all stood up as Garret and his group entered.

"This is the main activity room," Garret said. "We do most of our work at the workstations. We strategize and have work meetings at this table."

"But you do not get together to eat here, do you?" Sandi asked.

Garret ignored her comment. "These people are the rest of the exploration team. Everyone take a seat at the table, and then everyone can introduce themselves and explain what they will be doing."

Sandi, Marc, Garret, and Akhtar each found a seat. "Everyone here knows who you are and why you are here," Garret said to Sandi, Marc, and Akhtar. "Marvin, you can start," Garret said to the man who sat next to Sandi.

Marvin was a Watcher. He wore a powder-blue jumpsuit with strange hieroglyphics on the right side of his chest. His skin was light, and his hair was medium brown. He was tall and well built, a good-looking man. "I am Marvin," he said as he stood up. "I will be the navigator on the flight. My job is to get us to the right place and back. I will also be the one monitoring the areas around you while you are down. During the training period, I will show you some of the instrumentation we will be using to detect any possible threats to you." Marvin nodded to a woman sitting next to him.

"My name is Alexandra, but everyone calls me Alex," she said. "I will be the pilot of the shuttle pod that will take you down and pick you up. I will also assist Marvin on the monitoring devices." Alex was also a Watcher. She wore a lavender blouse and a tan, knee-length skirt. Her skin was fair. She had short blonde hair and blue eyes.

Next to her was another woman. Her skin appeared to be tanned. She was a Watcher with a thin, angular face. She wore a white sleeveless pullover and chocolate brown pants with a matching brown-and-white polka-dot sash tied around her waist. "My name is Carol. I will be in charge of collecting records, meaning I will go down with you, take photos and recordings, and gather necessary data in the field. On ship, I will assist in using the data to prepare demos and other assists to follow the path from the HSS when possible."

Next to Carol was a Thinker dressed in a charcoal-gray jumpsuit. To Sandi, all Thinkers looked alike. However, in this light, the slight green tint Thinkers in the dy-emeralite city had was not evident—in fact, this Thinker's face had an almost metallic look to it. "I am Seamiel." Sandi was fascinated with the way his small mouth moved as he spoke. His thin lips seemed to move with exaggerated precision, and his voice had the watery sound of the other Thinkers. "I will be in charge of onboard records. We have very sophisticated observation equipment to help us gather information. The shuttle pod will make nighttime flights near the surface to gather more data. We have computer systems to create three-dimensional holograms of the areas you will be traveling through. We have onboard viewing rooms that will allow you to see the areas in 3D. With any luck, this data will allow you to pick your trail and provide information you need to figure parts of your path without having to go down."

Next to Seamiel was a male Watcher in a yellow polo shirt with beige pants. He had short, wavy, dark brown hair. His eyes were light brown. He appeared to be a little overweight. "Hi. I am John. I will be in charge of housekeeping and the galley. I will prepare meals, keep you supplied with clean clothes, and keep everything clean and orderly. Naturally, I will be the most important person on the team." Sandi felt more at ease after his attempt at humor.

Jektu sat next to John. "You all know Jektu," Garret said. "He will go down with the surface team whenever that is necessary. Next to Jektu is Roger. He will be the pilot and captain of the mission."

"I will coordinate with Banks Island in North America and the Severnaya base in Russia," Roger said. "We will make trips to those base stations as needed."

Sandi was sure Roger was a Watcher, though he looked African. His skin and eyes were black. His hair was also black and tightly curled. He wore a teal-colored jumpsuit.

The next man was the last man around the table. He had dark skin and looked very much like Akhtar. "My name is Bandar. I am a Watcher. I have worked in Pakistan for thirteen years. I am familiar with the area we expect to be searching, and I speak all the local dialects. I will take care of any coordination with locals."

"Okay," Garret began. "The surface team will consist of Marc, Akhtar, Sandi, Jektu, Carol, Bandar, and me. We will spend the next five days on extensive training. You will learn how to live on the HSS and how the surface excursions will be done. Six days from now, we will be stationed over northern Pakistan, and the search will begin in earnest.

"With any luck, most of the mission will be aboard the HSS. We will only take the chance of going down when it is absolutely necessary. We are embarked on the most important mission in Earth People history and arguably the most important in Sun People history also. Good luck."

During the training, Sandi spent a lot of time reviewing the three-dimensional displays of Pakistan east of the lovers' cave. She was frustrated and losing confidence.

One day, near the end of the training, Ronaldo came to the base station and called Sandi, Marc, Akhtar, and Garret to a meeting. "As you all know, we are in a critical period in the history of the Earth People. Recently, it has come to our attention that Stanford University is working on a machine called an interferometer. When it is fully operational, it will be able to gather accurate information about conditions below ground from a flying plane. All our tunnels and population centers would be visible to it. We have Watchers working to slow the research down and Thinkers working on ways to overcome this technology.

"According to an informant in Solero's group, he is speeding up plans to create a worldwide disaster before interferometers are operational. According to our informant, Solero is also aware of Marc's unpublished report. It is possible he has information about the status of our search for the Heart of the Bison. If he knows, you can be sure he will do everything in his power to stop you. We cannot challenge Solero without exposing our informant. Because of this added level of danger to the mission, I have come to give you an opportunity to withdraw."

"What do you think Solero will try to do, and what are you prepared to do to prevent it?" Marc asked.

"We have sophisticated technology to provide cover, and we do have someone in Solero's organization to keep us informed about what he is doing. I am reasonably confident we will be able to protect the mission, and everyone involved, but I cannot make a guarantee."

"I have come too far to turn back now," Sandi said.

"After being kicked out of Mogadishu, I promised myself that I would never again be kicked out of a fight before the mission was accomplished," Marc said.

"I have exactly the same feeling for the same reason," Akhtar said.

"I can speak for the entire Council when I tell you we are grateful for your decision. Be assured we will do all we can to protect the mission."

Sandi felt brave and important during the meeting, but later, she quietly wondered what she was doing. Thankfully, Marc would be with her. Ronaldo and Garret may be queasy about using violence if needed, but Marc would have no compunction about it, and he was trained for that kind of fight. Solero's people would not find it easy to stop Marc.

Four—March/April 2003

Finally, the training was done, and it was time to return to Pakistan. As they entered the HSS to prepare for takeoff, there was a low, almost unnoticeable hum. Sandi took a seat at the round table between Marc and Akhtar. They had just taken their seats when Sandi felt the machine begin to move. "What is going on?" she asked.

"We are maneuvering out of the base station," Garret said. "When we are clear, the mass compensators will kick in. You will not feel any motion then." In the HSS, the mass-compensating chairs were located around the round table. They were computer controlled, and it was not necessary to squeeze handles for them to work.

A few minutes after takeoff, the warning lights turned from red to yellow.

Marvin stood up. "Come over here. I have something to show you."

Sandi, Marc, Akhtar, and Garret followed him to the end of the large room. The floor dropped down about two feet to a row of six chairs that faced a large, circular window that covered about 180 degrees on the underside of the HSS and curved under their feet so they could look straight down. "Take a seat," Marvin said. Sandi followed Akhtar down two steps to the row of seats.

The window gave a clear view of the earth below. Sandi could see the curvature of the horizon. "Marvin is familiar with the part of the earth we will be traveling over," Garret said. "He will describe the areas we are going to fly over."

"We are north of the Arctic Circle near the North Pole," Marvin said. "Our flight plan will take us over the Bering Strait, along the east coast of Russia, and over Japan. It will be daylight over the North Pacific, and we will be headed southwest. When we reach the thirty-fourth parallel, at the south tip of Japan, we will turn west. It will be a long arc, but we will be going fast enough that you will feel the centrifugal force of the turn unless you are in the mass-compensating chairs."

"Will we need to get back in the chairs then?" Sandi asked.

"No, it is a very wide turn, so the force is not that great. We will follow the thirty-fourth parallel across China, Tibet, and Kashmir and then into northern Pakistan, where we will park above the search area. As we travel west, we will be going faster than the earth's rotation, so the sun will set behind us. It will be dark when we get over Pakistan. When we are over Kashmir, we will have to get back in the mass-compensating chairs for the rapid deceleration as we come up on the surveillance position. Most of the flight will be at sixty-four miles above sea level. The surveillance position will be fifty-seven miles. We are just going over the Bering Strait now. The Diomede Islands are in the center." Sandi could see blue all across the curved horizon. Land was to her left and right. She could see two islands below. In the center of the blue in front, she could make out a large island coming over the horizon.

"The island coming up on the horizon is Saint Lawrence," Marvin said.

As they passed over it, the HSS began a slow turn to the right. "We are making a slight course correction. The large body of water to your right is the Gulf of Anadyrskij on the Russian coastline."

Though the sun was low on the horizon, it was bright daylight. Sandi could see two large fingers of water going inland from the gulf. Then the blue of the Pacific on her left turned white as they flew over clouds covering the earth below. "Under the clouds is the Russian Komandorskije Island." As they passed beyond the clouds, Marvin continued, "To your right is the Russian coastal port of Petropavlovsk."

Sandi looked where Marvin was pointing, but she could not see the city. The land where he was pointing was at the tip of a large peninsula. From there, she could see a string of islands stretching out in front of her, going all the way to the horizon. As they flew over them, Sandi could see they formed a large arc. "We are flying over the Kuril Islands now. These islands stretch to northern Japan. The water to the right of the islands is the Sea of Okhotsk, and to the left is the Pacific Ocean."

Soon, Sandi could see land to her right. Then a very large island appeared on the horizon in front of her.

"The large island in front of us is Hokkaido, the northern island of Japan."

As they approached, Sandi could see that the land on the northern part of Hokkaido was divided into squares. They were not agricultural—they seemed to be more like cities, although she was too far up to see buildings or roads.

"Below us are the cities of Abashiri, Kushiro, and Asahikawa. We will be flying over the Sea of Japan as we leave Hokkaido. Japan will be to your left. To your right, you will see the ocean curve around the end of the land. On that point is the southern-most port of Russia, Vladivostok. South of that is the Korean Peninsula. We will be flying over South Korea, and from there, we will start the wide curve onto the thirty-eighth parallel."

The Korean Peninsula was clearly visible as they approached it from the northeast. From just sixty-four miles up, everything looked peaceful and clean. "Seoul is to your right but is a bit too far to see. The land across the sea to your left is southern Japan. We will be starting our turn east now," Marvin said. The force of the turn made Sandi lean in her seat. "We will be heading over China. The big city to your left is Shanghai."

As they sped west, the sky got progressively darker. Sandi could see a wide angle in the direction they were flying and from the horizon to almost straight down. Unfortunately, she could not see the sun setting behind her. By the time Marvin announced that they were over Tibet, it was dark.

"We are over Kashmir," a voice said over the intercom. "Please take your seats at the round table. We will be decelerating in four minutes."

Sandi sat at the table with everyone else. In just a couple of minutes, the voice came over the intercom again. "We are now safely parked fifty-seven miles over Pakistan north of Islamabad. From the observation seats, you will be able to see the lights from Islamabad clearly to the south. The sun will be rising in an hour and a half. We want to put you down forty-five minutes before sunrise."

"That was spectacular," Marc said. "But why didn't we just fly down from the North Pole over Russia?"

"Our protocol is to not fly over Russia or the United States in wartime. The United States' attack in Iraq has put us under the war protocol. Our protocol is for political expediency, because Russia and the United States are on high alert about their airspace. It is unlikely we would be detected, but it is better to just skirt around. It makes for fewer explanations."

Sandi sat in awe. She had just raced the sun and won! They had traveled about thirteen thousand miles in less than an hour! Even as they were en route, the visions of the Earth below seemed unreal. Now it was already like a dream. She walked to the observation deck. The night sky twinkled with more stars than she had ever imagined. The dark crescent of the earth's horizon loomed before her. The darkness below was broken by scattered lights. To the south, she could see a field of lights that had to be Islamabad.

"Quite amazing, isn't it?" Marc was standing beside her.

"Amazing," she agreed.

Sandi watched as the eastern sky brightened, and the colors of the earth began to appear.

"We can see the sun on the horizon from here long before it can be seen on the ground. It is time to leave," Garret said. "Ready?"

Sandi started from her reverie. "Do you fly this high often?"

"Actually, this is a first for me. It is pretty incredible."

"I just never guessed the earth could be so beautiful. I mean, in real life, it is much more spectacular than the NASA movies you see."

Sandi followed Garret to the small shuttle pod that would take them to the surface. During the time Sandi, Marc, and Akhtar had been trained to live in and work from the HSS, the shuttle pod had been modified to carry the whole crew, including the pilot.

It took a few minutes to get everyone settled into the mass-compensating chairs, and then Sandi felt the shuttle pod begin to move as it exited the HSS. There were no windows. The panel in front of her had orange, red, and purple lights. On orange, she grabbed the handles. On red, she tightened her grip, and on purple, she squeezed as hard as she could. During training, she had practiced the sequence until she was totally comfortable with the timing and the strength of her grip. This time, it was for real!

In less than two minutes, all three lights changed to yellow, the signal to let go of the handles. She could feel the shuttle pod slowly bank as it glided into the ravine at the appointed landing spot. The door opened, and Sandi followed Garret and Marc into the antigravity beam. She had practiced the maneuver until it was second nature to her. As soon as the last of the ground team touched down, the shuttle pod shot up and out of sight.

Jektu led the way down the ravine. The team had decided to start near the secret entrance to the ceremony cavern. Based upon Jektu's intuition, the team followed the stream east from the cavern to the Indus River. The Indus River valley was a well-populated agricultural area.

Each member of the group had a knapsack with water and food for the day. They were all dressed in Middle Eastern attire. Sandi wore a plain, brown abaya, which was a dress with long sleeves and a hemline at her ankles. She wore a matching hijab on her head.

When they reached the valley of the Indus, they turned north. Jektu led the group, but Sandi could tell that he was tentative about the direction he was going. At times, Sandi had a sense they were going in the right direction, but at other times, she was confused.

As they traveled, Carol stayed in communication with the HSS. It was her job to see to it they avoided detection. They passed farms and villages, but always under the guidance of the HSS. Jektu also used his powerful senses to help them stay hidden from the people in the area. As the sun set, the HSS directed them to a pickup site. Shortly after dark, the shuttle pod silently glided in and picked the members of the expedition up. Sandi was frustrated. Nothing she had seen during the day gave her any assurance that they were on the right trail.

Near the end of the third day, the river turned from north to northwest. When they returned to the HSS, Garret stopped Sandi on her way to bed. "Did you sense anything as the river turned westward?"

"No. Why?"

"You said before there was something important along a river running east and west. There are not many places where the Indus flows east and west. I know this is not exactly east and west, but it is about as close to that as it gets. In anticipation, we have done some advanced reconnaissance of this area. We have used many different imaging methods and some advanced computer modeling. The team is getting worn down from starting before sunrise and working till after dark. I think it will be productive to take a day off tomorrow and spend some time in the viewing room to examine what we have found."

Sandi was feeling run-down. A day of rest was welcome. As she ate dinner, something about the river turning west bothered her. Her feelings became chaotic and fearful; there was something she wanted to avoid along that stretch of river.

Sandi had a fitful night, plagued by strange dreams and cold sweats. Even though the wake-up call was much later than normal, she was as tired as ever.

"How did you sleep?" Garret asked.

"It was a terrible night. There is an old energy in that place," Sandi answered.

"What kind of energy?" Marc asked.

"I do not think it is the Heart of the Bison."

"Then what is it?" Garret asked.

"I think someone was raped there. But what is really weird is I get this sense the woman was punished ... like they both were punished very severely."

"Where do you think that comes from?" Garret asked.

"I do not know ... perhaps from nowhere," Sandi answered. She could not figure out how her feeling would have anything to do with things she had learned about the Heart of the Bison.

After Garret returned from breakfast, Sandi went with him to the viewing room. On the screen at the front of the room was a bird's-eye view of the valley. There were six comfortable chairs in front of the screen with foldout writing desks. There was a joystick on the right arm of each chair.

"This is a flight simulator. You can control it with the joystick," Garret said. "It will let you move in and around the valley to any position and angle you want. Sit here and give it a try."

As Sandi took the controls, all the seats moved forward, and the screen in front of the seats became a tunnel. As the seats moved into the tunnel, the landscape of the valley surrounded them in a realistic three-dimensional display. When she looked up, she saw a slightly cloudy sky, and when she looked down, she saw the valley below. "The simulator is seven hundred feet high," Garret said. "You can use the joystick to fly around the valley at any elevation."

The three-dimensional effect was so realistic it was hard to believe it was just a display. Sandi pushed the stick forward, and the seats rotated forward. It was as though the floor fell from under her, and she began to drop. The sensation of going into a dive was so real that she nearly threw up.

"Let go," Garret ordered.

As soon as Sandi released the joystick, the simulator righted itself. A dial on the dash showed "ALT 218 feet ... 66.5 meters." The ground was noticeably closer.

"What was that?" Sandi asked breathlessly.

"You just fell about five hundred feet," Garret said. "The platform we are on rotates and dips to simulate the altitude a plane would take while making these maneuvers. Also, the seats are mass-compensating chairs that exactly duplicate the sense of acceleration you would feel while making these maneuvers."

"If it keeps up, I am going to get sick."

"You will get used to it. When you press the simulator to move faster than a plane could go, all actuators shut down, and the simulation skips forward. And do not worry about crashing. The simulator will not duplicate that."

It only took a few minutes for Sandi to get the hang of how to operate the joystick. For over an hour, she explored the whole valley. She only lost control three times. There was a sizable cave on the north side of the valley.

Sandi was able to get within ten feet of the ground. At that elevation, she could make out insects that were on the ground when the data was collected. But when she tried to glide into the cave, the simulator refused to go in.

"We could not collect data in the cave from the fly-bys," Garret explained.

Marvin came in as Garret was talking. "Are you getting anything?" he asked.

"Nothing so far," Sandi said. "I just do not seem to get the feelings from movies. We will probably have to examine the inside of the cave on the ground. Sorry."

"We have gathered infrared, sonar, and some other databases you have not heard of," Marvin said. "That information has allowed us to plot the path of the river at different geological times. There seems to have been some kind of major change in the riverbed at about the time of the death of the lovers. We have plugged that information and databases of typical biosphere during that time period into an advanced computer simulation that can show the valley as it looked back then."

Marvin pushed some buttons on his desk, and the valley morphed into something entirely new. Sandi flew around it with the joystick. "It feels kind of familiar, but I am just not getting anything," she said.

"Let me bring up the valley before the rapid change in the riverbed," Marvin said.

Everything stayed pretty much the same, but the path of the river changed drastically in several places. Again, Sandi flew around the valley. "Nothing," she said. Then she flew to a spot in front of the cave. She felt something there, but she could not get the details.

"There are some other things that we can try," Marvin said.

"No, wait a minute," Sandi said. "That pond at the bottom of the hill ... it must be an old oxbow from the river."

"Right," Garret said. "Do you want Marvin to bring up the time period when the oxbow was part of the riverbed?"

"No. It is not that. It is the pond. Somebody did something important with the pond. I need to go down to the cave and the pond."

"We will do that when we go down tomorrow," Garret said.

"What would that valley look like if it were full of water?" Sandi asked.

"It would take quite a lot of water to do that," Marvin said.

"Yes, but could you simulate that?" Garret asked.

"It will take some time."

"It is lunchtime now; could you have it by this afternoon?" Garret asked.

"Sure, no problem."

"Okay, Sandi and I will get some lunch and rest while you prepare it," Garret said.

"I am all for that," Sandi answered.

"You play. I work. Just great," Marvin said.

After the lunch ritual, Sandi played chess with Marc for an hour. Then Marvin had things ready. Garret and Sandi returned to the viewing room. Sandi used the joystick to place herself in front of the cave. Sandi felt something very strange as she looked at the water. "You can increase or decrease the amount of water with this lever." Marvin indicated a lever on the side of the joystick.

Sandi used the lever to adjust the water level up and down until it seemed most familiar. "I feel like it was water like this that saved the Spirit Fire."

"You believe the Spirit Fire was in that cave?" Garret asked.

"I do not know. I just feel that water saved the Spirit Fire. Water like that, but not a lake or a river … a large body of water full of debris. Like a flood, maybe."

Sandi spent another hour fiddling with the simulator, but nothing she tried improved upon her feelings. She would have to go down to see it in person.

The next morning, the shuttle pod dropped them off at the foot of the hill below the cave.

"I am really thinking or feeling something different … something familiar about this place," Sandi said as they started for the hill.

"Do you think it has something to do with the water?" Garret asked.

"I am not sure. I think it is something to do with the dream I had about a valley with mammoths."

"The side of the hill is too exposed for everyone to go up," Garret said. "You, Marc, and I will go. If we are spotted by someone from a distance, no one will think much of three people on the side of the mountain."

The cave was about two hundred feet up from their location. The slope to the entrance was steep. They had to zigzag across the face of the hill as they walked up. The opening was fifteen feet wide and about twelve feet high in the center. The sides of the opening sloped up from the ground on the sides to the peak. It looked like a triangle. As Sandi slowly walked in the entrance, she could see that it was big enough to have provided a home for a clan of ancient humans. Inside, it widened to about thirty feet. It went back forty-five to fifty feet. The temperature was noticeably cooler. The floor was dirt and relatively flat.

"There has been a lot of recent activity in this cave," Garret said when they were all inside. The cave had several food wrappers and the ashes of a recent campfire. In one corner near the back, there were piles of dried human feces. "If there are any artifacts in this cave, it will take some digging to get to them."

"This can't be what you describe as the Heart of the Bison, but it is the kind of cave that ancient people used," Marc said.

Sandi stood in front of the cave and looked across the valley. There were several agricultural areas laid out with rectangular fields. A road meandered down the middle. The Indus River cut a path up the valley between the road and the cave where she stood. Several cars and a couple of trucks crawled along the road.

In spite of all of the signs of modern man in the valley below, Sandi felt an ancient story. "I think this is the cave of my dream," Sandi said.

"Maybe your dream has something to do with the rape," Garret suggested.

"I do not understand any of this anymore, and I wonder if I can help you at all. Do you really think maybe I am some reincarnated ancient Cro-Magnon from the Alliance?"

"Sit down, and I will explain," Garret said.

To the right of the cave, there was a low projection of decomposed granite. Sandi sat on it with her legs crossed. She leaned back against the rock face. As Garret began to talk, Sandi began to get a mental picture of the valley.

"You understand the difference between inherited knowledge and learned knowledge?" Garret asked.

"You mean instinct and education? Yes, I know the difference."

"One important characteristic of the ancient Neanderthals was their brains were large. Most of that brain capacity was located behind the frontal lobes in the areas of instinct."

The vision of the valley became clearer in Sandi's mind. The vision was similar to Marvin's pre-flood simulation.

"Instinct is evolved knowledge carried in a shorthand form in the DNA," Garret continued. "Some traumatic experiences can be registered in DNA. If that helps the next generations to avoid danger, it can be passed forward."

In Sandi's mind, the river was not in the right place, and there were small differences in the skyline around the valley. The foliage was different, too.

"Instinct is general and develops over ages. Memories from traumatic experiences are more specific. I think many ideas of reincarnation come from such memories. In the case of the Ancients, those memories are much stronger."

"Do you have those memories and instincts?" Sandi asked.

"No. My brain has been developed to favor the frontal lobes like Sun People. However, the rudiments are still there. The point is Sun People have some of the same abilities at varying levels."

"Maybe so, but why are my memories important to you? You are trying to find Neandertal artifacts, not Cro-Magnon," Sandi said.

"Suppose your ancestors were part of the Alliance, and you are remembering stories that were told to them for so many generations they imprinted themselves in the DNA. The imprint in the DNA could conceivably be passed through many generations without finding structures in the brain that allow someone to communicate with the memory. Now, for some reason, those structures are put together in your mind."

In Sandi's mind, there were bends in the river that reflected sunlight. Sandi gradually realized there was something very important about the rape and a bend in the river.

"The historical period we are interested in was a time when there was cooperation between Earth People and Sun People," Garret said. "With your talent and Jektu's abilities, we should be able to find what we are looking for."

The valley became clear to Sandi, but it was more of an idea of the valley than an actual detailed picture.

"There was water below this cave," Sandi said.

"You mean like what you had Marvin simulate?" Garret asked.

"No, not that or the river … it was the oxbow pond below the cave. There is no pond now, but the bog below the cave has the crescent shape of an oxbow pond filled in with sediment."

Suddenly, Sandi got a clear mental picture. "No. It is not the pond. There is something about the pond, but this is different. The black rocks came from the stream at the edge of the pond."

"Are you sure?" Garret asked.

"I am very sure. Perhaps they were washed down when the river made the oxbow. The stones were found when that bog was a pond." Sandi stood up. As soon as she got up from the rock, the mental pictures vanished.

"Let's take a closer look at the bog," Marc said.

Marc took some measurements of the cave and made some notes and a sketch before they went down to the stream.

At the bottom of the hill, the other members of the group gathered around, and Garret explained Sandi's feeling that this area was the source of the black stones. Everyone began examining the area around the stream.

Marc used a small hand shovel to dig in the stream about two feet downstream from where the water came out of the ground. He found several angular rocks, and then he found two, hand-sized, rounded black stones about thirteen inches deep.

Sandi was excited. "These are the same as the rocks that were buried with the baby!"

"Are you sure?" Garret asked.

"Yeah, I am sure of that."

"That means that they probably came from somewhere along this river," Marc said.

"They came from this very spot," Sandi said. "If your Kectu put the rocks in the grave, she got them right here. She lived in this cave."

Garret started back up the hill without saying a word. Sandi looked at Marc. He shrugged his shoulders. "Now what?" Marc said as he started to follow Garret up.

"I do not know. Wait, I am coming with you," Sandi said.

Akhtar, Carol, and Jektu stayed at the foot of the hill examining the spring and the remains of the pond.

When they caught up with Garret, he was standing at the entrance and staring into the cave. He turned and looked out over the valley. Sandi could see tears in the corners of his eyes. Garret walked into the cave and began picking up the trash.

"What the ..." Marc exclaimed as he reached the cave.

"Shush!" Sandi responded.

Sandi turned to look out over the valley. She felt a sensation of dire threat. Then she felt a relief. She closed her eyes, and she saw the whole valley filled with water. It was like the simulation Marvin had made, but it was different in several ways. It was as though the water was giving her time to escape, but from what?

"You seem preoccupied." It was Marc.

"This whole valley was flooded with water at some time."

"Are you talking about a lake?" Marc asked.

"No, the water was moving ... like a flood or something."

"That would be impossible," Marc said. "Way too much water. Not even the worst monsoon in history could fill this valley with moving water."

Garret came from the cave and threw some trash to the side. "The oldest traditions of our people say Kectu brought the Spirit Fire from its original home to the Heart of the Bison. The stories say the Sun People wanted to destroy the Spirit Fire, but it was protected by water."

"I still don't see how this wide valley could be flooded," Marc said. "It may have been a lake if the outlet was closed, but I don't see any evidence of that, either."

"Perhaps something supernatural like the dividing of the Red Sea," Garret said.

Sandi interrupted, "You know, the first vision or memory I had of this place was after I had seen the Spirit Fire."

"If this was Kectu's home, it was the first home of the Spirit Fire," Garret said.

"What did Cro-Magnons have to do with the first home of the Spirit Fire?" Sandi asked.

"The only Sun People person to live here was the Guardian," Garret said.

"Then I should not have any connection to this place," Sandi said.

"Our belief is that there is something supernatural about the Spirit Fire."

"You think the Spirit Fire is talking to me?"

"I had a strong suspicion when we first came up, but now I am sure this is the first home of the Spirit Fire." Garret's voice was soft and reverent. "When you look out on this valley, you see what the Spirit Fire saw. You know the story of the people who gave the Spirit Fire life. I do not know how that knowledge could come to you except from the Spirit Fire. Do you?"

Sandi did not answer. She was confused and bewildered.

"I believe there is something supernatural about the Spirit Fire," Garret said. "The Spirit Fire connects Sun People and Earth People. The Spirit Fire originated as a gift from Mother Earth at a time when Earth People were dying out all across the land. It was the spirit of cooperation between Earth People and Sun People in the warmth of the Spirit Fire that preserved Earth People.

"Long ago, when the Spirit Fire was in danger of being lost forever, it connected with Small Beaver … a Sun People man. He led the expedition and directed the battle that rescued the Spirit Fire. You saw the Spirit

Fire in the cave where Small Beaver first saw it. Something reached out to him, something that caused him to risk his life for what the Spirit Fire stands for. Now something has reached out to you. Perhaps what you sense comes from the Spirit Fire itself."

"What makes you think that the Spirit Fire is supernatural?" Marc asked.

"I would not call it supernatural. It is the natural force for life this planet was formed with. It stands for cooperation between Sun People and Earth People. However, on a larger level, it stands for peaceful coexistence between all peoples, and between men and the world they live in."

Sandi remembered when she had first seen the Spirit Fire. There had been something powerful about it. And then it occurred to her that the Spirit Fire had first been ignited in this very cave over twenty-five thousand years ago. Somehow, it had gotten to a cave in Alaska.

"Now, as at the time of Small Beaver, there is a danger to the Earth People and the Spirit Fire," Garret continued. "Solero wants to use war to find peace. Everything could be lost if he succeeds in his plans. Something about the Spirit Fire reached out to you. It reached out to you just as it reached out to Small Beaver."

"Well, I don't buy any of that," Marc said. "Saying that this was the home of your Spirit Fire would be wild speculation at best."

"From a purely logical standpoint, it may not be possible to prove it," Garret answered. "Jektu and I will spend the night in the cave. I want to see if the place triggers any memories with him."

"What about me?" Sandi asked. "I may be just a Sun Person, but so far, I am the one with the memories of this place."

Garret thought a few seconds as he paced back and forth. "You are right. You and Marc should both stay. I will call the HSS and make the arrangements. I will bring Jektu down. The others will go back tonight."

Five—April 2003

Marc and Sandi moved back into the cave as Garret started down the hill.

"I've wanted to talk to you since we were first taken in the flying saucer," Marc said.

"What do you mean? We have talked."

"I know, but some things I didn't say because I could never tell if we were really alone. I'm sure that they have had us under constant surveillance."

"So, what did you want to talk to me about?" Sandi asked.

"I don't know if these guys are aliens, Neandertals, or something else entirely."

"Going by what I have seen and my own sixth sense, I would say they are who they say they are," Sandi said.

"Maybe so," Marc agreed. "What I have to say still holds."

"What?" Sandi asked.

"Well, it's obvious that you're developing feelings for Garret."

Sandi could feel her face heat up. "Is it that obvious?" she asked.

"It is to me, and I think it is to Garret."

"Why does that concern you? Apparently, it would not be the first time there was something between Neandertals and Cro-Magnons."

"You have stressed more than once that you want to have children and a normal life. Unless you are ready to give up on all of that, you should reconsider where this is all heading."

"Am I hearing this from you, Marc? I thought we had gotten past racial prejudices."

"Well, this is a bit more than a racial question. It's almost like a different species."

"Neandertals are Homo sapiens, and you are the one who has proven interbreeding is possible."

"That was over twenty thousand years ago, and we don't know for sure about that. They have been evolving and changing DNA rather aggressively over the past five thousand years. Even if you could have children with him, what would they look like?"

"I do not know, but who says we will ever get together?"

"Are you prepared to live in a dy-emeralite tunnel the rest of your life?" Marc asked.

"Garret is a Watcher. I think Watchers must live in our world."

"Suppose you move into your white-picket-fence life and have a couple of children. Suppose something happens. Say, for some reason, Garret is a suspect in a crime … not that he would be guilty. Suppose that he is forced to give DNA. Well, his DNA is going to raise some eyebrows and create some serious questions. Or even your children.

They will have medical exams. Maybe someday they will need to have their blood typed. What do Neandertals have? A? B? O? Or something very different? You could be setting yourself and your kids up for some serious questions and heartache."

Sandi could think of no answer to Marc's questions. They were considerations she had not thought about. She felt confused and even a little betrayed. She knew her feelings for Marc were more than just professional, but it was like family, a brother, not the same as the way she felt for Garret. Marc treated her in a way that was also more than just professional, and that just added to her confusion.

Sandi walked out of the cave to look over the valley. As she watched, the shuttle pod flashed in. Garret and Jektu took some things out, and Carol and Akhtar got in. When it was loaded, it zipped away. Sandi still could not get over how quickly it could come down and fly back up. Garret and Jektu had started up the hill. Sandi felt a great urge to get this all out in the open, but it would be too awkward to talk with Garret about her feelings around Marc and Jektu.

Garret and Jektu brought food and blankets for the night. They opted not to have any kind of fire in the cave for fear of drawing unwanted attention. Garret and Jektu left the cave to eat alone. Sandi could not stop thinking about the problems Marc had pointed out. There were some things she could not wait to know.

"Garret," Sandi said when he returned. "How many Watchers do your people have in our world?"

"I could not say. Why?"

"Just curious. Would you say ten? Fifteen? A hundred? A thousand?"

"There are many. Some are in governments of major powers, some are in business … oil, for instance. Some are in all kinds of research. I do not know how many, but surely more than a thousand."

"So, what is a Watcher's life like?" Sandi glanced at Marc, hoping he would not say anything to allude to the conversation they had just had. She could tell he was listening intently.

"What? You want to know if it is cloak-and-dagger espionage?"

"For instance, do you live in our world all of the time? Maybe 50 percent? What?" Sandi asked.

"Every assignment is different. I can only speak for me. I spend ten to ten and a half months in your world each year."

"What is your life like? What do you do in your spare time?"

"I am dedicated to anthropology in this world. When I am not on a dig, I spend almost all of my time studying."

"What about sports? Movies? Other normal outside interests?"

"I watch sports on TV. I like basketball, tennis, and some football. I always watch the Olympics on TV. I do not much care for movies. I arrange to go to plays in New York or Los Angeles whenever I can. I keep up with the news on TV, but that is about all. Why all of these questions?"

"Just idle conversation," Sandi answered. "I mean, here I am helping you with something that apparently is quite important, and I do not know much about you at all."

"I suppose my life would seem boring to most people in your world. But I am really interested in the work I do. It is recreation to me."

"What about the time you spend in the dy-emeralite world?" Sandi asked.

"I spend some time debriefing. I am in contact all year, but I sit down once a year face-to-face to review goals and progress."

"What is your goal?" Marc asked. Sandi wished that he would stay out of the conversation, but it looked like he wanted in.

"Until now, my goal was to learn all I could about paleontology. Of course, everything is changed now."

"In what way?" Sandi asked.

"Now we are on the trail of the Heart of the Bison. Now, for the first time in five thousand years, that goal seems within reach. My goal is to find the Heart of the Bison."

"After you are debriefed, what do you do? What kind of recreation do they have in the dy-emeralite tunnels?" Sandi asked.

"There are a number of things, but for me, I get most rejuvenated spending time with the children."

Sandi's heart sank, and she could not think of the next question.

"How many children do you have?" Marc asked. Sandi hated that the question had been asked, but at the same time, she was glad that Marc had asked it.

Garret chuckled at the question. "I do not have any children of my own. I work with the children at the training center. You would call it a school, I guess."

"What do you do with the children?" Sandi asked, feeling relieved and hoping that it did not show.

"I teach. I play. I just associate. The magic of the world is in the children. They believe in magic. For them, everything is possible. Their excitement for life rubs off on me."

"Do you want to have children of your own?" Sandi asked.

"Have you read *The Republic* by Plato?" Garret asked.

"No," Sandi said.

"I have," Marc said.

"Do you remember about children?"

"It has been a while," Marc answered. "It seems that all of the children would be raised by the State. They would be turned over to State schools sometime after birth ... like maybe after they were weaned or something. Oh! And everyone would be born at the same time of the year. ... like maybe in the spring or something."

"You remember pretty well," Garret said.

"You mean you use Plato to show you how to raise children?" Sandi asked.

"Certainly not," Garret said. "The fact is Plato is a latecomer. Much of his philosophy likely came from Watchers, anyway.

"Back in the Ice Age, life was very difficult for the Earth People. The Ancients are attuned to their bodies. They can tell exactly when the females are ovulating and are susceptible to becoming pregnant. When they mate at that time, they call it ... a rough translation would be 'baby mating.' That means the consequence of mating is pregnancy. Mating at any other time of the cycle is called 'play mating.' Play mating is mostly for enjoyment.

"Back in those times, life for newborn children was extremely hard. Chances for survival were best for babies born in the spring. It was natural to develop rules that females could only baby mate in summer so all babies would be born in spring.

"During baby mating time, there were strict rules about who baby mated with whom. It was very important for fathers to know who their children were. Fathers had a commitment to provide for the children they fathered and for the mother until the children became old enough to help provide for themselves. Though the man had to provide for his children and teach his sons to hunt, Earth People did not split into nuclear families. The women and children formed a close-knit group that stayed near the cave, while the men ranged far to hunt for food. They were gone much of the time, and when they were at the cave, they generally stayed to themselves.

"Sotif changed all of the rules of baby mating. From that time to today, the selection of partners for most baby mating has been based upon the development of certain traits we want to build in our people. Baby mating partners are selected by a committee of people who are skilled at breeding for those traits. The restriction on the time of year for baby mating was done away with long before the time of Sotif.

"When children are weaned, they are turned over to the central training system to be cared for and taught by people who are skilled and nurturing. Adults are given up to six weeks each year to spend with the children. So, you see, we have a system that is very much like *The Republic*. Our government is also like *The Republic*. You would think Socrates and Plato had spent a couple of years in our culture before they formed many of their ideas. Of course, we did have Watchers in ancient Greece. It is likely some of our ancient culture rubbed off on the Greeks."

"So, have you baby mated? Are some of the State's children yours?" Sandi asked.

"No, I have no children in any form."

"So, then your people would never get married and have children in a nuclear family?" Sandi asked.

"I like to think we are a large community family," Garret said.

Sandi sat against the wall of the cave, thinking. She had not considered just how totally different Garret's culture and beliefs would be. Marc was right. A contented relationship with Garret was impossible for her. Such an easy, cool conclusion to draw, but somehow, it did not ease the fire in her heart.

Sandi looked out on the valley. She saw a herd of many animals coming. She could see mammoths, woolly rhinoceroses, and other animals from the Pleistocene era. The herd was led by a giant aurochs. Sandi knew that they were coming to destroy. They were stronger than she. There was nothing she could do.

Suddenly, a great flood came down the valley. The herd was washed down as the whole valley filled with the floodwaters. Sandi saw that the aurochs had climbed onto high ground. She knew that the flood had given her a chance to get away, but the aurochs would form another herd to come after her. Her only chance was to find a place where the aurochs could never catch her.

The water left the valley, a new river flowed, and everything was different. The aurochs followed the river downstream to rebuild his herd. Sandi ran up the river looking for a new home. Soon, she found a mammoth with one tusk. He told her to follow a stream running east from the river. She followed the stream many days until it dried up. She continued traveling until, one day, she came to a beautiful valley. In the valley, she encountered a giant bison. The bison told her that she would be safe in the valley where he would protect her.

Sandi woke excited. The sky was gray; the morning sun had not yet risen. The men were sitting together at the entrance to the cave. Akhtar and the rest of the crew were there. "I have seen it!" she exclaimed.

"What are you talking about?" Marc asked.

"I have seen the way to the Heart of the Bison and the valley where it is!"

"Where?" Garret asked.

Sandi explained her dream. When she described the valley of her dream, Jektu said that her description was similar to his memories of the valley of the Heart of the Bison.

"I am sure that this valley was flooded at a time when the people in this cave were in grave danger," Sandi said.

"Well, I haven't seen any evidence that this valley was ever underwater," Marc said.

"It was a short time," Sandi explained. "Maybe less than a day."

"Sandi, you know that's impossible. No kind of storm could dump enough water to fill this valley. It must be symbolic of something. Besides, it's just a dream," Marc said.

"I know what you are saying," Sandi said. "But there is something so real about the dream. I know there were an aurochs and a bison. The aurochs is symbolic of the enemy, and the bison is symbolic of the cave and a protector. There was a mammoth with one tusk, and it pointed the way to the Heart of the Bison. The people escaped from the aurochs behind a wall of water that filled this valley. I cannot explain it, but I know the water is not symbolic. I know the water was real, and the path is real, and the mammoth is real, and I think I can follow it all."

"There is a story about a great flood in the *vidus* of my people," Akhtar said.

"Well, most old religions had floods in their mythology," Marc said.

"Which way does the path go to the Heart of the Bison?" Garret asked.

"We start going upriver, but the one-tusked mammoth said to follow a stream going east, so that is the way to start." Sandi felt a surge of confidence.

"Do you know how far upriver the stream is?" Garret asked.

"No, and I do not know what the path would look like exactly. I think I will have to walk it. From here, it starts by following the river upstream, but in the dream, the mammoth sent us up a side canyon."

"Do you know what the stream looks like?" Marc asked.

"I do not know, but the river is still large when we turn off. It is weird. The path does not follow the main river, but I am sure it leads to the source of the water that saved the Spirit Fire."

"We should get started," Garret said. Sandi walked behind him down to the stream, watching his body move. There was nothing in his walk that betrayed his origins. How could he be so different … so unlike her and her people? She tried to imagine what it would be like to be with him. She knew that he could never be hers. Play mating … that would be sex for recreation with no commitment. Baby mating would be worse. It would be assembly-line production of children for the State. Neandertals had never known the closeness of a traditional family. She thought of her parents. How sad it would be to have lived without the closeness she felt with them.

The day started with high hopes, but as they traveled upriver, Sandi had none of the feelings she had experienced at the cave. Nothing seemed familiar. At about noon, they came to the first tributary going east, but it just did not seem right. Then, shortly after passing it, she began to reconsider. All afternoon, she was plagued with doubt.

Her confusion only increased when the shuttle pod picked them up. It was time to return to Banks Island to restock and refuel the HSS. Sandi slept late the next morning. After breakfast, Garret took her to an impressive control room. "We have done a great deal of electronic and digital recognizance of the tributaries going east from the Indus. We are hoping you will get some indication of which one to take by studying them."

Sandi spent two days studying the holographs and handling samples of rocks, dirt, and plants that were collected from each of the tributaries. She had a vague feeling about the canyon just north of the one she had seen in the field, but she couldn't be sure about it.

The morning of the third day, they flew out of Banks Island at the same time of day by the same route as the first trip out. From sixty miles up at the speed they traveled, the Earth seemed small and manageable. The team was dropped off at the second tributary going east before sunrise.

"What do you think of this stream now?" Garret asked.

"I thought I would be more certain. It seems right, but I cannot say for sure. I am so sorry. I know you are investing a lot of time in this. I keep thinking we should have gone up the first one. I do not know what I am looking for. I expected more feeling about the direction."

"Jektu sees something on the side of the hill," Jektu said. "Jektu thinks Garret and Marc must look closer." Jektu pointed toward the bottom of what appeared to be a recent landslide.

"You might as well check it out," Sandi said. "I just cannot decide where to go." She turned to Garret. "I am really sorry. I know it is still early in the day, but I just do not know where to go. The only thing I am sure of is that we have to follow a stream from the east."

"Marc, you and Jektu check it out while Sandi and I work out a plan for today," Garret said.

Everyone else followed Marc and Jektu to the face of the slide. This was the first time Sandi had had a chance to talk with Garret alone since her conversation with Marc. She could not think of a thing to say.

"We have the day to explore. I suggest we start up this canyon and see what happens," Garret said.

"That could be a big waste of time."

"We are stuck down here until the evening pickup. That gives us all day. We can go up this canyon or follow the river up farther. Either might be a waste of time, or we could find something. Waiting here is a waste of time for certain. I say we follow your first hunch."

"Back at the cave, when I had the dream, everything seemed simple and straightforward. I really thought I would be guided to just walk straight to the Heart of the Bison. We have not made the first turn, and I am already lost."

"Do not get discouraged. What is your gut feeling?"

"When I first saw this stream, I felt this was it."

"Then why do you doubt it now?" Garret asked.

"I need to find something. You know, something I can recognize … something to guide me. I do not see anything I recognize. The more I look, the more I think … well, if there is nothing here that I recognize, I guess this must not be the place to turn, so then I guess we should keep going on up the Indus."

"I do not think you are going to see anything you will recognize. Twenty-five thousand years have passed. Your dream is at least that old. Everything will be different. You are going to have to listen to the promptings of the Spirit Fire. Do not let misgivings cloud your intuition."

"I know there is something special about the Spirit Fire, but I cannot make myself believe in a supernatural power from it."

"Sandi, there is one thing I am sure of, for whatever reason, you are here. What you have can lead us to the Heart of the Bison."

"What are you saying?" Sandi asked.

"You know what I am saying," Garret answered.

"We should go up this valley?" Sandi asked, knowing what the answer would be.

"Right."

"But it is so hard," Sandi said. "Memories from DNA I can almost buy into. But power from the Spirit Fire? I know I felt something when I first saw it, but no matter how long it has burned, it is just a fire. Sorry."

"A fire, yes," Garret said. "But there is more to it. It has energy from all of the ashes of all of my people for over twenty-five thousand years."

"That is okay for you and your people, but for me, the feeling is not that strong. I just worry if we go wrong, we could never find it. It could be years of backtracking, and then I could lose the feeling, and then what?"

"If you do not trust what you have, we *will* spend our time backtracking. Then you will lose this gift because of doubt."

"Look!" Sandi pointed to the hill. Marc was signaling them to come. Garret and Sandi walked toward Marc and the others. The terrain was rough, and several times, Garret took her hand to help her along. She felt like a high school girl every time he touched her.

When they reached Marc and the others, Sandi could see that they had found the remains of a mammoth skull.

"Look at this," Marc said. Pointing to the skull, he showed where the bone had grown around the hole where the tusk on the right side had been, but on the left side, the hole was clean.

"This mammoth lost his right tusk some period of time before he died, but he still had his left tusk when he died!" Sandi exclaimed.

"Well, I would say that's a pretty good guess," Marc said.

"This is the one-tusked mammoth that told the people where to go!" Sandi shouted, unable to contain her excitement. "Now he is telling *us* where to go."

Sandi spontaneously hugged Garret. She stepped back. "You were right. I just need to follow the feeling. I need to follow the feeling," she repeated. "Okay then, we follow this stream up the canyon!"

Less than an hour after they left the mammoth skull, Marc said, "Hold it."

"What?" Garret asked.

They were looking east up the canyon from the stream they were following. The canyon narrowed ahead of them. The north side had a smooth contour, shaped somewhat like a concave crescent. The side on the south was steeper. A ledge protruded out two-thirds of the way up the south side.

"I've seen something like this before," Marc said.

"What are you talking about?" Sandi asked.

"Look!" Marc pointed to the north side. "The crescent shape is nearly eroded away, but you can still make it out."

"So?" Garret said.

"Sandi, you can tell if rocks have been misplaced, right?" Marc asked.

"You know that," Sandi said.

"Well, if rocks that should be down here by the stream are up on that ledge on the south side, you would know. I mean, you could tell, couldn't you?"

"Usually, yeah, I suppose so," Sandi answered. "What are you getting at?"

"Back in the late fifties or maybe early sixties, there was a big earthquake in Idaho. A river flowed through a canyon like this. At one place, there was a campground along the riverbank. The earthquake caused the whole north side of the canyon to break away and slide down. It did not tumble or roll down. It slid as a mass. The bottom of the mass was pushed across the canyon and up the other side.

"The slip plane on the north side left a crescent shape. Some of the camping equipment and vehicles were found near the top of the slide on the south side. My dad's family went to see the slide when he was a boy. A lake formed behind the slide where it dammed up the stream. I have seen the pictures of him at the slide. Some of them were taken far enough away so that the picture clearly shows the crescent shape and the dam that was created. The ledge there on the south looks like the south edge of that dam." Marc pointed to the south side of the canyon. "The crescent on the north here looks like the crescent slip plane on the north of the dam in Idaho. That dam was called Earthquake Dam. When my dad went to see it, there was already a large lake behind the dam. They called it Earthquake Lake.

"In the picture, there is a lot of heavy construction equipment, and there were huge pumps pumping the water out of the lake. They were racing to tear the dam down and drain the lake. Here was a dam and a lake already built for them by nature. Why do you suppose that they were racing to tear it down?"

"Why?" Sandi asked.

"Because earth-filled dams have to be engineered. They have to have a strong keyway in the bottom. They have to have certain slopes upstream and downstream. The fill has to be compacted and impervious to water. Without these engineered features, it is just a matter of time before the dam breaks. They had to tear it all down before it could break. We have found the source of the water you dreamed about!"

"You think this was once a dam?" Garret asked.

"It's hard to tell, because it was so long ago. There has been a lot of erosion, so the features are a bit muddled. But if the rocks on that ledge came from the bottom of this valley, I would say that there is no doubt that there was a dam here with a lake behind it. I don't know how big the lake was; we'll see as we go up the valley. If the dam failed, as I'm sure it did, it would have drained very rapidly. That would have caused an incredible flood all down the drainage from here past the cave and out onto the plains south of there. Depending on how big the lake was, it could have filled the valley in front of the cave. Well, I guess Sandi's dream is more literal than symbolic. Makes a person wonder about reincarnation."

"Maybe not reincarnation ... maybe *inspiration*," Garret said.

Sandi did not say anything, but she wondered about the power of the Spirit Fire.

Sandi and Marc climbed to the ledge on the south side. It was clear, even to Marc, that the rocks on the top had come from the bottom of the canyon, because they were rounded and worn as they would be only if they had been in the stream at the bottom of the valley.

"Look at the size of that basin upstream," Marc said. "There's no doubt that it could store a lot of water and judging by the width of the bottom of this valley, the river coming down was much larger than the stream flowing now. It could have filled that basin in just a few years."

By the time they got back to the streambed, it was getting dark. The team waited there until it was dark enough to shuttle up to the HSS.

The next day, they stayed aboard the HSS to examine details of the canyon. Marvin created a computer simulation of the dam and the lake behind it. From sophisticated programming, he was able to determine how high the dam would have been, and from the topography behind it, he determined how much water it would have held. Then Sandi sat in front of the virtual cave in the simulator, and Marvin had the dam break. The water rushing down the valley in front of the cave was just as Sandi had seen it in her dream.

It was almost scary for Sandi to realize how literally her dream was being verified by the archeological data they were finding. Was there some Mother Earth law that allowed the Spirit Fire to speak to her?

From that day forward, the path they were to follow came to her in clear feelings, though the land was not familiar to her. She was not following a vision of what the path looked like; it was a sense of the direction to take. No more did she allow doubts to confuse her. After leaving the confines of the ancient lake, Sandi turned the search to the southeast.

"Are you sure about this direction?" Garret asked. "Because our legends all say Kectu took the Spirit Fire east."

"The main direction out of the Indus River was east, but I am sure the path turns south. I'm not sure how far it will go south. Maybe it will turn east again."

"Maybe that's why all of our current research going east has not found anything Jektu remembers," Garret said.

In spite of Sandi's confidence, progress was slow. Each day, Sandi went down to follow the trail. At night, she reviewed holograms and samples of the trail ahead. Sometimes, she felt confident enough to skip forward, but most of the time, she had to pick up the trail in the morning at the point where they had left off the previous day. Days were grueling and long. She relished each trip back to Banks Island. They took two days each trip to recoup and review their progress.

Six—May/June 2003

One afternoon, Sandi felt a strange excitement. "There is something important around here," Sandi said. In front of them, there was a cave in the side of a hill. There were a lot of pine trees around, though it was not a thick forest. They had not seen any sign of civilization all day.

They were in a forest. "Here," Sandi said. In front of them, there was a cave in the side of a hill.

"What is this?" Marc asked. "This isn't the kind of cave that people would live in. It's too low on the hill. It's too exposed, too small, and there's not enough protection."

"You are right," Sandi agreed. "But there were people here all the same." Sandi walked into the cave. It was small, only about twenty feet by twenty-five feet. The cave was completely empty with no signs of ever having been used as a habitation. "I need to spend the night here," Sandi said.

"Then we will stay here tonight," Garret said. "It is big enough to give us a good place to get some sleep. I will call and have the shuttle pod bring supplies for a camp."

No one could find any evidence in the cave, but Jektu found several piles of rocks that formed a semicircle in front of one side of the cave.

"Some early structures were constructed by digging holes in the ground to stand logs in," Marc observed. "They were held in place by placing stones around the logs. These rocks could indicate that someone set poles in front of this cave to hold animal skins around the entrance. They could have effectively increased the livable size of the cave by about 30 percent."

After dinner, Sandi curled up on a cot inside the cave. She fell asleep almost immediately.

Sandi soared over a tree-covered mountain. Raven wings held her in the cool air. She banked and circled above the trees. A group of strange people worked at the entrance to a small cave below. She landed on a branch and watched strong men dig holes in a semicircle in front of the cave. Women cut and spread meat to dry in the light of a low sun. Others brought fruits, vegetables, and herbs. When the holes were dug, the men chopped down straight trees and put the trunks in the holes. The women sewed pieces of mammoth skin. The men stretched the skins over the poles and tied them in place. The fire in the cave had power to protect the people.

Sandi woke from her dream. The sky was gray. Garret and Marc were starting a small fire. Sandi walked to the fire. "Is it okay to have a fire here?" she asked Garret.

"A small campfire would be alright. The HSS has scanned the area. There is no one within three miles. If anyone starts coming this way, we will no know well in advance."

"How can you be so sure?" Marc asked.

"The HSS has the best surveillance technology in the world. It is designed for just this kind of work. How did you sleep, Sandi?"

"I dreamed a large group of people were preparing this cave so they could spend the winter in it."

"What people?" Garret asked.

"I believe it was Kectu and those who were running with her. It is as you said. The more I follow the trail, the more information I get, and the more certain I am."

"According to the Sotif stories, those who ran from the Sun People spent the winter in a cave along the way. This must be it," Garret said. "We must be more halfway there."

Progress remained slow but steady. Occasionally, they encountered areas where it was dangerous to travel in daylight. If Sandi had a good idea of the direction, they would wait until the shuttle pickup and skip over the problem area to start the next day. One morning, shortly after they had started, they came to a wide valley. Sandi was certain that the path would take them to a point on the skyline about twenty miles away. There were few signs of human habitation in the valley below, but, because Sandi was sure of the direction, they decided that it was not worth it to walk so far. Shortly after lunch, Sandi noticed Carol sitting alone under a tree.

"Kind of a boring day," Sandi said.

"Yeah, kind of."

"You and Alex are the first women I have been with since I got to the dy-emeralite world. There were no women at any of the meetings I had with Ronaldo."

"Women have an interesting place in our world."

"How do you mean?"

"Well, there is no such thing as a law or regulation about what women can do or cannot do. It is all a hereditary thing. For instance, there are clans of Ancients that live in caves in Russia and Canada. The roles of women among the Ancients are totally set by their instincts. The men lead. They hunt. They make all the important decisions. The women stay near the cave. They bear children. They do as the men say. Their responsibility is to bear children, care for them, and gather what food they can. The Ancients mate and have babies just like they did in ancient times. They call it baby mating. That is not a law or rule; it is just the way they are made. You cannot get a female Ancient out of that role, even if you try."

"So, then they are not part of the breeding program?" Sandi asked.

"No. From the beginning of that program, there have always been clans of Ancients that were left as Mother Earth made them. They are sort of our anchor."

"What about females in the other groups?"

"Gatherers are very much like the Ancients. Although the women can go out with the men to make pickups when some of the supplies they are bringing in can be packed in small backpacks, women's roles are more on a domestic scale than roles for male Gatherers. Female Gatherers are like the Ancients as far as their interest in other roles is concerned. However, childbearing for the Gatherers is controlled by the Breeding Council, and their children are raised by the State."

"It seems to me Gatherers are pretty much perfectly suited for going out into the world to bring in supplies. Why would they be in a breeding program? What are they trying to change?"

"I never really thought of that," Carol replied. "I think it is just the way things are."

"I have also seen several Watchers that look like different races of Sun People. If you have already duplicated Sun People, why would Watchers still be involved in the breeding program? Should they not begin to form Sun People family units, even in your caves?"

"It is pretty complicated to make changes in Earth People laws, especially in things that are spelled out in the *Wisdom Skins*."

"What is the role of female Watchers in the Earth People world?"

"There are no prescribed role differences among Watcher females or Thinker females. Males and females do exactly the same work and have the same responsibilities. Women do not seem to get into leadership roles, but I think they have some of the genetic force regarding roles from the Ancients that it is not totally bred out. However, some Watcher and Thinker females have started to enter the political scene, and some hold high positions in local government. I think it will not be too long before you find them on our national scene. Many Watchers live in your world. In those cases, they pretty much live by the rules of the culture they are in."

"What about Kectu? It seems she was a very important person even though she was a female."

"That all goes to the Ancients. There are two really important people in an Ancient clan. One is the leader. He is usually the strongest male, and he makes almost all the decisions for the clan. The other is called the shomot. He is usually a little older. He is in charge of spiritual things ... stuff like the ceremonies to Mother Earth. He spends his time like everyone else in the tribe unless some problem arises that requires intervention by Mother Earth. In addition, during the winter, the shomot must tell all the ancient stories of the Earth People. Only males who participate in the hunts get to hear these stories.

"On really rare occasions, and I mean *really* rare, some important changes in the clan are needed ... changes to carry forward and become part of the stories of the Earth People. When this happens, Mother Earth picks a female counterpart to the shomot. She is called the shorec. A female is chosen, because the females are the ones who bring the future to the clan by bearing the children."

"About how often does a shorec appear?"

"The last one in the stories of the Ancients was Kectu, about twenty-five thousand years ago. There are a lot of people who think we are approaching a time when another shorec will be needed. There are people watching all the Ancient clans closely for signs of a new shorec in one of them. I do not know what they will do if they find one. In some ways, I would like to see that, but mostly I am pretty skeptical."

"The things I have read say Sotif started the breeding program. He was not a shorec."

"He was at the end of the Alliance. His title was "History Man of the Alliance." There have always been laws against crossbreeding between Sun People and Earth People. The history man was an exception to that rule. He was always a crossbreed, because he was the spiritual leader of the Alliance. I think with a history man, there was no need for a shorec."

"I think the whole breeding program ought to be ditched. It seems you have pretty much gotten everything out of that is worthwhile. You ought to stop trying to make yourselves more different from each other and celebrate the things that bring you together."

"Maybe so. I see your point, but that is a Sun People perspective."

One day around noon, several weeks after finding the winter cave, Sandi led the group over a ridge. Below them was a valley running east and west about a mile wide with a stream meandering down the center. Much of the valley was clearly being used for agriculture. There were several fences around areas of deep green. There appeared to be a small town about four miles east. A low bridge crossed the stream about a half mile southeast from where they were standing. A narrow dirt road running up the valley crossed the stream from the south side to the north side at the bridge. Occasional clumps of trees could be seen scattered along the stream. Sandi thought of her trip to the forest when Marc wanted to be sure they were on Earth. What a contrast this valley was! The air was hot, dry, and odorless. The sun beat down from a pale blue, cloudless sky. The only relief from the heat came from a mild breeze caressing her shirt, which was damp from sweat. But there was something about this valley, something more special to her than the Pacific Northwest.

Across the valley, a low mountain covered with low vegetation climbed for several hundred feet above the valley floor. It was considerably higher at the west end of the valley where the skyline dropped sharply going east and then more gradually from there until it dropped again at the east end. Using her imagination, Sandi could see the outline of a bison facing west. The top of the head at the far west end, the sharp rise to the powerful shoulders dropping to the sloping back going east down to the rump. There were a few trees in random locations. However, at a spot west of the steep drop-off from the shoulders about halfway up the hill, there appeared to be a clump of trees that stood out as a large green dot on the mountainside. Sandi immediately realized this was the valley she'd dreamed of. The Heart of the Bison was here!

As Sandi grasped the significance of what she was looking at, Jektu shouted, "This is the place of Jektu's memories! There is the Heart of the Bison." He was pointing at the dark spot Sandi was staring at.

Garret immediately called the HSS.

Chapter 5

The Heart of the Bison

One—June 2003

Garret put the communicator in his pocket. "Okay, the order is for us to go back to that stand of aspen we just passed and wait for the shuttle pickup. We will put a crew down at the location of the Heart of the Bison tomorrow morning."

"No. It is not that far. We can make it in a few hours. We should go now and confirm it," Sandi said.

"It is a risky crossing, and it will be late afternoon by the time we get there. We take a risk of attracting unwanted attention when we walk up the hill. It is exposed."

"No. We should go now!" Sandi said.

"I think that Garret is right on this one," Marc said. "It's an open walk up the side of the hill to the spot where you want to go. It's not worth the risk to gain just a couple of hours."

After about forty-five minutes in the trees, Marc noticed small herd of goats with a goatherd driving them toward the valley. He was passing about a quarter mile from the trees. "Shouldn't the HSS have warned us about that?" Marc asked as he pointed to the herd.

"We can stay hidden here. I do not think he will see us," Garret said.

"Yeah, but the HSS should have let us know he was in the area," Sandi said.

"Let me make a call," Garret said as he pulled his communicator from his pocket. "Field crew calling HOB. Come in, HOB." Garret tapped his communicator on his pant leg. "HOB, come in." Garret looked around at the members of the crew. He tried several more times but got no answer.

"What is it?" Marc asked.

"Something has happened. I am not getting any answer."

"Solero?" Sandi asked.

"I do not know."

"We have got to go now! We have to get to the Heart of the Bison! Something awful is going to happen if we do not get there!" Sandi exclaimed.

"I'm with Sandi!" Marc agreed.

"Me, too," Garret said.

Everyone started walking to the hill, but soon they were all jogging. Once they reached the bottom of the hill, the pace slowed. It was still a long walk. They had to go east to the bridge before going back west to the dark spot. Sandi had a sense of how the valley should look and smell. There should have been a cool forest with the smell of trees and loamy earth. Instead, the air was hot, and the ground was cultivated with fields of beans. The shape of the hill was so familiar; there could be no doubt that this was the right place. As Sandi started up the hill, her adrenaline was pumping. After climbing to the place they had seen from across the valley, they walked over the top of an outcropping to a level space behind the clump of aspen trees. There were some small trees near the point where the outcropping joined a nearly vertical face. A lizard scooted over the rocky ground and into the bushes around the trees. Behind the foliage, Sandi could just make out the outline of what once was an opening into the mountain. The entrance was filled with rocks.

They cleared some of the brush away. "Look!" Marc shouted. "See the way these rocks fit together? This isn't natural." He began pulling more brush away.

"We should leave the brush in place for now," Garret said. "You can see there is an entrance to a cave here. According to our traditions, this could be the Heart of the Bison. We should not expose this for others to see."

"Well, you're right about that," Marc said. "So, what are we going to do now?"

"I have called the HSS a couple of times. Something is still wrong with our communication. Hopefully, the shuttle pod will be down looking for us after dark."

As they talked about what to do, Sandi was attracted to a flat rock at the end of the outcropping. She sat on the rock and looked out over the valley. As she looked at the valley, she felt this was Kectu's home and the center of the Alliance. Suddenly, she saw some off-road vehicles coming over the hill near where they had entered the valley. "Someone is coming!" she shouted.

Garret ran to her. "Where?"

Sandi pointed to the vehicles and the dust they created.

"Everyone behind the trees," Garret ordered.

"Probably someone just driving up the valley, but we'd better alert the HSS so they can position for a quick pickup," Marc said.

Garret made another call on his communicator. He got no answer.

"What is it?" Garret asked Jektu.

Jektu said something, but there were several words Sandi could not understand. The blood seemed to drain from Garret's face. "There are three jeeps and a Humvee. They are not just innocent farmers. Everyone stay down! Hopefully there is just a communication problem, and the HSS is monitoring this."

After they crossed the bridge, the vehicles turned directly toward the outcropping where the crew was hiding. The images of the original crew bleeding at the time of the first terrorist attack crept into Sandi's mind. She began to shake as the vehicles quickly closed the gap.

"We have been spotted! Emergency pickup! Now! Now! Now!" Garret screamed into the communicator.

The vehicles reached the bottom of the hill and began picking their way up. Several men jumped out and began running in front of them.

"Where are you? Respond!" Garret shouted into his communicator.

Sandi looked up in the sky, but there was no sign of help. In just minutes, they were surrounded by twelve men carrying guns. They wore black jumpsuits with ninja masks.

"On your faces, on the ground!" the leader shouted in a muffled voice.

As soon as they were down, the invaders quickly bound their hands behind their backs with flexible plastic handcuffs and took their backpacks and other gear, which they put in one of the jeeps. One of the men ran a long rope through the crew's arms and attached both ends to the bumper of the Humvee.

"Do not move," the leader said. This time, his words were clear.

"Sluma! What are you doing here?" Garret shouted.

"I knew it would be hard to fool you," the leader said. "Okay, everyone stand up."

"What are you doing?" Garret asked as he stood up.

"You did not think Solero was going to let you ruin his plans, did you?" Sluma said as he pulled his mask off. The other men also took their masks off.

"You cannot get away with this," Garret said. "I have already reported the find, and I have made the emergency call."

"Your messages have all been intercepted. What do you think brought us here? The HSS had some unexpected malfunctions with its gyroscopes and communication devices. It had to make an emergency return to Banks. Of course, Marvin is going to really catch it, but there was a false reading on the gyro. It was all just a terrible mistake. An EMF will be dispatched, but unfortunately, it will not find anything. And then everyone will be saddened and disappointed that you disappeared ... probably victims of some terrorist group. The message about the Heart of the Bison never made it through. Terrible situation."

"So, what are you going to do with us now?" Garret asked.

"What the hell is going on here?" Marc demanded.

"It seems you got caught in a power play on the wrong side," Sluma said.

"Undo my hands," Garret demanded. "Earth People do not kill Earth People. You are going to have to let us go sometime. It might as well be now. Maybe I can help you out of some of the trouble you are in."

"We have our friends, Garret," Sluma said, nodding in the direction he had come from. "We have been monitoring you ever since you started this search. Our friends have the coordinates, and they will be here tomorrow. Then we will see what they want to do. Sun People terrorists, you know. You can never tell what they might do."

"What Sun People are you talking about?" Marc asked.

"We have our connections. I am sure you know plenty about that."

Sandi felt a cold chill at the tone of Sluma's voice.

"This is all wrong," Garret said. "Let us go."

"That cannot be done. We have to do a thorough search. My men will need to go through all your pockets. I hope you will cooperate."

As the men approached Jektu, he kicked one to the ground. It took six men to wrestle him down. They cut his clothes off, because they were not able to keep him still to get into his pockets.

Sluma went through the pockets of Jektu's ripped clothing. "This is much better," he said. "I hope the rest of you will be more cooperative … maybe not you," he said to Sandi.

In just a few minutes, all the prisoners were searched, and all of their possessions were collected. One of the men gave Jektu some pants. He could not put a shirt on without removing his handcuffs.

"Okay, Garret, I do not know how this will all work out," Sluma said. "We are kind of working on contingencies here. No one wants to kill anyone. But you have to be kept out of things until Solero gets control. Once that is done, we will make a concession."

"If Solero gets control, he will put us in a war," Garret said.

"There will be a war, but it will be a Sun People war. When all the Sun People that want war are through killing one another, those that are left might be peaceful. Then everybody will be happy. Then even you might agree."

"In the interest of the day when I might agree, how about cutting these handcuffs off?" Garret said.

"Nice try, but you know that is not going to happen."

Sluma and his men examined the bushes in front of the blocked entrance. They were as interested as Garret's men had been.

"You know what that is?" Garret asked in a tone that implied that he knew what the answer would be.

"You are going to tell me that it is the Heart of the Bison," Sluma answered.

"Right. It will prove that Sotif did not just make up the *Wisdom Skins*. You know that means the Points of the *Wisdom Skins* are also true."

"So what? Ancient rules and laws are no good in the world the Sun People have created."

"That is rich. How does Solero propose changing to new laws without a shorec?"

"No one is going to wait around for a witch from the Ancients to tell the Earth People what to do. That is all part of the Sotif mythology. We are well beyond that as a race. Now shut up."

At dusk, Sluma and his men spread out around the vehicles to eat their dinners alone. While they were eating, Sandi noticed some bats coming from the hill above and behind the cave entrance. "Look," she whispered to Marc.

"There must be an entrance to the cave up there," Marc whispered back. "What do your legends say about other entrances to the Heart of the Bison?" Marc asked Garret.

"The legends talk of openings above that released the smoke from the Spirit Fire."

"How can that help us now?" Sandi asked.

"Maybe it is no help at all, but on the other hand, if we could get free during the night, we might be able to disappear before Sluma's friends arrive," Garret said.

"How could we get up that steep climb in the dark?" Sandi asked.

"It will be a full moon tonight, and I think I can see a way around. We will take the rope if we manage to get free. The big problem will be getting up the face without knocking any rocks down. Fortunately, they do not have any of the Ancients with them, and we do. There is no way we could sneak away from an Ancient. Jektu will be able to tell if any of them are stirring, plus he will study the slope and find the best path up."

After eating, Sluma's men returned and set up a small camp.

Garret spent much of the evening talking to Sluma, trying to convince him that the discovery of the Heart of the Bison changed everything. Sluma seemed to waffle at times, but in the end, he would not relent.

Sandi noticed that Jektu spent the evening studying the hillside. When it finally got dark, she could not sleep. Garret was next to her. "You awake?" he whispered after the camp had quieted down for the night.

"No, of course not," she whispered back. The moon was just coming up.

"Sluma will probably break camp early to meet his terrorist friends on the way. He is not going to want them to get close to the Heart of the Bison if he can help it. I do not think that things will be good for us if he turns us over to terrorists."

"What are we going to do?" Sandi asked.

"Jektu has bitten through Marc's plastic cuffs. Marc is disconnecting the rope right now. As soon as he is done, we will all leave together. If we are very quiet, we can get out of the camp unnoticed. If we can get in where the bats came out, there might be a chance. I am sure there must be a hole up there that drops into the Heart of the Bison. If this rope is long enough, we might be able to get in and back out. If Sluma's men do not see the opening or where we tie the rope, we can escape after they leave."

"You said he would not use the guns. So, we should just get the guns and take them prisoners."

"They would resist, and there are too many of them for us to physically take them."

"We would have the guns."

"They know we would not use them."

"Marc and Akhtar would."

"I cannot agree to that. Besides, we still have the problem of the terrorists that are coming."

"Your plan is not all that good, you know," Sandi said.

"Sluma will not kill us, but his friends most likely will. I am not trying to scare you, but we have to get away."

Just then, Marc came with both ends of the rope. He had a large knife. He cut Garret's cuffs and handed him the knife. Garret helped Sandi get to her feet. Garret coiled the rope as he pulled it from everyone's hands. The prisoners silently left in a group. When they were about fifty feet from the camp, Garret cut all the plastic cuffs off. "Where is Marc?" he whispered. No one answered. "We need to get away. It will be light soon. Jektu has found a path up, but we will have to be very careful not to knock any rocks down or make any noise."

Sandi followed Jektu. The moon was so bright it created shadows. Jektu went slowly as he zigzagged across the almost vertical slope. As he went, he silently cleared the path of all loose rocks and debris. It was fascinating to watch him as he worked. There were soft sounds as the crew members occasionally slipped on the soft, gravelly path, but the sounds did not carry back to the camp. Sandi could see Marc was coming up behind the main group.

The moon had reached the high point in the sky by the time they crept over the crest of the cliff. The ground still sloped steeply toward the top of the mountain, but the going was easier. Sandi could see the silent camp below in the moonlight. The group waited at the top until Marc caught up.

It had taken them several hours to quietly sneak up the cliff. Sluma and his men would be able to climb it much faster in daylight without worrying about noise.

"I got a flashlight and a rifle," Marc said. "Where is the entrance to the Heart of the Bison?"

"I do not know, but it should be close," Garret said.

Once they were out of sight of the camp, they were able to use the flashlight. It only took Jektu a few minutes to find the opening. He had sensed the hole from the smell of air coming out. It was near the bottom of a seven or eight-foot vertical rock face. It was concealed by several bushes.

Marc shined the light down the opening. "It looks like it only goes down about fifteen feet. We'll be like fish in a barrel down there," he whispered.

"It must turn or something. No bats would live there if it was just a hole. I will go down and check it out," Garret said.

"Okay, but hurry," Marc said.

Garret took the flashlight and started down the hole. He disappeared to one side when he got to the bottom. The light in the bottom of the hole got dimmer, and then it began to get brighter. In just a few minutes, Garret's head came back in the hole. "This tunnel goes about ten feet on a downward slope. Then it drops into a large cavern. Tie your end of the rope off, and I will see if it is long enough to reach the bottom of the cavern. Sandi, you follow me and hold the light as I go down."

The tunnel was roomier than it looked. At the edge, Garret dropped the rope. Sandi could see the end dangling in the air, but she could not tell how far it was from the end of the rope to the floor of the cave. "Now what?" she asked.

"I am going to climb down."

"The rope does not reach the bottom."

"I know, but I cannot tell how close it is unless I go down."

Garret maneuvered to get his feet over the edge. "Sandi."

"What?"

"This is the Heart of the Bison. Do you realize I am the first of my people to go in for almost five thousand years? I am the first in, and you will be the second."

"We will be a team like Ronaldo said ... a team of Earth People and Sun People. It is kind of like starting a new Alliance," Sandi said.

Garret put his hand on her shoulder. "You are right. I like that. It carries weight." Garret started down, and Sandi shined the light on the floor as he let the rope slide around his feet.

"It is only about three feet from the floor," Garret said. Then he dropped to the floor. "Tell the others to come ahead and then you come down next. I will help you at the bottom."

Sandi crawled back and whispered out of the tunnel. "Garret is in."

"Sandi, you go next," Marc said. "Akhtar will follow to hold the light for you."

"Why me?"

"We don't have time to argue," Marc said.

"When will you come?" she asked.

"The camp is awake," Marc said. "The sun is coming up, and they are all scurrying around looking for our trail. It won't be long before they figure out that we climbed up. I got the gun, so I'll come last. Now go!"

Marc was right about one thing—there was no time to argue. Sandi slid down and easily negotiated the turn. She held the rope tightly as she inched down the steeply sloping tunnel. After what seemed like a long time, her feet dangled in midair.

"Loop the rope around your feet and begin to lower yourself," Akhtar said. He was holding the flashlight, which gave an eerie light to the large cavern where Sandi hung in the air. She could feel her heart beating against her ribs.

"Keep coming," Garret encouraged. "I will get you at the bottom."

Finally, she felt his arms around her as he lowered her to solid ground. This was an alliance she could support, but too soon, he let her go. Carol came next, followed by Bandar, and then Akhtar, who brought the light down.

"Where are Jektu and Marc?" Garret asked.

"They are having some sort of broken-up argument," Akhtar said. "I gather from Jektu's signs that he wants to be last in case he gets stuck, but Marc wants to be last, because he has the gun."

Just then, they heard the muffled sound of Sluma shouting. Garret shined the light up to the ceiling. Two feet came through the hole in the ceiling—and then two legs. It was Jektu.

"Garret, you come out of there! This is the only way out. If you do not come out, we will just have to come down and get you!" Sluma shouted.

"Is everyone okay?" Marc shouted from the hole in the ceiling.

"Yes," Garret answered. You had better get down here!"

Marc fired a shot back to the entrance. Sandi screamed. Marc shouted, "Come ahead! I'm Sun People, and I guarantee that I *will* shoot anyone who comes down that hole."

"Garret, you know the memories and the traditions," Sluma's voice came down. "The Heart of the Bison has a chimney. This must be it. The only other way out is blocked. You will never get it unblocked before you starve. Even if you do the famine ceremony, you will not make it. Send the gun up and come out. We will protect you until Solero takes over."

"No deal, Sluma!" Garret shouted.

Marc had started down the rope, and he was almost at the bottom of the rope when he suddenly dropped to the floor of the cavern, and the rope followed him down. "Are you all right?" Sandi asked.

"I'm fine, but it doesn't look like we're going back the way we came."

Garret turned the flashlight off. A faint light came from the hole in the ceiling. The cavern was bathed in a soft glow that allowed Sandi to vaguely see the shadowy figures of the others, but not enough to see how big the cavern was.

"Turn the light on," Marc said. "Let's see what we have."

"I do not want to run the batteries down until we have a plan," Garret answered.

"Well, how can we make a plan if we can't even see where we are?" Marc said.

"I suppose a quick look around will not hurt," Garret answered. "But let us talk first. I did some looking while people were coming down. This cavern is about a hundred fifty feet by seventy feet. There are two major tunnels leaving it, I mean, two tunnels that are not blocked. From our traditions, one of the tunnels leads to an underground river, which appears out of the rocks and disappears back into them. The other tunnel goes to a lot of small dead-end tunnels and caverns but nowhere else. There are two tunnels that are blocked off. One goes to the History Room, which is a dead end. The other one goes to the outside, but it is long, narrow, and full of rocks. At least that is the way it was five thousand years ago. There is no other way out."

Suddenly, everything went totally dark. "Sluma blocked the chimney hole," Marc said.

"Okay. I am going to shine the light slowly around the cavern. If anyone has any ideas, speak up," Garret said.

Even with the light on, Sandi could not tell much about the space they were in, but there were plenty of signs people had lived in the cave long ago.

"See that?" Garret said. "See the loose stones? That is a tunnel that the people blocked. There should be another one." Garret continued moving the light. "There it is!" he said as the light rested on another tunnel blocked with loose stones. "One of those tunnels goes out of the cave, and one goes to the History Room." Garret's voice was shaking. Sandi couldn't tell if it was from excitement about being in the Heart of the Bison or fear about never getting out.

"Well, let's pick a tunnel and start digging out," Marc said.

"According to the stories, it would take months. The batteries will die in a few hours. We do not have food," Garret said.

"sometime this people must do a famine ceremony," Jektu said.

"What is a famine ceremony?" Sandi asked.

"A last act of desperation," Garret said. "We will find a way out."

"The famine ceremony is where you eat people," Sandi said. She hoped she was wrong even as she said it.

"In ancient times, it was sometimes necessary in order to avoid starvation. The famine ceremony is no longer necessary. At some point, Ronaldo is going to figure this out," Garret said. "Look. There is one of the open tunnels."

"Well, which tunnel is the river going down?" Marc asked.

"I do not know," Garret said.

"Okay. Let's start down that one. I'm much more concerned about being stuck in the dark than starving. The faster we find a way out of here, the better," Marc said.

"I told you, there is no way out. One tunnel is a dead end, and the other is blocked."

"You have a lot of faith that Ronaldo will find us, but it appears that he lost us. I don't much care for staying here on that bet. You said that there was a river in one of the tunnels. That means a way for the water to get in and out."

"None of us is a fish," Sandi said.

"Well, maybe the river has dried up in the last five thousand years," Marc responded. "Besides, there has been a long drought in Pakistan. It's likely that the water level in the river will be low."

"Marc is right," Garret said. He started walking at a rapid rate to one of the openings.

Jektu said something to Garret about Marc leaving something behind. "Marc, Jektu has a problem with us carrying a gun. He has a point, because we should not need it once we start down the tunnels. He is sure it will lead to bad luck for the whole group. Earth People do not use guns."

"I think we should keep it in case some of Sluma's friends follow us. They will have to keep their distance if we have a gun. It would be our only way to protect ourselves."

"Maybe so," Garret agreed. "But only if terrorists come down. I can assure you Sluma will not show any Sun People where the Heart of the Bison is. He will not come down himself. Earth People do not use weapons."

"Well, I'm not Earth People, and I'm afraid that I will have to insist. We don't know what we may find in these caves."

Jektu sat down and said, "Jektu go with a ... ... not!" He was emphatic, and he sat down. All the other Earth People in the group sat down with him.

"It seems we are not leaving this spot unless you leave the gun behind," Garret said.

Marc reluctantly put the rifle in a small alcove.

"Which tunnel has water in it?" Garret asked Jektu.

"Jektu smells water there," Jektu answered, pointing to the tunnel on the right.

Not far up that tunnel, they found a stream of water trickling in the bottom of a deep channel.

"The traditions say there was a river here, but I do not think this is enough water to call it a river," Garret said.

"Look at the watermarks," Marc said. "That much water would've had a large exit. There's a good chance that we'll be able to follow this out."

"Marc is right. This is our way out," Garret said.

Garret started downstream with the flashlight at a rapid pace, but those behind could not see well enough to keep up, so he had to slow down. For the first hundred feet or so, the ceiling was low, and Sandi had to walk bent over. Then it got higher, but the light was getting noticeably dimmer. Finally, Garret stopped and turned the light out. "We will take a break and give the batteries a rest."

Sandi was happy for the chance to rest a little, even though it was pitch-black. In the dark, with only the sound of people breathing and the trickle of water running in the streambed, she thought about the Heart of the Bison. Through the paintings of the ceremony cavern, she had felt a connection to the people who had created them. The Heart of the Bison was so different. It was plain—no paintings—only an empty circle of rocks that had once been the hearth of the Spirit Fire. Here, she felt a different connectedness—decidedly stronger—a connection to some power or essence that she couldn't define. In the ceremony cavern, she was looking into history—here, she was home.

"Okay, we should get started again." It was Garret's voice. "From now on, when there is a straight stretch, I will turn the light off, and we will feel our way along in the dark. Everyone will have to tie the rope around his or her waist. That way, we will all stay together."

Much of the time, they traveled in the dark. Their progress was excruciatingly slow. Sandi began to feel panic growing in her mind. She could not keep track of time. Then the batteries gave out, and they were in total darkness.

One of the men had a watch with a florescent face. It was surprisingly visible in the darkness of the cave. Garret attached it to the back of his belt, so it became a beacon that others could follow as he stumbled and felt his way along the stream. The rope kept everyone together as they worked their way down the tunnel. Sometimes, one would fall, and then everyone would stop until he regained his feet. Trying to negotiate the trail in the dark helped Sandi keep her mind off questions that did not have comforting answers.

Sandi concentrated on the dim green light and listened intently to the men's conversations. Some were joking. There was comfort in that.

Sandi had no idea how long they had been stumbling through the dark, but she hoped it was still daylight outside so they could see light if they passed an opening. Suddenly, her thoughts were interrupted as she saw faint motions in the dark in front of her. Then she was sure that she could make out the bodies of the others.

"There is light coming in from somewhere," Garret said.

"Can you tell where?" Marc asked.

"It is directly in front."

Soon, Sandi could make out the sides of the cave. The pace began to pick up as the light made it possible to see the path ahead.

"This is it," Garret said. They were standing at the edge of a pool of water. It was about twenty feet wide and thirty-five feet long. The wall of the cave completely encircled the water, except for the tunnel they had come down. The surface of the water on the far wall, just right of center, glowed with a gray light. Over the water on the left side three thin slivers of light shown through cracks in the ceiling. There was no way out!

"This is the end of the cave," Garret said.

"Not exactly," Marc said. "That light at the other end must lead to daylight. Because of all the water that used to go through here, the opening out must be large."

"What are we going to do?" Garret asked. "Jektu cannot swim at all. I am only a novice. What about the rest of you?"

"I consider myself to be a better than average swimmer," Sandi said.

"I learned in the army," Akhtar said. "I haven't been in the water in years, but it's not a thing you forget."

"I swim a little," Carol said.

"I can swim a little on top of the water, but not underwater," Bandar said.

"Well, the only way out is through the water," Marc said.

"How far do you think?" Garret asked.

"Don't know," Marc answered. "It can't be too far, or we wouldn't see so much light. I'll find out."

"If you try to get out, how will we know if you make it?" Sandi asked.

"Well, to start with, I'll just explore a bit. I'll make several dives and see what it's like down there and how far I can get."

Marc dove in from an outcropping above the light. After a couple of minutes, his head popped out of the water.

"Not far down the tunnel, the light is bright, and it dances like sunlight is shining through ripples on the surface. This time, I'm going all of the way."

After ten minutes' rest, Marc stood up. "Okay, I'm ready. There isn't a strong current one way or the other, so if I make it out, I'll be able to make it back after a rest. Don't expect to see me for about a half hour."

Marc swam out and climbed on a rock ledge above the light. He took four deep breaths. "Do not get hyperventilated," Garret warned.

"Right," Marc said. "Here goes!"

Marc took one last breath and dove into the water. Sandi sat against the side of the cave. She was probably the best swimmer, except for Marc. If he did not come back, she would have to follow. Suddenly, the thought of losing Marc hit Sandi. She had not realized how important he was to her. It was more than depending on him to find a way out; he was a friend.

"How much time?" Sandi asked Garret.

"Eighteen minutes and thirty seconds," Garret answered.

Sandi wondered just how good Marc was. He was older than he had been in the military, and he might not be in good condition—maybe not as good as she.

"I am going to have to follow him," Sandi said.

"He said to wait thirty minutes. It is not twenty yet."

"I know, but he should have been back by now. I am just going to swim out to the rock so I will be ready to go."

"You should not be too impatient," Garret said. "Just give him some time."

Sandi waded into the water. It was colder than she had thought. "How much time now?"

"Nineteen minutes."

Sandi swam to the rock from which Marc had dived. The light was much brighter looking directly into the water than it had seemed looking at it from the shore. She could see a sandy bottom, and she could easily see the entrance the light came through.

"Twenty minutes," Garret shouted.

Sandi decided to wait thirty minutes as Marc had said. She pulled her knees up to her chest and wrapped her arms around her legs to preserve body heat.

As Sandi looked into the water, she could see the light begin to flicker. A couple of seconds later, she could see someone swim out of the tunnel, and then Marc's head broke the surface of the water. Everyone cheered and clapped as he gasped for air.

"What are you doing there?" Marc asked when he noticed Sandi on the rock.

"I was getting ready to go looking for you."

"Well, that's not going to be necessary. Let's get to shore."

Sandi dove in and swam to the side of the pond with him.

"It's not too far to swim underwater. On the other side, you come to the surface in another cave, but it's only about twenty feet to the outside of that cave. Outside, there's a large pond. There are man-made gates that let the water into irrigation ditches. There's a wide valley below like the valley in front of the Heart of the Bison. There are cultivated fields and some farmhouses in the distance. There's nothing near the cave, but someone operates the gates that direct the water. The sun is shining, but it's well past noon. There's a smaller cave near this one where we can build a fire and get some rest. We can worry about food tomorrow, after we have rested. We should try to get everyone out before dark."

"How are we going to get everyone out?" Garret asked. "I cannot swim well, and Jektu cannot swim at all."

"I know. Once you're in the tunnel, it's open. You don't need to swim. You can pull and kick yourself along the rocks. You just have to make sure … you can't panic when you start to run out of breath. Then, at the other end, I can pull you out."

"This is not going to work," Garret said. "Some of us are not used to being underwater. What if we panic down there?"

"What if I pull the rope through? I think it's long enough to reach. Then we can tie the rope to each person. I can pull them from the other side to make it faster."

"I can help pull them down to the tunnel and get them started in," Sandi said.

"You will have to bring the rope back each time. It will be dark before we get everyone out," Garret said.

"Well, I don't think we should try it in the dark. Maybe we can't get everyone out tonight, but if I can get Akhtar out before dark, maybe he can scavenge around and get some food. At least that way, we will have food in the morning when the rest get out. The sun is still up. If we hurry, we still might get everyone out tonight."

"Some of us may be able to get out just by pulling on the rope, hand over hand, if it is secured at the other side," Sandi suggested.

"Who thinks they can get through that way?" Garret asked.

After some discussion, they decided that Carol, Bandar, and Jektu would require help getting through. Marc would take the rope through. Akhtar would follow him when the rope was secure. Garret would go next, and then Carol. Sandi would help Carol tie the rope around her chest, and Marc would pull her through. Marc would bring the rope back to get Bandar, and then he would bring it back again for Jektu. Sandi would wait till last so she could help the others get started.

Sandi walked into the water with Marc and Akhtar. All three climbed on a ledge near the source of the light. Sandi and Marc dove in together. In the dim light, Sandi could see the gray sides of the cave that led to the outside. Marc signaled the direction he would take. Sandi found a ledge where she could hook her feet for leverage, and then they both swam back to the surface. After a quick review of their plans, Marc dove in with one end of the rope. The rope played out slowly. After a short time, it stopped, with several feet left. In a few minutes, there were two strong tugs on the rope. "Okay, Marc has the rope tied off and is ready. You wait here," she told Akhtar. "I'll go down and brace myself. When I get set, I will give the rope a tug. Then you dive in. I will hand you the rope and help you get started."

Sandi dove into the water, picked the rope off the bottom, hooked her feet, and gave the rope one strong tug. She could see Akhtar dive in. It was just a couple of seconds, and he was with her. She handed him the rope and sent him on the short distance into the lighted tunnel. For the first time since the battery had died, Sandi felt hope. Her ears hurt from the pressure, but she was happy to be doing something to help. She waited to see Akhtar pulling himself along the rope and kicking his feet, and then she swam to the surface.

Garret swam out and climbed on the ledge with her. Sandi was shaking from the cold.

"Marc had some matches in a waterproof container. There should be plenty of wood for a fire in the other cave. Just hang on, and you will be warm soon," Garret said.

"Okay, I am ready," Sandi said. When she dove in, the water was cold but not so bad. After Garret had gone down the tunnel, Sandi picked up the end of the rope and took it back to the ledge with her. Carol swam clumsily out to the ledge and climbed on with Sandi. She tied the rope under her arms. This would be a tricky move. "When I tug on the rope from down there, you jump in. I will pull you down, so do not panic. I will help you into the tunnel, and Marc will start pulling you through as soon as I pull twice to give him the signal. It will take a few seconds to get the slack out of the rope. I will be with you until Marc starts to pull you out."

"Okay. I am ready," Carol said. Sandi dove in the water and gave the signal. Once Carol was down, it took Sandi precious seconds to get the rope taunt enough to send the signal to Marc. She held Carol and watched the rope slide into the exit. Finally, Carol was pulled behind the rope. Sandi gasped for air as she broke the surface of the water. There was nothing to do now except wait for Marc to bring the end of the rope back. She swam back to the bank to wait. She was shivering as she got out of the water. Jektu and Bandar snuggled up to her as they waited. "Are you afraid of the water?" she asked Jektu.

"Jektu is more afraid of dying in this cave."

"You are used to caves," Sandi observed as much as asked.

"Jektu is used to caves with light. Jektu is used to caves with food. Jektu is not used to dark caves with no food."

Sandi was proud of how well she understood Jektu's ancient language.

After about fifteen minutes, Marc's head popped up. When he got to shore, he joined Sandi and the others in a communal hug. His body felt cold to Sandi, but in a few minutes, he began to warm up, and his breathing slowed.

"Well, the sun is reaching the horizon, but it'll still be light for a while after it goes down. I've got the system down pretty good now."

"That will be good, because I do not think I can make it through the night in this cold," Sandi said.

Bandar was next. Marc seemed to be pushing himself as the light got dimmer.

The light was noticeably dimmer when Marc came back for Jektu.

"Maybe I should just follow you out when you take Jektu."

"Well, I've seen the work you're doing," Marc said. "It would be safer for you to wait until I bring the rope back. It's just one more trip for me. Akhtar built a fire in the cave I found. He also killed a goat and is cooking it. I've had some food, and I'm feeling pretty good. Be patient, and the next thing you know, you'll be sitting beside the fire, eating a warm meal."

"I think I can make it out alone," Sandi said.

"Maybe, but I know the way really well now. I can pull you out pretty quickly. It would be very risky for you to try it alone. Besides, the little bit of food I've had has given me more strength."

They both had to help Jektu get to the rock ledge. Sandi and Jektu sat in each other's arms as Marc swam back into the light. After Sandi dove in and got things set, Jektu jumped in. She had to admire him for his bravery. He had no experience underwater, but he showed no sign of panic. Sandi watched as he disappeared down the tunnel of light. It was nearly dark. After she climbed on the rock and caught her breath, she dove back in and started into the tunnel. She had not gone far when the hamstring on her left leg cramped. At first, she started to panic but quickly realized that she would drown if she did not remain calm. Using her arms, she pushed herself back out of the tunnel and swam for the surface.

Her lungs were bursting when she finally made it. She filled her lungs as full of air as she could, as much for the buoyancy as for the oxygen. Using her arms, she started toward the shore. Her left leg screamed in pain as the muscle pulled tighter. It was not far, but the distance seemed insurmountable. Each time she tried to use her right leg, it also started to cramp up. Finally, she got to the side. She found a rock to push her leg against to stretch the muscle out. It was a relief when the muscle finally released, but it kept twitching. Any move sent it back into a tight spasm. She was cold and hungry, but when she tried to curl up to preserve the heat in her body, her leg started to cramp again. There was still a faint light in the water, but she was sure she would not be able to get through the tunnel in her current condition.

Soon, she could see it was nearly dark. Something must have happened to Marc! The light was almost gone!

Suddenly, a head popped up in the water. Sandi was so relieved that she started to cry.

"Oh, my God!" It was Garret's voice.

"W-w-w-where is M-M-M ... "

"Marc had a problem with Jektu." Garret put his arms around Sandi. He was wet, but his body felt warm. The heat from his body seemed to flow into Sandi. Garret pulled her to a corner. He put his arms around her and rubbed her back and arms, creating more heat with the friction.

"W-w-w-what ab-b-b-bout M-M-Marc?"

"Jektu panicked in the tunnel. Marc had to go down and get him out. It was a fight. Marc inhaled water as he got Jektu out of the tunnel. Akhtar and I had to jump in the water to pull them out. They both needed mouth-to-mouth to revive them. They are okay, but Marc could not make a trip back. The rope was frayed, and, in the panic, Jektu broke it. We got half of it, but in the bad light, I could not find the rest of it. I decided that I had better try to get back, anyway. And it looks like it was a good thing that I did."

"W-W-What are w-w-we going t-to d-do?"

"We cannot try to get out now. It is dark, and you are all done in, and we do not even have the rope. We will have to spend the night and try in the morning." Garret untied a makeshift bag made of torn clothing. "We got a goat, and we had a small fire. We cooked some of the goat. I brought you some. Sorry, but it is wet." He sat down, pulling Sandi into his arms.

The inside of the meat was still hot. Sandi slowly started to eat, savoring every bite. Garret also brought some tomatoes.

"I almost did not bring food. I thought we would get out tonight, but Jektu insisted. I guess he realized that you would be very tired. He thought I would also need some time before starting back. It is a good thing I listened to him. You are freezing."

"I am so cold. I think I will never be warm again," Sandi said, but she was already feeling a little warmer.

"Stop thinking about the cold."

"I cannot think of anything else."

"Tell me what it was like growing up with a father and mother," Garret said.

"I do not know how to explain it to someone who never had parents."

"I would think you must have had a close relationship with your mother."

Sandi had never really thought about her mother in the sense of a relationship. "Do not get me wrong," Sandi began. "I love my mom, and there were some great times when she taught me about being a woman and shared thoughts about girlfriends, and boyfriends, but she is not the kind of person who really gets in there for you when you need it. My strongest relationship has always been with my dad. He was always there, giving advice, helping with homework, challenging the schools and my teachers." Sandi took a bite of the meat and followed it with some tomato. "My dad and I used to go on father-daughter dates at least once a month. Sometimes, it was to a movie, and I liked that, but sometimes, we just went out to eat. That was great. He would ask about what I was doing at school or with my friends. It was fun just talking, even if we were just eating a hamburger at McDonald's. You know what I mean."

"No, I guess I do not," Garret answered.

"Oh, sorry. You know, it all depends on who your parents are. Lots of my friends did not have it so well."

Garret gave a good-natured laugh. "We are going to have to get out of these wet clothes, or we will both freeze."

Sandi was too tired and weak to argue. Garret removed all her clothes except her underwear and laid them out on the rocks, and then he did the same with his clothes. They curled up together. Garret's skin felt hot and comforting to her. Talking about her family had taken her mind off the cold.

"You are a very hard man to understand. Did you know that, Garret?"

"How do you mean?"

"Well, it is like sometimes you really seem to care about me, and then other times, you are really distant."

"Does that matter to you?"

"I do not know. I mean, yes, I do know … or not. I mean, I keep getting these feelings about a closer relationship with you, and you seem to encourage it, and then … I mean, for no reason at all, you are suddenly distant. So, do you have feelings for me?"

"What you said about us starting a new Alliance … for me, I would like that."

"But?"

"But things are a bit complicated right now."

"How so?"

"For one thing, we are in a rather emotional situation. I do not think it is a good time to be thinking about relationships."

"And what else?"

"Would you just trust me? We can have this discussion after this whole Solero thing is over."

Sandi knew Garret well enough to know when she had hit a stone wall. She took her time finishing the food, wondering about Garret's complication. It was a strange menu, but it seemed perfect to her. By the time she had finished, she felt warmer.

As she ate, Garret described the valley and the cave where the rest of the team was camped. She drifted off in his arms.

Sandi lay on her back with her hands crossed above her navel and her eyes closed. The surface under her was soft and cool against her bare skin. She stretched her left arm on the ground beside her with the palm down. She could feel the soft grass folding gently under the weight of her hand. It seemed she could feel its greenness through her palm. The breeze gently brushed across her naked skin, carrying the smell of wild jasmine. Someone on her right side was softly breathing. She opened her eyes. A cotton-ball cloud floated quietly through the sky above. Garret was beside her, on his left side, his head resting in his left hand, supported by his elbow in the grass. He smiled. In the fingers of his right hand, he held several blades of grass. Slowly, he lowered his hand until the grass lightly touched her breast. He circled her nipple with the grass, sending chills throughout her body. He raised his hand and let the blades drop one at a time onto her stomach as he kissed her nipple. He leaned down and put his right palm on her right knee and gently massaged it. He raised his palm and lightly touched the inside of her leg with his fingertips, moving up her leg until he had his palm on her pubic bone, his fingers gently stroking her. She sighed, closed her eyes, and gave herself to him.

Two—July 2003

Sandi woke in the warm glow of her dream. When she opened her eyes, she was in Garret's arms. "What time is it?" she asked.

"Seven thirty," Garret answered. "Time to get up. How do you feel?"

Sandi was sore and stiff. She stood and stretched as Garret tried to get up. "Ouch!" Garret moaned. "Wow! I feel like someone slept on me," he said jokingly.

"Oh! I am sorry," Sandi said. "Here, let me rub your back."

Sandi rubbed Garret's back while he leaned his hands against the side of the cave wall. His muscles were tight and stiff. She could feel the knots as she rubbed.

"Do Watchers have families?" she asked.

"What?" Garret asked.

"In the caves, Earth People do not have families like in my world, but you have a lot of Watchers. I mean, if you live in our world, it seems that in order to blend in with us, you should have families like we do. You know, get married … have children … that sort of thing."

Garret was silent.

"Well?" Sandi persisted.

"Actually, there are some Watchers that have done that. There are advantages, but there are risks."

"What risks?"

As Sandi waited for Garret to answer, Marc's head popped up in the water. Garret and Sandi ran to the water's edge. Marc waded out. "Anybody ready for breakfast?" Marc asked. He had a very strange look on his face.

"Oh, my God!" Sandi exclaimed as she realized that she and Garret had not dressed. She had been intent on figuring out how to question Garret about family life. She ran to her clothes. They were still damp and cold, but she quickly wiggled into her pants and pulled her kurti over her head.

Garret was more composed. "There was no way we could have stayed here all night in those wet clothes without getting hypothermia," he said as he walked to get his clothes.

Marc took Sandi out first. Her lungs were bursting when her face broke through the surface of the water. It was only about three strokes to the edge of the pool they were in. Just as she and Marc reached the side of the pool, Garret's head popped up behind them.

Before she had time to think about how cold she was, Akhtar came from behind a rock and handed her a large dark blue wool cloth. She realized it was a burka. After Akhtar helped her put it over her head, she slipped out of her wet clothes underneath it. The sun was painfully bright outside the cave. Marc led her to a small cave around the side of the mountain. The rest of the crew was there.

"Akhtar and Bandar had a very busy night," Marc said. There were loaves of bread and other prepared foods, along with her burka and a few other items of Middle Eastern dress. The smell was indescribably welcome to Sandi. Garret took part of a loaf of bread and some of the cooked meat and left the cave. Sandi sat by the fire with Marc while she slowly ate the food he gave her.

"No one else is hungry?" Sandi asked Marc.

"We all stuffed ourselves with the food when Bandar brought it. At least, I think we did. Akhtar and I did. These are the weirdest people I have ever encountered. Fortunately, Bandar and Akhtar were able to beg, borrow, and steal enough to get us fed and replace some of our clothing."

This eating ritual is a complication, Sandi thought. "What are we going to do now?" Sandi asked.

"Well, I don't know what's going on, but I don't think Ronaldo has much control right now. The HSS that was supposed to be taking care of us messed up. I would sure like to know where it is now," Marc said.

Garret returned to the cave after a short time. "Okay, everyone is out safely. It looks like we are on our own now. We do not have any of our equipment, and they took my communicator. We have very little food and no transportation. The fact that the HSS did not intervene when Sluma captured us means that Solero has achieved some control. I doubt he has had time to oust Ronaldo, but I am confident our discovery has forced Solero to move ahead on his plans."

"What if they send someone in the Heart of the Bison to get us?" Marc asked.

"I do not think Solero will do that right now. He will not send Earth People in with guns. They would not use them, anyway, and Sluma knows Marc has a gun and will use it. That means he would have to send his terrorist friends in, but he will not send Sun People into the Heart of the Bison. Solero will take some time to orchestrate the discovery of the Heart of the Bison to his advantage.

"We know Solero has several assets in place. But he will have to create some pretext to wrest control from Ronaldo before he can implement his war plans. If he succeeds, we will not be able to stop the destruction that will follow."

"What exactly is his plan?" Marc asked.

"We only know the generalities that I have explained already. He will use his Watchers to arm and coordinate major terrorist organizations to use weapons of mass destruction to destroy Sun People culture and governments."

"How much destruction are we talking about?"

"The worst-case computer models predict complete financial collapse over the whole world, a death toll of over five billion, an energy collapse, civil unrest, and governmental collapse. The post-war situation is of a divided world of small clans led by warlords, anarchy outside the clans, and some areas of the world may be uninhabitable because of radiation. The world would be an agrarian economy ruled by barter. It would be a world where decent people would be ripe to accept any leadership that could bring organization and law to the chaos. And who do you think could do that?"

"Solero?" Marc said.

"Exactly," Garret responded.

"So, you are saying that Solero and his people could destroy the world?" Sandi asked.

"What I am saying is the world you live in holds an imbalance of hate and envy mixed with a technology for destruction that has never existed before. It is a powder keg just waiting to be set off."

"I do not think that is true," Sandi said. "Most of the people in the world love peace."

"And they are willing to fight and kill for it," Garret pointed out.

"Sure," Marc said. "Don't you think that peace and freedom are worth fighting for?"

Garret let out a sigh. "Yes, of course you are right. But that is the trap of war."

"What do you mean?" Sandi asked.

"War has been a major part of the history of the Sun People for thousands of years. What good does war do?"

"It could stop a man like Solero from getting power," Marc said. "You don't really believe that he can succeed, do you?"

"It is all computer modeling at this point," Garret answered. "The models are based upon assumptions, equations, and models of models. I personally think there are a lot of problems with the assumptions and equations. Suppose Solero is wrong and the plan only kills one billion instead of five billion. Would that make you feel better?"

"So, what are good people supposed to do?" Sandi asked.

"That is the trap. There is nothing you can do. You are in it."

"And your people are not?" Marc asked.

"We believe if we keep ourselves out of war, there will come a time when we can lead Sun People out of the trap. This is important, because Solero wants to put us in the trap. He wants to make a preemptive strike."

"And how would you stop him?" Marc asked.

"Our people are a republic. The battle now is for the hearts of the people. The strength of the position of peace rests with the ancient teachings. The Heart of the Bison supports those teachings. I am confident the actual proven existence of the Heart of the Bison will defeat Solero. That is why we must get to Ronaldo as soon as possible. A great deal of your world and all of mine hang in the balance."

"So, you are saying the fate of the world depends on us, and we are stuck in the middle of Pakistan," Sandi said. "A bit melodramatic, you know."

"I did not intend to overstress the point," Garret said.

"Well, what do you propose to do?" Marc asked.

"Our major ports of entry to my world are north of the Himalayas. I do not know of any way to cross them in time. Fortunately, we have one port of entry south of the Himalayas. It is near Saharanpur in India."

"How far is that?" Marc asked.

"I am not sure, but something like three or four hundred miles."

"Are you crazy?" Marc exclaimed. "You're not even going to be able to get across the border into India."

"On our way here, we passed about forty miles east of Islamabad. I can make contact with Watchers there who can help us."

"How far is that?" Sandi asked.

"I am guessing eighty to a hundred miles from here."

"Okay, that's more like it," Marc said. "Let's get started."

"I need some time to myself," Sandi said.

"Sure, but not too far," Marc said.

Sandi walked around the side of the hill and carefully climbed to where there was a clump of bushes she could hide behind. As she got to them, she saw Jektu hunkered over something, maybe his breakfast.

He'd listened in on the meeting just a few minutes before. He must have left just as Garret was finishing the explanation of his plan. The breeze was in her face. Jektu was so intent that he had not noticed her. She looked closer, and then she saw he was talking into a communicator! That was strange, because she was sure if Garret knew about it, he could try to put in another call to have them all picked up. Curious, Sandi carefully crept closer until she could hear Jektu's side of the conversation.

Sandi overheard Jektu saying, "Does not know Garret's plan." He paused, listening, and then said, "Jektu thinks Garret will go ——" Again, he paused. Sandi strained to hear as he continued, "Sluma left after Jektu —— Rajel —— night?" Jektu put the communicator inside his clothing. Sandi jumped up and ran back to the camp. She looked back and saw Jektu was running behind her.

Sandi got back to camp first. "Sluma is coming!" she breathlessly shouted as she ran in.

"Where?" Marc shouted back.

"Take it easy," Garret said. "What are you talking about?" he asked Sandi.

"Ask Jektu," she said. Jektu came into camp behind her.

"What is Sandi talking about?" Garret asked Jektu.

"Jektu believes there must be war. Earth People must save Earth People."

"You know that is the trap," Garret said accusingly.

Jektu said something about traditions and not letting Earth People die.

"What is he saying?" Marc demanded.

"It looks like Jektu is in Solero's group. Have you contacted Rajel?" Garret directed the question to Jektu.

"Jektu called Rajel last night. Jektu told Rajel the people are free. Jektu called Rajel this morning. Jektu told Rajel, Garret goes to Islamabad."

"Okay," Garret said to the group, "last night, Jektu told Solero's general, Rajel, we got out. I am sure they have contacted Sluma, and he is on his way. Jektu also told him we are going to Islamabad. If we get away from Sluma, I am pretty sure a welcome will be prepared for us there."

"What are we going to do?" Sandi asked.

"Jektu, give me the communicator," Garret demanded.

Jektu took the communicator from his clothing. Suddenly, he twisted it in his hands and threw it on the rocks.

"Where would he get a communicator?" Marc asked.

"They must have put it in the clothing they put on him after they searched him."

"Look!" Akhtar shouted.

Sandi could just barely make out three vehicles about a mile away.

"We have to get out of here!" Marc shouted.

"We will have to climb up there!" Garret shouted, pointing up a steep incline behind the cave. "We have to go where they cannot follow in their vehicles. We will have to outrun them on foot."

"Can't you fix the communicator?" Marc asked.

"They are built tough. You can throw them around and even take them up to fifty feet deep in water, but when they are broken, there is no fixing them."

Without another word, Sandi started up the hill. Akhtar followed. She heard Marc ask Garret what to do about Jektu. She did not hear the answer. She could see Garret and Marc talking to Jektu. At the top of the hill, they caught up. "What happened to Jektu?" she asked.

"Jektu is not evil. He just has a different point of view. He will not be coming with us," Garret said.

"Did you kill him?" Sandi asked Marc.

"We should have, but Garret wouldn't go for it. He ran downhill, and we ran up."

"We are going to be caught," Sandi said.

"I do not think so," Garret said.

"Why not?" Sandi asked.

"Sluma used terrorist contacts to help them travel in Pakistan, but they never intended to turn us over to them. Sluma was in on the plan for us to escape during the night. Jektu was going to help us find the smoke hole our legends talk about. The plan was for him to be the last one down, and then instead of going down, he was to pull the rope up. They were going to drop food and water to keep us alive until Solero got control, and then we would be rescued. Marc insisted Jektu go down the rope first. At first, Jektu refused, but when he could tell Sluma was coming, he knew there would be a confrontation, and Marc had a gun, so Jektu had to quickly come down the rope so Marc would follow. Sluma should have told us he would provide food, but he was upset when Marc started shooting. He planned to let us stew in the dark overnight and then start dropping food and water. They gave Jektu a communicator in case we could not find the smoke hole into the cave, and we decided to run away across country.

"Jektu turned us in last night so we could be prevented from getting word to Ronaldo. This morning, when he found out about our plans to make contact in Islamabad, he put in another call to Rajel to update him. The terrorists have joined Sluma. Jektu knows if we are caught now, the terrorists will kill us. He is not prepared to let that happen. As long as he knows we are no threat to Solero's plans, he will not lead the terrorists to us. Jektu will cover our tracks from the cave and lead them to believe we are still headed to Islamabad. They will be looking for us all along that path, so we have to go in a different direction."

"So, we are not going to Islamabad now?" Sandi said.

"No. Unfortunately, that plan has already been compromised."

"Then what are we going to do about Solero and the war?" Sandi asked.

"I wish I knew. We are getting out with our lives, but that is only because Jektu knows we cannot do anything to stop Solero's plans."

"We are stuck because you can't get over the Himalayas?" Akhtar asked.

"That is pretty much the gist of it," Garret said. It was strange to see Garret stuck.

"There's a pretty large town named Sialkot just a few miles down the highway we crossed on the way to the Heart of the Bison," Akhtar said. "I have some contacts there who can provide money. If I can find someone to fly us over the Himalayas, where do you need to go?"

"Do you know someone who could do that?" Garret asked incredulously.

"Just where do you need to go?" Akhtar asked again.

"We have to get to Lake Baikal in southern Russia. From there, we can get into the dy-emeralite underground. There is a small AGL substation in the Stanovoy Mountains about five hundred miles northeast of the entrance near the lake."

"How far from here to Lake Baikal?" Marc asked.

"About 2,400 miles, I think."

Sandi felt her heart sink. "We will never make it, will we?"

"Can't you just put out a call for an AGL when we get to Sialkot?" Marc asked.

"We did put out the call before Sluma captured us. Somehow, it was intercepted."

"I have a friend in Peshawar who used to smuggle American goods into the Soviet Union," Akhtar said. "Since the breakup of the Soviet Union, he has used his contacts to smuggle goods into Russia. One of his drop points is on the southern shore of Lake Baikal. He has an old Cessna that he used."

"A Cessna can't fly that far," Marc said.

"My friend has refitted the plane with extra tanks, and he has refueling stops set up in Kazakhstan. I think those stops are still active. I don't know if he can still pull it off, but as soon as we get to Sialkot, I can contact him. We just might be in luck. He has to fly around the west end of the Gory Kara-Aryktau mountain range to get around the Himalayas. I'm not saying he can do it now with the Americans controlling the airspace around Afghanistan, but he was able to get around the USSR radar and border controls."

"Well, it's the only thing we've got. Lead on," Marc said. Marc seemed very cool, very military.

Travel was more difficult than it had been on their way to the Heart of the Bison. They did not have the protection of the HSS. They could not follow the roads, because only Akhtar and Bandar could speak the language.

They reached the hills overlooking Sialkot late the next day. The food they had was gone. Sandi was famished, and her body was so tired and sore she could not walk another mile.

Akhtar went into the city alone, while the rest remained hidden in the foothills. Sandi closed her eyes, and everything went dark.

Someone was shaking Sandi's shoulders. "Okay, Sleeping Beauty, time to get going." It was Marc's voice. Sandi opened her eyes and quickly realized she was in the hills of Pakistan, but it took a few more seconds to remember the situation. The sky was gray, but she didn't know if it was late evening or early morning. As she started to get up, the soreness and fatigue in her muscles made her movements slow and stiff. She hoped it was not morning. "What time is it?"

"Well, it's time for us to find a real bed and get a good night's sleep," Marc said.

That sounded so much like what normal people did that Sandi had a hard time processing it.

"Akhtar is back, he has a vehicle, and he has made arrangements for a place to spend the night," Garret said.

"A vehicle?"

"Yes, it is about a hundred yards over there," Garret said.

Sandi looked in the direction he pointed, and she could see what looked like a station wagon. Her eyes burned, and she felt like crying, but she held the tears back. She nodded her head, and they all started for the car.

Sandi didn't pay much attention to the roads they traveled. Finally, they arrived at a small house in an area where the houses were close together. Inside, it was clean. A woman set food on the table. She did not say a word, and she disappeared after leaving the food on the table. Sandi ate the food in a dream. It tasted strange, but it was good. Akhtar showed her to a bathroom. She took a hot bath and then fell into a soft bed. The house had a strange smell to it, but Sandi liked it—and then she was asleep.

Three—August 2003

Sandi woke up. The room was full of sunlight. Her bladder was about to explode. She got out of bed, still hardly able to move. It had been a dreamless night. She thought of the pioneers who had crossed the great plains of America and had then struggled through the Rocky Mountains on foot. *Impossible*, she thought.

She put on a clean pair of white pants and a light brown kurti that she found at the foot of the bed. Then she stretched her tired muscles. She smelled something very good, and she realized she was famished.

The room was about ten feet by twelve feet with one window covered in plain white curtains. They were closed, but they let a lot of light in. She had been sleeping on a narrow bed. There was an old beat-up dresser with a mirror. She looked in it. She could hardly recognize the haggard-looking woman who stared back through red eyes. She looked around, hoping to see a comb. No luck. Then her bladder forced her to move.

Sandi quietly opened the door. There was a short hall that opened to what she thought was a kitchen. Garret and Marc were sitting at the table. Garret was the first to see her. He stood and said, "Good afternoon."

"Afternoon?"

"Yes. You will want that door," Garret said, pointing to a door across the hall from her.

Sandi opened the door. It was as if her bladder had eyes! As soon as she saw the toilet, she almost lost it before she could get in and close the door.

Afternoon! How long had they let her sleep? Too long and not long enough!

Sandi ran her fingers through her hair to shape it some. Then she walked to the kitchen.

"Hungry?" Marc asked.

"Yes. What time is it?"

Sandi sat at an empty place, and the woman from last night brought her some hot rice with meat and spices in it. Sandi had no idea what the woman had worn last night. Today, she had on a very ornately brocaded blue abaya with a matching hijab. The food smelled good. "Thank you. Thank you for everything," Sandi said.

Akhtar said something to the woman in Punjabi, and the woman answered in broken English, "You are welcome."

Sandi smiled. The woman smiled back and then left the room.

"About one thirty," he said in answer to her questioning look.

"One thirty! Why did you let me sleep so long? How can we save the world if we sleep all day?"

"What *we?*" Marc said. "Garret and I have been making plans while you got your beauty sleep."

"You will need all the sleep you can get," Garret added.

"So who is going to tell me what is going on?" Sandi asked.

"Well, Akhtar contacted his friend last night," Marc began as Sandi began to eat the food. It was delicious. "The guy called back this morning. It's all arranged. He'll pick us up near here at five thirty and fly us back to his base. Then tomorrow, we take off at 2:00 a.m."

"How far is it to the pickup?" Sandi asked.

"We are not sure," Garret answered. "Akhtar will take us to the pickup location in about an hour."

"Who is going?" Sandi asked Garret.

"You, Marc, and I will fly to the Russian entrance to my world. Once we get to Ronaldo, he will make arrangements to pick up the rest of the team. Akhtar has asked to be part of the team."

"Team for what? We have found the Heart of the Bison. That was the goal."

"There still is a lot to do," Garret said. "Once Ronaldo gets things straightened out with Solero, we will need to go back, open the History Room, and transfer part of the Spirit Fire to the Heart of the Bison."

"It all seems so simple," Sandi observed sarcastically as she continued to eat.

Akhtar took the passengers to a secluded field that was a two-hour drive from the house. The plane came in flying low about fifteen minutes later. Sandi and Garret sat in the two backseats, and Marc sat in the front, because he was an experienced pilot.

The plane was flown by an old gray-haired man. Before they got on the plane, Akhtar explained that the pilot who would fly them to Lake Baikal was much younger, but he was a good, experienced pilot who knew the route very well. The flight to Russia would take up to sixteen hours of flight time with one refueling stop along the way.

The flight to the base was less than two hours. There was a small farmhouse near the field where they landed. Sandi was not hungry, but in spite of all of the sleep she'd had, she was suddenly tired again. She dropped right off to sleep as soon as she got into the bed that was provided in the farmhouse.

Garret woke her at 1:45 a.m. She felt alert and refreshed. Garret gave her a skirt and blouse. "How about some slacks?" she asked. She hardly ever wore dresses in the field.

"I can get you some slacks, but here is the thing. We will be sitting in those seats right next to each other for two flights of about eight hours each. Mohamed has managed to get a hospital bedpan for you to use, just in case you need something in the middle of the flight. So, you can imagine sliding the bedpan under your dress, or you can wear slacks and …"

"I get the picture," Sandi said. "Who is Mohamed?"

"He is the pilot who will take us to Russia."

"Okay then. I can change my clothes without your help."

Garret grinned and left her to change. "Such modesty after what we have been through," he quipped as he closed the door.

Mohamed did not look older than twenty. They had something to eat, and then they went to the plane. Mohamed had a printed checklist of things to look at before taking off. He checked all of the fuel tanks with a dipstick. He checked all of the controls.

"This kid does not seem to know what he is doing," Sandi said as she watched him go over the list.

"He's a good pilot. I taught him everything I know," Akhtar's pilot friend said.

"Maybe, but I get a bit concerned about someone who still has to use a written checklist to prepare for takeoff," Sandi commented.

"I have flown that plane for twelve years. The checklist he's using is the one I use myself. When you know a lot is when you can become so familiar you forget something. A lot of pilots don't use a checklist. Some of them are dead over stupid mistakes. Time to get on board." The passenger side door was open.

Sandi crawled in and took her seat. Garret sat beside her. A nearly full moon shone as they took off down a dirt runway with no lights.

"We will be flying close to the ground all of the way," Garret said. "They used to fly over Afghanistan through lower mountains. They cannot do that now … not with the US military there. The ride through these mountains will be a lot more exciting, but the distance is shorter."

Garret was right. It was like no roller coaster that Sandi had ever ridden. The sun was rising as they reached the point where they were going to cross the Himalayas. The mountains on both sides were higher than the plane. Some of the passes they flew through appeared to be only about a hundred yards wide. Several times, she was on the verge of throwing up. The plane made turns that were so tight it seemed the plane would roll over. At times, the engine roared, and the plane climbed steeply. At other times, the engine went almost silent, and the plane fell. It twisted and turned and climbed and dove so much that Sandi could not stay oriented. When she looked out, the wings seemed to be flapping like a bird. She could not look at the mountains, because the plane passed so closely, she was sure they were going to crash. They flew from grassy foothills, up through deep forests, past the tree line to cross the snow-covered Himalayas, and then they flew back down through the same scenery on the other side. As they crossed over, she felt like they had flown over the top of the world. Then she thought about the HSS flight. Once they had crossed over the mountains, Mohamed flew the plane right against the foothills. He flew in and out of gullies and up and down ridges.

It was nine hours and forty minutes after takeoff when they set down in a field. Dust clouds billowed out behind the plane. "Where are we?" Sandi asked Garret.

"If everything went per plan, we are near a village named Kajna in Kazakhstan. We will get something to eat and rest here until dusk, and then we will be off again. Most of this leg will be smoother flying. Mohamed will follow a GPS, and we will be flying in the dark. The last couple of hours will be through mountains again. We will be landing of the south edge of Lake Baikal near a Russian town called Babushkin. By then, it will be daylight. Babushkin is about a hundred miles from my friend's home in Ulan Ude. He will make arrangements to pick us up. It will take three and a half hours to get us from Babushkin to the Lake Baikal entrance to our caves. We should be in by noon tomorrow."

The rest in Kajna was good. Mohamed took off in the dark with just a couple of lights at the end of the field they used as a runway. The seat was already uncomfortable before they got in the air. Somehow, Sandi fell asleep and did not wake up until the plane began weaving through the mountains again. The sun was up but very low in the sky. Many times, they passed into the shadows of the mountain as they flew along the foothills. Finally, they got a glimpse of the lake. It was a deep gray-blue color that reminded Sandi of Garret's eyes. Forested mountains were on three sides. To the north, the water went to the horizon. "Are we there?" Sandi asked.

"I think we still have a ways to go," Garret said.

"How big is this lake?" Sandi asked.

"You will probably be surprised to know that one-fifth of all of the fresh water on the surface of the earth is in this lake," Garret said.

"No!" Sandi exclaimed. "How come I have never heard of it before? What about the Great Lakes?"

"Lake Baikal is three hundred miles long and fifty miles wide. Pretty large, but small compared to the Great Lakes. However, Lake Baikal is six miles deep."

"Six miles!" Marc exclaimed. "That's over thirty thousand feet deep." He whistled.

"I think my legs are numb from the lack of blood. I hope we land soon," Sandi said.

When the plane finally landed, Sandi had a hard time standing. Garret spoke a little Russian. He made arrangements for a ride in a hay wagon to the highway. They waited two hours, and then a Russian van arrived. Garret spoke a few words in Russian with the driver. The driver drove them to a meeting spot an hour and forty-five minutes from the pickup site. Severo Kirsanov, Garret's contact, was waiting for them there.

After talking to Severo, Garret explained the situation. "Severo says there is a squad of guards from Rodlu City in the station. They say they are looking for some contraband they believe someone is trying to sneak in. They check every group of Gatherers and the packages they bring in. We will not be able to get in unnoticed. My guess is Solero has put out an alert. He undoubtedly knows Sluma has not found us. He is taking no chances."

"Will your friend help us, and do you trust him?" Sandi asked.

"I trust him. We will have to force our way past the guards. They have scheduled their time so there are always two watching. They relieve the guards every six hours. The next change is in two and a half hours. Severo has arranged to have a couple of his friends quietly take the two guards prisoner right after the guard is changed. That will give us six hours before the squad discovers what has happened.

"An hour and fifteen minutes after we get in, the tram to the Stanovoy substation will leave. When it gets there, the EMF usually takes off within an hour. It is an hour and a half from takeoff to landing. From landing at Banks Island to Rodlu City is two more hours. That puts the timing very tight."

"They would have to fly through Russian air space, wouldn't they?"

"That was the big HSS. The smaller EMFs fly lower and maneuver through blind spots."

"Why doesn't your friend just arrest the next set of guards and give us more time?" Marc asked.

"The guards make a coded call to headquarters at every guard change. We cannot count on more than the six hours. It is possible Solero will have agents waiting at the Rodlu City station when we come in."

"What can he do to us there?" Marc asked.

"I do not know. It depends on how many followers he has in Rodlu City. He will be stretched thin across Asia to try to stop us from getting in. He will have to move men to Rodlu City. That could take a couple of hours, assuming he has enough men. I just hope we can make it in before he finds out. I have some people I can contact when we get to Banks. They might be able to help us at the station, but it could get pretty complicated."

"What about the place where you took me out?" Marc asked. "That was close to the place where we met Ronaldo."

"We do not have an EMF station near there," Garret said. "But that gives me an idea. If we can convince the EMF pilot to fake an emergency landing near there, we would be on a direct emergency frequency. The emergency response is locked in. Solero cannot intercept communications on that system. Everything is automatic, and the communication lines are extensive. If we go there directly, it will eliminate the trip in from Banks, and that could save us an hour and a half and maybe more. We will just have to convince the pilot to help us. That could be tricky, but everything is a risk from here in."

Everything went as Garret planned. They completed the phony crash landing. In just a few minutes, a group of men came from the forest. Garret knew the leader.

"Garret?"

"Hello, Sid."

"The news reports said you and all of your party were captured by terrorists," Sid said in surprise.

"I suppose that was reported by people from Solero's group."

"He was the one who ordered the AGLs into the field to try to rescue you," Sid said. "They swarmed over the area, but they did not find a trace. How did you get here?"

"It is a long story. The EMF is not damaged. You can report the problem was minor, and the EMF is okay and on its way to Banks."

"What is going on?" Sid asked.

"Sid, we found the Heart of the Bison," Garret said.

"How? Are your sure?"

"We were inside. I saw the Spirit Fire hearth."

"What about the History Room?"

"There was a sealed tunnel just like the traditions say."

"How did you get away from the terrorists? How did you get here?"

As they walked through the forest, Garret explained everything that had happened. "We have to get to Rodlu City," he concluded.

"That will not be easy. Four of Solero's men showed up here two days ago. They say they are increasing security in all the outposts because your group was captured, and someone in your group may have given information to the captors about Earth People and our security. They are watching everything and searching through every package that comes in. We are on the highest alert."

"We will have to figure a way in."

"It is worse than that," Sid said. "Solero has really stirred things up. He claims your people may have compromised us to the Sun People. He says this proves how much at risk we are. He has increased security, and he has called for an emergency vote to approve his plan to create worldwide war among the Sun People. There is a rumor that terrorist groups have already placed weapons of mass destruction in twenty-seven major cities around the world."

"We know about his computer simulation, but there was no indication it was more than just a 'what if.' How could he have the plan so far advanced?" Garret asked.

"I do not know. Some say he has his own terrorist machine going, and there are a lot of people who are commending him for doing it now that the danger of exposure has been demonstrated."

"How much time?" Garret asked.

"It may already be too late. Ronaldo has called for a Council meeting to have a special vote this afternoon."

"How could something like that be organized so quickly?" Garret asked.

"Solero had great foresight. There are several Majority Party members who have been talking about supporting Solero. As I understand it, if Solero gets the approval, a major worldwide signal will be sent in a day or two. Everything is coordinated to happen four days after the signal."

"What is the signal?" Garret asked.

"I do not know, but it will be something spectacular ... a major story on CNN. There are many different terrorist groups involved all over the world watching CNN. When they act, it will be all at once."

"What if Solero does not get the vote?"

"If he gets the vote in the Council, he will have the support of the people. However, all he really has to do is send that signal, and then it is out of control. I do not know what the signal is or how many of our people would be involved in sending it. Once the signal is sent, the players are all Sun People. There is no abort signal."

"We have to stop Solero," Garret said. "Somehow, I have to get to Ronaldo without Solero knowing. With the information we have, Ronaldo will win the vote and dismantle the whole plan."

"Most of the people are against war," Sid said. "They support Solero because of the constant fear of depending completely on hiding, but if you have really found the Heart of the Bison, that would change everything."

"I made several calls, but all of my communications have been intercepted. I have to get inside and get to Rodlu City."

"There is a convoy of ten Gatherers going in today," Sid said. "I think, with some inside help, I can get two or three people in."

"How can you do that?"

"Solero's men check everything that comes out of the decontamination chamber. I can move large backpacks in there. They only watch that area when someone opens the outside door. I can put the three backpacks under the video camera, where they cannot be seen. You can hide in the large backpacks the Gatherers carry in. When the Gatherers get into decontamination, they can quickly exchange backpacks behind the camera. Then, after Solero's men have checked the Gatherers and have gone back to their office, we can let you out. Once you are past the checkpoint, it will be easy to get a tram to Rodlu City. The increased security is just at the entrance."

When they got to Rodlu City, Garret went ahead to talk to Ronaldo and set up a meeting. Sandi and Marc waited about four hours in the room they had stayed in on their first trip to Rodlu City. Finally, Sandi and Marc were ushered into the oval meeting room. The scene in the faux window was set to a forest on the Yukon River.

Ronaldo sat at one end of the long table. Seated on the sides of the table near Ronaldo were members of each of the different types of Earth People. A very handsome Watcher was seated at the other end of the table. A similar group of Earth People sat at the sides of the table near him. Between the two groups, there were four empty chairs on each side of the table. A Gatherer ushered Garret and his group to the empty chairs.

When they were seated, Ronaldo spoke. "We have invited you to meet with the Council about the Heart of the Bison and other related subjects." Sandi sensed something major was about to change in her life. "The Council is made up of two parties," Ronaldo continued. "Each party has an elected leader. He chooses a Watcher, a Gatherer, a Thinker, and one of the Ancients to serve with him. The two leaders are chosen by a vote of the people. The Majority Party makes all decisions relative to the laws and government of the Earth People. However, the Minority Party is given certain powers that allow it to have some influence, which guarantees everyone has representation in government.

"The Council has been under tremendous pressure from the Minority Party to take aggressive actions to protect the secrecy of our world. The purpose of this meeting is to determine if the Heart of the Bison has been found. I will be asking you some questions. Solero, the Minority Party leader, will also be allowed to ask follow-up questions." Ronaldo nodded to the end of the table. Sandi's head snapped to look at Solero. He nodded his head at her and smiled. Something about his smile relieved some of her tension.

"I am glad you were all able to get here," Ronaldo said. "Garret has told me a great deal about your recent adventures. Sandi, tell me about how you found the Heart of the Bison."

Somehow, that did not seem important right now. She wanted to know what the struggle with Solero meant for Earth People, Sun People, herself, and most importantly, what it all meant for her and Garret. "I do not know exactly what to say. I just had an idea about that first cave. Then I dreamed of a flood and a mammoth with one tusk. After we found the mammoth, I just knew where to go. I did not exactly remember anything. I was seeing the mountains for the first time, but as we went, I could tell where to go. It was not like seeing and following a trail. It was more like just knowing the directions ... general ... like knowing where to head on the horizon."

"So, you really had no actual knowledge you were on the path to the Heart of the Bison," Solero said. His voice was warm, and his tone seemed to express genuine interest in what her answer would be.

"That was true all along the path until we came over that last hill. Then it was all different."

"How?" Ronaldo asked.

"How? I am not sure," Sandi said. "It is like … I mean, I do not remember ever seeing anything like that before, but when I saw it, it was familiar, and I knew it was the right place."

"What about the inside?" Ronaldo asked.

Sandi began to cry. "I do not know what this is!" she exclaimed.

"You felt something," Ronaldo said.

Sandi sniffed and dabbed her eyes with a handkerchief that one of the men gave her. She put her elbows on the table and ran the fingers of her left hand through her hair. The emotion was a surprise to her. She had not felt it coming. "We had just been attacked. People were sliding down the rope. There was a gunshot. I should have been frightened, but instead, I felt secure and safe.

"When Garret shined the light around, nothing about the inside of the cave was familiar to me. It is not a pretty cave. It is nothing like the ceremony cavern. But in the plainness of it, I was home. That is all I can say. I was *home*."

"Apparently, you just had a very emotional scare," Solero said empathetically. "As I understand it, you had previously seen close friends and coworkers gunned down by terrorists. Then you were captured, and there was an indication you were going to be turned over to terrorists again. Then, in the night, you managed to escape into this cave where you must have felt you would be safe. Do you not think your feelings … the ones you just described … came as a consequence of the incredible emotional state you were in rather than anything specifically connected to the place itself?"

Sandi looked at his disarming posture. He was very good. She felt like she wanted to make him right. His argument was sensible. "I see your point, but it was more than a sense of security or the relief of having gotten away. I did not have a feeling of having escaped, because at a real level, we were still trapped. The feeling was more than just a feeling of safety or relief. It was a sense of being home." Sandi gave a little nervous laugh. "Come to think of it, by the time the feeling really hit me, we were lost in a dark tunnel."

"Why would you have a feeling like that?" Solero asked. "Even if the cave were the Heart of the Bison, what would that be to you?"

"I do not know," Sandi answered.

"Thank you. You have been very helpful," Ronaldo said. She had been cut off abruptly, but she was glad she did not have to answer any more questions from Solero.

"Jektu, tell us about your discovery," Ronaldo said.

Sandi had not noticed Jektu was there. He stood up from a chair against the wall. Without thinking, Sandi gasped audibly.

"We picked Sluma and Jektu up in Lahore, Pakistan, with one of our fastest AGLs after Garret explained what had happened," Ronaldo explained. "Jektu?" Ronaldo said.

"Jektu did not know how to find the Heart of the Bison," Jektu began. "Jektu followed the woman Sandi. Jektu saw the valley. Jektu saw the Heart of the Bison. Jektu knew this was the valley of Jektu's memories." Sandi understood all Jektu said. The language was simple and easy now that she had the hang of the syntax.

"Jektu went inside the cave. Jektu saw that this was the cave of Jektu's memories. Jektu saw the mighty hearth of the Spirit Fire. Jektu saw the tunnel to the History Room. The tunnel was full of rocks."

"Are you sure this cave is the Heart of the Bison?" Ronaldo asked.

"Yes, Jektu is sure."

Sandi was impressed with the honesty of Jektu's answers. It was clear that Solero wanted to discredit the idea that the Heart of the Bison had been discovered. Even though Jektu agreed with Solero, he completely confirmed they had found the Heart of the Bison. Sandi could see the Council members believed him.

"Did you understand what he said?" Ronaldo asked Sandi.

"Yes," Sandi answered.

"You have learned his language very quickly," Ronaldo said.

"I have worked hard," Sandi responded.

"Did you have any memories or dreams of the inside the Heart of the Bison?" Solero asked Sandi.

"In the dark, it was hard to see much except what was in the light beam, but nothing looked at all familiar to me."

"We are through with this issue," Ronaldo said. "Should the Council prepare a declaration the Heart of the Bison has been found?" Ronaldo posed the question to the Council.

Solero interrupted before the vote. "I cannot say Jektu is mistaken, but before a declaration of this magnitude is made, we must send a team in to examine and document the Heart of the Bison. The History Room must be opened, and the History Wall paintings must be examined and compared to the *History Skins*."

"Is this the will of the Council?" Ronaldo asked. Each member of the Council put a white cube on the table.

"So says Ronaldo, so it shall be."

All the Council repeated in unison, "So says Ronaldo, so it shall be."

The members of the Council stood together and put their right hands on their left shoulders. They all left except Ronaldo.

When they were gone, Ronaldo addressed Marc. "You used modern survey equipment to gather data in the ceremony cavern."

"Yes, we got what are called point clouds. A computer can use them to create a three-dimensional, digital duplicate of the surface of very complicated structures."

"We are familiar with survey techniques, but we do not have anyone who can use that kind of equipment. Would you do a scan of the Heart of the Bison for us?"

"The Heart of the Bison is much larger than the ceremony cavern, and besides, my equipment was lost when the terrorists attacked."

"Garret told us about your work in the ceremony cavern. We sent an EMF back to recover all of your equipment and data."

"You have all of my notes and data?" Marc asked.

"We have it all, and it is yours, but if you do the Heart of the Bison, that will be ours. You would have to leave that data behind when you leave."

"You mean you plan to let us go with all of our stuff?" Marc asked.

"Of course," Garret said.

"When?" Sandi asked.

"You are not prisoners," Ronaldo said. "But if Marc agrees to help us with the Heart of the Bison, we would like you to stay until that is done," Ronaldo said to Sandi.

"Well, I don't much like being used as a pawn by a strange race of people ... Neandertals, for God's sake," Marc said.

"What are you going to do when this is all over?" Garret asked Marc.

"What do you mean?" Marc asked.

"When the survey is done, and this threat from Solero is put to rest, you are going to have to leave. We will give you the ceremony cavern data, and I suppose when the politics of the region are right, you will go back to the cavern. But my question for you is, what are you going to say about the Heart of the Bison and the Earth People?"

"Well, what if we say that we're going to tell everything and that we'll bring our people to open the Heart of the Bison?" Marc asked.

"The only way we could fight something like that would be to so thoroughly discredit you that you would never be believed. We have Watchers who could help. It is against our law to keep you here against your will. I hope you understand we would have to attack your reputation."

"What about using your electromagnetic ray to confuse us?" Sandi asked.

"That works to mess up short-term memory. It is not effective on long-term memory. In this situation, it would probably do more harm than good. We have to depend on your word or our ability to discredit you. We hope you will not try to expose us. Once we control Solero and his people, there will be no threat to your world. The existence of the Heart of the Bison will forever confirm our laws against war."

"When do you plan to let us go?" Marc asked.

"Our law does not allow us to hold you. You can leave anytime. We will take you to a safe place in the Middle East any time you say."

"So you say, but what if I say, let us go right now?" Marc asked.

"You can go now, but I am asking you to scan the Heart of the Bison and help us defeat Solero."

"If I say no?" Marc asked.

"I would make arrangements to take you back to Pakistan immediately."

"What about my equipment and data on the ceremony cavern?"

"I would like to hold the data, but I will not be able to. But I could, by rights, demand a copy of the ceremony cavern data. That would take some time to decide. You do not have to wait for a decision. I could make the copy and you can go."

"We want to leave right now," Marc said.

"Speak for yourself," Sandi said.

"It will take about six hours to prepare …"

"What do you mean, 'Speak for yourself,' Sandi?" Marc interrupted.

"I want to hear what Ronaldo has to say before I make up my mind. So, what were you saying about six hours?" Sandi asked Garret.

"Six hours to get everything arranged for you to leave," Garret said. "I can send the order as soon as this meeting is over. Akhtar wanted to come back when we picked Jektu and Sluma up. He is in Rodlu City. You will all have to learn the cover story. We also have to prepare Kelvin for the trip. He is not as healed as we would like him to be, but with a little preparation, he will be ready to travel without serous risk to his recovery. You will be taken to your quarters until things are arranged. Once I start the cover story, we reach a point where you cannot turn back."

"I don't want you to copy the ceremony cavern data. It's my data," Marc said to Garret.

"We put up the money and opened the political doors. We feel we have purchased something by that," Ronaldo said.

"You got your Heart of the Bison. That should be enough."

"I do not think so," Garret said. "We can put it before the Council. But you would have to stay until it is resolved. Once you leave, there will be no coming back."

"So, it's leave now without my data, or wait an indefinite time to get it?"

"No, you can leave with your data, but we will make a copy for ourselves," Garret said.

"Okay. Make your copy and get us out of here."

"No!" Sandi said. "Go ahead and check out what you have to, but do not make any arrangements for us yet. Let us think about it."

"We cannot keep anyone against his or her will. Our cover story involves all four of you. It would take some time to revise the preparations that have been made. That means you have to leave together if you want to go now."

"You think about it," Ronaldo said. "We will leave you for a short while. Please make your decision quickly."

Four—August 2003

"What are you doing, Sandi?" Marc said after they were left in their room. "Let's get out of here while the gettin's good."

"Marc, I really want to see this Heart of the Bison. And I think we should help Garret. Besides, you were all for rushing back here when we were trapped."

"Well, yeah, I was for getting out of there and getting Garret back to fight his fight, but I'm not for getting involved personally in it. And besides, you've already seen their cave. We are even with Garret. He saved us, and we gave him the Heart of the Bison."

"You are right. Everything you say is right, but Solero is organizing to destroy the world. The Heart of the Bison will stop him."

"Are you really falling for that far-fetched destroy-the-world idea?"

"Have you ever heard a tune that reminds you of another tune from when you were young?"

"What are you getting at?"

"You hear a tune like another tune you heard when you were young, but you cannot quite remember it, and you know the tune meant something to you back then. If you could think of the tune, you would know what it meant, and you are just on the verge, but it will not come. You get this feeling, and it is some kind of heartache, but you could face it if you could just remember the tune."

Marc looked at Sandi in her eyes. "What?" Sandi said.

"You're still thinking about Garret, aren't you?"

"What are you talking about?"

"You want to help him because of your personal feelings for him."

"Maybe I do have some feelings for him. So what? I am not a schoolgirl. There is something to what Ronaldo said. And Marc, there is something almost palpable about the Heart of the Bison. Something I can almost … and I cannot walk away from it."

"You think that you're really a descendent of that legendary Small Beaver? Do you have any idea how crazy that all is?"

"The logical mind is a great thing, Marc. It is a good thing you have it. You can follow your logic … fine. But, for me, there is something above logic. I cannot walk away from that any more than you can walk away from logic."

"If they tell me that I can go and take my data, I'm outta here. I will not say anything about their secret world. That should be enough to satisfy them."

"I am staying," Sandi said.

"Well, I don't think that they're giving you a choice. If I go, you'll have to go, too."

"Maybe not … if I ask to stay forever. They could just say the terrorists killed me."

"You can't help them. Staying would mean never seeing your family again. Do you love Garret that much? Do you think he cares for you that much?"

"I am not thinking about Garret now. I am thinking of the Heart of the Bison. There is something there I need to know. Plus, I want to see Solero defeated."

"Maybe you don't want to think about you and Garret, but you'd better think about it."

Marc sat down at the table, and Sandi sat in silence—thinking about it. It was true she could not deny her feelings for Garret, but she knew that it was not why she wanted to stay. As outrageous as the war threat sounded, something rang true about the danger. If she left now, and Solero's plans were implemented to any degree, she would not be able to live with it. But that was not the reason, either. She could not explain the reason to herself. It was pointless to try to explain it to Marc. Then she thought about her parents and knew she could not let them think that she was dead. There was no solution.

Sandi and Marc waited in strained silence for about four hours for Garret to return.

When Garret finally returned, Akhtar was with him. "Hope you have not been bored while I was away," Garret said.

"What about my data?" Marc abruptly asked.

"It is the Council's opinion that the data are yours."

"What does that mean?" Marc asked.

"It means if you do not want to leave us a copy, we cannot force you. Your equipment will be cached at the lovers' cave. There is no good explanation that would explain you being a prisoner of terrorists and carrying the equipment this long. You can take the data with you. We have prepared a story for you to learn and repeat. All the archeological artifacts will remain with us. It will be assumed the terrorists destroyed them. You will be dropped off the day after tomorrow near Saidu in northern Pakistan. We will give you a trail of data to support the back story we are providing."

"I am not going back," Sandi said. "Not until the Solero problem is resolved."

"It does not work that way. The back story is worked out. It is everyone or no one. Akhtar wants to stay, too, but he will leave if Marc leaves."

"You can just send me out? Just like that?" Sandi asked.

"If Marc wants to leave now, there is no choice. We could possibly revise the back story, but that would take time. Information has already been released. We would have to work out some ways to debunk that information and replace it. It could take several days."

Marc looked at Sandi. "You really want to stay that much?"

"More than you can imagine."

"Well, I'd hoped that I could influence you to get out of this mess," Marc said to Sandi. "You know I wouldn't leave without you. What about you, Akhtar?"

"You remember Mogadishu. Your president took you out. I know you had to go. I had to leave, too. Even today, it eats at me. No matter what happens to Solero and his plots, if we leave now … you know what I'm saying."

"Akhtar is right. I'll help you gather the data," Marc said to Garret.

"Are you sure?" Garret asked. "You realize you will not be allowed to keep any of the data on the Heart of the Bison or the History Room, and you have to promise you will never say anything about it to anyone."

"You mean it? You agree to stay?" Sandi said to Marc.

"Well, I don't guess that all of my great discoveries will be much use to me if Solero succeeds in his plan."

Sandi hugged Marc. "Then it is settled. We are going back to the Heart of the Bison."

"What about Solero?" Marc asked.

"You should have seen his face when I showed up at the Council meeting. Lying is not a thing Earth People do well. Ultimately, he had to admit he had intercepted our message. Marvin has been working for Solero. It was Marvin who sabotaged the HSS. They had to return to

Banks on a faked emergency. Another EMF was supposed to go out, but those orders were intentionally messed up by Solero's people. We were missing before they could straighten it out. Solero knew we were trapped, but he did not have direct knowledge of the fact we were trapped in the Heart of the Bison. He had Sluma keeping track of our progress with a cover to give Solero plausible deniability about what was going on. Solero's activities will be severely curtailed while his actions with regard to the HSS are investigated. His communications have been cut off. He is in house arrest."

"What about Jektu?" Sandi asked.

"He helped Solero because he believed Solero's arguments for war," Garret said. "He has been relieved of all of his responsibilities. Ultimately, he will be sent to live in one of our Ancient colonies with a clan that lives in a remote area of Russia. There, he will live just like our ancestors lived before the Alliance. This is not a punishment. It is a life he is perfectly suited to ... one that conforms to his natural instinct and inherited knowledge."

Sandi could hardly believe she was going back to the Heart of the Bison. She had read about Small Beaver in books Ronaldo had provided. She was impressed, but her sense of connectedness seemed more tied to the Guardian. Perhaps the Guardian was more real to her than Small Beaver because she had actually found his remains.

Chapter 6

The History Room

One—August 2003

An EMF took Sandi to the Heart of the Bison. Marc had gone ahead to set up his equipment. When she got to the water entrance, there were underwater lights and frogmen. They had a small, one-person, submersible vehicle that could be pulled through the opening. An HSS was stationed far above for surveillance.

Sandi rode through the tunnel in the submersible vehicle. It was claustrophobic, but it was better than trying to swim through. When she got out of the vehicle in the cave, Marc was waiting for her. The first thing she noticed was the tropical smell that came from the Earth People's air-filtering devices.

"What is all of this?" Sandi asked as she stepped from the vehicle into the shallow water near the water's edge. Equipment was scattered around the edge, and several men were stacking it up.

"It's surprising how fast these people can mobilize. This is the in-cave staging area. All my equipment is here. We will be starting back up the tunnel any minute now."

"It is really strange to see this all lit up," Sandi said. "It is funny, but in the dark, I felt this space was much bigger."

"Yeah, so did I," Marc said.

"What is all of this equipment for?" Sandi asked. "We did not have this much stuff when we did the ceremony cavern."

"They plan to bring in about fifteen of the Ancients to clear out the tunnel to the History Room, so that means a lot of food and sanitary facilities. And then there's the equipment to move the rocks that the Ancients will be pulling out of the tunnel and batteries for their lighting. The real problem has been getting all of this stuff in without attracting local attention. They have an extensive network of sensors all around the area outside to back up the HSS so that they can tell if someone is wandering too close to our operations. What've you been up to?"

"I have been studying the writings of Sotif. I also visited the Spirit Fire again."

"What do you think about all of this?" Marc asked.

"It is like being in a Jules Verne novel, except, actually being in it, I have feelings I just would not have expected."

"What?"

"Some of it feels … I do not know, exactly … familiar."

"Yeah. I get that sometimes," Marc said. "It's one of the things that attracts me to paleontology. It's like finding a rock tool and knowing that it was made by habilis. And I hold it, and I already know what Homo habilis looked like and something about his world, and then I can almost feel what he probably felt when he used that tool, and then I feel connected … like maybe he was my direct ancestor. Stupid, but …"

"The connection of the atheist?"

"Nah, I don't believe in atheism," Marc said.

"Maybe it is the memories. I would not be surprised if all people have some traces of the memories. Maybe it is so faint and so deep most people cannot see it. Maybe they just feel it occasionally."

"And what about God?" Marc asked.

"Everyone has a God … Jehovah, Jesus, Allah, Buddha, the Great Spirit. I believe the complications of living organisms and the DNA molecule require much more than even four billion years of accidental chemical reactions. And that is before you even consider self-awareness, intelligence, and memory. Some kind of intelligence must have guided it, but I do not know what name to put to it."

"Intelligent design?" Marc asked.

"Maybe."

"Science will explain everything sometime," Marc said.

Just then, Garret came up to them. "Science makes models to explain things, but it explains nothing. It is as much faith based as any religion.

People think they accept science by knowledge rather than faith, but it is faith ultimately."

"Garret, where did you come from?" Sandi asked.

"I was coming down the tunnel. I just overheard Marc's comment."

"What do you mean that science is based on faith?" Marc asked. "It's based upon research, and precise mathematics, and reproducible phenomena. There is no faith in that."

"Newton had precise mathematics and reproducible phenomena, but his laws were superseded by the Theory of Relativity. That theory runs into problems when applied to electromagnetism. Throw gravity, black holes, string theory, and ultimately the hoped-for Theory of Everything into the pot and all you have are theories and a faith they will explain what science, so far, has not."

"It's just a matter of time until all will be discovered and proven," Marc argued.

"Is that what you *believe*?" Garret asked.

"Sure, don't you … wait a minute. What are you implying?"

"You have *belief* in your science … faith."

"What do *you* believe?" Sandi asked Garret.

"I believe science resides in Mother Earth, and the memories are the closest connection to God we will ever have. Are you ready to go to the Heart of the Bison?"

The tunnel to the Heart of the Bison was brightly lit. Travel was faster than it had been when they stumbled through on their escape—it only took about a half hour to reach the Heart of the Bison. The large, open space was about two hundred fifty feet by two hundred feet. The floor sloped gradually from Sandi's left to her right where the other unblocked tunnel out was. The opening into it was so big it was almost an extension of the main cavern. On the other side of that opening, Sandi could see a large, circular hearth. She walked over to the side of it.

"This must be where the Spirit Fire was," Sandi said to Garret.

"Did you read how Sotif burned his face with the last hot coal of the Spirit Fire when the warmonger doused it?" Garret asked.

"Yes." Sandi's voice was barely a whisper as she contemplated the incredible drama that had occurred on this spot more than five thousand years ago.

"No one has touched this hearth since Sotif intentionally burned his face," Garret said.

"I was thinking about the same thing myself," Sandi said.

It was not just that the hearth had been undisturbed that sent chills up Sandi's spine. Sandi had seen sites that had been undisturbed for much longer than that. She was deeply moved by the fact that she knew exactly what had happened and why the Heart of the Bison was closed off and abandoned.

Sandi looked around the cavern. According to Sotif, people lived in this cave for many thousands of years. Sotif's stories told of many stone dwellings in the cave, but the Earth People had taken them apart to block the path to the History Room. In the bright lights, Sandi could see the outlines of the foundations to the structures that had been destroyed. She tried to imagine the desperation that had caused the people to destroy their dwellings.

"I guess that must be the tunnel to the History Room," Sandi said, pointing to where people were setting up digging equipment.

"You can easily see the two tunnels that are filled with rock," Garret said. "Jektu told us which tunnel goes to the History Room when he was debriefed. We have done some high-altitude mapping of the hillside, and, coupled with directions and measurements we have taken from the inside, we have confirmed that the other blocked tunnel exits the hillside about seventy feet out."

"How long do you think it'll take to open the tunnel?" Marc asked.

"I do not know," Garret answered. "Most of our people who have studied Sotif's writings believe his people took from one to three weeks to fill it. They all agree there was a great sense of urgency, so they probably worked in shifts around the clock. We will set up a conveyor belt, and we have jacks and hydraulic lifters. I estimate from three to five days."

"Well, this cavern is pretty big," Marc said. "It'll take more time for me to scan it than it took to do the ceremony cavern. And we don't know how big the History Room is. I'll need a lot more storage media."

"We have already put that request in. You will have plenty."

"When will they start working on the tunnel?" Sandi asked.

"Everything is nearly ready," Garret said. "They will start in an hour or so and work twenty-four hours a day."

For four days, Sandi carefully went through the cavern looking for archeological evidence. Even though the cave had been cleaned by the warmonger, she found significant evidence of habitation, including an abundance of arrowheads.

Garret was interested in the arrowheads. There were two distinct types, providing evidence that there had been a significant battle between two different cultures in the cave. This agreed with Sotif's description of the battle preceding the destruction of the Spirit Fire.

After Marc and Sandi finished their breakfasts, Marc helped Sandi catalog a small pile of artifacts before going back to his survey. "These come from the last of the side caverns," she told Marc.

"When you look at the stacks of wood and listen to the stories, you would think that there was a very large population living in this cave, but then, when you add up all of the artifacts you have found, it doesn't add up to very many people at all," Marc said.

"The writings I was studying before we came here explain the warmonger was afraid if he left any of the Neandertal bodies or their possessions lying around, they would use their powers to come back. He burned their bodies in smelting hearths they used for copper, so even the bones were reduced to ashes. He collected their possessions and destroyed them also."

Garret rushed up, obviously very excited. "They have broken through to the History Room. They will have the tunnel cleared in a couple of hours."

"Oh, can we go in?" Sandi exclaimed.

"I'll get my equipment ready," Marc said.

"No one will be going in today. Ronaldo and some members of the Council will be here tomorrow. They will bring hot coals from the Spirit Fire and start a new Spirit Fire in the Heart of the Bison. Then they will do the ancient ceremony of the ashes to sanctify this Spirit Fire. No one will go into the History Room until the Spirit Fire is burning in its home."

"You mean you're not even going to take a peek to make sure that it's the right room?" Marc asked.

"It is forbidden to have any light in the History Room that does not come from the Spirit Fire," Sandi said.

"That is right," Garret said. "I am impressed. You made excellent use of your study time."

"You mean that I'm going to have to work in there with flickering torchlight?" Marc asked.

"We have good gas lanterns that will provide a bright, steady light. After the ceremonies to open the History Room are completed, the gas lanterns will be ignited with the Spirit Fire for your work. After your work is done, the History Room will only be lit by the fire torches, as it was in the past. Meanwhile, we will make preparations to go into the room tomorrow."

The rest of the day, Sandi went through the motions of doing her work, but all she could think of was the History Room. If they found the paintings Sotif had talked about, it would be the greatest archeological find in her lifetime—an unbroken history of a great alliance that had lasted nearly twenty thousand years.

When the crew members gathered around the central camp near the Spirit Fire hearth, the camp was unnaturally quiet. It seemed that everyone was contemplating the deep significance of the chasm of time they were on the verge of crossing.

It was normal for all the members of the work crews to spread out around the cave and the side rooms when it was time to eat. Sandi and Marc speculated a lot about what that meant. Marc insisted that they ate live rats. That didn't make sense, because it didn't explain why they didn't eat with one another. Sandi was surprised when Garret asked her to eat dinner with him.

"Of course," she answered. She stood and shrugged her shoulders at Marc.

"Why not?" Marc said. "Go ahead."

Sandi followed Garret to a secluded spot just inside a small cavern. She sat against the wall with her knees drawn up. "So, what is the occasion?" she asked.

"What occasion?" Garret asked innocently.

"We have known each other for … oh, my God, I have lost track of the time … and this will be the first time we have eaten together."

"We have known each other only a short time relatively, but it seems longer to me."

"What do you mean by longer?" Sandi asked.

"It is like I know you much better than I would have thought in so short a time."

After a pause that seemed to last forever, Sandi lifted a fruit bar to her mouth.

"No! Wait!" Garret exclaimed.

"What?" Sandi asked.

"I planned what to say, but then ... it is really hard. You just do not know."

"What do I not know?" Sandi asked.

"It is just difficult."

"Okay," Sandi said. "Let me say something. I have very strong feelings for you. Is it the same with you?"

"Yes," Garret answered.

Sandi had expected a few more words than just *yes*. "Before, you said it was complicated. So, are you saying there is a chance for us?"

"It is difficult, because our cultures are so different."

"What is the difficulty?"

"Sex has different meanings in our culture. In ancient times, sex among Earth People was divided into two classes. Casual sex was called play mating, while sex for children was called baby mating. There was no such thing as marriage. The family did not form a unit. The commitment was only that the father would provide for his children and train his male children to hunt.

"At the time of Sotif, our breeding practices were changed to develop the special kinds of people you have seen. Children are no longer raised by parents. Baby mating is directed by experts in breeding and no longer represents a commitment. As our family structure and the place of baby mating changed, we developed a way to express closeness that did not involve sex.

"In ancient times, the people of the clan helped take care of one another. We did not have blenders, and yet our diet consisted of tough meat and fibrous vegetables. The people of the clans who had good teeth chewed food and passed it mouth to mouth to those who had lost their teeth. This is a fairly intimate process.

"After the time of Sotif, the act of eating gradually took on a quality of intimacy that is more important to us than sex. For Earth People, the act of sharing a meal together has become the sign of an intimate relationship."

"So, then the fact that you have asked me to eat dinner with you means you want to share intimate time with me … almost like sex."

"Yes," Garret said.

"Are you thinking of passing chewed food between us?"

"No. That is the historic source of the custom. Nobody passes food anymore. We have blenders now."

"So then if we eat together, it means something special," Sandi said.

"Yes," Garret answered.

"You are a man of many words," she kidded. She looked at Garret eye to eye and took a bite of her fruit bar. Garret took a bite of his.

Sandi did feel something. Perhaps it was the way Garret looked back at her. "Does this mean we are engaged or something?"

"We do not have marriage, but it means we are sort of a couple."

"What does that mean?"

"We could live together and share our lives. Sort of like being married in your world, but without the children."

"That would be too sad, Garret. That is not the kind of life I could accept."

"I meant that is how it is in the caves … in the dy-emeralite cities, as you call them. Everything is different for Watchers who live in the world. There are many completely normal families of Watchers all over your world."

"Are you saying we could live in my world as man and wife and have our own children?"

"Yes, we could get the clearances. You are a paleontologist just as I am. What would be better for creating a cover?"

"What about children? Do you not have to have permission from the breeding committee, or whatever it is?"

"No, it is not the same for Watchers who live above ground. We try to blend in. I personally would love to have my own children."

"But they would be half Neandertal. I mean, what if they looked like Neandertals? I mean, that is okay with me, I guess, but life would be kind of difficult for them."

"Do you ever worry that a poodle's puppy will look like a wolf?"

"No. What is your point?"

"All dogs came from wolves. You came from Homo erectus. Do you worry your children will look like Homo erectus? I come from the accepted idea of what a Neanderthal looks like, but that is no more in my genes than Homo erectus is. If we have children, they will look like you and me."

"But if they had their DNA checked for some reason, then what?"

"There are minor DNA differences, but they are within the expected differences between different populations of Sun People. There are some markers our geneticists can find, but that is because they know they are Neanderthal. Earth People are not a different species. Even if Sun People find the markers in fossils, they would assume those markers in modern men only prove Neanderthals and Cro-Magnons were able to breed together before Neanderthals disappeared."

"So, you are saying we could live a normal life with a house and children?" Sandi asked.

"Kind of normal," Garret said. "I would still have my annual trips to the dy-emeralite cities. I would have assignments and so forth."

"That sounds like living with a spy. Would you want to complicate your life by being married to a Sun People woman?" Sandi asked.

"My life responsibilities would not be different. I would still have my career. It is no different than any man in the Sun People world being willing to accept the responsibilities of marriage and raising a family. The answer is yes. I want to do that with you more than anything."

"Well, in my world, friends and acquaintances eat together. In fact, even strangers eat together. In my world, personal intimacy is expressed through sex. You would have to change your preferences to blend in. I cannot see me changing. We would be living in my world. You should blend in and be more like we are."

"So, I have already been told," Garret said.

"By whom?"

"All Watchers have been told to act more … normally. Most have accepted that advice. I have just been kind of slow. For me, going into McDonald's is like if you walked into an orgy in a bordello."

"So, where do we go from here?"

"Right now, is not a good time to be thinking about that. As soon as we resolve this Solero thing, I will officially start the wheels rolling."

"How long would that take?" Sandi asked.

"I hope you do not think I am presumptuous, but I have made some inquiries. It would take a few days to a week for papers and physicals."

"Physicals?"

"Yes, anyone who has lived outside the caves would have to pass a physical before engaging in a sexual relationship."

"Oh. So, in a few weeks, we could be married?" Sandi asked. It all felt so businesslike.

"Not exactly," Garret said.

"What else?" Sandi asked.

"We should just start at the beginning. Sandi, I love you, and I want to spend my life with you. Will you marry me?"

That felt much better. "Yes!" she exclaimed and threw herself into his arms.

Sandi slept in Garret's arms all night. "Okay," Sandi said when Garret opened his eyes. "It is time for you to start adjusting to Sun People customs."

"What are you talking about?" Garret asked groggily.

"I want you to have breakfast with me, Marc, and Akhtar."

"Oh, I do not think so. I am not ready for that."

"You will never be ready. Come on. You have to start before you are ready."

"Not now," Garret pleaded. "Give me some time to prepare."

"You will have to figure out how important it is to be with me. Then you will be ready," Sandi said. Garret did not answer. Sandi could not believe that he could just sit there. It had all seemed so simple, but clearly, it was not. Sandi left him and went back to have breakfast with Marc and Akhtar.

Marc was quiet and withdrawn. He finally broke the silence. "What happened last night?" he asked.

"Not what you think," Sandi said.

"What do I think?" Marc asked.

"Earth People are not allowed to have sex with people outside the caves without having a bunch of tests first. They do not want to take AIDS into their caves, I guess."

"So, what did happen? And don't tell me nothing. I see how nervous you are."

"We talked about the things you and I talked about."

"What things?"

"About marriage and having kids. It would not be a problem. There is not much difference in the DNA. He is allowed to get married and have kids and do everything Sun People do. In fact, they encourage their Watchers to do that."

"Well, I suppose you are happy about that," Marc commented.

"I really think he is the man for me."

"This is a really strange decision," Marc said. "It's not just the Neandertal thing. You don't know anything about that culture. It's bound to cause problems. What if Solero wins? You could find yourself allied with the wrong side in a dangerous struggle."

"I know more about the cultural differences than you think. You are right; I could not live according to the Earth People culture in their dy-emeralite cities, but the Watchers do not live that way. They follow the customs of the country where they live. And if Solero wins, you and I both will be aligned on the side opposing him no matter what else happens."

"You hear stories of American women marrying Muslims from the Middle East," Marc said. "They think they are in love and that their love will overcome cultural differences. Then the next thing you know, the man disappears with the children, and the woman is left alone trying to have governments help get her children back from some Middle Eastern country. What would happen if Garret disappeared into the dy-emeralite world with your children? How would you even try to get them back? Who would believe you if you told them that a Neandertal took them in a flying saucer piloted by an alien-looking Neandertal to a cave guarded by Neandertal Bigfoots?"

Sandi did not answer at first. It was just one more problem she still had to think about. "I do not know what I would do. Before I do anything, I will study the writings of Sotif. If Ronaldo wins this argument, the people will remain under the guidance of Sotif's writings. If Ronaldo does not win, who knows what the world will be like, or where Garret will fit in it? At some point, a man and a woman must trust each other. If we just focus on cases where trust is abused, who would ever get anywhere? I know trusting Garret is a leap of faith, but on the other hand, I do not believe he has ever lied to me. I thought he did, but I can see now if he does not want me to know something, he just refuses to tell me. There is at least honesty in that approach."

"Maybe he doesn't lie, but he isn't above misleading, and I'm not sure what the difference is."

"I guess it still goes back to trust," Sandi said.

"Well, Sandi, if you do decide to go with him, I can only wish you the best of luck. I'm only saying that you should be very sure about what you do."

"Thanks," Sandi said. "I will be careful. You have given me some important things to think about."

The early morning was filled with activity at the watery entrance to the Heart of the Bison. Three EMFs brought dignitaries, implements, costumes, and artifacts. All these things had been unloaded and brought in before sunrise. By midmorning, everything in the Heart of the Bison was ready.

Workers had installed a large cover over the Spirit Fire hearth. "What is the point?" Sandi asked Garret as she pointed at the cover.

Garret was distracted. "Garret!" Sandi said.

"Oh! Um, the Spirit Fire will burn wood. That will produce smoke and heat that would go out of the hole where we first came in. Someone would surely notice it. The hood will filter and cool the fumes from the fire. There is one like it back at the Eastern Spirit Fire."

"I did not notice it," Sandi said.

"This one is temporary. Eventually, they will install a bigger one supported from the ceiling. It will be camouflaged, so it will look natural."

"I thought you were going to plug the holes in the Heart of the Bison with dy-emeralite."

"We will, but that just makes it more necessary to filter and clean the air to keep it breathable."

"Oh," Sandi said. "You seem very … um … I do not know, maybe distracted is the word. Is something wrong?"

"I guess everything is okay," Garret answered, but the tone of his voice said something else.

"You guess?" Sandi asked. "Come on, what is wrong?"

"I just did not think Ronaldo would bring the whole leadership of the Majority Party here. I guess they are all anxious to be part of the Spirit Fire ceremony and see the Heart of the Bison and the History Room. I mean, this is the biggest thing that has happened to Earth People since Sotif reunited the Eastern and Western clans."

"But?" Sandi asked.

"But with all the trouble with Solero, I would leave some senior officials in place just to be sure no vacuum of power is left behind. Look, they are ready to start," Garret said.

As he spoke, Sandi heard the soft beat of a drum. She followed Garret to a place near the Spirit Fire hearth. The dignitaries stood at the edge of the hearth on the north side. Tinder and wood were in place almost directly across from them.

The sound of the drum grew a little louder. Ronaldo appeared and walked to the edge of the hearth. He wore leather leggings and moccasins. Across his chest was a vest of woven reeds and grasses. His shoulders and arms were bare. On his head, he wore a tall, straight hat of fluffy animal fur. Some large bird feathers hung from the hat over each of his shoulders.

He tapped the drum three times slowly, followed by four rapid taps.

"Sedco must bring the Spirit Fire to Ronaldo," Ronaldo said after the last drumbeat, speaking in the language of the Earth People.

An old man of the Ancients stepped forward with a wooden box. "Sedco brings Ronaldo a live ember from the Spirit Fire of the East. Sedco brings Ronaldo a living ember to make a sister to the Spirit Fire of the East. Sedco testifies to Ronaldo that this ember comes from the flames of the Spirit Fire. Sedco testifies to Ronaldo that the living ember burns with all of the promises of Mother Earth." Sandi understood the words that the old man spoke. The cadence and rhythm of the ancient language gave a very ancient feel to the ceremony.

Ronaldo took the ember from the box in his left hand. He held his hand above his head. Sandi gasped. He was holding it in his bare hand! Then he pushed the glowing ember into his cheek. Sandi could smell burning flesh. When Ronaldo removed the ember, Sandi could see the blackened flesh with ragged lines of red.

Ronaldo was shaking as he put the ember in the tinder and blew on it. With his first breath, the tinder burst into flames.

Ronaldo faced the people who were gathered to witness the ceremony. The ugly, blackened wound on his face wept with watery-looking blood. "Ronaldo has returned the Spirit Fire to the Heart of the Bison." Ronaldo held his bleeding, burnt hand above his head. "Ronaldo will always carry the mark of the Spirit Fire. Bring the ashes," Ronaldo commanded.

Sedco brought a large animal skin bag. As the Spirit Fire blazed up, Ronaldo added the ashes to the fire, one handful at a time.

"In the time of Sotif, the Spirit Fire ashes were taken from the Spirit Fire of the West to become part of the Spirit Fire of the East. The Spirit Fire of the East became whole. The ashes Ronaldo holds come from the Spirit Fire of the East." After placing the last handful in the fire, Ronaldo said, "Now this Spirit Fire of the West has the ashes of all of the Earth People from the beginning of the Alliance. Now the Spirit Fire of the West is a true Spirit Fire. Now the Spirit Fire of the West has the spirit of Kectu's sister. Now the Spirit Fire of the West has the spirit of the Earth People." Ronaldo stood in silence in front of the Spirit Fire. No one spoke for about five minutes. Then Ronaldo said, "Now the Ceremony of the Ashes is done."

An Ancient handed Ronaldo a simple wooden box about the size of a shoe box. He held the box above his head so that all could see it. The cave became silent as attention was focused on Ronaldo and the box he held. "Lekto, the shomot of the Earth People, has prepared this sacred box to carry a bone from Kectu's grave," Ronaldo said in English. "The Thinkers will use the bone to map DNA from the great shorec, Kectu. We will disturb the sanctity of the grave as little as possible. The box will remain on the full moon spot of the hearth of the Spirit Fire until Kectu's grave is found." Ronaldo set the box carefully on the Spirit Fire hearth.

One of the Earth People dressed the burns on Ronaldo's face and palm. When the bandages were placed, Ronaldo came to where Garret, Marc, and Sandi were standing.

"Did you understand the words of the ceremony?" he asked Sandi.

"Yes, I did," Sandi answered. "You seem so sure that you will find Kectu's grave. The whole thing will be totally anticlimactic if it is not there."

"It is good you understood. I am not worried about the grave. I am certain it is there. The priests are preparing the torches to enter the History Room. Today, we will see the paintings and study their meanings. We will find the bones of Kectu and Shekek.

"Tomorrow, we will light the room with the lanterns and photograph everything. Then Marc can begin his work. When the torches are ready, we will go." Ronaldo returned to the Spirit Fire hearth.

"What were they saying?" Marc asked Sandi.

"Mostly, the old one was testifying to Ronaldo that the hot coal does come from the actual Spirit Fire that has been burning since the days of the great shorec, Kectu. Ronaldo used hot coals from the Spirit Fire in the East to start this fire in order preserve to the fire's continuity. Then Ronaldo put ashes from the Spirit Fire in the East into this fire to preserve the historical connection to the ashes of all the Earth People whose ashes have passed through the Spirit Fire since its beginning. Now that the flames and the ashes come from the Spirit Fire in the East, this new fire is a Spirit Fire ... a fire that has burned continuously since the time of Kectu."

"Why did Ronaldo burn his face and hand with the coal in the fire?"

"No one said anything about that," Sandi answered. "But according to the writings of Sotif, back when the original Spirit Fire was put out in this very hearth, Sotif found the last hot coal. He held it in his hand and used it to burn a scar on his face. It was kind of a symbol that the warmonger could not destroy the Spirit Fire. Ever since that time, these people have been looking for the day when the Spirit Fire would burn again in the Heart of the Bison. This is probably something like the Second Coming for them. Maybe Ronaldo just wanted to have a mark for being the one to finally put the fire back."

"Well, I suppose that it's a good political move, considering the problems with Solero."

"Do not be such a cynic," Sandi said.

"I know that I'm a cynic, but it's one of the things you like about me," Marc joked.

Finally, Garret came from the group that was preparing to enter the History Room. "Ronaldo has agreed both of you may enter the History Room."

Sandi was speechless. If everything she had read in Sotif's writings were true, she was about to see the oldest book ever written. Sure, it would be in the language of paintings, but it would talk of traditions and stories from twenty-five thousand years ago. It was more than a few cave paintings that might depict a single hunt or other event. These would be paintings representing a history of nearly twenty thousand years!

"When you go in, please do not say anything." It was Garret talking. "No one knows what condition the room is in. For my people, this is the most sacred moment in thousands of years. Whatever we find, Ronaldo wants complete silence."

"That's good for me," Marc said.

"Me, too," Sandi said.

"Then follow me," Garret said.

Ronaldo stood at the entrance. "On this day, Earth People will reunite with the source of our history. We will find the remains of the great shorec, Kectu, and we will find our history painted on the walls of this cave. A small bone will be taken to our labs in Rodlu City in order to map her DNA."

Ronaldo was first to enter the tunnel. He carried a burning torch from the Spirit Fire. Behind him were four of the Ancients, each carrying two torches that were not burning.

Sandi could feel her heart beating against her ribs as she walked down the tunnel. Suddenly, the line stopped. There was a noticeable breeze coming down the tunnel at her back. The dim yellow light from the nearly smokeless torch flickered in front of her. The smell of burning animal fat filled the air, reminding Sandi of the ceremony cavern. It had been over five thousand years since humans been in this room, but it had been almost twenty-five thousand years since the first human had entered the room to make the first painting!

Sandi knew there were plenty of cave paintings much older than the paintings she was about to see, but the stories behind the paintings in this cave were still told among living Earth People.

Finally, the line moved forward, and at last, Sandi stepped into the History Room. All the torches had been ignited with the fire of the torch that Ronaldo carried. The light was not bright, but it did clearly light the room. To her right as she entered the room was a wide, high, flat wall. Sandi involuntarily sucked in a deep breath as she stared at the wall. It was covered from the floor to a level about thirty feet high with a wide variety of paintings. It was a panorama of varying scenes, almost like looking at the Sistine Chapel, except the paintings were clearly done by many different artists in different styles. The paintings were faded, but the details were clear. The first painting of Shekek's genealogy was just as Sotif described it in his writings. Kectu and the Guardian were shown at the top. Their daughter, Tuka, and the boy hunter, Sky Man, were shown below. From them came Shekek. The painting clearly showed that Shekek went with Kectu and the Guardian to start a new people—the

Alliance. Tuka and Sky Man did not go. There was no escaping the conclusion that the lovers she had found were Tuka and Sky Man!

Where the thought came from, Sandi could not tell, but the truth of it was so clear she gasped and almost blurted out, *Oh, my God!* Suddenly, it hit Sandi with emotional power and conviction that Sotif's writings were more than just ancient stories and traditions—they were history!

As Sandi looked at the pictures before her, she was able to recognize several of the stories she had read from Sotif's writings. The large, panoramic painting depicting the Alliance when it covered the world from the Middle East across Asia to Alaska and Canada was prominent a little more than halfway up from the bottom of the wall.

Sandi's eyes burned, and she felt tears running down her cheeks. This was not just the history of Earth People. It was the history of the great Alliance between Earth People and Sun People. It was her history as much as it was Garret's! There was a bond between her people and Garret's people—a bond older than any other bond in this world. If only the world could know this—that people as different as Neandertals and Cro-Magnons had been able to live in peace and cooperation for more than twenty thousand years! The warmonger from the West had invented war and brought it to destroy what had been a true Eden. No wonder Sotif warned so strongly against war.

Two Ancients carefully dug into the floor of the cave at the base of the genealogy painting. They found a skeleton! Though Sandi expected them to find it, she was shocked when they did. One of the men carefully removed a bone from the tip of the little finger on the left hand. Then they buried the skeleton and returned the floor to its original condition. "Those who are to care for Kectu will bring the box," Ronaldo commanded. His voice was filled with emotion.

Several men left the History Room to get the box that had been prepared to carry the bone fragment.

Sandi realized the skeleton must be the shorec—Kectu! Kectu was the mother of the female lover. All the legends and stories of the survival of one clan of Neandertals were tied together and proven by the paintings she was looking at. She had found the lovers, she had found the entrance to the ceremony cavern, and she had led Garret and his people to the Heart of the Bison. It was humbling to think about it.

No one had spoken all the time they dug up the bones. Sandi had lost track of time. There were twenty or more people in the room. The cares of the world were suspended. Sandi felt sorry for Marc and Akhtar. They were the only ones in the room who could not recognize the stories and history of the Alliance in the paintings on the wall. Sandi was glad for the time she had taken to study the writings of Sotif.

Suddenly, all the Ancients jumped and turned to the entrance. Then Sandi heard it—muffled sounds like distant gunfire!

Two—August 2003

"Let's get out of here!" Marc screamed. Sandi followed him down the tunnel. As he reached the entrance to the great cavern of the Heart of the Bison, Marc stopped and peeked into the cavern. Sandi looked around his shoulder. There were six men dressed in black in the center of the cavern. They each had what appeared to be an automatic rifle. Three of the men who had gone to get the box lay dead on the floor.

Suddenly, two men ran from behind a rock into the tunnel that led to the river. All six men began firing at them. Sandi stumbled back into Akhtar, who was standing behind her. "Don't make a sound," he whispered in her ear.

"I hid the rifle in that alcove over there," Marc said to Akhtar. "I'm pretty sure that it's still there." Marc dashed for the alcove about twenty feet away. Four of the men with guns ran after the men who had run into the tunnel. The other two held onto the end of a rope as another man began to descend from the opening in the ceiling with a gun and a grenade launcher strapped to his back.

Sandi heard gunfire coming from the tunnel where the men had run. Then she jumped and screamed as loud gunfire went off close to her left. It was Marc! The two men holding the rope and the man on the rope all fell dead without returning fire. Marc and Akhtar ran to their bodies and picked up their weapons. Then they ran to the tunnel.

Marc fired into the tunnel, and someone returned fire. In the meantime, another man had started down the rope. Sandi shouted, "Marc, the rope!"

Marc turned and fired two shots. The man shouted something in Arabic and fell from the rope. The rope began to ascend to the ceiling in a jerky fashion.

Garret stood beside Sandi. "What is happening?"

"Marc has killed at least four men who came down on a rope. Four others ran into the tunnel to the river. Marc and Akhtar are over there. The men were talking in Arabic. We are being attacked by terrorists again!"

"I was afraid of something like this," Garret said.

"You said Solero would not send terrorists in here."

"That was then. Now Solero knows the Heart of the Bison has been found and all the Majority Party members of the Council are here. His level of desperation is pretty high."

As Garret spoke, Ronaldo came out of the tunnel to the History Room. "What is going on here?"

"Solero must have found out about the History Room. We have been attacked by terrorists," Garret said.

"He would not dare," Ronaldo said.

"Maybe, maybe not, but they are here all the same, and they came to kill," Garret said.

"Sandi, get the weapons out of the center of the cave and bring them to me!" Marc shouted.

"I will get them," Garret said. He ran to where the bodies were, picked up an armload of weapons and ammo, and carried it all to Marc.

Sandi ran out and pulled another ammo belt from one of the bodies. There was a dark pool of blood all around the four bodies. The odor of gun smoke and blood made her nauseous. There was no way to get the ammo belt off without getting blood on her hands. It was sticky and warm—she began to dry heave. She took the ammo to where Marc and Garret were. Akhtar was about fifty feet down the tunnel, using a large boulder to hide from the terrorists. Thankfully, the smell of gunfire quickly became more powerful than the smell of blood.

Someone fired out of the tunnel, and Marc returned fire. "Four guys ran in there," Marc said. "One of them is lying dead in the open. I know I hit another one. He must be hurt really bad if he is alive. I don't know about the other two. I think I hit one of them. We can keep them bottled up there, but it would be really dangerous to try to go down that tunnel. We're trapped again."

A voice came from the ceiling. "Drop your guns and surrender to my men. We will take you as hostages and let you live. If you don't surrender, we will kill everyone."

"Tell your men to surrender to us, and we will not kill them!" Marc shouted.

"Don't be foolish. We have found the water entrance. We are bringing our men in now. You won't be able to hold them back, and then you'll all die."

"What do we do now?" Sandi asked.

"We can sit tight here as long as the food lasts," Marc said. "But at some point, we have to find a way out."

"What about opening the entrance?" Sandi asked.

"That would take too long," Ronaldo said as he joined them.

"You have a better idea?" Marc asked.

"Can you keep them back for now?" Ronaldo asked.

"Let's put more light down the tunnel," Marc said. "Then I can see both ways, and if anyone comes down from the ceiling or up this tunnel, I can keep them back."

"I have contacts in the FBI and US military," Ronaldo said.

"Watchers?" Marc asked.

"Not exactly. I have worked with your government since the 1940s. They think I am an alien. If I can contact them, they will get us out of this. Solero does not know about this relationship. It is top secret among both Earth People and Sun People. If they get us out of here, I will trade certain information about Solero's plans. The important thing is that it is better for them to continue believing we are from another planet. I am asking you to maintain that cover story. You do not have to tell any lies … just do not offer any information." He spoke directly to Marc.

"You won't have any problems with me," Marc answered.

Ronaldo looked at Sandi. "Me, either," she said.

"What about Akhtar?" Ronaldo asked Marc.

"He is military. You can trust him."

"Okay. The problem is how to communicate from inside this cave. The rock is too thick here. Maybe we could follow the river upstream."

"I do not know if this will help," Garret said. "The Ancients can hear what is being said by the terrorists above. Some of the Ancients understand Arabic. The terrorists do know about the river and where it comes out, but none of them knows how to swim. They are watching the opening, but they are not sending anyone in."

"There's not much rock cover at that entrance, and there are some seams that go to daylight along the left edge of the water," Marc said. "Could you get a signal out from there?"

"Yes, I did get a signal back to our base when we came in," Ronaldo said. "Solero will intercept anything I send to my people, but I should be able to communicate with my military contacts on a secure satellite frequency from there."

"Okay then, we're gonna have to ferret those guys out," Marc said. "Someone is going to have to watch the ceiling in here and shoot anyone that tries to come down."

"Nobody here knows how to use a gun," Garret said.

"I'll show someone. It's not really that difficult. If anyone tries to come down a rope, he'll be a sitting duck. They know that, so I don't think they'll try anything. Besides, your guys can hear if anyone starts down. Just shoot at the hole in the ceiling if they drop the rope in again, and that should send them packing."

"Show me," Garret said.

"Me, too," Sandi said.

"We cannot participate in this war," Ronaldo said.

"What war?" Garret said. "We are under attack right now. It is like the stories that talk about how the Earth People helped at the Heart of the Bison massacre."

"That is how it starts," Ronaldo said.

"Maybe they will not send a rope down," Garret said.

"How about if one of the Ancients comes with me and Akhtar to be our eyes and ears?" Marc said. "He can just point, and we'll do the rest. It's either that or just wait until Solero initiates his plan."

Ronaldo walked into the tunnel to the History Room.

"He cannot okay it. He has left me to implement Rule Seven. Show me how to use the gun," Garret said.

Marc gave Garret and Sandi a quick shooting lesson. They both fired their guns at the hole in the ceiling for practice.

When he was done, one of the Ancients came forward. Garret said, "Marc, Sendo will help you find the terrorists. He can signal with his hands."

Marc fired a rifle grenade into the tunnel to the river. Marc and Sendo ran into the tunnel under the cover of the smoke and dust from the explosion.

Sandi waited nervously with her gun pointed at the ceiling. There were gunshots and explosions in the tunnel. A voice came from above. Both Sandi and Garret responded by shooting their guns into the opening.

There were more shots in the tunnel, and then it was silent. Sandi and Garret hid behind some rocks and pointed their guns into the tunnel. Sandi was shaking. She took several deep breaths to calm herself. Just as she saw two figures coming down the tunnel, she heard Marc's voice. "It's okay; the tunnel is clear."

Sandi let out an audible sigh of relief. She had the gun ready, but she could not make up her mind whether to shoot or let the terrorist take her prisoner. Sendo and the four other Ancients came close behind Marc and Akhtar.

Ronaldo held a short ceremony in the History Room to put the bone fragment into the box, and then everyone came out of the History Room. Marc led the way to the entrance while Akhtar stayed behind to watch the ceiling. It took less than an hour to get everyone to the spring. Ronaldo was able to make contact with one of the generals he knew.

They waited about two hours in the cave. Then they saw the shadows of someone coming through the tunnel from the outside. Sandi was relieved when she saw that they were US Special Forces.

"Send someone to get Akhtar," Garret said when the first of the Special Forces entered the cave.

"Well, it's going to take you some time to get back to Rodlu City," Marc said. "This isn't going to be like an EMF trip. Someone is gonna have to stay here to make sure that the terrorists don't take control of the cavern. I'll go back. Akhtar and I will keep watch. We have food and water, and we can take turns sleeping."

"Marc is right," Ronaldo said.

"No. It is too dangerous," Sandi said.

"You don't have to worry about me and Akhtar. We're both trained soldiers. We can take care of ourselves." Marc gave Sandi a big hug. "I appreciate your concern, though. Now you'd better get going."

Sandi felt a great loss as she watched Marc walking down the tunnel. She could not imagine what she would do if anything happened to him.

Ronaldo insisted Sandi and Garret be among the first out. When Sandi came out of the water, one helicopter and seven marines were on the ground. Four Arabic terrorists were sitting cross-legged on the ground, and a fifth was being interrogated. When Garret came out, Ronaldo pulled Sandi aside. "It is going to take about thirty more minutes to get everyone out. We cannot wait that long. We are leaving now on one of the helicopters. Oh, and keep your face down, the fewer people who see you, the better."

"What about the rest of your people and the prisoners?" Sandi asked.

"Our people will be taken to a secret base where we can make arrangements to pick them up later. The US military will use the terrorists and their radios to cover up the fact that we have escaped for as long as possible. The prisoners will be taken to a military base in Afghanistan, where they will be interrogated. Ultimately, they will be turned over to Pakistani authorities. That will help to explain the military action in Pakistan."

"How long can they keep the fact of our escape bottled up?" Garret asked.

"It depends on how much information they get out of the prisoners," Ronaldo said. "The longer our escape is kept secret, the better."

When they took off, the noise in the helicopter was much louder than Sandi had imagined it would be. They were not able to hear one another talk, even when they screamed. Those who had to communicate wore earphones and microphones. They were shuttled from the spring to an air base in Pakistan, and from there, they were flown by jet to a base in Germany. Ronaldo's contact was already there.

"General, it is nice to see you again," Ronaldo said to the graying old man.

"Ronaldo, in trouble again, I see," the general responded. He wore a civilian suit and tie.

"Not nearly as much trouble as you," Ronaldo responded in a serious tone.

"So, you said. You said that there are major terrorist attacks in the works. I'm going to need the details."

"It will be by the same rules. No publicity about any of it."

"You got it."

"This much I already know," Ronaldo began. "It is going to start with several accidents to soften the country up. The terrorist connection to these actions will be deeply covered to keep your alerts at a low level."

"What kinds of accidents?" the general asked.

"The first will be a giant blackout of New England and parts of Canada. The biggest in history. That will be a signal to many differing terrorist groups around the world to begin operations."

"Oh, my God!" the general exclaimed. "The blackout is happening now."

Ronaldo's eyes widened. "Things are happening faster than I thought. What about a worm attacking government computers all across the country?"

"I have seen some intelligence about that. But it isn't nationwide."

"I can give you the codes that will stop it. What about the oil transmission line in Arizona?"

"Nothing there."

"Okay, I do not have exact intelligence on that, but you need to get people to watch it and also the oil line from Alaska. I have coordinates on that. It will be attacked right after the Arizona line.

"There will be a big increase in forest fires all along the West Coast. You need to get as many men as possible there. Unfortunately, I do not have information that will allow you to get to the source. There are too many groups involved. There are several sniper events planned for the East Coast, but for that, I have information on sources. If you act quickly enough, you will be able to stop most of them. Following all of this, there will be a major explosion at the Scattergood plant in Los Angeles. That will be a signal to all the other groups around the world for the final attacks. If Scattergood goes off, there is nothing I can give you that will stop everything in time."

"What are we supposed to do about all of this?" the general asked.

"I have some communications problems. I need to get to Seattle as quickly as possible. I can get all the information you will need once I am there. But this is class one."

"Totally undercover," the general said.

"Totally. That includes the men here. They did not see anything. When you uncover the plots, confiscate the weapons of mass destruction, and break up the groups, it cannot hit the news. It is like it never happened."

"Seattle?" the general asked.

"Yes," Ronaldo said.

"You don't have your own transportation?"

"I need your help on this, and I need the fastest jet you have. When I get there, I will give you an electronic transfer of all of the information you will need to disarm this situation through our info website."

"Get ready. We will have you in the air in fifteen minutes."

"Sandi, I want you and Garret to come with me," Ronaldo said.

"Why?" Sandi asked.

"I have my reasons. Please get ready."

Sandi was excited about being involved in something as important as this all sounded. But this was not a game! She didn't know what kind of plane they were loaded onto. The seats they had were improvised. Obviously, the plane was not designed to carry passengers.

They were in the air twenty minutes after the talk with the general. According to Ronaldo, they were flying at several times the speed of sound. He was definitely a man with influence. Less than four hours after takeoff, they landed at an airport near Seattle.

A man was waiting for them with a helicopter. They flew out of Seattle, going north to Canada. After two hours and fifteen minutes, the helicopter landed in a meadow in a forested area.

From there, Ronaldo led them through the woods for about an hour and a half. They did not walk fast by Sandi's standards, but she could tell that Ronaldo was pushing as hard as he could. They finally reached a cave where Ronaldo entered a code on his communicator. What appeared to be a solid rock wall slid open.

"I was worried Solero would have changed the codes," Garret said.

"He did," Ronaldo said. "I have a secret code that overrides all of the other codes."

Suddenly, three large Gatherers blocked the entrance. They were surprised to see Ronaldo.

"What is going on?" one of the Gatherers asked. "Solero told everyone you and the Council were led into a trap in the Middle East by Sun People with a lie about the Heart of the Bison. Sun People hope to put us in disarray by killing all our leaders. How did you get away?"

"Solero has misled you," Ronaldo said. "I need to get to Rodlu City as quickly as possible. You must not tell anyone that we are here."

"What did happen?" the Gatherer asked.

"I will tell you this. I have been to the Heart of the Bison and the History Room."

The Gatherer seemed stunned. "I have lived to see this great day?"

"Now is a great time for Earth People. Old prophecies are coming to pass, but there is much to do first," Ronaldo said.

"I will make the arrangements," the Gatherer said.

As soon as they settled in the vehicle that would take them to Rodlu City, Ronaldo turned on a communicator. Solero was addressing the Earth People.

> The security we have enjoyed for centuries is beginning to break up. Even some of our own people have brought Sun People to fool and mislead us. They tricked the leadership of the Majority Party with a claim they had found the Heart of the Bison. It has been documented there was a trap to capture our entire leadership in one move.
>
> Everything possible is being done to locate them. I am afraid we have to assume the worst.
>
> We have the names of the conspirators, but they are not communicating. We should assume they have joined with the Sun People, and they will give the Sun People all of the information they need to invade our caves and subjugate or kill all of our people.
>
> Therefore, as leader of the Minority Party, I have taken several actions to deal with the current emergency. I have only done what is absolutely necessary to ensure our safety until we can install a new government according to the principles of the Republic.
>
> I have ordered all entrance codes changed. I am initiating our Sun People destabilization plans to deflect Sun

People away from our people. I have declared Garret Chambers and several of his colleagues to be enemies of the Republic. Should they ever fall into our hands, they will be tried and dealt with as traitors.

This interim government will deal with these emergency situations. When things have been stabilized, elections should be scheduled to rebuild the Republican government as outlined in the *Wisdom Skins*.

It is truly unfortunate Earth People have been put into these desperate measures by the treachery of our own people. However, we are not caught totally unprepared. Some important provisions have been made. I will now explain some details of our plans.

Always, when the Earth People have been threatened with extinction, there has been someone to lead them through times of peril. When Earth People were on the verge of extinction, Kectu gave us the Spirit Fire and the Heart of the Bison for our protection. When the Sun People began to systematically kill off all Earth People, a great leader, Rodlu, came to save the Earth People and help hide them from the Sun People.

Now the Earth People are threatened again. This time, our own people have betrayed us. Now the Sun People will once again seek to destroy the Earth People.

I recognized the potential for this danger many years ago. Those who should protect all Earth People did not heed my warnings at the Council meetings. These leaders have now followed wild stories about the discovery of the Heart of the Bison and have placed themselves in the hands of our enemies.

Over the past years, I have fought in the councils of government for more realistic preparation for the inevitable conflict with the Sun People. It has been a frustrating battle. However, I made secret preparations to protect Earth People. It is precisely because of these preparations there is now hope for Earth People.

I have put in place a network of Watchers who are prepared to turn the violent nature of Sun People against themselves. I have already set in motion a series of events that will cascade into a worldwide terrorist conflagration that will deflect all interest from Earth People.

Sun People will turn their high-powered weapons of destruction against themselves until their ability to provide government and order will be destroyed. When that happens, Earth People Watchers will be positioned to take control. Then Earth People will rule all Sun People according to the precepts of the *Wisdom Skins*. Then Earth People will be safe forever, and war will cease to exist on Mother Earth.

Now everyone must support the interim emergency government. For the next several months, all our attention and resources must be directed at implementing our emergency plan so Sun People governments will not be able to act against the Earth People.

As soon as the security of the Republic is assured, elections should be organized to establish a permanent government. I personally have no plans to run in an election. I only step in now because of my familiarity with the plans to protect the Republic.

Thank you all for your support and faith in me and those who work with me as we confront these perilous times.

Ronaldo turned the communicator off. "I know Solero," Ronaldo said. "His foremost goal has always been to rule. If his plan works, he will find an excuse to postpone elections indefinitely."

"What do we do now?" Sandi asked.

"Just make an announcement the government is back," Garret suggested.

"It will not be that easy," Ronaldo said. "If I just walk in now, there will be chaos and confusion. We do not know how much control he has over his war plans or what possible contingencies he could implement. We must totally compromise his plot without alerting him. I have access to the complete details of his plan. I have already made arrangements to convey the plan to my Sun People contact. In the next few days, those who have sided with Solero will begin to realize his plans have collapsed. I will take advantage of that confusion to turn his people against him. Then I will be in a position to take control and have Solero and his coconspirators arrested."

"What about Marc?" Sandi asked.

"I cannot get to him until I have wrested control from Solero. Solero must believe we are all still trapped in the Heart of the Bison. As long as he believes that, he will suspect a traitor in his own organization as his plan begins to fail. This will add to his confusion and make my work easier. Marc will be a great hero among my people."

"And what if the terrorists kill him while you are working your plans?" Sandi asked.

"I do not know this man very well," Ronaldo said. "Though he is a warrior, I like him. You know him better than I. If the choice were left to him to die and stop Solero or save himself and let Solero lead terrorists to use weapons that could kill most of the population of the world, what would he choose?"

Sandi thought about Marc and the things he had told her about Mogadishu, and she realized that he would always choose to stay and fight if the cause was right.

"Are those the only choices?" Garret asked.

"I do not know of any way to save him without tipping Solero off," Ronaldo said. "Marc has ammunition and guns. He knows how to use them. The terrorists have only one way in. They can only come one at a time. I do not think Marc is in any grave danger for the next few days."

"Marc was crushed when he was called out of Mogadishu. He could not face himself if he were pulled out now. If he had a choice, he would choose to help Ronaldo," Sandi said to Garret. "What do we do now?" she asked Ronaldo.

"You must stay hidden until I have secured the government," Ronaldo said. "I may need your help, and I will call on you if I do."

Three—August 2003

Sandi spent the next day alone in a room studying various writings of Sotif and feeling useless. The more she read, the more she was amazed at the depth of the Neandertal culture. In many ways, it was as foreign to her as aliens from another planet would be. The ceremonies dated from Stone Age thinking, which did not seem to allow for changes, and yet the Earth People had made significant changes. The whole breeding program was different. But how much real change was there? It was disconcerting that Garret had refused to eat with Marc and Akhtar. She wondered if there was any hope at all that she could make a happy life with him.

Someone knocked on her door. "Come in," she said.

Garret came in. "Solero is sending poisonous gases to the terrorists at the Heart of the Bison. They are going to gas everyone there so they can make sure Ronaldo can never get out."

"How do you know this?" Sandi asked.

"I know people who know people," Garret said.

"What can we do?" Sandi asked.

"I have arranged for an EMF. I have connections. Solero is using conventional methods to deliver the poison. He has a head start, but we can move faster."

"We?" Sandi asked.

"Someone has to swim in to warn Marc and take air tanks to him and Akhtar. I do not know anyone who can swim well enough to get into the cave except you."

"What about you? You got through when you came to save me," Sandi said.

"I am going to have to drop you off. I must handle another problem near Lake Baikal. Believe me, I would handle this if I could."

"And what am I supposed to do?" Sandi asked.

"There are still some air tanks inside the cave near the water entrance. You must swim in and take air tanks to Marc and Akhtar so they will be able to breathe when the gas is dropped in."

"That is it?"

"I do not know any other way," Garret answered.

"What does Ronaldo say?"

"I do not have time to make contact with him. I am going to use my own connections. Rule Seven."

"Why are you doing this?" Sandi asked.

"Come on. We can talk on the way."

Even though Solero thought Garret was trapped in the Heart of the Bison, he had put his picture and notices out to detain him in order to make the people feel the threat that he could be leading Sun People to the entrances. After much secret travel from one place to another, they were finally on the EMF. Although it had seemed like a lot of time, less than two hours had passed.

When they released the handles of the mass-compensating chairs after takeoff, Sandi asked Garret again why he wanted to risk so much to save Marc.

"There are actually three reasons," Garret said in answer to her question. "Reason three, if the terrorists gas Marc and then go in, they will find that Ronaldo has escaped from the Heart of the Bison. That could be bad for Ronaldo. Reason two, I like Marc. He has risked his life for this cause. I do not want him to die like that." Garret was silent.

"And reason one?" Sandi encouraged.

"You told me you love me," Garret began. "A lot has happened since then, and a lot was happening at the time. I know Marc has strong feelings for you, and I suspect, before all of this happened, you had some feelings for him. When this is all over, if you decide to be with me, I want to make sure your decision is made with all options open to you. I do not want you to ever have to wonder, what if?"

"Which reason is most important?"

"You are," Garret said without hesitation. "But for all those reasons, what we are doing is vitally important. We are going considerably faster now than on that first trip, and we are taking the shortcut over Russia. We will be there in about forty minutes."

Sandi thought about the first trip when they had escaped from the first terrorists. Was it this lifetime? So much had happened. Could it be true that she had finally found the right man for her, and he was a Neandertal? The thought made her laugh under her breath.

Chapter 7

Home

One—August 2003

As they flew to their destination, Garret seemed consumed with problems. Sandi watched him as he met with the other members of the group. He had been faced with a very important decision—to wait for direction or risk acting on his own. He had decided to act to save Marc, partly so she would be able to choose freely. She ticked off all the qualities she wanted in a man, and Garret met every one of them.

While she waited, Sandi picked up a volume of the *Wisdom Skins*. She found the section on the Points of Law and began studying them. Point Four on the trap of war was particularly interesting. Then Sandi moved to Point Five. She could hardly believe what she was reading! It was clear and plain, but if it were true, Garret had lied to her! Not just a small lie—Garret had lied about the very basis of a relationship with him!

"Hold onto the handles," Garret said. "We are about to decelerate."

Once again, Sandi held the handles and squeezed. When the release light came on, Sandi let go. She was about to ask Garret to explain Point Five when the pilot broke in. "We have got real trouble."

"What is it?" Garret asked.

"We are in surveillance range of the target area. There are trucks unloading fifty-five-gallon drums. Our instruments detect a powerful nerve gas. They are moving them up the side of the hill to the opening of the cave right now. We may be too late."

"Can we stun them?" Garret asked.

"No, the camp is too big, and they have shoulder rockets that could mess up our controls."

"Quick, get us to the entrance!" Garret said.

"Garret, I need to know about Point Five," Sandi said.

Garret looked like a rabbit caught in a spotlight for a second. "Sandi, this is not the time. Listen to me. You must get into the cave as quickly as possible. There is scuba gear near the pool inside the cave. When you get in, put a wet suit on. If they are using nerve gas, it can get through your skin. Put the wet suit on and use the face mask. Then take two suits and masks to Marc and Akhtar. Go as quickly as you can. You take one set of air tanks. You will all have to share coming out."

"It is too far," Sandi said.

"You start calling for them as soon as you get in. They will hear you and start from the other direction. The gas will be behind them. You can do it! You have to do it."

"But Point Five," Sandi said.

"No time now." Garret grabbed her and pulled her into the gravity beam. When she and Garret reached the ground, they were alone. "What happened to the Americans who got us out?" Sandi asked. "I thought they would still be here."

"They had to leave to avoid complications with the Pakistani government. It is up to you, Sandi!" Garret said as he nudged her to the water. "Get him out and get yourself out. Do not take any chances."

"What do we do when we get out?"

"I have to secure some things at Sotif City. You hide and wait here. I will be back before long."

Sandi took a deep breath and dove into the water. It was shockingly cold. As she swam and pulled herself through the watery tunnel almost in a panic, she could see the divers had done a lot of work to open the tunnel for their equipment. When her head broke from the water, she took a deep breath. The air seemed clean. She swam to the shore and found the suits. The area around the entrance and the tunnels was still lit with the LED lights they had left connected to batteries. It was a struggle to get the tight-fitting suit on. Sandi strapped an air tank to her back and grabbed two more full suits. She started running down the tunnel with her flashlight. Breathing and running with the air tank was difficult. She took the mask and respirator off her face and ran as quickly as she could, shouting for Marc every ten or fifteen steps.

Suddenly, she heard gunfire. She put the mask back on and began breathing through the respirator again. When she reached the Heart of the Bison, she took a deep breath, pulled the respirator out, and screamed, "Marc! Marc! This is Sandi! Where are you?" Then she put the respirator back on to breathe in.

Someone walked toward her. He was wearing a wet suit with goggles and a mask. He took the respirator out of his mouth. "They have dropped some kind of gas. Don't breathe the air." It was Marc. "How did you get here?"

"It is a long story." Sandi breathed in through her respirator and took it out to speak. "There is an EMF waiting. What is going on?"

"Well, I thought that they might try something like this, so I had Akhtar go back and get us a couple of air tanks and suits. It's a good thing I did. A few minutes ago, they dropped several drums of something. They followed it down. I shot them." Marc breathed in through the respirator as he talked. "They must have been surprised that someone was still alive. They just dropped a couple of more tanks." He pointed to the center of the Heart of the Bison. There was a rope hanging from the ceiling, and two bodies dressed in some kind of safety gear were on the floor at the bottom of the rope. There were six drums that were blown open near the bodies.

"They're gassing everything up pretty good," Marc said.

"There is no telling what different kinds of gas they will be dropping," Sandi said. "We should go. Garret will be waiting."

"Look!" Marc shouted.

Sandi saw the rope moving. Then a man's legs appeared from the ceiling. He slid down tentatively. When he cleared the opening, he slid rapidly down until he was just above the floor. He was wearing an environmental suit. Almost the second his descent stopped, there was a loud explosion in Sandi's ears, and the man fell to the floor in a heap. Akhtar stood with a smoking gun ten feet from Sandi.

"I don't think these suits will protect us very long. Let's get out of here," Marc said.

As they hurried down the tunnel, Marc pulled his mask off and dropped his air tanks. "The poison has not had time to get this far."

Sandi dropped her tank and mask, too. "What's going on in the real world?" Marc asked as they jogged down the tunnel.

"Solero gave the signal to start the terrorist attacks, but Ronaldo gave enough information to his contacts in the United States military to stop everything. I cannot tell if Ronaldo or Solero is running the dy-emeralite world."

"So, Ronaldo really is connected?" Marc said incredulously. "Imagine a whole culture and civilization, and our intelligence people have known about it and kept it secret. That just blows my mind."

"If you believe Ronaldo, they do not know about the culture or the dy-emeralite cities. They just think the Earth People are aliens, and maybe they are. I do not know whom to believe about anything anymore," Sandi said.

"Well, aren't you the cynical one all of a sudden?"

"As soon as I think I have found someone I can trust, it turns out that he is a liar. If he will lie about one thing, he will lie about everything."

"What're you talking about?"

"Garret has been lying to me all along."

"Well, he's a Watcher, isn't he?" Marc said. "That sort of implies living a lie."

"That is different," Sandi said. "They do all of that with the fine art of deception. He flat-out lied to me about us."

"How so?" Marc asked.

"I told him how important it is for me to have a normal life."

"You must know that life with a Watcher can't be normal. It's living with a spy," Marc said.

"Of course, I know that, and we talked about it. He told me we could be married and have children of our own. He even told me the DNA difference is so small no one could ever tell they were half Neandertal. He said other Watchers have already married and had children in our world."

"And so?" Marc said.

"I have studied their law. It is absolutely forbidden for any one of their people to ever have children with one of our people. There are no exceptions."

"What does Garret say about that?" Marc asked.

"I only discovered that little problem as we were on our way here. He has not said anything yet."

"Garret doesn't always tell everything that's going on, but he hasn't lied to us so far."

"What? Are you taking his side now?"

"I've had a lot of time to think. I went back to the History Room. I read some of the books they brought. This is archeology in a whole new paradigm. This is science on a whole new level."

"What are you getting at?"

"When this is over, I don't think that I want to go back to my old life. I've been seriously thinking about staying in the dy-emeralite cities and working with their scientists."

Sandi stopped. "Are you crazy?"

"Maybe. But I've never thought about marrying one of them," Marc said dryly.

"Enough talk." Sandi picked up her pace down the tunnel.

"There is something else I have been thinking about," Marc said as he caught up with her. She did not slow her pace.

"Well, are you going to tell me?" Sandi finally asked.

"It's going to sound crazy," Marc said. "But you just said that Garret told you that other Watchers have married and have had children. Did he say when that started?"

"What difference would anything he says make? It is all a lie, anyway."

"Maybe it is partly true. I mean, you didn't read anything that said Neandertal Watchers couldn't have children with other Neandertal Watchers, did you?"

"I got the impression there are Watchers with children in some places," Sandi answered in a bored tone.

"Hm," Marc said.

"Hm, what?" Sandi asked.

"Well, I've been thinking that the Earth People have some unexplainable connection to the Earth. They predict weather and earthquakes. Have you ever been in an earthquake?" Marc asked.

"No," Sandi said. "Where is all of this leading?"

"I suppose their ability to predict earthquakes must come from some close connection to the Earth itself. Something like your ability to know if rocks are in the right place ... an unexplainable sense of the Earth."

"Maybe there is such a sixth sense, but I have never seen them predict an earthquake," Sandi said. "They could be lying about that, too. Do you not think so?"

"Everybody I know would say, 'Don't you think so.' You never use contractions."

"Is there some rule of English that says you *have* to use contractions?" Sandi asked defensively.

"No," Marc answered. "I just wonder why you never do."

"You already know why. It is a rare form of dyslexia. And what does my condition have to do with the Neandertals' connection to the Earth? What has it got to do with anything?" Sandi could feel herself getting angry, but she didn't know why.

"Well, you are the first person I've ever heard of having contraction dyslexia," Marc said.

"Maybe if you had been dropped on your head out of a moving car when you were a baby, you would have a better understanding. Come on, we are almost there."

"I wonder if they drop all Earth People on their heads when they're babies."

Sandi stopped short. "What?" she almost whispered.

"Well, your dyslexia is very rare among Cro-Magnons, but I don't know if you've noticed … Garret, Ronaldo, and every other Neandertal I have spoken with have it."

It seemed Sandi's heart was in her throat. She turned to Marc and tried to say something, but no noise came out. Marc looked back and nodded.

"Impossible!" Sandi heard herself shout. "My birth certificate is totally in order. It is certified. I knew all my grandparents. Our family goes back for generations. This is crazy!"

"You're probably right, but then, if you were one of them, Garret would not have lied about getting married and having children."

"It is not only crazy," Sandi said, "it is foolish. Let us get out of here before the poison gas does any more damage to your brain."

"Right," Marc said. "*Let's* get out of here." He put a large accent on the contraction. Sandi did not answer, but the contraction echoed in her mind.

Sandi did not want to talk about Marc's stupid idea, so she remained silent as she, Marc, and Akhtar hid in the small cave near the springs that came from the cave.

"Should we be waiting here?" Akhtar said. "They'll find we've left the Heart of the Bison, and they'll be coming down the cavern and around the hills."

"Well, I don't think that they'll be sending anyone down the rope soon. They know that we have guns and that we have some kind of protection from the gases. They'll wait awhile. But if Garret doesn't show up pretty soon, we'll have to get out of here," Marc added.

"Garret will be here," Sandi said.

"Well, I hope sooner than later," Marc said.

Garret and the EMF arrived a few minutes later. On the flight back, Sandi tried to ignore Garret, but she found her gaze continuously drifting back to him. He was in a serious conversation with two other men. They were listening to a communicator and talking animatedly. Occasionally, Garret glanced over and smiled at her. His smile was so disarming; it made her heart beat faster.

Marc was crazy to think she was one of them. If she were so different, surely, she would have noticed something. And what about her family? Garret had said Watchers having children was a recent thing. Sandi had parents and grandparents. What did Garret mean by *recently*? Could her father and mother be Watchers? No, that was impossible. There would be no reason to keep her in the dark about that, and they take annual trips to the cave world.

All the way back, Sandi thought about her life. Her childhood had been normal. She had had her share of friends, and generally, she had gotten along with everyone. She had been a little better than average in academic classes. She was a tomboy, but not to any extent that made her stand out. She could not be a Watcher and not know it. Surely, a Watcher would have to know it from a young age. There would be special training and preparation. Her parents could not be Watchers. They never took annual trips to the dy-emeralite world or anywhere else, except the annual trip to Vernal, Utah. She always went with them. There was no dy-emeralite world there.

"We made it back in time," Garret said as they disembarked from the EMF at the Banks station.

"In time for what?" Marc asked.

"When Ronaldo got my message, the terrorists were going to use poison gas to invade the Heart of the Bison, he realized his time was running out. He had been working in secret to regain control of the news, the police force, and the media. Solero had infiltrated everywhere. Ronaldo was able to step up his timetable. Solero has been arrested. There have been mass arrests at all levels. There will be a lot of investigation and more arrests, but Ronaldo is in charge now. He will be making a speech to the whole country in about five minutes. We can listen to it in the lunchroom."

"Then the terrorist war is over?" Marc asked.

"Solero's war is over before it even began," Garret said as he led them to a room that was already full of Earth People. "The Sun People war with terrorism has not changed. However, the information Ronaldo gave to the US government will eliminate all of Solero's contacts. The weapons of mass destruction Solero had helped them to amass will also be quietly destroyed."

"Then you could announce to the world what you have done," Sandi said. "It seems now would be a good time to reunite Earth People and Sun People to make a safer world."

"No," Garret said. "The Sun People are in a war. Now is not a good time for Earth People to make a decision to join one side or the other. Earth People cannot participate in the Sun People war. It is a trap."

"But you already did," Sandi said. "You passed information to help us capture and disarm some of the terrorists."

"No. All we did is undo what Solero started. That is more than some of our scholars wanted to do, but we had to undo our participation. Now that has been done, and we have to drop out."

"What about the contacts you have in the US military?" Sandi asked.

"These contacts were originally established to help hide our existence," Garret said. "We maintain them solely to keep our existence secret. We have no intention of telling them who we really are until we see they have escaped the trap of war."

"What about things *you* said to me that are untrue?" Sandi asked. "And what things do you have no intention of telling me to keep me in the dark?"

"Point Five?" Garret asked.

"Exactly," Sandi answered. She watched his face closely, but it revealed nothing.

"I will explain it all after Ronaldo's speech," Garret said.

There was always something more important than the explanation Sandi needed. Garret's face appeared open and confident. Sandi could not help thinking that whatever his explanation was, he was sure that he would be able to convince her again. *Not this time*, she thought.

Ronaldo's voice came through the communicator.

> We have been through a very trying and dangerous time. The *Wisdom Skins* and the *History Skins* have been challenged. Those who want to put the laws of the *Wisdom Skins* aside have claimed Sotif made up the stories of the Alliance so he could control the Earth People. These people have said there is no History Room in the Heart of the Bison. They say Kectu and the Spirit Fire gave Earth People the power to survive, and no Alliance was needed. They say the Points of law of the *Wisdom Skins* do not apply to Earth People in today's world.
>
> Solero has led this faction, intending to put aside all the teachings of Sotif and create new teachings. Solero has already violated Point Four and has attempted to involve Earth People in the trap of war. Fortunately, Solero and his people have been found out and arrested.
>
> In the time of extinction of the Earth People, a Sun People holy man came to help unite Earth People and Sun People in the great Alliance. He was the Guardian. In the times of the warmonger, a Sun People warrior came to the aid of Earth People and saved the Spirit Fire. He was Small Beaver.
>
> Now in our time, another great Sun People warrior has come to aid Earth People. He is called Marc Metcalf. He

fought the terrorists Solero sent to kill me and the rest of the Council. Marc will always be remembered, as the Guardian and Small Beaver are remembered.

It was partly with Marc's help that Earth People have found the Heart of the Bison and the History Room. The Heart of the Bison and the History Room are exactly as Sotif's writings say. The Spirit Fire has been returned to the Heart of the Bison and burns there now.

Ronaldo paused, letting that sink in.

The ancient History Room has been opened to the Earth People again. Several Earth People played important roles in the discovery of the Heart of the Bison. All these people will be honored in a celebration in three months.

Information sheets are being prepared to give details and explanations. All the information will be available in four hours and will be posted to our intranet web pages. For now, we are working on plans to tunnel into the Heart of the Bison to restore it and the History Room. This is a great time for all Earth People. I am happy and privileged to live in this day of discovery and fulfillment of prophesy. Thank you all for your continued support.

"How about an explanation now?" Sandi demanded. She was only vaguely aware of the things Ronaldo had said. Her mind was elsewhere.
"Come with me," Garret said.
"Whatever you say to me, I want Marc to hear," Sandi said.
Garret considered the request. He seemed to be experiencing some inner conflict. "Okay," he finally said.
Garret led them to small office off the lunchroom. It had a wooden desk with a communicator and a computer screen on it. There were no

windows, and the walls were made of softly glowing dy-emeralite. Sandi felt an inexplicable chill seeing the mixture of her world and Garret's in the office. Sandi picked a blue chair on one wall and sat down. She watched Garret but said nothing.

Marc sat in a chair next to Sandi, and Garret pulled the chair from behind the desk and placed it about six feet in front of them. "Okay, Sandi, what do you want to know?"

Sandi was sure she was about to find out something, but it all seemed so normal and casual. Would all of this be another lie? How would she ever know? "Tell me about Point Five," she said.

"Point Five of our law sets down rules for mating. These are the rules that direct us on how to use the basic laws of nature to develop and improve skills and characteristics that are important for our survival. I suppose the most important part of the law, as far as you are concerned, is where it says no Earth Person must ever mate with a Sun Person and produce offspring."

"Offspring ... kind of a cold word, would you not agree?" Sandi said. She was not going to make this easy.

"I did not make the word up," Garret answered.

"What if one of your people breaks the law and has a half-breed child?" Sandi asked so Marc could hear the answer.

"You have read the *Wisdom Skins*," Garret said. "You already know the answer."

"The child would have to be killed," Sandi said to Marc.

"That's barbaric," Marc said. "It's not the child's fault."

"Perhaps you are right," Garret said. "It all depends upon what the definition of what life is and what is valuable life. But Sun People are in no position to judge Earth People in this regard."

"What do you mean?" Marc asked.

"Sun People have a long history of setting out to kill other Sun People. When they decide to do it, they just invent a new definition of human life and then proceed to kill those who are not included in their new definition."

"What are you talking about?" Sandi asked.

"Let me give you some modern examples," Garret said. "The United States entered World War II after the Japanese attacked Pearl Harbor. They sent an army to the Pacific Theater to kill the Japanese, but they did not kill Japanese people. No, they went there to kill 'japs.' In Europe, they killed 'krauts.' In Vietnam, your soldiers killed 'gooks,' and now they fight 'terrorists.' When the terrorists kill you, they are killing 'infidels.' When Hitler killed, it was Jews. You make it easier to kill one another by creating dehumanizing names."

"The fact that we have to invent dehumanizing names to make it easier to fight a war may be just because we have a reverence for life," Sandi argued. "At least we are not killing innocent children."

"I have one word to answer that," Garret said.

"What?" Marc asked.

"Fetus," Garret said. The silence hung in the air.

Finally, Sandi said, "No, wait just a minute. A fetus is not a human being. It is just … a … a fetus. It is potential to be human, but not human."

"It is not human?" Garret asked incredulously. "You can examine the DNA in great detail. It is not a frog. It is human, and it is alive."

"No," Sandi said. "It does not have arms and legs. It does not have feelings and thought. It is not human yet."

"Of course, it has arms and legs. The second the DNA is complete in the fertilized egg; the arms and legs are there in the code. As soon as the fertilized egg leaves the fallopian tube, it searches for the wall of the uterus, and as soon as it finds it, it attaches. If it is not fertilized, it does not search for or attach to the wall of the uterus. The unfertilized egg has no ability to think or feel. There is a drive in the fertilized egg to find nourishment. That shows thoughts and feelings on a cellular level … thoughts and feelings that are totally appropriate for a human at that stage of development. Although the thoughts and feelings of a newborn may be incomprehensible to an adult, they are totally appropriate for the newborn. When does a human fetus become a human being and gain the right to life? Answer me that."

"I do not know," Sandi said. "Some say the first trimester, some say later."

"The reason Sun People cannot come to an agreement about when the fetus crosses over from potentially to actually being human is because there is no scientific or scriptural basis to measure such a change. Why? Because there is *no* dividing line. There is only one reason to pretend there is a dividing line."

"What is that?" Sandi asked.

"It is obvious," Garret answered. "Those who set the line between prehumen and human want to kill those humans who are on the downside of their arbitrary line. There is no other reason. The truly pathetic thing is you let those whose agenda is to kill the developing human be the ones to define and set the dividing line. If a man is accused of murder, and the punishment for his crime is execution, what standard does your government have to meet before the man is killed?"

"What are you getting at?" Sandi asked.

"The government has to prove beyond a reasonable doubt the man is guilty. The small human you want to kill is only guilty of being accused of not being human. It would be consistent with your sense of justice to require proof beyond reasonable doubt that a fetus is really not human before you kill him or her. You cannot prove the existence of the imaginary line between human and prehumen. You cannot even agree where it is. At least Hitler had a very easily defined line. But just because his line was legal and politically correct in his circles did not make it right. And just because, among Sun People, taking the life of an unborn child is legal and politically correct does not make it right."

"What about a woman's right to choose?" Sandi asked.

"All the woman is choosing is to get rid of an inconvenience in her life. But that is not fair to the rest of the people. What about a man who finds being married to a woman is inconvenient? If a woman can get rid of an inconvenient unborn child by killing it, why cannot a man do the same with an inconvenient wife?"

"That is silly," Sandi said. "You are twisting everything. What about the child? It is not fair to put it in a world where it is not wanted."

"Why not give the child a chance to find someone who wants it? Why not let it live until about two years old? Then, if no one wants it, you could very humanely put the child to sleep. As it is, many abortions are brutal, prolonged deaths for the unfortunate victim. Also, you would have the benefit of being able to harvest many organs that would save lives and alleviate pain and suffering. Since the determination of when a developing human actually becomes human is totally arbitrary, you could just arbitrarily set that dividing line at two years old. It looks different than an adult. It does not think and feel in the mature way of an adult human being. It is not a change in concept ... only a change in application of the existing concept.

"And that is where we are. We decide the child is a half-breed, and that is how we define human life ... theoretically."

"What do you mean *theoretically?*" Sandi asked.

"Sun People who have lived on the surface of the Earth focus on the right of the individual woman to choose. Earth People, who live in caves, focus on the right of society, as a whole, to choose. Sun People have killed millions and millions of unborn children. ...excuse me, *fetuses* ... based upon an arbitrary definition of life. Earth People have a law to kill a half-breed. However, that law has never been implemented, and there is some serious doubt it ever would be, and if it were ever implemented, it would be done through abortion, anyway. So, Sun People have a law that has been used to kill tens of millions of unborn children, and we have a law that has not been used. Who is the monster?"

"But if we were married, and I got pregnant with your child, your society would kill it. That is where you lied to me. You said we could get married and have children and live a somewhat normal life."

"I did not lie to you at anytime. We can have a normal life with our own children."

"How?" Sandi asked. "I do not see exceptions to Point Five."

"Let me make a call first, and then I will explain," Garret said.

Marc and Sandi stepped out of the office. "So, what do you think now?" she said to Marc.

"Well, this is a strange turn of events. I guess that I'm going to have to rethink my stand on abortion."

"That's not what I'm talking about, and you know it!"

"I know. Garret said that there is some doubt whether the law would be enforced. So, I wonder how that works. Maybe he can get some kind of dispensation on Point Five."

Garret was gone about ten minutes. "Years ago, there was couple in Englewood, Colorado," Garret began when he returned.

"I have been through Englewood a thousand times," Sandi said. "It is like a suburb of Denver. What has that got to do with anything?"

"This man and woman were both Watchers," Garret continued, ignoring her question. "In the late sixties, Denver was experiencing a lot of tremors related to subsidence caused by pumping oil from deep reservoirs. The man worked for a company that specialized in drilling deep wells to pump water into the oil aquifers to stabilize them as the oil was being removed. In 1974, they had a baby girl."

"That is the year I was born," Sandi said. "But my parents had nothing to do with drilling, and I was born in California."

"This baby was born as part of a program to create second-generation Watchers," Garret continued, unfazed by her comment. "When the baby was six weeks old, the parents took her to Rodlu City. Since 1968, all Earth People children have come to Rodlu City for a special ceremony. As part of the ceremony, a DNA sample is taken and put on file."

"Why?" Marc asked.

"In the mid-1950s, our Thinkers concluded it would be possible to map out the entire genome for humans. Quite ironically, they succeeded in 1962, the year Watson and Crick got the Nobel Prize for discovering the double helix model. In 1963, our Thinkers began work on changing DNA in plants to develop hybrids to grow in special underground gardens with artificial light. In 1965, they concluded they could improve on Earth People breeding by manipulating DNA directly. Starting that year, they began collecting DNA from all Earth People. In 1967, they began the ceremony to collect DNA from new babies. The DNA goes into data banks, where it is analyzed to determine DNA patterns for attributes our people want to develop.

"After the ceremony, the family headed back to Denver with their daughter. On the road from Salt Lake City to Denver, they had a terrible accident just outside of Vernal, Utah. They ran off the road, and by the time the accident was discovered, coyotes had partially eaten the man and woman and had apparently carried the baby's body off someplace to eat it.

"We were able to provide papers and claim the bodies of the parents. It was a sad thing we were unable to find the body of the baby. It is our religion that each person must be cremated when they die so their ashes can be mixed in the Spirit Fire. It is almost like being baptized for a Christian ... it is sort of our ticket to heaven. You can understand how devastating it was to those who knew and loved her parents when they could not find the body of the baby.

"Although there are several Watchers who have had children, they are all accounted for. You can imagine our surprise when, one day, we found an adult Earth People woman totally embedded, but not on any of our records."

Sandi was struck dumb. She just stared at Garret's eyes.

"Samples of the woman's DNA showed she is the missing baby, without a doubt. She was not killed. Somehow, someone found her and raised her."

"No!" Sandi shouted. "This is just another lie! You are like a water faucet gone wild. You change from hot to cold practically every time we meet."

"I am sorry about that. It is a perception, but my feelings have been rather constant."

"How is that?"

"It started when you followed Jektu and me into the forest. I really admired you for your courage. You are a very beautiful and charming woman. The time we spent walking alone through the forest began to win me over. Then when we lit the ceremony cavern, I had to pull you by the hand to the altar. As we stood there, I relaxed my grip, but we still held hands. It was a very emotional time. Then you started squeezing my hand so hard it was painful. Something happened … you let go and our hands dropped. When you let go, I knew the emotions I was feeling had as much to do with you as with the cavern. But then, there was the complication of Point Five. So, I tried to pull away. But that was not so easy with all the events that pushed us together. I knew a relationship with you was out of the question, so I tried to smother my feelings. Then I noticed how you talk, and so I got some DNA from your room in Rodlu City. But then I could not get it tested because everyone said it was impossible for you to be Earth People. When we were trapped in the cave overnight, holding each other to stay warm, I knew I was hopelessly in love. I was hoping I could get permission to have a life with you because of all you had done to find the Heart of the Bison. When I talked to Ronaldo, he was totally against it. But as we talked about how you talk and the fact that you picked up on the Earth People language so quickly, he agreed to okay the DNA test. When I called to inform him we had opened the History Room, he gave me the results of the DNA test. Then I knew we could be together. That is when I invited you to eat with me.

Until that time, I could not allow anything physical to happen, not even a kiss. So, whenever a possibility of that kind of closeness happened, I pulled away. That night in the cave, I had to hold you to warm you. I so much wanted more."

"So why did you not tell me all this in the cave when you invited me to eat?"

"I knew you would have to know, and I knew it would not be easy for you to accept. There was just too much other stuff going on at that time."

"You are so clever with your asinine arguments and stories. I want to go back to my world! I will not stay in a world of baby killers."

"That is not fair," Garret said. "Please think about this."

"Do not talk to me." Sandi turned to Marc. "Do not let him talk to me anymore."

"Sandi," Garret said.

Marc stepped between Garret and Sandi. "You said that you would let her go. You're going to have to give her some time. Maybe even time away from here."

"You have to talk to her," he said to Marc. The resignation in his voice was deep.

"Tell him there is nothing any of you can do," Sandi said to Marc.

"Are you sure that you are ready to make a complete break?" Marc asked.

"There is nothing anyone can say! All of a sudden, out of nowhere, he is trying to make me think I am a Neandertal and my parents are not my parents. No way can that be true! And suddenly he tries to play on my emotions by claiming he has been in love with me all of this time." Sandi pounded the table and stood up. "I cannot trust a thing these people say. I do not believe in any war threat. It has all been smoke and mirrors." She turned to Garret. "This breeding program is pure nonsense, especially for Watchers. And you all think you can just sit in comfy little caves until Sun People suddenly discover peace. You are all as crazy as loons. You are going to have to put your pants on and *do something*!" Sandi paced and let all the built-up anger and frustration flow. Then she spoke in a calmer voice. "Maybe Solero was right ... not about war, but maybe it is time to take a serious look at the information in the so-called *Wisdom Skins* and think about making some changes." Then she turned back to Marc. "Just listen to me ... talking as if any of this is true. I do not need any of this crap! I just want to get back to something normal. I do not ever want to come back here, wherever *here* is."

"Well, I don't that think there's anything you can do about this," Marc said to Garret. "But I'm having second thoughts. I think that I want to stay and work with your scientists."

"It is both or none," Sandi said.

"Well, I don't want to leave," Marc insisted.

"I am not staying. I do not care what either of you say," Sandi said to Marc. "You will just have to leave with me."

"That will not be necessary," Garret said.

"What?" Marc asked.

"We have been doing a lot of work with DNA in the past few weeks. We have had several breakthroughs with the Iceman DNA. DNA is interesting. You can track DNA from daughter to mother through mitochondrial DNA. You can also track men from son to father through the Y chromosome. We have been able to get a genome map of the Iceman that is 96 percent complete. We have been particularly successful with his Y chromosome. Comparing the Iceman DNA, especially the Y, to Marc, our Thinkers have been able to say there is only one chance in several hundred thousand that Marc is not a descendent of the Iceman through an unbroken line of fathers and sons. According to the traditions, Small Beaver was the Iceman's only son. Therefore, Marc is a direct male descendent of Small Beaver."

"Oh, now that is too much!" Marc said.

"You are free to examine all of the evidence. However, our Council is convinced. Therefore, if you want to stay, they will not force you to leave. We owe this to you personally, and we also owe it to your forefathers. Here, the Council has decided this is yours."

Garret handed Marc a small stone dagger point hanging from a leather thong.

"Now what do you think?" Sandi said. "How does it feel to suddenly be genetically part of all of this madness?" Marc looked at her and then at Garret. He tied the thong around his neck without saying anything.

"Get me out of here! You are all crazy!" Sandi shouted.

Two—September 2003

The Denver Daily News

Yesterday was a celebration for the Earl and Jan Hartwell family of Arcadia. After spending months in the hands of terrorists in the Middle East, their daughter, Sandi, was released unharmed. She and members of the archeological team she was working with were attacked by terrorists. Several members of the party were killed at the time of the attack. Sandi and four others were taken hostage. Sandi is one of three of the hostages that were released. No word has been received regarding the whereabouts of the two remaining hostages, Professor Marc Metcalf, the leader of the group, and Garret Chambers. Many fear they may have been killed. Jan was too emotional to grant an interview. Earl thanked all of those who helped negotiate the release of their only child ...

Sandi put the paper down. It had been a joyous day to finally be in her home and back with her family. She, Akhtar, and Kelvin had been dropped off in Pakistan six days ago. The back story had been changed. Marc and Garret were still listed as missing. It was such a relief to see Kelvin. He was weak, but in good physical condition. He was getting better and planned to continue in his career as a paleontologist. Akhtar left to go back to Pakistan two days ago. Sandi had been released to come home the day before.

There had been a lot of debriefing and physical exams. The whole experience was beginning to seem unreal.

Sandi had avoided talking to her parents about her experiences. They were just overjoyed to know she was safe at home.

At breakfast the next day, her mother finally asked, "Did they ... hurt you in any way?" The question was clumsy, but the meaning was clear.

"No, Mother, there was nothing like that. I was treated very well. The group that attacked us was brutal. If I had stayed with them, I am sure something awful would have happened. We were taken by another group that treated us well. The last time I saw Marc, he was in good health and good spirits. I do not think he will be hurt." Tears brimmed in her eyes. "I am not ready to talk anymore about what happened. Just know I was treated well and with respect."

Sandi spent three weeks at home telling her parents only generalities about her time with the terrorists. Her story was crafted so she did not have to lie. She thought constantly of the implications of the story Garret had told her and of the things Marc had alluded to. It had all been too much to believe—flying saucers and aliens in caves. That whole Point Five thing—Garret's people clearly had a law requiring the killing of innocent children. But Garret had turned it all back on abortions, making it seem like she was the one in favor of killing babies—absurd! Then he had tried to turn her life upside down by making her one of them, and he'd even claimed she was not part of her own family. Why did she still have feelings for him? What if it was all true?

It seemed she was constantly being hounded by local and national news reporters wanting to do stories about the terrorists and how she survived. The story she had to tell was crafted and nuanced so she didn't have to tell blatant lies, but it wouldn't stand up to inquisitive reporters looking for a sensational, salacious story.

One morning she came in from a walk. Her mother met her at the door. "Sandi, I got another call from a reporter.

"You know I do not want to talk to a reporter."

"I think you should at least talk to this one; her name is Shari Darling."

"Shari Darling? Why is that name familiar?"

"I thought you might remember it, though you were a teenager involved with school at the time."

"I am still not sure about what, but it is certainly a memorable name."

"Back then, there was a serial killer in Salt Lake City who raped and killed small children. He wrote poems about it."

"Oh yeah, now I remember. The year after it happened, we discussed it in one of my classes. He thought he was greater than God. His poetry was not very good, but some was pretty complicated, with palindromes and acrostics."

"Shari was kidnapped and tortured."

"Yeah … I do not think I want to do any stories about my experience, but I think I will give her a call."

"Hello, Shari Darling."

"Hi ... uhm ... my name is Sandi Hartwell. You called?"

"Ms. Hartwell ... thanks for calling ... I'm a little surprised you called. The reason I called you is that I sort of know what you are going through ... in a way. You see, I was kidnapped and beat up. The man had a giant lens like a magnifying glass, and he was going to use it focus the sun's rays on me to slowly burn me to death."

"I do remember that. I guess that is the reason I called you back. But this more of a curtesy call. I really do not want to talk about the things that happened. I am ready to get on with my life."

"I know that feeling. I'm not quite ready to discuss those things about myself, and it has been many years. I'm writing a book about women who have been through these kinds of traumas, but my focus is their coping mechanisms and steps to getting on with life."

"That is interesting, but I was not mistreated, except for the first hour or so."

"But your experience was difficult. I suppose that is why you have turned down many writers who want to do an in-depth story."

There was something about her tone and the empathy it expressed Sandi. "I was involved with people ... others that were in the situation with me. It is great to be out of it now, but ... well it is not something I want to talk about."

"Of course not. I have been interested in variations of the aftermath of these types of trauma, and I have developed a support group. Members are scattered around the country. Many of them want to remain anonymous, and I honor their wishes. It's early now, but please contact me if you have difficulties adjusting and want someone to talk to."

"I might just do that. I have your number if I decide to join."

"Thank you. I hope to hear from you."

"Thank you. Bye.

"Goodbye."

Sandi hung up the phone. It was a short call with no pressure, but somehow, Sandi felt a connection. What would Ms. Darling think if she knew her problem was that she was in love with a Neandertal who wanted to make her believe she was a Neandertal?

Three—October 2003

Sandi stood in front of the cave. The valley stretched before her, and the river ran as a silver ribbon through the valley. The blue waters of the oxbow pond lay below her. A small group of strange people gathered. An old man was making a fire. Sandi could see that it was hard work. She could not understand why, because there already was a fire. After the new fire was burning, the old man took a baby girl and buried her in the dirt. Then he moved his new fire over the spot where the baby was buried. The old man spoke to the clan in the language of the Ancients. "The spirit of the baby becomes fire. This fire is lucky for the clan. This fire must not burn out. This fire is the spirit of Tid's daughter. This fire will travel to far places. This fire will come back to the cave. This fire brings the peace of Mother Earth." A woman and a young girl ran from the group to a tree. They huddled together and cried for the baby girl. They sadly accepted the beginning of the Spirit Fire.

Sandi woke in a sweat. She had hoped with the defeat of Solero, she would be free of these strange dreams. Then she realized no Sun People were in her dream. She understood the sounds they made as words. Could the dream have been an inherited memory, or had she created it from the stories Sotif had written about the Alliance and the beginning of the Spirit Fire? Or could it be the Spirit Fire telling her about its creation? Then she knew the name of the old man. "Sotak," she said reverently. The name Sotak was not in the writings she had read. Sandi felt she had just woken up in an ancient world threatened by, but by what? "The aurochs," Sandi whispered to herself. A powerful feeling crept in her heart. Somehow, she knew there was something else for her to do—something in the dy-emeralite world. But there was no way to get back; Ronaldo had made that clear when she made her decision.

"What's wrong? You don't look well," her mother said when Sandi entered the kitchen. The smell of freshly brewed coffee was familiar and comforting. That and the sound of her mother's voice brought her back to her world. "What do you want for breakfast?" her mother asked.

"I am not really hungry. I did not sleep very well," Sandi answered.

"Still having nightmares about the terrorists?" her father asked. "The psychologist said you may have them for a long time. Do you want to talk about it?"

"No, it is not that. It … I just did not sleep well. I think … I do not know. Maybe it is school and … you know …"

"If it's not the terrorists, what is it?" her mother asked.

"Have you ever felt like you somehow did not belong?" Sandi asked.

"Where do you think you don't belong?" her father asked.

"I sometimes think I do not belong to my life. Do you know what I mean?"

"Whose life could you belong to?" her mother asked.

"Is this a feeling you have always had or is it something that has come up since you were kidnapped?" her father asked.

"If I am honest, I would have to say I have had similar feelings before, but the feeling is stronger now," Sandi responded.

"You shouldn't worry about it," her mother said. "I'm sure it will go away when things get back to normal." For Sandi's mother, all problems would vanish if they were ignored long enough.

"Sandi, how about you and I going out for an Egg McMuffin?" her father asked.

"Yes," her mother said. "A father-daughter date would be good. You haven't done that in years."

Sandi looked at her father's face, and she could tell he had something he wanted to say.

After they got their order and sat down, Sandi's father started the conversation. "This morning, what did you mean that you don't feel like you belong to your life?"

Sandi decided to just lay it all out. "I meant I do not feel like I belong to your life, or Mom's life."

"I don't think I know what you're getting at."

"I think I was adopted."

"What brought that on?" He had not denied it.

"Was I adopted?"

"The answer to the question is definitely no."

His answer sounded just like something Garret would say when he was trying to deflect the conversation. "Let me rephrase the question. Am I your biological daughter?"

Her father sat silently staring at her, and that told her more than anything he could have said. Sandi let him think about what she had said. Finally, he responded, "I guess I always knew this day would come."

"What day, Dad?"

"Our Sandi was born in San Francisco where I was going to school."

Our Sandi? she thought.

"When she was six weeks old, we decided to take her to Denver to visit my mother and show her off to my family. On the way, we stopped in Salt Lake City for a night, and the next day, we headed east on Intestate 40 toward Denver. We had dinner in Vernal. We thought we could get to Craig, Colorado, before getting a motel for the night. We left Vernal on Highway 40. After we had driven a while, your mother picked Sandi up from a travel crib we had attached to the backseat. When she got her out of the crib, Sandi did not respond. It must have been some kind of crib death, but your mother insisted she was just sleeping."

Sandi could feel her legs beginning to shake.

"I convinced your mother we should take Sandi back to Vernal to see a doctor. On the way back, I saw a car coming from the other direction. All of a sudden, it swerved off the roadway and flew into the desert in a cloud of dust. I did not see any other traffic on the road, so I stopped the car. Your mother and I raced across the highway and out to the car. It was off the road and over a small rise where it was not visible from the highway.

"I went to the vehicle to see if anyone was hurt. The car had rolled over several times. There was no one in it. I found a man and woman nearby. The man was already dead, and the woman was critically injured. She was saying something about a daughter and something about finding her earth people family." Sandi gasped. "I never understood what she meant by earth people. It may have been some kind of hippie commune ... they were still around back then. I promised her I would try to help.

"Your mother came over, and she held the woman's head in her arms. I was going back to the car to get our first aid kit when I heard a baby crying. It was you. You were lying in a blanket in the dirt. It was some kind of miracle that you were not hurt. As I picked you up, your mother, I mean, *Jan*, came over the hill from the wreck."

"Please do not refer to her as Jan. Whatever else may have happened, she has always been Mom to me."

"Thank you," her father said. "Your mother said the woman was dead. When she saw you crying, she said, 'See, I told you Sandi was all right.' She took you from my arms and sat by the side of the road and began to nurse you. I guess you were hungry, because you just settled in.

"I didn't know what to do. Our baby was dead, but there was no way your mother would accept that. You looked a little like Sandi, even though you had more hair.

"Back at the car, your mom changed your diaper and clothes. She did not even notice your birthmark, or if she did, she didn't say anything."

"How did you know about my birthmark?" Sandi asked. It was a dark brown mark in her crotch.

"I changed your diapers and gave you baths hundreds of times when you were a baby. It's a fairly obvious birthmark. But your mother and I never talked about it. I don't know if she just ignored it, or if she was so upset at the time that she just mentally made it part of our Sandi."

"What did you do with your baby?"

"I reported the accident anonymously by phone in Vernal. We spent the night there and left the next day. Our baby was in the back. I didn't know what to do with her. We stopped at a campground near Dinosaur National Monument for lunch. By then, your mother was totally involved with you. I took Sandi, wrapped in your blanket, to a quiet place. I buried her in the park there. I placed some stones to mark the grave."

"How could you dig a hole?" It seemed like a stupid question to Sandi even as she asked it, but all the details seemed important.

"I always carried a shovel in the car. It was a habit I got into growing up in Denver. Many times, I needed a shovel in the winter when my car would get stuck in snow and ice. I gave your mother an excuse that I wanted to take a walk. She didn't notice I took the baby and the shovel. It took me more than an hour to dig the hole deep enough. I spread leaves and branches to disguise the grave but left stone markers that I would recognize should I come back. When I got back to the car, your mother was worried and upset that I had been gone so long." Tears flowed down his face.

"I have carried this terrible secret ever since that day. That tiny baby we had to leave in a makeshift grave is my flesh and blood. There was no one to mourn for her but me."

Sandi's eyes were running, too—not just for the baby, but for her biological parents who had died alone. "So that is why we always took a family vacation to Vernal every year. You always said it was because you were interested in the dinosaurs and the museum there."

"That has always been my private pain. I hired a detective to find the earth people commune, because I'd promised your biological mother I would. She wanted you taken to those earth people. It turned out that all your parents' paperwork was forged. Someone claimed the bodies and took them away. The detective was able to follow the paper trail to Seattle, and then it all disappeared. He couldn't find anything about them or any earth people. The car plates were from Oregon, so he mostly looked in Oregon and around Seattle. The detective told me he thought your parents were illegal aliens or something. I was happy with that result. I don't think I could have given you up.

"I have lived in mortal fear of this day. There was always the chance some blood test or some other medical test would uncover the truth. Now the only thing is to find a way to break this news to your mother. As many years as I have had to try to figure that out, I still do not know how to approach it."

"You do not need to put her through that," Sandi said. "Now I have a story to tell you."

"What?"

Sandi took a couple of moments to gather herself. "I had a whole battery of physical tests done because of what happened with the terrorists. As part of that, some DNA tests were done on my blood. The results went into a data bank. My biological parents' family was monitoring DNA data for medical research they were doing. They discovered my DNA matched the patterns for their family and realized I was related to them. At first, that was very puzzling, because they knew all their family. Then they realized part of their family was missing. One of their brothers and his wife had been killed in an auto accident near Vernal, Utah, in 1974. The baby was missing, but everyone thought it had been carried off and eaten by wild animals.

"Before they said anything to me, they did research on me and my family. They discovered my parents had a baby girl in San Francisco in 1974, but they knew it could not have been me. They thought I must have been mixed up with the other family's baby on the trip through Utah.

"Until they saw my DNA, they all believed I was dead. They brought the evidence to me, but I just could not believe it. The last time I talked to them, I told them they were crazy."

"Now what?" her father asked. He seemed beaten down.

"The people who are my family live mostly in Washington and Oregon. They are happy to have found me, but they are not going to make any kind of demands. What I am saying is there is no reason to tell Mom anything. The secret is completely safe with these people, and there is nothing positive that can be gained by telling Mom anything."

"Are you sure about this?"

"I have gotten to know my biological family well enough to know they will not be making any kind of trouble for us. The only reason I pushed you for answers is because I personally wanted to know. Everything they said was just so unbelievable, but now I see it is true. These people have connections that can make sure it never comes to light. You can stop worrying about that. There is just one thing."

"What?"

"I sort of feel like the baby in the desert is my sister. I would like to go to her grave with you sometime."

Her father hugged her. "Yes, of course," he said. "I don't know how my detective missed finding them. I thought he did thorough research."

"He was right in his assumption. They are illegal aliens. Their ancestry goes back through Europe, but they sneaked in from Russia. They are not Russians, and they have no connection to the Russian government, but they do not want to be found. I could not find them now, even if I wanted to.

"I am happy you and Mom are my parents. My life has been all I could have hoped for. And is it not ironic that my interest in paleontology comes from our trips to Vernal? After all, it was that interest that led me into the situation where my biological family could find me. I guess I owe that to Sandi."

"Hello, this is Shari Darling."

"Hi, this is Sandi Hartwell."

"Sandi, I'm so glad you called."

"I just need to talk to someone, but what I have to say is confidential; it cannot show up in a magazine article or a book."

"Perfectly fine. As I said before, there are several women in my group who want their privacy protected. How can I help you?"

"I cannot tell you details of what happened. Suffice it to say, I was not just sitting around waiting. I was involved in … let us just call it an adventure. This involved other people, and I fell in love with one of them."

"You weren't gone a long time; I mean it probably seemed long, but …"

"I know, but when you are in a situation where your lives depend upon each other, something is built, and it really seems … seems real."

"You're right; my husband and I sort of depended on each other during the serial killer period, and that's when our relationship morphed."

"The feeling was strong and mutual, but then … ohh!"

"It'll be alright."

"He told me something, and I knew it was a lie, and he wanted me to change my whole life for the lie … it felt like it was a condition put on me … I had to believe it or else. So, I made a decision. I left him. And now, I find out it was not a lie … he told me the truth. But I cannot undo my decision."

"But, why not?"

"His life was in the Washington Oregon area, but because of what happened, he has changed his life. He is now in a place I cannot find."

"He knows where you are?"

"Yes, but his new life bans him from coming to me."

"Listen Sandi. If this love is as you say, and he shares it; he will come to you. If he doesn't come; it just was not meant to be."

"Do you really believe that?"

"Yes, I do."

"Well, it gives me something to think about. Thanks."

"I'll check in on you, if that's okay."

"Yes, please do. Thanks. Goodbye."

"Bye for now, Sandi."

If only she could latch onto that hope. She had closed the door permanently, according to Ronaldo. Suddenly, it dawned of her, she was a Neandertal, after all. They would have to reach out to her some time.

Four—October 2003

Sandi loved to jog in the early morning when she could think with a clear mind. Her conversation with her father had given her a lot to think about. She finally knew she belonged to the Earth People, but life in the dy-emeralite cities was impossible for her. However, she would not be able to answer basic questions about herself without reconnecting with that world. If only she knew how to contact them. Garret was primarily interested in the Heart of the Bison; he might never come back to this world. How ironic that the very thing she had helped find would be the barrier that separates them. But if Shari was right, he would surely come. Ronaldo could not keep her out. There were important ceremonies—the ceremony of the ashes, ultimately.

Sandi was running through a small neighborhood park. She sat on park bench to catch her breath. The leaves on the trees had nearly all fallen. Those that were left were brown, no longer showing the bright red, purple, orange, and gold colors of September. It seemed her life had turned brown, and she did not know what to do about it. She saw a patch of grass that was still green. Slowly, she walked over to it and kneeled on one knee. She closed her eyes and laid the palm of her hand on the grass. It was soft, and she imagined she could feel the green and smell wild jasmine. *If only Shari were right*, she thought. She stood up, and, wiping tears with the heels of the hands, she started for home.

Sandi jogged up the steps of her house and went into the kitchen. Her parents were seated at the table eating breakfast with—

"Garret! What are you doing here?" Sandi shouted.

"Having breakfast with your parents," he casually answered.

"He is a very strange man," her mother said. "He insisted we should be already eating when you got home."

Sandi could hardly believe what she was seeing. "Does this mean what I think it does?" Sandi asked.

"Come on, Sandi. Have something to eat," Garret said as he pushed a serving dish full of scrambled eggs to her.

"What are you talking about?" Sandi's mother asked.

Sandi put some of the eggs on her plate and slowly put a fork full into her mouth. Garret also put some eggs in his mouth. They both started chewing while staring at each other.

"Mrs. Hartwell," Garret said. "It means your daughter and I are on the verge of developing a serious relationship."

"Sandi?" her mother asked.

"I, for one, do not know what this means," Sandi said to her mother. To Garret, she said, "I think you should talk to my father about this."

"About what?" her mother exclaimed.

"I can tell you this," Sandi said to her father. "Garret is from Oregon. I think before anyone talks about serious relationships; you should get to know him better. I think a man-to-man talk is the right place to start."

Sandi could see her father had picked up on the hint. "Sandi is right. I think there are some things Garret and I should talk about relative to career, family, and so forth that would best be discussed man-to-man."

"Isn't that just a bit old-fashioned?" Sandi's mother asked.

"It is," Earl said. "Nevertheless …" Earl stood up and motioned to Garret. Both men went to the den.

Sandi calmly helped her mother clean up the breakfast dishes, though her emotions were dancing all through the house. Her mother was all questions about Garret and how Sandi felt about him. Sandi still had too many of her own questions to think much about her mother's questions. She gave general answers with no information—a skill she had picked up from conversations with Garret. When they had finished the dishes, Sandi's father came from the den. "Sandi, could you come in for a minute?"

"Um, I guess so."

"I don't think I like all of this secrecy," Sandi's mother said.

"Just give us a few minutes," her father said.

Sandi felt like a kid on her way to the principal's office. Garret was sitting in a chair in front of her father's large oak desk. There were two other chairs. Sandi sat in one, and her father sat in the other.

"I told Garret I know you found your family in Oregon. He says he knows that. He says he knows your family, but he has danced around all my questions and hasn't given me any useful information about himself or your family. He says it is not for him to explain, but it seems to me there is more to this than either of you have told me. Garret says you will explain."

Sandi just looked wide-eyed at Garret.

"Do not worry," Garret said. "Everything is going to be all right."

"I will trust you, Garret," Sandi said. "But you are going to have to trust me, too."

"What do you mean?" Garret asked.

"If you are talking about having a relationship with me, I want to tell my father everything. We cannot live a whole life that is a lie."

"You are right, of course," Garret said. "I knew you would have to. It is not like our people to live a lie. Ronaldo also knows this. It has all been discussed and agreed to."

Sandi turned to her father. "I ... we have to tell you something that is impossible to believe. To start with, I love Garret. I do not think I can be happy living my life without him. What we must tell you is ... it is necessary for you to understand something about me, but it is something you cannot tell another living person ... ever. I am telling you this, but I want you to understand my happiness depends upon your keeping it secret."

"For crying out loud, Sandi, you know I'll do anything that'll make you happy," her father said.

Garret nodded to Sandi. "Tell him everything you think he must know."

"That is everything," Sandi said.

Garret nodded again.

Sandi's father sat expectantly as Sandi searched her mind for the words. Finally, she said, "I was never held hostage by terrorists." The surprise on her father's face was clear. "You know how you always put down stories about alien kidnappings?" she asked, not knowing what to say next.

"I hope you are not going to tell me you were kidnapped by aliens. Don't even start on something like that."

"No, there are no aliens," Sandi said. "I have found that out for sure. But there is something to the stories. There are no aliens, but what I am about to tell you is more ... or at least as strange as aliens. Just let me tell you the whole story without interrupting."

"Let me just make a small interruption," Garret said. "You will find this all extremely unbelievable. However, I am prepared to prove to you, beyond a doubt, that everything she is going to tell you is true."

Sandi looked at Garret in disbelief. He nodded. Sandi told her father about the terrorist attack and how they were saved by an electromagnetic floater. She explained the machines were called AGLs and they were based on a small island north of the Arctic Circle.

"When you say you will prove all of this, does that mean you will show me one of the AGLs?" Sandi's father asked Garret.

"That has already been arranged," Garret answered.

"I don't understand any of this," Sandi's father said.

Sandi explained about the dy-emeralite cities and the underground world.

"Who are these people, and where do they come from?" Sandi's father asked.

"They are called Earth People, and they come from this Earth. In fact, my parents who died in Utah were Earth People. That means I am also one of them. They lived in this country, but they were not from this country. Several of these people are in countries all around the world."

"What is the point of all of that?"

"Their culture is in the underground cities, but some of their people live here."

"Spies?"

"Maybe. I mean, yes, I suppose you could say that."

"For the sake of discussion, let's say I buy into this," her father said. "Who are they, and why do they put their kind in our world with phony paperwork?"

Sandi could tell he was stringing her along to humor her. "It is harder and harder for them to remain hidden in their world," Sandi said. "They are afraid of what might happen to them if they are found. So, they embed people all around the world to make sure their cities are not accidentally discovered."

"That sounds subversive to me," Earl said.

"It is subversive," Garret admitted. "But it is not an aggressive action. Anything we do is to help people, or it is something benign. For instance, I was with the archeological group, because I was looking for information about my people's archeological history in the area where Marc was digging."

"Tell me about your history and who you are," Earl demanded.

"Thousands of years ago, we decided to hide from other people. We have developed a society and culture based upon life underground."

"You buy into all of this?" Sandi's father asked her.

"I know how strange this sounds," Sandi said. "Garret says he will prove it to you. I have already seen the proof. I know it is all true."

"Oh, man!" Earl stood up. "This is the weirdest sort of brainwashing I have ever heard of! Who are these Earth People?"

"These people are Neandertals," Sandi said.

"Oh, that's totally impossible! You say that you are one of them. Look in the mirror. You know enough about paleontology to know how impossible that is."

"You are right. The mirror tells me I could not be a Neandertal. Most of the people I met in the underground city look like you and me. But I saw others. Some have very large heads with large eyes and no hair. They are short and incredibly thin with long legs and arms. Others are tall and large and covered all over with thick hair. I saw others that look exactly like Neandertals must have looked back in the Ice Age. It is a lot like seeing a Saint Bernard and a poodle standing with a wolf."

"Just like people started with wolves and bred them into many different kinds of dogs, the Neandertals bred themselves into many different kinds of people," Garret said.

"This is just goofy science fiction. I'm not even going to begin to poke the obvious holes in all of this. What have you done to my daughter?" Earl demanded of Garret.

"Hear her out for now. I will prove it all later."

"Could you just assume that it is true? I am telling you I am in love with Garret. I want to be with him."

"What about you?" Earl asked Garret.

"I have several reasons for coming here, but the most important reason for me is because I love Sandi. I first began to have these feelings before I realized who she is. That was difficult, because our laws would never allow us to have a normal life."

"How did you find out who she is?"

"We call Neanderthals, Earth People, and the modern men above ground we call Sun People," Garret began. "Earth People have always had a close relationship with nature. When I heard how Sandi can connect with rocks well enough to tell where they come from, I should have suspected right away there was something Earth People about her, but I did not. We have very good records of where our Watchers are and who they are. It just did not occur to me there could be one running around unaccounted for. Then, after hearing her talk over a period of time, I began to get the wild idea somehow she was connected."

"What do you mean by, 'after hearing her talk'?"

"Earth People brains are not wired exactly like those of Sun People when it comes to language. None of us can figure out how to use contractions. I am sure you have noticed that about Sandi's conversation."

"It's a kind of language dyslexia caused by an accident she was in as an infant," Earl said.

"You have put a name to it," Garret said. "All of the Earth People have it. I do not know of any Sun People who have it.

"Ancient Neanderthals inherited their language … they did not have to learn it. People like Sandi and me still have that inherited language, but it is buried deep. After being exposed to the ancient language, Sandi picked it up right away.

"When we began to suspect Sandi's heritage, we procured a sample of her DNA. The tests showed she is full-blooded Earth People. We already knew a Neanderthal family was killed in an auto accident near Vernal, Utah, in the 1970s. There was a baby girl whose body was never found. The only explanation for Sandi's existence was that she must be the missing girl."

"How could you know about our involvement in that accident? Earl demanded. "I just told Sandi about it a few days ago. Did you tell him?" he asked Sandi.

"No. I told you, I heard about the accident before you told me anything." Sandi said.

Earl raised his eyebrows. "It's pretty funny this guy would show up with that information right after I revealed it to you," Earl said.

"Dad!" Sandi exclaimed. "I first heard that story from Garret's people, not from you. That is why I was asking you."

"We thought the baby was carried off and eaten by animals. I can assure you when Sandi's DNA results were in, we were as surprised as you are, Mr. Hartwell," Garret said. "But I did not come to cause tension in your family. I can prove everything I have told you. Will you let me do that before you doubt Sandi?" Garret asked.

Earl frowned. "I'll listen to the rest of your story. Then you can show me your proof."

"I can show you an AGL. I can give you a ride in one. I can show you our cities. If *you* see those things, could you decide?"

"You've been in the flying saucer and their underground caves?" Sandi's father asked her.

"I have been in their AGLs several times. I spent most of the time I was gone in their cities," Sandi answered.

"I want to see this for myself. I think Sandi should stay with her mother, and if I don't return, she can do whatever is necessary."

"That can all be arranged," Garret said.

"How can I be sure you will not brainwash me or something like that?" Earl asked.

"You know Marc Metcalf," Garret said. "What if he came with us?"

"Where is Marc?" Sandi asked.

"He is outside in my car. Let me get him, and he can explain everything."

"He is here now!" Sandi exclaimed as she stood up.

"Wait a minute," Earl said. "You can't bring him in here. That would create too many questions for your mother," he said to Sandi.

"We could meet you in the park down the street," Garret said to Sandi.

"Okay, we'll meet you in about fifteen minutes," Earl said.

"Well?" Sandi's mother said as they all came out of the den.

"It looks like we will be seeing a bit more of Garret," Earl said.

"But that does not mean anything serious ... at least not yet," Sandi said.

After Garret left, Earl made an excuse for Sandi to run an errand with him. When they got to the park, Sandi saw Garret sitting at a picnic table with someone. As she and her father got out of the car, the two men got up and started walking toward her. About halfway across the parking lot, Sandi recognized Marc. Sandi ran to him. When she got to him, she threw her arms around him. "I thought I was going to be locked out of the Earth People world!" she exclaimed.

"Well, you're one of them, Sandi. You can never be locked out."

"How have you been?" Sandi asked. "Are you coming out?"

"I still find that every day is a new challenge. I have no plans to return to the Sun People world ... not yet. I have only come to see you and to convince you to reconnect with the Earth People as a Watcher living in this world. But all of that is best explained by Garret."

"Maybe. I mean, I just do not know what to do," Sandi said as they walked back to the picnic table.

"Hello, Mr. Hartwell," Marc said as Earl caught up to them.

"We thought you might have been killed."

"No," Marc said. "Terrorists did attack us, and they killed most of my team, but Garret and his people were able to save Sandi, Akhtar, Kelvin, and me."

"They saved you with a flying saucer?" Earl asked.

"You told him?" Marc asked Garret.

"I have tried to explain what happened, but it is a far-out story, and he is having a hard time with it," Sandi said.

"They have an incredible story about flying saucers and Neandertals. I don't know what's going on here, but I haven't fallen for it," Earl said.

"Well, here's what I know. There's an entire civilization hidden in underground population centers in a crescent from Oregon up through Alaska into Russia and China. I have only seen two centers myself. One is in Canada, and the other is near Lake Baikal in Russia. There are people there who look like you and me. There are others who look a little like the pictures of aliens you sometimes see artists conceptions of, with big heads and eyes. There are some who are big and hairy look like Bigfoot. And there are others who look like Neandertals."

"You've seen all of these different kinds of people?" Earl asked.

"I have seen them, touched them, and communicated with them. So has Sandi. They are real."

"And what about those flying machines?"

"They have developed flying machines that look like flying saucers. I've watched them fly, and I've ridden in them."

"They can't be flying around in flying saucers. People would see them. They would be on radar."

"People have seen them," Garret said. "They have even shown up on radar a few times, but we do not fly them except when it is necessary. We have some good materials to avoid radar detection now."

"You believe this Neandertal stuff?" Earl asked Marc.

"I've seen the DNA results. I'm no expert, but what I have seen leaves no doubt in my mind. Sandi is a Neandertal."

"Why are you still with them? Are they holding you?"

"I'm not a captive. I never was. Neither was Sandi. I have carefully evaluated my life. I have no family and no close friends. My life has revolved around science and paleontology. With these people, I can follow my interests. I do not have to jump through political hoops or chase funding. Perhaps someday, I will come back to this world, but I will always maintain ties with Garret and his people."

"What about Sandi?" Earl asked Garret.

"I do not know the answer to that. I have come here to see what Sandi wants."

"What would life be like in your world? Would she disappear into some cave with you?"

"Life in the world of my people would be completely different," Garret said. "However, many of my people live in your world, and they follow your customs. I am one of those. Sandi would also live in your world. I have come to ask her to marry me. If she agrees, we would live in the state of Washington. We would both work in the field of paleontology."

Sandi couldn't believe what she was hearing. Garret was asking for her hand. She had left that world and hadn't agreed to this new proposal.

"What about children?" Earl asked.

"We would have children. They would be raised in your world. They would attend your schools and live normal lives, except for two months each summer when they would attend our schools in a place, we call the Heart of the Bison. There they would learn their history and their culture."

"I don't care how smart you are, your people won't be able to stay hidden forever. What are your plans just in case you are found out?"

"It is our belief that at some time we will be able to join with your people in a peaceful alliance. Part of the reason for keeping people in your world in all walks of life is to facilitate that transition when it comes."

"When will that be?"

"I cannot answer that question," Garret said. "It is a very complicated process. I am not sure we will live to see that day, but I think it is possible our children, your grandchildren, will see it happen."

"You haven't said anything to me about marriage," Earl said to Sandi.

"Because I thought I would never see Gar … no one has asked me … no … I mean … I have to think about this. Things are not that eas … I mean, you do not know everything."

"Caught you off guard, didn't he?" her father said. Then, before she could respond, he asked, "Sandi, are you sure you love this man?"

"Yes, I love him, but it is not that simple. That is all I can say. It is complicated." She looked at Garret as she finished.

"Tell you what," Earl said to Garret. "You show me this AGL and leave Sandi to think about this. I would give her advice, but I clearly don't know enough … not about this story. You show me what you have to show me. And I'm not going to be gone for months. You can show me in one day … a weekend at most. I'm not going to be gone long enough for you to brainwash me. I go, I see, I come back. You give me your proof, and then we'll see what advice I give Sandi."

"I need to talk to Garret alone for a minute," Sandi said.

When they were alone, Sandi began, "Those things I said before I left about … you know … that I disagree with a lot of things in the *Wisdom Skins*. I was not just spouting off. I really believe that. So, um, do you still think there is a possibility for us?"

"There are three factions in our society. There are those who say the *Wisdom Skins* are the final word of law and cannot be changed. That is the smallest group, by far. All the rest would agree with you. Most of them say we should just make the changes that are necessary to update our system. Of course, that creates questions of what to change, who decides, and how the changes can be made. Solero's views are the radical extreme of that group. He would through them all out and start a completely new system. The majority of Earth People realize some changes in the breeding program and the isolationist stand we take regarding Sun People are needed. They believe those changes should be initiated by a shorec."

"So, you just wait around for one to appear?"

"The popular belief is that the life force contained in the natural law we call Mother Earth will provide that when it is necessary. Our Thinkers are working on the genome for Kectu. When that is done, the DNA of the Ancients will be checked to see if any of them match."

"Why?"

"There is a prophesy that a daughter of Kectu will come to be a shorec. The Ancients still have the original Neanderthal brain, which connects most directly to Mother Earth. We call upon the shomots from the clans to lead in matters that relate to Mother Earth because of that connection. Obviously, when a shorec comes, it will be through one of the clans of the Ancients."

"Suppose one matches … are you just going to make her a shorec?"

"No. A shomot will have to do that."

"So, you are still just waiting around."

"The writings of Sotif include stories that are told as fact and stories that are legends. One of the Sotif legends states the winter after Sky Man was saved, Kectu, Tuka, and Sky Man were faced with starvation. Somehow, Kectu was able to manipulate the Mother Earth laws so food was dropped from the sky. This predates Moses by over twenty thousand years, but perhaps they both used the same principle.

"We do not look at Mother Earth as a being, but as a law. The whole world, as we know it, depends upon scientists being able to manipulate the laws of electricity. Light, machines, entertainment, travel, communication ... it all comes from knowledge of how to use the laws of electricity. There are also laws of life. Medical science uses them. Sun People call it biology. We call it Mother Earth. But there is so much to Mother Earth that lies completely outside of simple biology. Our Thinkers are looking at those legends and miracles from Sun People and Earth People history to find a way to manipulate the laws, as Kectu and Moses did. It may have something to do with prayer and faith. But the hope is we can use whatever they used to help bring a shorec to the people to lead us through those changes. This is an important time.

"However, the main point I am making is your belief in the need to change aligns you with the norm in Earth People culture."

"Well, shorec or no, I will be arguing for changes. I may even be interested in getting involved politically."

"I could never see it any other way with you. And just maybe your calling is to get in politics to help make those changes."

"What do you mean?"

"The fact that you were raised in Sun People culture, and then showed up in time to stop Solero by finding the Heart of the Bison, and the fact that Marc played a part of it, and he is a descendent of Small Beaver. You know there are no coincidences. Something is going on with the Mother Earth life force."

Sandi put her palms together with her fingers interlaced. "Maybe. We will see."

Five—October 2003

Sandi sat at the table while her mother fixed breakfast. "Are you absolutely sure about Garret? I mean, you haven't really had what I would call any normal time together. You just met him, and then you were on that campout, and the next thing you know, you were all prisoners. I've heard of strange relationships growing out of the stress of being a hostage." Sandi's mother always called archeological digs campouts.

"It was crazier than you could imagine in many ways, but in other ways, it was like normal. We had some real problems to resolve, but you can really get to know someone when you have to face problems."

"Yes, I guess I know what you mean. In fact, you are sort of a solution to a problem yourself."

"What do you mean?"

"When I was a very young girl in my early teens, I had a terrible infection. It left my womb badly scarred, and the doctors told me that I could never have children of my own. I had always wanted to be a mother from the time I first started to play with dolls. When the doctors told me I couldn't, it just made my desires all the stronger.

"After your father and I were married, we tried to have children, but it was just like the doctors said. Oh, I got pregnant several times, but they all ended in miscarriages. I can't tell you how devastated I was each time my tiny child could not find a welcome home in my scarred womb. I was heartbroken, and your father decided to give up, but I convinced him to try one more time. You were that last try. I had to be bedridden for the last five months. Time and time again, I started to bleed. Several times, I was put in the hospital and given drugs to stop contractions. I had to have several blood transfusions. This put you at risk for problems with your heart, or liver, or brain damage. I was so exhausted, but I couldn't give up till you were born. Sometimes, I wonder how I ever did that. After you were born, the doctors discovered there were several problems. Most of them didn't think you would make it to be a toddler. I worried about that every minute of the day and night. Several times, you had to have emergency care. We went on a trip to see your father's family in Denver when you seemed out of danger. Then, right out in the middle of nowhere, it looked like you had died. I couldn't believe it. I couldn't accept it. Then there was a terrible accident, and I held a woman in my arms as she died. It was too much. I just gave up ... it was all out of my hands. The next thing I knew, you were okay, and I was nursing you beside the road. That's when I realized that, for me, things work out better when I just let fate ... or God, or whatever, take care of problems. It always works out better for me. I know some people have to really struggle. Your dad, for instance, when we got to Denver, he decided right there to only think positively about your health. We started a new life in Denver. We never went back to California, and we never saw any of those doctors again. We didn't tell our new doctor about your problems or the other treatments back in California. We just wanted everything to be positive. It was a miracle. The Denver doctor approached everything as if you were normal, and then you were! Now you are making plans to be a bride ... probably a mother."

Sandi sat back in her chair. While her father was off finding proof of the dy-emeralite world, she was finding out who her mother really was. She had always thought of her mother as being weak, because she ran from or ignored problems. Now she could see a different woman, and now she could understand better why her mother was the way she was. She also gained a deeper appreciation for how her father had handled Sandi's death.

"You know something, Mom?"

"What?"

"I love you. Thank you for telling me that. It gives a deeper meaning to some of the things I have been going through myself."

"Really? Then I'm glad we had this little chat. And you are sure about you and Garret?"

"More sure than I have been about anything so far in my life."

"Then there isn't much else you can ask for. I'm happy for you and Garret. He's a lucky man."

Sandi and Garret were married two months after he and her father got back from his trip to the dy-emeralite cities. Sandi had talked to Shari several times and she came to the wedding. Sandi and Garret stopped for a day near Vernal on the way to Portland, Oregon, where they spent a week for their honeymoon. While they were in Oregon, they went to the dy-emeralite cities to participate in a celebration to honor those who had helped to find the Heart of the Bison. Marc received a special honor for his role in protecting the Heart of the Bison as a representative of the Sun People. Sandi and Garret were also honored for the important roles they had played in finding the ceremony cavern and the Heart of the Bison.

It was still difficult to accept that she was one of the Earth People, but she was beginning to recognize something deep inside of her that felt like a kinship to these people and their culture.

Sandi and Garret's first child was a girl born on November 17, 2004. They named her Kecland. The family moved to Seattle where she and Garret taught anthropology in a local high school nine months a year. The nanny who took care of Kecland was a Watcher. In the summers, Kecland went to the dy-emeralite cities to learn about her heritage.

One morning over coffee, Sandi asked Garret, "Are you satisfied with the life we live?"

"Sure," Garret said. "Why?"

"Lately, I have been thinking about all of the excitement and adventure we experienced while searching for the Heart of the Bison. Somehow, life seems rather tame since then. I am not sure what our goal is now."

"After that kind of adventure, life can seem a bit routine, but I am pretty sure you would not want to spend every year in a race to save the world."

"You are right, of course. And there are the annual trips to the dy-emeralite world and seeing the model of the Heart of the Bison near Rodlu City. I just do not know what it is, but somehow, it seems I should be doing something else with my life."

"What?"

"I guess it would make it easier if I could answer that question … so at least I would know what to look for. I am anxious for Marc to finish the restoration of the Heart of the Bison in Pakistan. Maybe when we go back to see it, I will get an answer. You remember I talked about getting into politics. Now that Kecland is older, I wonder if I should be look into politics. Nothing much has happened about the changes I talked about."

"You would have to spend a lot more time in the dy-emeralite cities," Garret observed.

"I could give up my job, but we would not have to move from Seattle. Could we deal with your work and Kecland's schooling?"

"We will look into it. I believe we could work around that," Garret said.

"Really?" Sandi began thinking about just how to start a new career.

On Kecland's fifth birthday, Garret and Sandi received an invitation to attend a special ceremony to celebrate the official opening of the Heart of the Bison and the History Room. Garret, Sandi, and Kecland flew in an EMF to Sotif City near Lake Baikal in Russia. They took the new tunnel to the Heart of the Bison. As Sandi stepped from the tram into the caverns connected to the Heart of the Bison, memories of the day the expedition was trapped crashed in on her. On this day, her feelings were so different.

"It is hard to imagine a day more important to the history of our people," Garret said.

"This is a great day for the Earth People, and now I know I am Earth People. But for you and the rest, it is something you have heard about and dreamed about all your lives. For me, this is all new. I cannot put my finger on it, but I feel something is incomplete."

The Heart of the Bison was as Sandi remembered. The only difference was the Spirit Fire had a circular ring of dy-emeralite around the outside with the same symbols that were around the Spirit Fire hearth in Alaska, but there was no fire. In addition, there was a circular platform of dy-emeralite in the middle about two feet in diameter and four feet tall with a grating on top. "Why is there no fire in the Spirit Fire hearth?" Sandi asked Garret.

"The fire burns over there." Garret pointed to a small fire about twenty feet from the hearth. "The Circle of the Spirit Fire hearth has been remodeled to be similar to the hearth in Alaska. They have added radial burners coming from the center like spokes on a wheel. They have valves to control which spokes are live so the fire will move around the hearth. The central hub has a burner that will burn constantly."

"That is quite a change from the ancient way things were done."

"There is a good reason for the change. Ronaldo will …"

"I know," Sandi interrupted. "Ronaldo will explain everything."

Garret laughed. "You got it."

As they approached the crowd waiting at the entrance to the History Room, a man walked toward them. "Marc! Oh, my God! It has been so long!" Sandi exclaimed as he hugged her.

"It's been years," Marc agreed.

"Here is my little Neandertal daughter, Kecland," Sandi said.

"I'm not Kecland," the little girl insisted.

"We call her Kec," Sandi said.

"What's a Neandertal?" Kecland asked.

"A special person," Marc said as he knelt and offered his hand. The little girl smiled and took it. "I'm Marc, an old friend of your mother's."

"I'm pleased to meet you, Mr. Marc," Kecland said.

"You're a very pretty girl," Marc said.

"Thank you. You're a handsome man," Kecland said, and her smile widened.

Marc smiled and winked at Kecland. "Did I just hear Kecla … I mean, *Kec* use contractions?" Marc asked Sandi.

"What're contractions?" Kecland asked.

"It's just the pretty way you talk," Marc answered. Clearly, Kecland was pleased with the answer.

"As you know," Sandi began, "Thinkers isolated the part of the DNA that affects Earth People's ability to speak as Sun People do. They are experts at varying DNA in plants and animals. This was the first time they had tried it with humans. As you can hear, it was quite successful. Kec's generation of Watchers will all speak perfectly."

"Things are always changing," Marc observed.

"I hear you have been a busy man." Sandi noticed Marc was wearing the Iceman dagger point around his neck.

"Well, I've been working with the Earth People on the Heart of the Bison and the History Room models."

"I know. I have visited them several times."

"It was very detailed, and I had to take several trips back here to get better data. The survey equipment that's available now is already a couple of generations ahead of what I used in the ceremony cavern. When those models were done, I came here to work with them as they worked out the final details for these caves. Now that these rooms are done, we are starting on a model of the ceremony cavern. A tunnel from the ceremony cavern to the Heart of the Bison is already under construction. They want to add it to the Heart of the Bison and History Room models back at Rodlu City. It will all be a memorial park dedicated to the Alliance. In a way, the park will be better than the original caves."

"How so?" Sandi asked.

"The models will be exactly as we found the caves. The actual Heart of the Bison and the History Room have been reinforced with dy-emeralite. They were expecting a major earthquake in this area, so they pushed pretty hard to get the dy-emeralite reinforcement in place. They blended the dy-emeralite and textured and colored it so it doesn't show, but every place they put it, the actual cave wall is behind it ... some places as deep as two feet. Fortunately, the reinforcement was completed well before the actual earthquake hit. There was no damage. The ceremony cavern was a long way away from the epicenter. They have checked it out, and there was only minor damage.

"We added a number of amenities to the Heart of the Bison. There are rooms scattered in the cavern where the tram station is. We had to put in places for visitors to eat and sleep. We also put in restroom facilities. They're all hidden in excavations made in the walls so everything looks like it did when we found it. We've also constructed a memorial to Kectu, the Guardian, Tuka, Sky Man, and Shekek. They call them the First Family of the Alliance."

"Where are they? What about the little boy? He was Kectu's son."

"He's not in the memorial. He wasn't part of the development of the Alliance. The memorial is just outside of the History Room. The life stories of the First Family are written using the symbols that Sotif invented. Fortunately for me, they put the English translation next to the original writing.

"The Thinkers acquired skeletons of dead Sun People with pictures of the people before they died. Then they worked with computer modeling programs to recreate the people's faces from their skulls. They started with the best forensic programs the Sun People have. Then their programmers revised and improved upon them so the computer images they create exactly match the photos. After they perfected the programs, they used them on copies of the skeletons of the First Family of the Alliance to recreate their faces. Look, it's time to go in." Marc pointed to Ronaldo.

Everyone assembled near a podium next to the Spirit Fire hearth. "The day our people have anticipated for thousands of years has come," Ronaldo began. Sandi noticed the ragged scar on his face from the Spirit Fire coal. It added a sort of dignity to his appearance. "The history of Earth People and the Spirit Fire is long. Recently, there has been much contention about Sotif and his writings. Now, with the History Room and its many paintings, we can prove Sotif's writings are history.

"The History Room has been exactly duplicated near Rodlu City in preparation for a memorial park. Today, you will see the actual paintings that preserve the history of our people. Using highly advanced technology to scan the paintings, we have found images on the painting of the First Family that had faded so they were not visible to the naked eye. With this technology, we have found how the original paintings were done and what materials and dyes were used. The faded parts have all been restored to their original brilliance. We know what others only believed.

"None of this could have come to pass without the help of Marc Metcalf, a Sun People scientist and warrior and a proven descendent of Small Beaver. That is as it should be. From the beginning, Earth People and Sun People have worked together to ensure life and prosperity for both peoples. In the beginning, the Sun People man known as the Guardian helped establish the Alliance. When the Spirit Fire was lost in Sotif's time, the Sun People man, Small Beaver, rescued the Spirit Fire. In our time, the Sun People man, Marc Metcalf, led the expeditions that discovered the trail to the Heart of the Bison. Marc risked his life to protect the Heart of the Bison and preserve it for all time.

"Not only have we discovered the caves of our history, but we have also recovered the remains the First Family of the Alliance: The Earth People shorec, Kectu and the Sun People Guardian were parents of Tuka. Tuka and the Sun People hunter, Sky Man were parents of Shekek. We have made several exact replicas of their skeletons. From the skeletons, we have also made effigies of the First Family of the Alliance here in the Heart of the Bison in a memorial to them. Those depicted in the memorial look exactly as they looked when they lived.

"According the *History Skins*, Shekek and Kectu were buried in the History Room. Not long after Shekek's death, the first history man of the Alliance, Puntif, was selected. In Puntif's time, the clan of the Alliance grew and spread from the Heart of the Bison. The special powers of the Spirit Fire were revealed to the history man, Puntif. Puntif initiated the practice of cremating the bodies of Earth People after death so their ashes could be put in the Spirit Fire. In the Spirit Fire, their spirits were released to Mother Earth. Then their ashes were taken from the Spirit Fire to be sprinkled in fields to produce ceremonial food for the Earth People.

"Puntif taught only when all of the remains of the First Family of the Alliance were together could Kectu and Shekek pass happily through the Spirit Fire.

"From the time of the beginning of the Alliance until the time of Sotif, the bones of Kectu and Shekek were in the History Room under the watchful eye of the Alliance with the expectation that the bones of Tuka, Skyman, and the Guardian would be retrieved and a Spirit Fire ceremony could be done. With the loss of the Heart of the Bison, the last of the First Family was lost. Only a miracle could bring them together.

"Now, after twenty-five thousand years, the miracle has happened. The bones of those who began the Alliance will be placed in the center of the Spirit Fire hearth, where they will burn continuously till the end of time."

At a signal from Ronaldo, six men placed a large wooden box on a special grate on the platform at the center of the Spirit Fire hearth. "The remains of the First Family of the Alliance are in this box. The box will burn away, leaving the ashes of their bones forever in the center of the Spirit Fire."

Ronaldo raised both his arms. "Lunto, the shomot of the Ancients, will ignite the Spirit Fire in its home in the Heart of the Bison." An Ancient brought a burning brand from the Spirit Fire. He touched it to the side of the Spirit Fire hearth. Flames ignited and raced to the platform, which sprang forth in flame. As the box began to burn, Sandi felt she was being transported back to the beginning of the Spirit Fire. Several of the Ancients brought the ashes of the small Spirit Fire and placed them into the hearth. They wore clothes the Ancients wore in their caves. It seemed to Sandi that everyone else in the cave disappeared, and only the Ancients remained.

After several minutes, Ronaldo broke the spell. "Before we go to the History Room, Lunto and I will take Garret and Marc on a tour through the First Family of the Alliance Memorial." Ronaldo nodded at Sandi. "I want Sandi to accompany me through the memorial. The people in this memorial are those who started the Alliance. The effigies in this memorial were created with computer models of their skeletons. Our Thinkers assure me they look just like the people they represent looked when they were alive."

Sandi followed Ronaldo to a wall near the entrance to the History Room. The wall slid open to what looked like a long hallway. On the right as Sandi looked in was a long wall of solid rock. On the left, there was an open display. It was the view that could be seen looking out over the valley of the Indus River from inside the cave, the birthplace of the Spirit Fire. Sandi recognized the mountains across the valley. It was so realistic she felt like she was back there on her search for the Heart of the Bison. However, the valley was different. It was recreated as it would have looked at the time of the creation of the Spirit Fire. Near the entrance, there was a fire with several Earth People Ancients sitting around it. The display was so realistic it was several seconds before Sandi realized the people were not real. She could not take her eyes from the fire. Something about it pulled her attention until suddenly she saw the face of a young Earth People girl flickering faintly in the flames.

"Is that the Spirit Fire?" she asked Ronaldo.

"It is actually not a fire at all. It is a hologram representing the Spirit Fire. Can you see the face in the fire?"

"Yes." The scene was like a rock that could tell Sandi its story. She looked away from the fire and saw a young Earth People girl standing near the cave entrance looking out over the valley. She was turned sideways so her profile was visible. She looked so young, and at first, Sandi could not guess who it was. Then she recognized the face.

"That is Kectu!" Sandi gasped.

"You are right. Our Thinkers took the image they developed from her bones and backed it up in age to about eight or nine years old."

"No, I mean, I know it is Kectu. I know, because I recognize her. I am not guessing. I know her face. I know her."

"How could you know her face?" Ronaldo asked.

"I do not know. I have never seen that face before … not in a dream or a vision or anything like that. It is so weird to see it for the first time, but to know that face as though I have always known it. And there is something more."

"What?" Ronaldo asked.

"She had a life of terrible confusion and sacrifice. She had a great sadness."

"How do you know that?" Garret asked.

"I did not know it a minute ago. I know it now, but I do not know what sacrifice. That is all I know. Wait! She had three children with three fathers. She loved all her children, but she only really loved one of the fathers. The death of her second child brought her to the depth of her despair. From that point, her strength grew until she could face her deepest fears."

"You are sure?" Ronaldo asked.

"Do not ask how, but I know it."

"It makes me very happy to know she was happy in the Alliance she created," Garret said.

"Oh no. The Alliance came after her. Shekek and the Guardian created the Alliance after Kectu died. She was happy, because she had helped save the clan from the Aurochs Man and because of her last baby. A baby girl."

"Who was the Aurochs Man?" Garret asked.

"I do not know. Wait! I know he was a man who wanted to destroy all Earth People. In that sense, he was like the warmonger who came later."

"The traditions say the Guardian and Shekek founded the Alliance. We have all assumed Kectu was there. Are you sure she was not?" Ronaldo asked.

"Kectu sacrificed everything to save the people of her clan. It was only after the Aurochs Man was defeated and her people were safe that Kectu baby mated with the man she loved and had the child she had hoped for. Her life of sadness and loss was allowed to end in happiness, but there was no Alliance when she died."

As they passed the Kectu display, they came upon another display. In it, there was a man holding an infant with a female standing next to him at the side of the oxbow pond. In the background, the ground rose to the cave where the Spirit Fire began. Sandi instantly recognized the man.

"This is the Guardian," Ronaldo said.

Sandi was entranced by his face. She recognized him immediately, but then something began to grow in her mind. Something was wrong. Almost everything was wrong! "His title was 'Guardian of the Ceremony Room,'" Sandi said.

"What?" Ronaldo asked.

"It was a title. It was an important position. His people did not call him 'the Guardian.' They called him 'Guardian of the Ceremony Room,' but his name is White Cloud."

"How can you know that?" Garret asked.

"I do not know how. The man is White Cloud. I know it. I know him. I love and respect this man." Sandi started shaking. "Something is happening. His face is wrong."

"How? Our Thinkers are positive they have it right," Garret said.

"They could not know what is wrong. White Cloud has a scar on his left cheek. It is four lines, one fat and three thin." Sandi paused. "The scar was very bad for him."

"Some of Sotif's notes mention a scar on the Guardian's face, but they do not describe or say where on his face. They also mention something else. Do you know what it is?" Ronaldo asked.

"He has a tattoo on his forehead. It looks like … it is a horizontal line with a half circle on top with five lines radiating out from the circle … a rising sun."

"Sotif writes of a hunter's tattoo on his face. Now we know what it looked like and where it was," Ronaldo said.

"Yes, it was a Hunter's tattoo, but Hunter was not just word. It was title, a special ceremonial calling, and it had to be earned." As Sandi talked, she made strange signs with her hands and fingers. First her left palm was down, and then she turned it up, and then she brought her arm to a square.

"What are you doing?" Marc asked.

"I do not know … a ceremony, a Hunter ceremony. How could I know that? I do not remember reading it in my studies."

"Besides the *Wisdom Skins* and the *History Skins*, there are many written communications between Sotif and Rodlu," Ronaldo said.

"Rodlu was the one who helped Sotif find the Spirit Fire in the East," Sandi said.

"Yes," Ronaldo responded. "Rodlu led the Earth People on the east side of the big water. Sotif stayed on the west side and led the people there. In those letters, Sotif talked about the Guardian. He mentioned the scar and the tattoo."

"So maybe I read about them in the letters," Sandi suggested.

"No, they are not available except in a special library in Sotif City," Ronaldo said. "And they do not describe the marks or say anything about a Hunter ceremony."

"The female is Kectu. Who is the child?" Sandi asked.

"It is their daughter, Tuka," Ronaldo said.

"No, that is all wrong," Sandi said. "White Cloud did not know Tuka. He lived with the Sun People. He did not know Tuka until she was grown. Tuka never saw this cave. She was born were she died."

"Where are you getting this information?" Ronaldo asked.

"When I see these people, I know. It is not just their stories. I know their feelings. When White Cloud found out about Tuka, he had deep regret that he did not know her. He saved Kectu and Shekek after Tuka and Sky Man were killed. He helped Shekek start the Alliance partly to make up for that regret."

"You know what you say could not come from memories," Ronaldo said. "What you say contains too much detail and too many feelings. This could not come from DNA memories."

"Perhaps those of the First Family have carried their stories from their bones to the Spirit Fire. Maybe their stories are flowing from the Spirit Fire," Garret said.

"Why would those memories come to me and not Ronaldo?" Sandi asked. Suddenly, before anyone could answer her, Sandi was filled with thoughts she couldn't hold back. "I know White Cloud's regret. It was deeper. Garret, do you remember when I found the home of the Spirit Fire?"

"Yes."

"I told you there was a rape. It was not a rape like we think of, because sex at that time period did not have the same meanings as today. White Cloud forced Kectu to mate. He did not know her. He ran away after, but Kectu slapped him and tore his face first."

"No, she could not do that," Ronaldo said. "It is absolutely forbidden for an Earth People female to hit a man."

"White Cloud spoiled something she had waited for. She hit him. She was sorry, but she was banned from her clan for it. She could no longer be the shorec because of it. This display is at the home of the Spirit Fire, but Kectu raised Tuka at the lovers' cave. Tuka was born at the lovers' cave."

"How do you know these things?" Ronaldo asked.

"White Cloud was punished, and he could never have another child, but he did not know Kectu was pregnant with his child."

"Where does this information come from?" Ronaldo demanded.

"White Cloud had been a great Hunter, but he could no longer be a Hunter."

"How can you know this?" Ronaldo asked in frustration.

"The chief, Sky Man's father, made White Cloud Guardian of the Ceremony Room, because he did a great deed."

"Sandi!" Ronaldo exclaimed.

"What?"

"Where does this information come from?"

The question jolted Sandi. "I cannot explain it. It is like the information is a mist around their faces, but not a mist you see with your eyes. It is a cloud of information that comes when I recognize their faces. It fills me, and I cannot stop it. I think there is much more, but I cannot quite put it all together."

"But how can these things be true?" Garret asked.

"There are things you do not know," Ronaldo said. "We cannot dismiss what Sandi says. Some of it is verified in Sotif's notes and letters. But there is more to it than that."

"What?" Sandi asked.

"All in due time," Ronaldo responded. "We should see the rest of the memorial."

"No," Sandi said. "I am afraid."

"What are you afraid of?" Marc asked.

"I am an Earth People woman. In Earth People culture, the men are the leaders. I am already contradicting their data. I do not know where this information comes from, but it goes against a great deal of work that has been done with study and science. A great deal of effort and expense has gone into this. Almost everything here is wrong! Who am I to say it is wrong? I should not see this until I can figure out where this information is coming from. What I am feeling could be all wrong."

"Do you feel you are wrong?" Ronaldo asked.

Sandi struggled with the question. She was telling Ronaldo that this fantastic memorial was wrong. How could she know that? "I am sure I am right, and that is the problem. I cannot back down from what I know. Knowing that creates doubt for me about the *History Skins*. The stories are old, but what I feel is new. I do not want to … I do not know what to do."

"If your stories are true, we need to hear them. We will give them serious study. Our best scholars will look into them. Our Thinkers will test them out. What you think are conflicts, we will work out. I want you to finish this tour," Ronaldo said.

"I do not know."

"This isn't like you," Marc said. "You grew up Sun People. Culturally, you're Sun People. Who cares what Earth People think about a woman's place? Don't let being Earth People make you into something you are not. Don't be afraid of your truth."

"Is that what you think it is? That I am afraid of truth?" Sandi asked. Sandi pushed past Ronaldo to the next display. It was the lovers' gravestone. The panorama in the background was a realistic, three-dimensional representation of the area in front of the lovers' cave looking toward the entrance. A young man stood by the gravestone. A small boy stood beside him reaching up to hold his right hand. The man's left arm was around the shoulder of a much shorter young woman.

"Do you know these people?" Ronaldo asked.

As she looked at the face of the young man, in her mind, she saw a young boy facing a bison. She knew him as though he were a brother. "You call these people Sky Man, Tuka, and Shekek," Sandi answered. "I know these people. They do not belong to the lovers' cave."

"Who do you say they are?" Ronaldo asked.

"The man is a great Hunter ... not a chief, but the son of a Sun People chief. His name is Sky Runner. He saw this cave only one time ... on the day of his death. His mate is Tuk, daughter of Kectu. She was never called Tuka. As a female, Tuk's name could only have one syllable unless she was the shorec. Kectu was the only shorec. Tuk was born in the lovers' cave after Kectu was banned from her clan and the Spirit Fire cave. Kectu had a son called Kopek in this cave. The rock you call a gravestone was put there by Kopec's father. He put it there for Kectu so she could have a rock to sit on to think. After a wild cat killed Kopec, Kectu was banned from this clan and this cave. She and Tuk were sent to the wilderness, because Tuk was a half-breed, and Kectu was unlucky. Kopec is part of the First Family of the Alliance. His death was the turning point I talked about before. His bones must be recovered and added to the Spirit Fire to make it complete.

"While Kectu and Tuk were in the wilderness, they saved Sky Runner from a cave lion. Sky Runner had a tattoo on his forehead just like White Cloud, but Sky Runner had another tattoo of a small hand, because he risked his life to save a Hunter. Sky Runner was also honored by having an imprint of his hand placed under the great aurochs in the ceremony cavern. Sky Runner had a large scar on his stomach from the cave lion that nearly killed him. Sky Runner and Tuk baby mated in the wilderness. They had a son. Sky Runner named his son Sun Fire."

"You speak with such confidence," Garret observed.

"These stories are clear to me. They are not visions or dreams. It all comes as knowledge." Sandi felt surer of herself than she had in many years.

"Why were Sky Runner and Tuk killed?" Ronaldo asked.

"I do not know. I know it was a mistake. Sky Runner's father buried Sky Runner and Tuk together. White Cloud was there when they died."

"Who was Sun Fire?" Ronaldo asked. "When was Shekek born?"

"In the ancient language of the Sun People, the translation of Sun Fire is Sheeme Keekee." Sandi said.

"You know that ancient language?" Marc asked.

"No, but I know the Sun People names and what they mean."

"Then who is Sheeme Keekee?" Ronaldo asked.

"Lunto knows," Sandi said.

"Lunto does not know this child," Lunto said.

"Say the child's name," Sandi said to Lunto.

"Lunto is an Ancient," Garret said. "He cannot make the Earth People sounds of that name."

"Say Sheeme Keekee," Sandi ordered Lunto. The tone of her voice surprised even Sandi.

"Lunto cannot," Lunto said.

"Try it!" Sandi ordered more forcefully.

"Shekek," Lunto stammered. Lunto stepped back from Sandi. He repeated with more confidence, "Shekek." Everyone looked at Sandi—no one spoke.

Garret broke the long silence that followed. "How could …? Where did …?"

"Sandi could not have made up these names and stories," Ronaldo said, interrupting Garret.

"I know these things. I do not understand them. Maybe they are not true. No, I know they are," Sandi said.

"The stories of our people come from paintings on the History Wall and Sotif's hieroglyphics," Ronaldo said. "These are not language. They are representations. They do not have sentences with subjects, verbs, and objects. The details are missing. Solero has had a powerful influence on the people. Even now, many are trying to give different interpretations to the pictures and hieroglyphics of our history. Now one truth, the *only* truth, is being revealed in a direct manner. It could come from Mother Earth, the Spirit Fire, or from the spirit of Kectu herself."

"Or it could come from energy fields caused by joining all of the members of the First Family in the Spirit Fire," Garret added.

"Wherever it comes from, it is a uniting truth," Ronaldo said.

"If that is true," Sandi said, "that information should come to a leader… not to a woman and especially not to a woman who grew up not knowing she was Earth People."

"These stories had to be revealed to someone with a clear mind … someone who grew up without learning the traditions as we teach them … a blank slate, as the Sun People say," Ronaldo said.

"I understand what you say, and I am almost convinced, but it is all very hard to grasp," Sandi said.

"Come, it is time to go to the History Room. The answer you seek will be found there."

Sandi walked from the memorial with Ronaldo. As she walked, she thought of Kopec. Years ago, when they had first found his bones, Sandi had wondered about this boy. Now she knew his name and how he died. Then a smile crept across her face. She knew a door had opened. The whole story of the beginning had been released. It came through the Spirit Fire from the bones of those who had lived it. She did not know it all now, but she knew that she would   all of the details of Kectu's sacrifice, why Sky Runner and Tuk were killed, and even the mystery of the Earth People man who was sealed in the tunnel connecting the Sun People ceremony cavern with the Earth People world. It was all part of the energy of the Spirit Fire and the Heart of the Bison, just waiting for her brain to decode it.

Ronaldo led the group back to the center of the Heart of the Bison. He stood in front of the crowd waiting there. One of the Ancients handed him a lighted torch. "The power of the Spirit Fire has revealed many details about the beginning of the Alliance. Now we will enter the History Room with a deeper understanding," he said to the crowd. "The flames that light our way come from the Spirit Fire." Ronaldo led the way down a corridor. Sandi recognized the corridor from her trip to the Heart of the Bison and the History Room more than six years ago.

Once in the room, the same awe she had experienced when she first looked at the ancient paintings filled Sandi. Earth People history—her history was laid out before her!

"Please, Sandi, come sit on this chair," Ronaldo said. He was directing her to a caribou antler chair at the base of the wall of paintings. The chair had a leather seat and back, and it was all trimmed in gold.

"I have asked Sandi to sit here for a reason I will explain shortly," Ronaldo said, addressing the assembled group. "We owe a great deal to Sandi Chambers for the discovery of these sites. It was she who found the grave of the lovers. It was she who directed Garret to the secret entrance to the ceremony cavern. It was she who led us to the first home of the Spirit Fire. It was she who led us to the Heart of the Bison and this History Room."

Now Sandi began to feel a little self conscious about this special recognition. Just a little mention back when they were praising Marc would have been sufficient. Many people had participated, and nothing would have ever been found without all of them.

"Sandi was chosen to show these things to us," Ronaldo continued. "This morning, Sandi has begun to reveal details about the beginning of the Spirit Fire, the Heart of the Bison, and the Alliance. She has an uncanny connection to the beginnings of those things that form the basis of our history and our beliefs."

Ronaldo pointed to the painting at the bottom of the wall. "Here is the beginning. This part of the painting shows the mating of an Earth People woman with a Sun People man. Just now, as we showed the First Family of the Alliance Memorial to Sandi, she recognized the likenesses of the members of that historic family. At the same time, Sandi was given information Earth People have not had for many thousands of years.

"The *History Skins* tell us the bones found under this painting belonged to the great shorec, Kectu. The *History Skins* also tell us the man who mated with Kectu is called the Guardian. Sandi has given us his name. It is White Cloud. He had the tattoo of a Sun People Hunter on his forehead and a scar on his right cheek. White Cloud died in the great ceremony cavern of the Sun People.

"The first painting at the bottom of this wall is called the First Family. It shows from the mating of Kectu and White Cloud, a female child was born. Thinkers used sophisticated X-rays and other devices to bring out faded colors of this painting. As they examined the painting, they found faint shadows above the heads of all the males in the First Family painting. They were able to restore those shadows. They are clearly visible in the restored painting, but we had no way of knowing what they meant."

Sandi gasped. Their meaning was perfectly obvious to her.

"With the information Sandi gave us this morning, we can now read the meanings of those symbols. The symbol above White Cloud's head is a jagged, horizontal line with broken, curved lines joined to form an oval above the jagged line. It is now obvious the jagged line represents the mountains on the horizon, and the curved lines represent a cloud in the sky above the mountains. The symbol represents the name of the man ... White Cloud.

"We have called Kectu's daughter Tuka in honor of her role as Shekek's mother. However, Sandi has pointed out she was not a shorec, and so she could not have a name with two syllables. The name she used was Tuk. The painting and the traditions say Tuk mated with a Sun People chief named Sky Man. Sandi has discovered his name was Sky Runner. The symbol above the Sky Runner representation is a jagged line with a stick figure above it. The jagged line is exactly like the line above White Cloud, and it represents the horizon. The stick figure is of a man who is obviously running in the sky ... Sky Runner. From the mating of Tuk and Sky Runner came a son named Shekek. In Sun People language, he was called Sun Fire. The symbol above his head is a jagged line exactly like the lines above the representations of White Cloud and Sky Runner. Over the horizon above Shekek's head is a circle with flames rising from it ... a sun on fire ... Sun Fire.

"The *History Skins* tell us Shekek was buried in the History Room near Kectu. Those bones have been found. The bones of White Cloud, Tuk, and Sky Runner have also been found. Our scientists have used advanced DNA methods to show the female of the lovers' grave is the daughter of the man in the ceremony cavern, White Cloud, and the female in the History Room, Kectu. The tests also show the male in the History Room, Sun Fire, is the lovers' son. There is no doubt we have the bones of Kectu, White Cloud, Tuk, Sky Runner, and Shekek. The relationships and locations of their bones match the descriptions in the *History Skins*.

"The greatest stories of our history are now proven facts. Never again will there be room for contention about how the Earth People were saved from the laws of extinction.

"The *History Skins* say Kectu and the Earth People shomot had a daughter in Kectu's old age. With so many things coming to fulfillment in our time, we are a blessed generation. But there is even more good news for Earth People. For many years, we have collected DNA from all Earth People. Our Thinkers have worked tirelessly to develop and build DNA genome data banks of our people to use in our breeding programs. One important part of Sotif's writing is that a day would come when a daughter of Kectu would restore the Alliance between Sun People and Earth People. Those genomes of the First Family have been compared to the extensive DNA data we have been collecting since the 1960s. Several strands of nuclear DNA matching Kectu's DNA have been discovered in the Earth People population. Our Thinkers cannot say with certainty they came directly from Kectu. However, there are sixty-seven Earth People that the Thinkers have statistically shown to have up to a high probability of being direct descendents of Kectu. Twenty-eight of those people are females.

"The problem with nuclear DNA is that it is split and recombined with each generation, as the father and mother each provide one-half of the child's DNA. Our Thinkers realized they would be able to increase the probability of connecting someone to Kectu through mitochondria, but that could only be possible if there were unbroken lines of daughters to mothers going back to Kectu. Incredibly, two of the twenty-eight females who have the highest probability of matching Kectu's nuclear DNA have mitochondria that also match Kectu. Our Thinkers have informed the Council these two females are daughters of Kectu with over a million-to-one certainty."

Ronaldo paused while each of those in the room thought about the magnitude of this revelation.

Sandi was awestruck at what she was hearing. What Earth People had found was equivalent to finding the Garden of Eden and the core of the apple Eve ate. To know there were two descendants of the ancient shorec, Kectu, was incredible! There were several females of the Ancients in the room. Sandi tried to guess which of them could be Kectu's daughters. What a world that could tie them back twenty-five thousand years!

"As Sandi revealed the true history of the First Family of the Alliance this morning," Ronaldo continued, "she, rightly, suggested this information should not come through a woman. In Earth People culture, only males are allowed to be spiritual leaders ... shomots. This kind of truth can only come through a shomot unless there is a shorec. It is no accident Sandi was the one to lead our people on the quest to find the Heart of the Bison and the First Family of the Alliance. Sandi and her daughter, Kecland, are the two Earth People who carry Kectu's ancient genes. Kectu has spoken through her daughter to lead us to the sites of our ancient history. Many thought a shorec could only be an Ancient because of the close connection Ancients have to Mother Earth. They were wrong. Sandi's connection to the roots of Earth People history through the power of Mother Earth is proven."

Sandi felt faint. Ronaldo looked at her and stopped speaking. A strange warmth began to spread in her body, and new strength filled her heart. For the first time in her life, Sandi knew exactly who and what she was.

"Kectu was a great shorec," Ronaldo continued. "She was tattooed with embers from the Spirit Fire on the day the Spirit Fire was made. According to Garret, Sandi and Kecland both have birthmarks exactly like Kectu's tattoo ... the mark of the shorec."

Suddenly, Sandi felt a burning on her birthmark. She saw a vision of a young Neandertal girl as an old man cut her genitals and rubbed ashes from a fire into the wound. The Spirit Fire was there with the old man, and the Spirit Fire was Kectu's sister. Sandi shook her head to clear her mind. She realized she was connected to the Spirit Fire from its beginning through Kectu.

"Kectu was made the shorec," Ronaldo continued. "She blessed the people with the Spirit Fire. Now her daughter has blessed the people with all the power of those days of the beginning. The Council has discussed this with all the shomots of the clans, and it is our unanimous decision that Sandi is the shorec by birthright and the birthmark she carries. Kecland will be the shorec after her. So says Ronaldo, so it shall be."

Everyone in the room repeated in unison, "So says Ronaldo, so it shall be."

Sandi looked at the paintings of the History Wall. The story of Kectu was at the bottom. Now there would be a new story—the story of Kectu's daughter—Sandi's story. A shorec could only come at a time of change. Sandi had already thought about changes, but they were small. There must be big changes in store—changes she would start, but it would take Kecland to complete them. She sensed Kectu's bewilderment and fear on the day she was made the shorec. It was a frightening prospect for Sandi to face with so little preparation. Garret stood beside her and put his arm around her. She would not face it alone.

For the complete story of Shari Darling's battle with the serial killer read: Dead Angels by Glen R Stott

www.ingramcontent.com/pod-product-compliance
Lightning Source LLC
LaVergne TN
LVHW091529060526
838200LV00036B/543